A Botanist's Guide to Flowers and Fatality

ALSO AVAILABLE BY KATE KHAVARI

The Saffron Everleigh Mysteries

A Botanist's Guide to Parties and Poisons

A Botanist's Guide to Flowers and Fatality

A Saffron Everleigh Mystery

Kate Khavari

CROOKED LANE

NEW YORK

Copyright © 2024 by Kate Khavari

Published in the United States by Crooked Lane Books, an imprint of The Quick Brown Fox & Company LLC.

Crooked Lane Books and its logo are trademarks of The Quick Brown Fox & Company LLC.

Library of Congress Catalog-in-Publication data available upon request.

ISBN (hardcover): 978-1-63910-278-5
ISBN (paperback): 978-1-63910-657-8
ISBN (ebook): 978-1-63910-279-2

Cover design by Nicole Lecht

Printed in the United States.

www.crookedlanebooks.com

Crooked Lane Books
34 West 27th St., 10th Floor
New York, NY 10001

First Edition: June 2023
Trade Paperback Edition: April 2024

10 9 8 7 6 5 4 3 2 1

*For my parents, Tracy and David,
who helped me find the villain*

Chapter 1

"Everleigh."

The rush of the train over the tracks and the subsequent rattle of the compartment doors were as harsh to Saffron's senses as the flickering sunlight coming through the grime on the windows. She blinked at the blur of the passing landscape.

"Enjoying your little nap?" asked the man sitting across from her. His brilliant green eyes were lit up with amusement.

Saffron ignored Lee as best she could. It wasn't easy, considering they were the only two people in the tiny compartment, and Lee was the most obnoxious combination of attractive and infuriating. Even in the shockingly steamy heat of August, his tan suit had not a wrinkle, and his golden hair was perfectly styled away from his face with a pomade that perfumed the close air of the compartment. Saffron, on the other hand, felt her lightweight traveling suit sticking to her back and legs. She was grateful that her straw hat hid her dark hair, similarly damp with sweat.

Saffron stood to open the window a crack, if only to get Lee to stop looking at her like she was his source of entertainment. Beyond the dirty window, rolling stretches of pink heather blooming across green plains gave way to dark trees.

Before her kid gloves touched the latch, the train jerked. The metallic whine of brakes pierced the clattering. Saffron nearly lost her footing, flattening her palms against the windowpane. She glared at Lee's hand on her elbow.

"We've arrived," he said easily.

She repacked her notebook into her handbag and slung it over her shoulder, then followed Lee down the tight corridor to disembark.

The train hissed steadily as they walked along the simple concrete platform adorned with a sign proclaiming Saffron and Lee had reached "Aldershot." Then it rolled away, leaving a ringing silence after its clattering faded. A chorus of insects took up a moment later, and Saffron found herself once again in an empty country lane surrounded by fields, with Dr. Michael Lee.

He withdrew a folded piece of paper from a pocket and squinted at it—he really needed eyeglasses—then looked up and down the lane. "Should be just around the corner."

Saffron pursed her lips. The lane went on for at least a mile in either direction.

Lee smirked. "Metaphorically speaking." He tipped his straw Panama upward and nodded to the south. "I suppose it's that way."

She couldn't help but wrinkle her nose. "You suppose?"

"Yes. The report said it was south of the station."

Saffron could already feel her temper climbing along with the temperature. Perspiration pricked along the nape of her neck. "You didn't check on a map?"

Lee heaved a sigh. "This was rather last minute, you know. I was only told we were coming here when I arrived at the North Wing this morning."

"That's no different from two weeks ago when I heard first about Theydon Mount. And yet I had time to check the map," Saffron shot back.

Getting lost in Hampshire might be a minor inconvenience to him, but it might mean something more serious for the boy they'd been sent here to help.

"Now, now, no need to worry," Lee said in a placating voice that made Saffron want to strangle him. "It seems we're saved from wandering these bucolic fields indefinitely." He pointed down the lane to an approaching cart.

They stepped to the side of the lane, and Lee raised a hand to flag down the man driving the cart, a large fellow in rough clothing, with a fraying hat shading a florid complexion and anxious eyes.

"You wouldn't be the folks down from town to see about the Evans boy?" he asked the moment his aged horse came to a halt before them.

"We are," Saffron replied. "Can you give us the direction?"

"I came to fetch you," the man replied. "Good of you to come. Local doctor wouldn't, the wretch. I work for the family. Climb up."

Wordlessly, Lee climbed into the back of the cart and offered Saffron a hand. They perched on two crates half buried in hay, Lee tapping his fingers on his black case all the while. The ride was brief but bumpy, and they soon arrived at an old farmhouse shaded by a massive oak tree.

Lee hopped off the cart and helped Saffron down into the dirt yard. The hulking cart driver led them straight into the house. The moment he set foot across the threshold, he tugged off his hat and called, "Missus Evans? I got the folks from London."

A feminine voice replied something Saffron didn't make out. Lee dropped his hat and gloves on the small table near the door, but Saffron kept her hat and gloves on. Niceties weren't something they usually had the time for, and she would likely be leaving again directly.

They followed the man deeper into the house, Saffron taking in the shabby home. It was messy, but not dirty, with children's toys strewn over the squeaking wood floors and threadbare carpets.

She entered the parlor at the back of the house, where Lee was already kneeling beside a sofa. He was examining a small child lying in the arms of a blonde woman not much older than Saffron's twenty-three years. The seven-year-old appeared to be sleeping. The woman's face was pale but determined, watching Lee like a hawk as he asked questions.

"How long has Joey been ill, Mrs. Evans?" Lee's voice was gentle as he opened his black doctor's bag and withdrew the small case where he kept his stethoscope.

"Abe found him at dawn when he went out to check the sheep," Mrs. Evans replied, her voice clipped with tension. "He was in the field, fitting. Abe brought him straight here. I didn't—" She took a shuddering breath, looking away from Lee as he applied his stethoscope to the boy's chest. "I didn't think anything of it when I saw he wasn't in his bed—he likes to get up with the chickens in the morning. He always collects the eggs."

Tears streaked down Mrs. Evan's cheeks, and her arms tightened around the boy.

"Joey, my lad, look just here for me," Lee instructed. He sounded almost cheerful, but Saffron knew better. He looped his stethoscope around his neck and withdrew a case that held his ophthalmoscope. Joey didn't respond, so Lee gently lifted his eyelids.

After a brief examination, Lee dropped his scope. His eyes met hers across the room. "Pupils are dilated."

Mrs. Evan's head snapped toward Saffron, confusion written on her weary face.

"Mrs. Evans, I'm Saffron Everleigh. I'm Dr. Lee's colleague from University College London. Before he can treat your son, I have to confirm what it is affecting him." Rather than wait for the perplexed expression to clear from her face, Saffron asked, "What did he touch or eat?"

"I don't know." Mrs. Evans's face crumpled. "I don't know, and he won't wake up. But he shakes so violently and he—he smiles like—"

"He smiles?" Lee asked sharply.

"Yes," Mrs. Evans whispered, her hands coming to cup her son's face. "He stops when the fit passes."

Lee stood abruptly and went to where Saffron stood in the corner. Her heartbeat tripped at the serious expression on his face.

"Everleigh," he murmured, "if he's still fitting, there's little I can do for him. I could give him a barbiturate for the convulsions, but it's risky with his breathing already depressed. He needs a hospital."

"Where is the nearest?"

"I'm not sure. But you need to find out what he ate."

"I know," Saffron said, annoyed even as fear rose in her chest.

"Doctor?" Mrs. Evans moaned, and when Saffron and Lee turned, she was gripping Joey tightly against her chest. The boy was shaking, his eyes rolling and jaw tightened in a horrific mockery of a smile.

"Dear God," Saffron whispered.

Lee was across the room in a moment, easing Joey out of his mother's arms and saying something in a soothing voice.

A hundred thoughts thundered through Saffron's mind. Flashes of their prior cases, accounts she'd read in medical journals and books of herbal remedies. Seeing the rictus mask on Joey's face had shocked her into numbness.

Her feet felt rooted to the ground, until Lee barked her name.

"Go," he mouthed before returning his attention to the fitting boy.

Saffron fled, her feet carrying her to the only place she could be of use—outside to hunt down whatever had done this to Joey Evans.

"Miss," called the farmhand, when they reached the sunshine of the front yard.

She paused in tugging off her kid gloves. "Yes?"

"I can show ye where I found him, if you like," he said.

"Yes, thank you." She slid her heavy buckskin working gloves onto her hands as she scanned the yard again. It was hard packed dirt, nothing but a few weeds managing to poke their little heads up. She looked at the farmhand, who was rolling his hat in his hands as he watched her. The mixture of doubt and worry creasing his face made her question come out more snappishly than she'd intended. "What is your name?"

"Abraham Grant. Folks call me Abe."

"Well, Abe"—Saffron tried to give him a confident smile, but her face felt as frozen as Joey's—"show me where you found him, then."

They passed through the yard and into the nearest field.

"Are there any snakes here?" Saffron called ahead to Abe.

"Haven't seen an adder 'round here for years. Sheep mostly scare them away."

"Any nasty spiders? An insect Joey is allergic to?" The expected answer was "no" to both questions, but it seemed prudent to ask since she was up to her knees in grass.

"None I can think of," was Abe's reply. He pointed ahead. "Just here. I wouldn't have seen him, but he was wearing his pirate kerchief 'round his head. It's red."

They stopped next to a fence of roughly hewn wood, where a smattering of long grass had been flattened. Saffron set her bag down at the corner of the fencing. Beginning closest to the place Abe had indicated, she began circumambulating the spot, moving a foot or so out each time. There was a lot of ground to cover, and she needed to examine every plant.

After ten minutes, the immediate area revealed nothing but grass and heather and a number of other wildflowers. She straightened, brushing down her skirt and readjusting her hat.

She'd just opened her mouth to ask her next question of Abe when a call from the house caught their attention.

"Be right back, miss," he mumbled before jogging off through the grass.

Saffron withdrew her handkerchief and patted her brow. She blew out a frustrated breath. Searching out culprits of accidental poisonings was not easy work, but this particular episode felt like finding a needle in a haystack, if the haystack were spread over miles and miles of overgrown farmland.

Unfortunately, there were a multitude of plants that caused convulsions. Deadly nightshade, foxglove, cardinal flower, honeysuckle berries, jimson weed—if only she'd been the one to get the report from Dr. Aster about this case! She could have taken a moment to review poisonous plants common to heathland.

Every moment she wasted was seconds that allowed whatever chemicals to progress further and further into Joey's small body.

She wouldn't wait for Abe to return. He might be driving Lee and Mrs. Evans and Joey to the hospital even now, and she'd be standing around, feeling hopeless.

She shucked her jacket and hung it on the fence, then hitched her bag over her shoulder and set off, eyes trained on the ground.

Time moved in a strange way when Saffron was searching out plants in the field. There was only her, the landscape, and her need to find what she sought. The sun's heat sunk into her clothes. Perspiration slipped down her back and beaded along her brow. She ignored it in favor of wracking her brain for the names for each plant her gaze swept over, pausing only briefly to wonder at ones she didn't recognize and hoping her lack of knowledge didn't spell doom. She didn't register the progress of the sun through the sky nor where precisely she was.

This work was so different from the structured management of the species in the university's greenhouses. It made her grateful for the hours she'd spent wandering the countryside with her father, examining whatever flowers they came across. Her experience had always been on the more pastoral side until she began her formal studies at the university.

Her feet took her faster and faster, expressing the urgency of her growing fear that her inadequacy would mean Joey's death. If they didn't know what was poisoning him, they might give him the wrong medicines, perhaps something that would compound the effects and worsen his condition.

She stumbled over a jumble of rocks obscured by the tall grass, and she fell to the ground with a grunt of pain.

As if awoken from a trance, Saffron looked about her, realizing that she was no longer in a field proper, but along the edge of a hidden creek bed trickling with water. She'd been so focused on what was just before her, she'd lost track of where she was.

Her left ankle twinged as she rotated it.

"Blast," she muttered. She carefully rose, only to have her knees grow weak at the sight not twenty yards ahead of her.

Small, lacy white blooms clustered above fernlike leaves, masses of them lining the creek, winsome and pretty to anyone not familiar with the toxins that lurked in every part of the plant.

Had her mouth not already been parched, it would have gone dry. How many times had her father warned her of thinking herself clever for finding a wild carrot or parsnip? How many a sheep or cow had been felled by one bite?

And there it was, growing as gaily as any wildflower.

Her ankle forced her to walk slowly when all she wanted to do was rush forward and search for any sign the plants had recently been disturbed. A cut stalk, an exposed section of roots, crushed flowers. Hemlock was one of the most poisonous plants that grew in England. Any part of it might have harmed Joey.

Her examination was swift; two segments of broken stalk, hollow within like a reed, lay in the grass just at the edge of the nearest clump. When she exhumed two of the smallest plants, she found the telltale pale roots that indicated she'd discovered hemlock water dropwort, a kind of hemlock that was equally poisonous as its more famous relatives. It was clear from the dirt-covered appendages that the nickname "dead man's fingers" was well deserved.

She wrapped the broken stalks and the roots of the plants in the leather sack she'd brought with her and set off the way she'd come, holding the samples far from her body. Eating the plant wasn't the only way to come to harm from it.

The twinge in her ankle soon became a burn, and before she'd passed back into the more orderly fields surrounding the Evans's farm, it was throbbing badly.

Saffron paused for a break, leaning on a fencepost and mopping her sticky face with her handkerchief. The insects cranked out their rhythms beyond the trees. The field shimmered with green and gold as a welcome breeze canted through. But there was no peace in it. Urgency tensed her muscles to move.

She didn't notice the figure of a man until he was nearly upon her.

Saffron shot to her feet, only to stumble on her weak ankle and swallow a yelp of pain. "Lee! You can't sneak up on me in the middle of nowhere. You might have been anyone!"

He came forward, hands raised in mock surrender. "It's your own fault you're in the middle of nowhere. You've scouted nearly a mile from the house. It took me ages to find you."

"Why did you find me?" Saffron eased her back onto the fencepost to alleviate the strain on her ankle. "Shouldn't you be with the Evanses at the hospital?"

"The nearest place was the military base just a few miles down the road. Abe brought me back to collect you." He nodded to the plants, which she'd set down at a safe distance from her legs. "I see you've had luck. What is it?"

"Dead man's fingers," Saffron said, glaring down at the plants. "I found a stalk had been broken off. Looked as if someone might have used it as a pea shooter—the stalks are hollow. It doesn't mean that it was Joey, but—"

"Is that a kind of hemlock?" Lee interrupted, looking curiously down at the lacy flowers. "Looks like that picture you showed me when we began this little venture."

"*Oenanthe crocata*, hemlock water dropwort. It belongs to the Apiaceae family, same as the plants traditionally known as hemlock." She pressed the handkerchief beneath the mass of her dark hair, which pressed heat on her neck like a hot water bottle. "I ought to have known. His smile, the rictus smile, that should have been more than enough to tell me. And the stream was the perfect place for it to grow. But any country boy ought to have known about hemlock of any kind. I wasn't permitted to leave the house at the start of spring without being able to pick it out as dangerous."

Lee shot her a wry smile. "You were raised by a botanist, Everleigh. From what Mrs. Evans told me, Joey is lucky if he has half her attention on a good day. After Mr. Evans was killed in action, she's been trying to run their farm on her own, with only Abe's help."

Saffron bit her lip. It was a horrible situation for all of them. Mrs. Evans would no doubt feel a great deal of guilt. And it was a miracle that Joey was still alive at all if he'd come in contact with hemlock, but how long would that miracle last?

She started forward, eager to do whatever she could in her limited capacity now the plant had been identified, but her ankle barked with pain, and she grimaced.

Lee was by her side in three strides. "What's the matter?"

"Nothing," Saffron gritted out.

"Don't play those games with a doctor." He looked her up and down, then frowned at her feet. She probably ought to have planted her foot back on the ground, but she didn't want to wince so obviously again. "Your ankle?"

Grudgingly, Saffron said, "Just a bit of a sprain."

"And a bit of a sprain will be quite the inconvenience if aggravated walking back a mile to the house. I would say I ought to take a look at it, but it's hot at Hades out here. Come, let me help you."

He accepted none of her protestations at him placing her arm firmly on his and began speaking as they started in the direction of the farmhouse. He kept her wretchedly slow pace as she attempted to walk normally despite the sharp throb in her ankle.

"It was only because the boy was practicing reading the news-paper that they even knew about the study," Lee said. "He read the advert and mentioned it to Abe yesterday. Apparently, he'd been fol-lowing him around through the fields like a little mimic."

The image of Joey as a vibrantly irritating child crossed her mind, causing her eyes to prick with tears. She blinked them away.

Lee patted the hand on his arm. "Come now, Everleigh. We've done good work here. Once we tell the doctors, they'll know what to do. With any luck, Joey will be up and badgering his caretakers before long."

Saffron couldn't honestly reply that she felt the same, so she said nothing. She nearly lost her footing at an unexpected dip in the ground, and Lee's grasp tightened on her arm, bringing her against his body. He was radiating heat just as she was. She glanced up at him as he resettled her. From this angle, his profile was noble, with a broad forehead and a straight nose neither too long nor too short. His sharp jaw was smooth, and his high cheekbones were pink with the heat. A bead of sweat threatened to trickle down his temple. She'd emerge from their cases sunburnt and sweat soaked, and he'd be the picture of urbanity. It was quite satisfying to see him less than perfect.

When he raised a brow at her staring, she asked, "Why didn't the local doctor attend Joey?"

"Mrs. Evans requested the fellow come right away, but there is apparently a long-standing unpaid debt keeping the doctor from treating any member of the Evans family." His voice dropped to a confidential murmur despite their isolation. "Mrs. Evans didn't have the coin to pay him anyway, though the stipend from the study will help. I spoke to the doctor at the military camp to ensure Joey's bill would be taken care of. That handy little letter was very convincing."

Any relief she felt tensed back to concern. The letter explaining the nature of the study from the university was useful, but it didn't guarantee anything. The compensation given to the poisoning victims for allowing Lee and Saffron to take their information and samples would be cold comfort if the little boy didn't recover.

But their job was done, or at least that is what Dr. Aster would tell her. They'd done what they were meant to do. And she hadn't been completely useless, even if she felt it now—she'd identified the plant.

These thoughts circled in her head throughout the walk back to the farm house. Something about the renewed knowledge of the lurking dangers in the shades of green, pink, and brown made the view less idyllic than before.

Chapter 2

University College London was quiet when Saffron and Lee stepped onto campus that afternoon. The hum of traffic was like a lullaby, muffled as it was within the quadrangle that formed the heart of the university. The tall, stony-faced buildings seemed to slumber beneath a blazing blue sky. Green leaves shaded the corners of the Quad, where flowers drooped in their shadowed beds. Saffron felt akin to the flowers; suffering in the heat brought on the sun they waited all year for. Saffron had been saturated with this highly anticipated work for weeks now and was, herself, drooping.

Still arm in arm with Lee, Saffron made her painful way toward the North Wing, a stately length of hall that bracketed the domed centerpiece of the campus, the Wilkins Building. She paused just outside the glossy black door of the North Wing, blotting her brow to allow herself a moment to brace herself for the three sets of stairs that separated her from the squashy couch in her office.

At Lee's meaningful clearing of his throat, she sucked in a breath between her teeth and made to open the door.

He did not move, drawing her back against his side. "As much as I appreciate you leaving your nasty little specimens about our work place, Everleigh, I would prefer not to maintain a cozy acquaintance with *that*."

Saffron looked down at her hand, which still clutched the leather bag. In her determination not to let Lee know how painful her ankle was, she'd entirely forgotten about the slightly withered hemlock.

Lee plucked the bag from her hands. "I'll just run this over to the greenhouses, shall I? Let Winters deal with it."

He strode off before she could agree. She pushed the door open, ignoring each stab of pain as she entered the quiet, cool hall. Her slightly uneven steps echoed loudly in the vacant stairwell. There had been a time when she would have missed the crowds of students and professors, perhaps when she was a bright-eyed girl electrified by the thrill of her first days as a student, but that time had long since passed. The summer holidays could not have come a moment too soon. The fewer people on campus, the fewer mouths there were to pass on whispers about the girl who'd gotten rid of her department head by getting him jailed for attempted murder.

The story wasn't entirely accurate, but Saffron wasn't necessarily averse to being known for sending a monster like Dr. Berking, or his horrible partner, alias Richard Blake, to prison. But it made life easier when the campus was quiet, and there was less for Lee to pick up on. The man was distractible enough without gawkers giving him fuel for his chattering.

Saffron unlocked her office door, and as she entered, she touched the little brass plaque that stated "S. Everleigh" in proud letters. Two steps to the couch, and she bit her lip on a whimper of relief as she sank onto the cool leather. She'd refused to remove her boot on the train, despite the terrible swelling, and contemplated taking it off as she shed her jacket. She winced at the sunburn on her arms. Gingerly, she propped her foot on the couch's arm and rested her head on the other, grateful that, for the moment, the office was hers alone.

Though she'd shared this space with Lee since nearly the day she received the keys, this was *her* office. After all, they were in the North Wing, the domain of the Biology Department, including Botany, not one of the many new buildings the university had bought up for medical studies, nor across the street in the hospital. Lee was occupying her space temporarily. And occupying it loudly. And messily. His desk was a small and battered piece of furniture that was snuggly fit into the little alcove she'd imagined she would one day fill with shelves full of her own research. Lee gave Dr. Maxwell, her mentor, a run for his money when it came to disorganization. Saffron never took it upon herself to organize his piles of books and files on his behalf, however. Her days of sorting papers, making tea, and taking notes for her colleagues were over.

For the moment, the whitewashed walls and dark wood paneling were pleasantly peaceful, if a little stuffy. She looked longingly at the two windows behind her own desk—a sturdy piece that was notably larger than Lee's—and considered hopping across the room to open them. Too much work, she decided, settling deeper into the couch cushions. The spurts of green that lined the windowsill caught her eye, as they always did. Small plant cuttings rested in test tubes she'd procured from a storage cupboard, and admittedly some of them were poisonous.

Her lips curved into a smile as she traced the familiar angles of the leaves sprouting from the noxiously yellow vine in the center of the sill. She had developed an odd affection for the xolotl vine, if only because it reminded her of the man with whom she'd survived it.

A knock rattled the door's glass, and Saffron arched her head back on the arm rest to glare at the frosted pane. She certainly wasn't getting up for Lee's benefit; the door was unlocked. When the knuckles rapped again, she groaned and sat up, spinning around to face the door. "For heaven's sake, open it yourself. I am absolutely not opening the door for you, you lazy—"

Her insult died on her tongue as the door swung open to reveal Detective Inspector Green.

"Inspector!" Saffron choked, scrambling to her feet.

The detective stood in her doorway with his homburg hat in his hand. He looked precisely the same as he had months ago when she'd harassed him with her ideas about Berking and Blake: tidy, medium brown hair over a bland face touched with lines. The only hint of personality was the shine of intelligence in his brown eyes. Those eyes were currently wrinkled into what Saffron could only assume was an amused expression.

Awkwardly, Saffron stood and hobbled toward the door. "I beg your pardon. I thought—well, no matter. Do come in."

"Don't trouble yourself," he said politely as he stepped inside and glanced around. "I understand congratulations are in order for your recent promotion. I'm told you're now a researcher for the Botany Department."

"Yes, thank you." Painfully, she crossed the room to at her desk. She gestured for the inspector to sit opposite her, and he did.

"I hear that Dr. Maxwell has taken an extended leave," he said with the air of a question.

It still jolted her some days, especially when she walked into the North Wing, caught up in her thoughts, and found herself outside of Maxwell's door, only to recall that her office was two doors down. "Yes, he did. I'm not sure when he'll return to the U." She shook off the touch of melancholy that thought brought on and added, "As a part of my graduate studies, I'm doing work in the realm of phytotoxicology, or botanical poisons. I've been working with a doctor to examine the effects of certain local botanical toxins more specifically."

"Sounds like important work," Inspector Green said.

Saffron couldn't help but smile. It was important work, even if it sometimes seemed like attempting to patch a sinking ship riddled with holes. For every case they attended, she was certain there were hundreds more. Dr. Aster, her department head, never told them how many reports of poisonings they received, only passed on which ones they would assist with.

It bothered her that she wasn't entirely sure what the arrangements were that provided her and Lee with such timely reports of poisonings, apart from the adverts in newspapers in communities near London. But she knew better than to press her notoriously taciturn department head for information.

When she and Lee had begun this venture six weeks ago, she was still reeling from the trial of Berking and Blake. It had been a rushed affair, to allow for the departure of the university's expedition crew to Brazil, so Saffron's attention had been split between the details of her new study and preparing to testify against the men who'd tried to poison her, Alexander Ashton, and the expedition leader's wife. Her role in the trial had been rather different from what she'd imagined, and now, weeks later, Saffron felt it was too late to ask Aster to confirm some of the fuzzier details of the study she and Lee had been assigned. It wasn't so much a study as a collection of case studies. Lee attended to victims of suspected botanical poisonings, and Saffron discovered the culprits in fields and gardens. They both collected samples, then wrote up a report and analysis of the plants and toxins involved and submitted it to Aster. She wasn't discovering new species, nor was Lee creating new ways of treating patients, but they were assisting those in need and getting some interesting field experience while doing it.

Saffron had to admit that she was delighted to be receiving such attention for her work from the new head of the Botany Department, rather than the lecherous attention the previous one used to give her. Even if that attention came with a partner she hadn't expected or wanted.

Saffron smiled appreciatively at Inspector Green. "The study definitely is informative. But please, tell me what brings you here."

The inspector tilted his head thoughtfully. "You'll remember when we wrapped up our previous business that you were less than impressed with the Yard's poisons expert. I believe your exact words were that you could do a better job." Saffron flushed at this, but he continued. "Now, I can't replace the man, but I'm within my power to seek alternatives when needed. I've been given a case, Miss Everleigh, and I want your help."

Saffron had to stop her jaw from dropping. Surely this was a joke. The inspector had resented her meddling and poking about in his investigation and had warned her off several times! Of course, he wasn't serious.

Before she had the chance to reply, he extracted a file from his pocket and opened it, handing her several photographs. "What do you make of these?"

The glossy photographs showed a bouquet in a crystal vase on a polished table. The other images were close-ups of the flowers.

"A bouquet?" Saffron asked. "Well . . ."

She examined the black and white images. The first thing she noticed was a long stalk of something drooping over the edge of the vase that bore small fruit that would fit in the circle created by putting her forefinger and thumb together. The crown on the tops of the immature fruits indicated these could only be one thing—pomegranates.

A cluster of small flowers under the pomegranate branch called to mind buttercups she might have searched out in the fields surrounding her grandfather's estate, competing with her father to see who might find the most perfect one. It was an unusual choice for a city-bought bouquet, not the least because it was included on her list of native poisonous plants. They had not yet had a case study with *Ranunculus acris*, perhaps because few would eat it, given the unpleasant acrid taste the plants were named for.

Next to it was a tower of doleful, speckled bells hanging heavily off to one side. It was *Digitalis*, foxglove.

A prickling sensation raced along her arms. Inspector Green was a homicide detective. Perhaps this bouquet had to do with a murder. She could believe it, with the toxic potential of the flowers that comprised it.

She flipped to the next photograph, more close-ups confirming that the little rounded flowers were buttercups. Though, as she squinted down at the photograph, something was strange about their stems. She retrieved her magnifying glass from her desk drawer and examined the photograph closely. "These stems were cut, nicked. That's curious."

"Why?"

"Buttercups are pleasant enough flowers, but the sap causes irritation. There are old stories of people seeking alms from the wealthy by faking skin conditions using the sap of buttercups to muster sympathy. The nicks on the stems look fairly regular. So that would mean the sender . . ." She peered up at him uncertainly.

"Meant to cause harm to the recipient."

There was a pause, during which Saffron rallied her relevant thoughts. "This bouquet isn't something you could easily buy from a shop. Foxglove is common enough fare for flower arrangements, but these buttercups are likely wildflowers, and a pomegranate branch . . . I've never seen such a thing in a bouquet."

Inspector Green removed from his file another set of photographs. "And these?"

Saffron searched the photographs quickly. They showed lush tube-rose and the delicate blooms of a rhododendron bush. She shuffled the photographs for a better detailed image. Another angle revealed a grim-looking flower she knew all too well.

"Aconite?" She glanced up at the inspector, who nodded.

The forlorn hoods of the aconite flower were nestled next to another familiar plant, one that was equally unpleasant. The broad, heart-shaped leaves of *Urtica dioica* were covered in tiny hairs that caught on skin and left behind histamines, according to Lee. They'd responded to a case of dermatitis as a result of incautious contact with stinging nettle.

She identified each plant to Inspector Green, whereupon he asked, "Would you mind writing it down?"

With the magnifier in hand, Saffron jotted down the components of the bouquets, lingering over the nettle. There was no way that had been included without the sender's knowledge that it was dangerous. When she was finished, she passed the paper to Inspector Green, who made a movement as if to leave.

"Inspector?"

"Yes?"

They looked at each other for a long moment before Saffron, gauging her luck, asked, "Have the recipients of these bouquets been killed?"

"They have."

She refrained from leaning forward across her desk in interest. "How did they die? Were they poisoned?"

"Strangulation," he said with distaste. "The other was smothered and suffocated."

"Oh." Saffron blinked. That wasn't at all what she'd expected.

The inspector allowed silence to fall in the warm room. After a minute, he cleared his throat and said, "It's unusual, no doubt. I recognized the aconite, thanks to your evidence in the Berking and Blake case, and thought there might be something to the flowers since they were present in both cases. I thought you might shed some light on them. For example, where would the perpetrator get these plants?"

Saffron considered, examining the photographs again. "Did these incidents happen this week?"

"No. The first was two weeks ago, the twenty-eighth of July. The second took place two days later."

"Ah." Saffron mulled over the dates, wondering why the inspector had waited nearly two weeks to ask her about the bouquets.

"All of these plants would be easy to find," she told him. "They would be in bloom, and they're mostly garden staples, like rhododendron. That's actually poisonous as well. Honey made from rhododendron flowers felled legions of Greek soldiers two thousand years ago. It's really quite funny; another army made the same mistake a few hundred years later."

Saffron caught the vague amusement on Inspector Green's face and cut herself off. She couldn't help but get excited. This conversation touched precisely on what she had been working so hard on. But this was about murder, so it called for circumspection.

Straightening up and folding her hands before her on the desk, Saffron said calmly, "Poisonous plants aren't uncommon, even in carefully planned gardens. Most people don't realize how many dangerous things are right under their noses. This person could have cut most of these plants from a garden or bought them in a shop. Apart from the nettle, no one but someone with knowledge of old remedies would grow that intentionally." When the inspector lifted an inquisitive brow, she added, "Nettles are covered with trichomes, needle-like hairs that release irritating chemicals into the skin, but they're also used to make medicinals for joint pain and diuretics."

He got out his notebook and wrote as he spoke. "So, we're looking for someone with access to a garden or a flower shop. Possibly someone with access to an herb garden. Anything else?"

"Whoever made this bouquet would also need access to a pomegranate tree that no one would mind was suddenly missing a branch." She felt like she was grasping at straws with that comment. She regretted she couldn't be more specific. "I couldn't prove if the flowers were from the same garden, even if I had the chance to see the flowers in person since they're different species. Do you believe they're from the same person?"

Inspector Green's expression cleared of whatever hint of amusement he'd worn throughout their interview. "We can't prove they're the same sender. Apart from that the black ribbons that tied both bouquets are an exact match." He stood, looking less severe. "Still, it's nothing definite. Telephone the station, or come by, if anything comes to mind. I appreciate your assistance."

Disappointed that she hadn't been able to provide him more insight than what he could have found in a flower guidebook, she asked quickly, "Can I keep the photographs, just for a few days?"

The inspector nodded and picked up the list of flowers. Saffron stood and accompanied him to the door, where they shook hands before he departed.

CHAPTER 3

Lee entered the office moments after the inspector disappeared down hall.

He sat on the couch, arm stretched over the top, as relaxed as if he'd been sitting there for hours. "Who was that?"

"An old colleague of mine," Saffron said lightly, crossing gingerly back to her desk. "Just stopped by to ask for some advice."

"From the university?"

"No." She flipped over one of the photographs, relishing her advantage. Lee was curious, she could tell.

"Oh, you're making me be a detective, are you?" He smiled slyly. "Fine, I'll detect. You haven't worked outside of the university, unless I'm very much mistaken. He had the air of a working man, so definitely not a university donor. Volunteer work perhaps? Didn't seem like the godly sort, so not a man of the cloth. He came for no more than an hour, as I haven't been gone that long. He brought you something, and it's on your desk. You keep looking down at it," he finished triumphantly.

She leaned her elbows on top of the desk to obscure the photographs. "All right, Sherlock, any deductions? Who is my mysterious colleague?"

He stroked his chin in faux concentration. "I say . . . that man is a police officer."

Saffron's mouth dropped open. "How could you possibly know that?"

Lee cackled. "I met him in the hall on my way back." She pursed her lips. "Well, what did he want? Did you get fed up with someone and slip them one of your ghastly samples? You're being hauled off to prison?"

"As I said, he came to consult me," she said with forced dignity.

"Did he bring you anything interesting?"

"Nothing to interest *you*." She shuffled around a few papers, avoiding looking at the photographs. Lee looked at her suspiciously but said nothing.

This was precisely the problem with this partnership, she groused as she flicked through her notebook. She'd expected a far less involved partner, one she saw maybe once or twice a week, not a man who sat practically on top of her in her office, mussing her books and papers, taking up all the air in the stuffy room. She shot him a severe look, only to catch him suppressing a smile as he thumbed through one of his medical textbooks.

After pretending to ignore the photographs for five minutes, sneaking glances when she thought Lee wasn't looking, she finally gave up. "Very well. Come and see what he brought me."

He was at her side in a moment, with a broad grin. "If you insist."

She showed him the photographs and described the mysterious bouquets. Lee examined them with the magnifying glass, leaning over her with utter disregard for her personal space. At least he smelled pleasant.

"I don't know half these flowers," he said, straightening up and leaning a hip on her desk. "Even with your edifying influence, I might only be able to pick roses out of a flower garden. I've sent my fair share of those to worthy gals." He winked; she rolled her eyes. "Roses are all well and good, I suppose, for the right woman. And the right sort, of course. Red roses can be dangerous things, though, and I'm not talking about thorns. Red speaks too loudly of love. I made that mistake in my youth. I believe her name was Lucille, and she was a first-rate girl, let me tell you . . ."

Saffron had long since stopped listening. Roses represented love. And there was rosemary for remembrance, of course. She'd memorized that bit of Shakespeare easily: *"There's rosemary for you, that's for remembrance. Pray you, love, remember. And there is pansies, that's for thoughts . . ."* It made Saffron wonder what each of the flowers in the bouquets were for.

"I'll just go to the library," she murmured, interrupting Lee's reminiscence about his past paramour.

"What, now? Why?"

"I want to look something up," she said noncommittally, gathering up her things.

"Well, if you're going to the library, I might as well come too."

The pain in her ankle hadn't lessened any, but it was far easier to ignore now she had something so fascinating to occupy her mind. They passed through the empty hall that connected the North Wing to the Wilkins Building, which housed the library. The octagonal Flaxman Gallery in the foyer of the building was utterly silent and still. The motes of dust suspended in the stagnant air of the high ceiling moved no more than the marble statue dominating the center of the room.

A musty rush of slightly cooler air washed over her as they passed through the glass-paneled doors into the library.

The long hall filled with tall shelves was equally noiseless, though the tables were dotted with a handful of late-afternoon researchers. Lee followed Saffron to a spot they frequented, the small botany section near the back.

"I thought we were going to look at something interesting," Lee groaned over Saffron's shoulder.

He wandered away. Saffron's eyes ran over titles she'd practically memorized over the years. No, nothing that would help here. She wondered where etiquette books would be, if any were in the university's library at all.

She found her way to the social section, and there she found what she was looking for. A small book sat lonely on the bottom shelf. It was called, rather wordily she thought, *Flowers: Their Language, Poetry, and Sentiment.* The book declared, *"No spoken word can approach to the delicacy of sentiment to be inferred from a flower seasonably offered."*

Saffron brought the book to the nearest table. She spread out the photographs in front of her. In the clear, blue-tinted light coming from the nearest window, she annotated the flowers in each bouquet with the interpretations offered by the book.

The bouquets became more meaningful, and concerning, with every turn of a page. There was a whole, alarming story written out in those petals. In her notebook, she wrote:

Bouquet One, strangled:
Buttercup—desire for riches, or childishness
Foxglove—insincerity
Pomegranate—conceit, or foolishness

She moved to the next bouquet, and found its flowers were just as meaningful.

Bouquet Two, suffocated:
Tuberose—dangerous pleasure, or a sweet voice
Rhododendron—danger, or agitation
Aconite—treachery
Nettle—slander, or cruelty

Biting the end of her pen, she puzzled over the last one. Several of the flowers had double meanings, but perhaps only one meaning was intended. For someone who'd been murdered, dangerous pleasure seemed more likely than a sweet voice.

She could hardly believe that anyone was actually interested in floriography anymore, its popularity having faded decades ago, but the combination of flowers told such a clear story, there was no way the bouquets had been assembled by accident.

"Not pleased with the flowers?" Lee asked, making her jump. He slid into a chair across from her.

She smoothed a hand over her notebook with a frown. "If I'm to believe in the Victorian tradition of secret messages via bouquets, then no, I'm not pleased at all. These are not happy flowers."

Without asking, he took her notebook and held it up to read. "No . . . not happy," he concluded, putting it back in front of her. "Well, shall we head back then?"

"Back to where?" Saffron asked, gathering up her things.

"The office, Everleigh—where we live these days."

Saffron shook her head. "No, I'll have to see if I can find another flower guide. I don't know if these are the only interpretations for these flowers."

"What? You're going off to investigate nasty bouquets? What about the study?" Lee's green eyes were incredulous. "And what of your ankle? You can barely walk."

Guilt touched her mind, but they had done what they could for Joey Evans, and her ankle would heal well enough, even if she did walk on it a bit more. Dr. Aster would expect a report tomorrow, but that could be done in the morning. It would be impossible to concentrate when she had evidence from two murders to investigate.

❧

"I'm home, Eliza," Saffron called from the front door of the flat.

"Yes, darling, I gathered from the door slamming," Elizabeth said, poking her head out from the kitchen. Her flatmate's sandy blonde bob was in perfect waves, her dark red lipstick impeccable, though it was late in the afternoon. "Have a pleasant day?"

"Considering there is a boy in Aldershot poisoned with hemlock"—she paused as she discarded her dusty hat and gloves on the little table at the door to the flat—"and there is every possibility I won't be able to walk tomorrow, I would say not a pleasant day." Her search for more information about floriography had been pointless; neither of the secondhand book shops she'd gone to nor the lending library had stocked anything about flowers, let alone an outmoded method of communicating with them, and she'd nearly brought herself to tears attempting to board a bus with her abused ankle. She'd given up and come home, displeased but not discouraged.

"No, indeed," Elizabeth replied sympathetically. Her expression turned shrewd within seconds as she added, "Lee isn't here, is he?"

"I left him at the U. You're safe from his overwhelming charms."

Elizabeth snorted and disappeared back into the kitchen. Her words were slightly muffled as she called, "No need to tempt fate by sending him into my orbit once again."

Saffron laughed and limped down the hall. "Oh yes. Two meteoric individuals such as yourselves will inevitably collide if you spend too much time together."

"It's bound to happen, you know," was Elizabeth's response as Saffron entered the small kitchen. "We are too spirited, too full of joie de vivre. He, the charismatic doctor, and me, the glamorous poet. You simply cannot have that much personality in one place."

Saffron smothered a laugh. Putting Lee and Elizabeth in the same room together had produced fascinating results, namely, an instant, inexplicable dislike on Elizabeth's part. Lee responded with overly courteous gestures that only served to further antagonize her. "Never mind about Lee. Guess who appeared at my office door today?"

Elizabeth was all astonishment as Saffron explained the bouquets and their supposed meanings.

"I can't say I'm surprised he came to you for assistance," Elizabeth said, going to the sink, where she began peeling a potato. "We all know that anything green and poisonous is your ideal occupation." Elizabeth cast her a dark look—she had not been overjoyed to learn Saffron would be continuing to study poisons—which gave way to a grin. "Well done, darling."

Saffron stood to help her prepare supper, but Elizabeth pointed to the kitchen door. "You've got to rest that ankle if you're going to get on with the bouquets. Besides, your post is in your room. You'll be most excited when you see who wrote you."

Saffron acquiesced, knowing she was as useless in the kitchen as her ankle was currently. Elizabeth, her lifelong best friend and flatmate since they'd arrived in London a few years ago, was the domestic one. Her self-taught cooking skills bordered on gourmet, and her partiality for cleanliness erred on the side of fanatical. Elizabeth kept house for the pair of them in addition to working as a receptionist and writing lurid poetry in her spare time. It suited Saffron just fine; her own domestic abilities were limited to the upper-class training of budgeting a large household, menu approval, and arranging flowers. Her mother and grandmother had certainly never anticipated Saffron living the life she'd made for herself, a scientist working in London.

In her cozy bedroom, Saffron managed to pluck her boot from her sore ankle with only one minor curse slipping from her lips. She settled on her bed to examine the swollen joint, but was immediately distracted by the letters Elizabeth had laid on the foot of her bed.

The looping, elegant handwriting on the smaller envelope, stating her name and address, gave her pause. This was definitely not the letter Elizabeth had been so gleeful about.

She picked it up, feeling immediately that the envelope could only contain a piece or two of her grandmother's expensive sheets of stationery. She opened it, then scanned the neatly written words.

And sighed.

She hadn't known what to expect when she'd finally told her mother and grandparents, the Viscount and Viscountess Easting, about her involvement in the poisoning affair a few months before. Her testimony had been needed to make the case, or so the prosecuting barristers had told her, and she had been more than willing to provide it. She'd had no intention of allowing those monsters to go free—or have lesser sentences because she was too afraid of public scrutiny.

But her grandfather had had other plans. One day, Saffron was rehearsing her answers to the barrister's supplied questions, and the next, her grandfather's solicitor, Mr. Feyzi, was knocking at the door of her office, telling her that she needed only to write a sworn testimony that would be read aloud in court. After a brief moment of hurt that her grandfather hadn't bothered to contact her himself, let alone inquire as to her well-being after being *poisoned*, she had agreed. Her study began the next week, and she'd been somewhat relieved that she wouldn't have to balance her time between the trial and her first independent work as a researcher.

This letter, brief as it was, was just another reminder of the renewed gulf of separation that had developed between her and her family. Her grandmother continued to suggest that she return home, not realizing that Ellington hadn't been Saffron's home for years. The only person Saffron regretted staying away from was her mother.

Saffron sat staring at her grandmother's letter for so long that her eyes burned, and she closed them on the biting words. *"You have proven your point,"* she wrote, *"that you are just as capable of wasting time with dusty books and dirt as your father was. Be of value to our family, and return here to see how you may be of service to your mother."*

Violet Everleigh was as loving and caring as one could wish a mother to be, but it was clear that her lively but fragile spirit had been damaged by the heartbreak of losing her husband in the Great War. Saffron's response to her father dying had been to delve into his passion, botany, and her mother's had been to sequester herself, as if she might avoid further heartbreak by hiding. It had been years since Saffron could recall her mother leaving her grandparents' house.

As much as it pained her to admit, Saffron's presence had not helped before she'd left Ellington, and it would not help her mother gain the courage to move beyond its doors now.

Her hand unconsciously moved to her aching ankle. She may not be of much use to her mother, but she was of use to others. She'd helped catch two would-be murderers and prevented them stealing money from the university, and she'd identified the harmful materials that Joey and a handful of others had consumed. It wasn't lifesaving—not like what Lee could do—but it was better than sipping tea in the parlor with dull suitors, coordinating the church fete, or knitting. Saffron grimaced. She *detested* knitting.

Despite their own frequent correspondence, her mother didn't know exactly what Saffron was doing at the university. The deception was a painful one, but it would only worry her mother to know that she was out in the field chasing down poisonous plants. Helping people was a goal her mother would always approve of. There was a time when she'd felt sure that her father would have felt the same.

She tossed the letter aside.

A large, battered envelope from Macapá, Brazil, beckoned to her. She traced her fingers along the messy scrawl of her name before carefully opening the envelope.

She first saw a photograph, folded in tissue paper. A group of men stood in three rows at a campsite surrounded by blurred trees. They looked seriously at the camera, their loose shirts and trousers in varying states of disarray. Dr. Lawrence Henry, broad and strapping as ever, stood at ease in the center of the group. Saffron squinted at the photograph, searching for a certain biologist among them.

She found him on the edge in the back. Alexander Ashton was nearly unrecognizable with his face partially obscured by a short, dark beard. What a pity young men didn't wear beards these days, she thought to herself, teeth sinking into her lower lip. His expression was serious, as it so often was, with his brows lowered slightly over dark eyes, the firm line of his mouth set. His black curls were a bit overlong and unruly. She examined the imprecise lines and shadows of his face for far too long before moving down to the rest of him. He wore no collar nor tie, allowing his shirt to part at his breastbone. He had a bandage around his hand, clearly visible with his shirtsleeves rolled up.

Saffron let out an appreciative sigh. He was very handsome with a beard. She put the photograph to the side and read the letter.

July 23, 1923

Dear Saffron,

Thank you for your last letter. It was a pleasant read as we went up the river to Santarém, where the Tapajós and Amazon rivers meet. The quote you included from Walt Whitman seemed especially fitting as we passed through miles and miles of wildness. The Earth does indeed feel incomprehensible and rude at times, but I feel as if I might be beginning to understand the divinity of the jungle, as he suggests. Though we've been here for nine weeks, our travels haven't even been a drop in the sea of trees and creatures and water that is the Amazon. I wish you could be here to see it.

Saffron's smile grew at those words. It was tempting to read something tender in them.

No new horrors have passed since Trumont was bit by that snake, as described in my previous letter. He's made a full recovery, by the way, and is supposed to be joining us in a few weeks, after we return from Santarém. I look forward to handing off the work his absence put on me. Your desired specimens are quite enough work already.

You'll be pleased to hear that I've located half of them, although I can't be sure of their constant supply as we can't harvest them until the month we depart. The strychnos, in particular, has been easy to find. Many of our guides have adamantly discouraged me from touching the fruit. They seem to think I'm going to eat it, so I learned the phrase for "I'm not going to eat it—I'm not an idiot," in the languages they speak. They appear doubtful.

A little laugh escaped her lips. His dry humor was always unexpected.

Due to the distance and the nature of our tasks in Santarém, I'm not sure when I'll next be able to send a timely letter. By the time you read this, we'll have come and gone from the city and won't return again for some weeks. According to Dr. Henry, we're likely to be murdered in our sleep by three different native tribes and attacked by several malicious creatures on this leg of the journey. I think the poisoning business rather set him on edge. I'll write if I'm not maimed by a venomous mango.

I hope your study is progressing to your satisfaction and you're well.

Yours,

Alexander Ashton

P.S.—The photograph I've included is the team I'm traveling with for the next month. I'm sure you'll notice right away the bandage. Not to worry: it was a brief disagreement with a jaguarundi over whether I'd be allowed to climb its tree. Apparently, I was not.

Saffron reread his message and returned to the photograph for an inordinate amount of time.

When Elizabeth called down the hall to her for supper, she tucked the letter carefully away in a drawer, with all the other missives from Brazil, and left the photograph out to return to later. She would definitely be spending more time contemplating Alexander Ashton with a beard.

CHAPTER 4

Two days later, Saffron telephoned Inspector Green from the university to share her possible interpretations of the bouquets. She'd hobbled around to every bookshop and lending library she could manage but had not had any luck finding another flower dictionary. Even without another source to confirm it, she could at least tell him the first bouquet seemed to be an accusation, and the second a warning of sorts.

It was an odd warning to give before murdering someone, she thought as she picked up the receiver. What sort of killer gave his victim a warning through flowers?

It made her hesitant to share her idea with Inspector Green at all. But she felt guilty leaving him with so little useful information when he'd specifically sought out her help.

She requested to be connected to the police station and settled onto the stool tucked into the minute telephone nook on the ground floor of the North Wing. She wrapped the cord around her finger as she awaited the connection, idly tracing the words scratched into the smudged white wall by mischievous hands.

The inspector's voice soon spoke into her ear. "Miss Everleigh, what can I do for you?"

With a deep breath, Saffron said, "I know it's a long shot, but I tried interpreting the bouquets using a Victorian floriography dictionary, and they both seem to have rather specific messages."

A man came to stand outside the nook, clearly awaiting the telephone. He was dark haired and plain, with his foot tapping impatiently on the black and white tile. She smiled apologetically at him.

After a pause, the inspector's voice asked, "What is floriography?"

Surely, he was going to think she was mad, presenting him with this bizarre idea. With bravado she didn't feel, she launched into her explanation. "It's the Victorian practice of sending messages through flowers. Coming right out and saying something was considered indelicate, so they sent specifically designed bouquets."

"Right," he said slowly.

"I looked up each flower, and according to the definitions, the first bouquet communicated wealth, conceit, and insincerity. The second, the one with aconite, seemed to be a warning of danger or cruelty. I know it all seems a bit far-fetched, but—"

The waiting man scoffed. Saffron inched her head out of the nook and fixed him with a glare. "Do you mind? This is a private conversation."

The man looked like he was going to object, but then he checked his wristwatch. He stalked off.

But the inspector was speaking, so Saffron hurriedly pressed the receiver back to her ear.

". . . according to the flower dictionary, these flowers were telling the victims something."

"Yes," Saffron said, straightening up at the flare of hope she felt because Inspector Green wasn't laughing at her. "But then again, someone could have thrown together bouquets that just happened to have flowers with these specific meanings, the majority of which were poisonous."

"But you don't think so."

Saffron released a breath, unsure of what to say. "Well, no. No one would walk into a garden and choose a pomegranate cutting or nettle when there are so many more pleasant things in bloom. And decoding them with the dictionary made the flower choices seem logical. They make sense when you consider them from a floriography perspective."

"Thank you, Miss Everleigh, that is . . . a unique insight that could prove to be helpful."

He sounded as though he were about to ring off, but now Saffron's curiosity had been piqued even further. "Do you know anything about the victims that could relate to the flowers, Inspector?"

He was silent for a moment, and Saffron held her breath. "The autopsies found barbiturates in the bodies of both victims."

"A barbiturate? Like veronal?" Lee had explained to her about barbiturate salts for the treatment of seizures in the aftermath of the Evans case, and she had, of course, heard of the calming drug known as veronal. She was sure her mother used it.

"And cocaine, in the body of the second victim."

Saffron blinked. "But don't they do the opposite? Cocaine stimulates, and veronal calms one down."

"Indeed," replied the inspector. "It is unclear whether the drugs are related to the murders. Plenty of people take veronal to sleep, and cocaine is not impossible to get one's hands on. I could imagine warning someone of using or abusing drugs. Cocaine and veronal both can be dangerous."

Unsure what else to say, she simply said, "I see. If there's anything more I can do, please let me know."

The inspector thanked her and rang off.

Saffron walked slowly back to the office, through the quiet halls. Strangling or suffocating a woman . . . There was something so grisly—so *visceral*—about preventing someone from breathing until they couldn't anymore. She shivered.

When she opened the door to the office, she found Lee leaning against his desk, oozing charm at a young woman in an outfit of pastel peach. Her bobbed red hair quaked with a little giggle.

Lee caught her eye and straightened up. "Saffron Everleigh, may I introduce Miss Lisa Dennis?"

"How nice to meet you, Miss Dennis," Saffron said, stepping inside and extending her hand. Miss Dennis was quite pretty, with pouting pink lips and brown eyes the color of toffee. She shook Saffron's hand limply. "Are you related to Dr. Dennis, Dr. Lee's colleague?"

"Oh yes," Miss Dennis replied in girlish tones, stepping ever so slightly closer to Lee. "My uncle was one of Lee's professors, once upon a time. That is when we first became acquainted."

"He recently left teaching to practice medicine again," Lee added.

Saffron couldn't help but smile at the look he gave her over Lisa Dennis's shoulder. His grimace spoke of a dull mind behind an attractive face. Lee liked pretty girls but mocked the dimwitted of either sex. "How nice. Are you also interested in medicine?"

Miss Dennis's pert nose wrinkled. "No, certainly not. I mean," she said with a little glance in Lee's direction, then continuing more graciously, "it's *frightfully* important and ever so fascinating, but I would be useless at such things. Though I do sometimes volunteer for the Ladies Council at St. Thomas's Hospital, of course, for their gala and such."

The girl stood there beaming at Saffron, who didn't know if she was meant to retreat or insist that Miss Dennis leave so she could rescue Lee. She didn't particularly feel like waiting around to see how much longer Miss Dennis would awkwardly smile at her, so she said, "Well, it was very nice to meet you, but I'm afraid I must dash off to the library. Dr. Lee and I have a report due soon." Smiling too sweetly at Lee, she asked, "Do you have that section for me to revise? I'd hate to keep you from your friend."

Lee handed her the file with a thin smile. "We must get cracking on the conclusion, you know."

"I can manage it myself, so you can spend time with your friend." She exited with a cheery wave.

Very little work was accomplished at the library. Amusement at Lee soon gave way to grim thoughts about what Inspector Green had told her, and she found herself puzzling over the bouquets' descriptions when she ought to have been writing.

When she returned an hour later, she found Lee sitting at her desk. Eyes narrowed, he pecked away on her typewriter.

"Goodness, why are you typing? You're going to waste good paper and ink!" Saffron chided.

He looked at her darkly over the Underwood's black and gold keys. "It was the only way I could get Miss Dennis to leave. She insisted on sitting and watching me work."

"I suppose she thought it'd be flattering."

"It would be if I was actually doing rounds in a ward or something. I think my typing gave her a headache, so she finally sighed off," Lee said, leaning into her chair with his arms spread wide in an idle stretch. "Now you're back, you can type."

"No, I think you ought to keep at it. Good to practice. Maybe someday you'll be good enough to do your own typing," Saffron replied in a falsely encouraging voice. "You, too, Dr. Lee, can be a typist."

"Golly, I can't wait," Lee muttered, squinting at the paper coming from the top of the typewriter. He plucked the paper out and brought it inches from his face to reread. "And another piece for the bin."

"It could be," Saffron said, coming to stand at his side to pressure him to vacate her chair, "that you need eyeglasses but are too vain to accept it."

Lee, unmoving, scoffed and changed the subject. "How was your telephone call with the inspector?"

The imagined vision of a glassy-eyed woman with gray skin rose once more in her mind. "The women who received the flowers were murdered. One was strangled, the other suffocated."

He stood and leaned a hip on her desk. "And?"

Saffron crossed her arms. "And? They were *murdered*! That's quite enough to be upset about, I should think."

"People are killed every day, Everleigh. Why take this one so hard?"

"Because they were killed brutally, and the murderer could be out there right now, picking more nasty flowers to send before killing someone else. Why shouldn't I take that seriously?" Lee just looked at her. Blue eyes glared at green eyes. "Not everyone can be as flippant about death as you."

Lee turned thoughtful, stroking a finger down his red tie. "Flippant? I wouldn't say flippant. I would say . . . understanding. When you've seen it as often and in such varied situations, death grows less ominous and more commonplace. Everyone dies, one way or another."

That was surprisingly philosophical, not that she'd ever admit it. "And some ways are absolutely ghastly and should be prevented."

"That is true. So, what will you do now?"

"What do you mean?"

Lee raised an eyebrow. "For the investigation?"

"Oh," Saffron said, surprised. "I don't know if there is anything else for me to do, apart from keeping an eye out for missing poisonous plants around the city. Or interviewing people with drug problems—perhaps they can give some insight into the second victim."

"Drug problems? Did the second victim die of an overdose?"

"No, but she was found with veronal and cocaine in her system. She was suffocated."

He made a sound of distaste. "Veronal and cocaine? And she didn't die mixing the two? Good Lord. Did she take veronal regularly?"

"I don't know."

"Did they find more in her medicine cabinet or drawers?"

Saffron frowned, uneasy. "I don't know."

"Was she old, young? Married? Scandalously entangled with anyone?"

His questions only brought home that the woman's life had been suddenly snuffed out, and she had nothing more than conjecture about floriography to help Inspector Green find the murderer. "I don't know. I just know she's dead now," Saffron said with a heavy sigh, sinking into her chair.

Lee clucked his tongue. "What sort of detective are you, Everleigh? The inspector came to you for help, after all. I'm sure you'd be more helpful if you knew more."

She rather doubted that. "More like I could entertain you more with gruesome details of a murder."

"Hardly," Lee said, crossing to his own chair. "I have a professional interest."

"How's that? You're thinking of becoming a police surgeon?"

"That's just autopsy after autopsy. My charm is wasted on the dead. You're clearly going to continue thinking about it, and that distracts you from our work."

Saffron withheld a snort. She was forever forcing *him* back on subject—never the other way around. "Who's to say that the inspector will even give me any details?"

"Did you try asking?"

She considered. "Actually, he did tell me how the victims died when I asked. But I don't want him to think I'm poking around." She didn't mention that was precisely what she'd done last time.

"Everleigh." He sighed, exasperated as he reclined back in his chair. "He invited you to consult on the case for him. He's essentially opened the door to poking."

Saffron leaned back in her own chair, thinking. She *had* done a fair job at investigating Berking and Blake for being completely inexperienced. She'd made some foolish choices, and she knew precisely what she should have done differently. And Lee was right, Inspector Green had come to her for help . . .

This time, she resolved silently as she turned to a fresh page in her notebook, it wouldn't end with drinking poison at gunpoint.

CHAPTER 5

The next afternoon, Saffron walked into the police station near King's Cross. Four floors rose above the busy street, each window decorated with a heavy stone cornice, and the entry to the station was marked by an elaborate carving of the royal coat of arms that stood over the door. The elegant exterior was not reflected inside. Plain tile floors, what could be seen between the boots of bobbies in navy-blue uniforms, were scuffed and stained. The walls had once been white, Saffron guessed, but had long since dulled to uneven gray. That and the close air, smelling of perspiring humanity and simmering with the low hum of conversation, made her feel as if she was walking into a crowded cave.

She gave her name to the desk sergeant, who called it back into the pool of desks behind him, and she settled on an open seat on the bench lining the wall directly inside the doors. There was no time to wonder what Inspector Green would make of her formal offer of assistance; she was immediately distracted by the exceedingly old man next to her describing all the reasons he was there to complain. After the first four, the desk sergeant spoke up.

"Leave 'er alone, Ned, she don't want to hear your whining," he said, sounding like he'd just stepped off a train from Cornwall. He winked at her. "'e's in here every day, telling us the world's ending."

Saffron gave him a small smile. It was the same ruddy-faced officer who'd been kind to her on previous visits to the station. "Thank you," she told him as a familiar young, blond sergeant emerged between a cluster of bobbies and called to her. "Hello, Sergeant Simpson."

Though he was well over the minimum height required to be in uniform, Simpson's peaches-and-cream complexion and the boyish roundness of his face made him seem a decade younger. The youthful admiration with which he'd regarded Inspector Green furthered the impression.

As they wove through the maze of desks, she asked, "Who is the sergeant at the front desk?"

"That's Johnson, miss," he replied over his shoulder as he elbowed through a pack of black-clad bobbies. "Been around here for ages, before the CID was formed. He's lasted through all the clean-ups, probably will outlast me!"

They stepped into the inspector's office.

The close walls were lined with filing cabinets, and cracks staggered across the ceiling. There was a map on one side of the room, and a lamp that looked as if the inspector had brought it from home to add illumination sat behind his desk. The man himself was sitting with hands knitted atop the tidy surface of the battered mahogany desk. He invited her to take a seat.

Saffron cleared her suddenly dry throat. "The woman who was recently suffocated," she began. "I . . . had a thought. Her flowers spoke of loneliness, dangerous pleasure. It sounded like a crime of passion, so to speak. I was wondering, did the woman have a lover?"

She was rather proud of herself that she'd managed to ask the question without embarrassment, but the way the inspector blinked at her made her wonder if she'd been too forward.

Slowly, Inspector Green replied, "Her household and her friends were mum on the subject, but they made it clear she was attached to someone. We need to nail down his identity."

"And the cocaine?"

"We found evidence of recreational rather than medical use. Her closest friends seem to share the habit."

Cocaine was no longer the omnipresence it had once been in the days before and during the Great War, but it certainly had not been stomped out like the government might wish. That being said, Saffron had no idea if it was easy to obtain. "So, the suffocated woman and her friends are involved in drugs. She receives flowers, which warn of dangerous pleasures. That fits together." It was surprising that the floriography *was* apparently relevant. Saffron frowned at the possibilities sprouting in her mind, like *Phyllostachys edulis* shoots. "But who killed her? A disappointed relation or friend? Her cocaine supplier or a lover? Or was her death unrelated?"

"All possibilities. Right now, we're looking to establish connections between the two victims."

"Who are the victims?"

The inspector's expression tightened minutely. Saffron said quickly, "I might know them or know a friend of a friend or something."

Behind her, Simpson shuffled his feet. Saffron bit down on a smile. Simpson had none of Inspector Green's composure, and he'd just told her that she might indeed know these people. Through the university, then? Or a different sort of connection?

Casually, Saffron said, "When I came down to London a few years ago, I did move a bit in society. I knew quite a few debs and their beaus, and my grandmother, Viscountess Easting, certainly made sure they knew of me. I might be familiar with them."

His continued silence felt like a dismissal. She drew herself up in her seat and clutched her hands together. "Inspector, two women have been murdered. I know what the upper class are like in these situations. They'd make it difficult if not impossible to find out the truth. If I can help, then I would like to. Who were they?"

After a considering pause, Inspector Green tapped a finger on his desk before reaching into the pocket of his plain gray suit for his notebook. He flipped to a page and read, "The first, who was strangled, was Mrs. Erin Sullivan. Thirty-eight, residence in Kensington. The second, Miss Bridget Williams, twenty-one, lived in Belgravia."

Saffron wracked her brain for recognition, but to her disappointment, she had nothing apart from noting that each neighborhood was on the wealthier side. "And the friends you mentioned? Miss Williams's friends?"

"Miss Lucy Renée Talbot, daughter of the late Baron Newton, Miss Caroline Genevieve Attwood, and Miss Amelia Jane Gresham."

Saffron didn't recognize any of those names either. It was possible they were simply younger than Saffron, but even more likely that they ran in more wild circles than Saffron had. Elizabeth, who'd had a similar upbringing of wealth and privilege before her family lost their fortune during the war, might be more familiar with the names.

"Who was the first victim, Mrs. Sullivan? What sort of person was she?"

"The wife of Mr. Gordon Sullivan, the head of the Camden Railway Company. No children, extended family lived out of the city. On a number of charity committees." Inspector Green took on a wry expression. "I was told by a number of her friends that she thought very well of herself for her generous work."

She'd endured many a tea and dinner alongside women who had nothing better to do than attempt to manage the lives of people they thought beneath them. "But I suppose no one stood out as having a particularly strong negative opinion of her?"

Inspector Green shook his head. "I believe they didn't care to cast the first stone."

Her lips twitched with the desire to smile, but she didn't want to seem as though she wasn't taking it all seriously. "And you said she was strangled."

He shifted in his seat. "She had been strangled with necklaces, costly ones. Diamonds, sapphires, gold, etcetera."

Saffron blinked at him. "She'd been strangled with her own jewelry?" That was bizarrely dreadful. "She wasn't strangled by hand? Then the necklaces were placed over top?"

"The ligature marks indicate it was done by a length of a thin material. Could be a soft but durable material, like thin silk cord, or a smooth length of chain, of which several were immediately surrounding the body."

"But wouldn't a chain break? If Mrs. Sullivan struggled . . ." The rest of her words fell away as she shuddered.

"The barbiturate we found in her blood would have likely prevented her from struggling." He shifted slightly in his chair, then added, "A few pieces of jewelry were found in her mouth."

A chill skittered over her skin at the image that conjured. "Did the murderer put them there?"

"That is what it looks like," Inspector Green said. "It suggests a strong personal motive."

"But it was also a robbery," Simpson added from behind her. "The lady's maid confirmed a few pieces of jewelry were missing."

It wasn't just about killing, but possibly money, then. The other victim was likely well-off too, living in Belgravia. "And Miss Williams?"

"By all accounts, she lived a charmed life," Inspector Green said, flipping pages in his notebook again. "Her father, Richard Haberly Williams, died when she was young. Her mother, Belinda Williams, née Berkley, was wealthy in her own right and died from influenza. Miss Williams lived off their fortune, and by all accounts did nothing but spend it."

"But there's nothing connecting the two victims?" Saffron asked.

"None thus far." The inspector gave her a wary look and continued, "Now, Miss Everleigh, because you are officially consulting, you may receive this information, but you are not to repeat it to anyone." Her guilt must have been obvious on her face, for his lips flattened into a grimace. "You've already told someone? I hope not that flatmate of yours."

Saffron grimaced. "No, just my colleague, Dr. Michael Lee. I believe you met him in the hall at the university the other day. It was his idea about the second victim having a boyfriend. He won't say anything. Or if he does, it'll just be to me, for hours on end."

Inspector Green shifted in his chair, folding his hands across his abdomen. "A doctor knows the strictures of confidentiality. Just impress on him the importance of discretion. I can't have you on the case if you're passing on information to outsiders."

"I understand," she said, nodding emphatically. "As I said, I just want to help."

That only served to make the inspector look more uncomfortable. "Right."

She saw that as her cue to leave. She stood. "If I learn anything, I will let you know."

"I'm not telling you to go out and investigate, Miss Everleigh."

"I understand. But if I happen across anything—"

Inspector Green's brow actually lowered a fraction. "I really do not—"

"—I will tell you." Saffron made for the door before he attempted more warnings or changed his mind altogether.

On her return to the university, Saffron found Lee in the library, bent over several large books and blinking sleepily. The warmth of the day hadn't penetrated the thick stone walls of the library, but the air felt especially close and still.

"Time for a lie-down, is it?" Saffron said brightly as she sat down at the long wooden table.

Lee sat up straight and rubbed his neck. "No, time for books with larger print. It's as if they don't want people to read them."

Saffron leaned forward and dropped her voice despite the fact no one was within earshot. "Lee, just how easy is it for one to get their hands on cocaine these days?"

To his credit, the non sequitur didn't stump him. With a smirk, he said, "Either you're thinking to grow a coca plant, or you've been thinking about those murders."

"I went to Inspector Green with my floriography idea. He gave me more details about the smothered woman who'd taken veronal and cocaine. He said her friends were also known to use it. Obviously, they don't sell it to just anyone the way they used to, but it hasn't disappeared entirely. Doctors still prescribe it, for example."

"They do, and it is much more carefully monitored these days. I avoid it whenever possible, both at the sickbed and during my own entertainments." Rather than make an off-color comment about his extensive evening entertainments, his honey-colored brows furrowed. He leaned his forearms over the volume he'd been falling asleep over. "My father—"

"That would be Dr. Lee Senior?"

Lee nodded. "Yes, good old pater. He's always thought it was a dreadful drug since it's so damn addicting. When the war began and everyone was buying little gift packets of the stuff to send off with their soldiers, he worked on my Uncle Matt to do something about it."

Saffron's own brows lifted. "Uncle Matt," as Lee called him so casually, was Matthias Lee, the Baron Carmichael, whose name was familiar across England as a wealthy and influential politician. His younger brother was Lee's father, and considering Lee spoke about his uncle more often than his parents, Saffron gathered they were quite close.

Lee continued. "My father told him all about the evils of the drug, the problems they were sure to see in their all-important fighting force. Uncle Matt gathered some of his cronies and took up the issue with the Army Council, and they passed the act prohibiting the free distribution of cocaine during the war. It wasn't hard to convince them; they were already seeing the effects of its abuse. Chest pains, confusion, paranoia, even seizures, not to mention the horrors of withdrawal. After the war, Uncle Matt and his friends pushed to make the rule stick."

"Yes, but how does one going about getting it today?"

"If I didn't know better . . ." She scowled, and he grinned. "How does one get anything of uncertain legality, Everleigh? One knows someone who knows someone else. It depends on who you know, where you live, how much coin you're willing to throw at the habit."

"Someone in your crowd. Young, wealthy, enjoys a good time."

Lee lifted a questioning brow. "You make an awful lot of assumptions."

"You go out to dinner and dancing twice a week and are usually to be heard crowing about your good times the next morning," she said impatiently. He'd done just that the previous day after stepping out with Lisa Dennis.

"Do I detect a hint of jealously, my dearest partner?" He ran his thumb along his jaw in mock thoughtfulness. "I know a chap or two who'd be happy to show you a good time if you're hard pressed for company."

Disgusted, Saffron snatched up her handbag and rose. "Never mind. I'll just go find someone else to ask since you're incapable of answering a simple question."

Lee laughed loudly, earning accusatory looks from the handful of people milling about the shelves. His voice dropped to an amused whisper. "And just who do you plan to ask about how the upper class get their hands on cocaine?"

Saffron opened her mouth, wishing to utter a scathing retort, rather than planning on doing so, when he half rose from his chair and snatched her wrist, dragging her back into her own seat. "Be reasonable, Everleigh. Give me more information, and I'll see what I can come up with, hmm?"

Reluctantly, she sketched out for him the information about the two victims and the friends.

Lee hummed, mouth twisted with distaste. "So, poor Miss Williams was friends with a few honoraries, they're all using, and she ends up asphyxiated with a pillow. There's a tidy solution, isn't there? The supplier did it."

"Possibly. What has that to do with Mrs. Sullivan, though?"

He shrugged. "You know, I've seen Lucy Talbot around. I'm not surprised that she has a taste for the ticklish white stuff, though you'd think the peroxide she uses on her hair would have done quite enough to her poor brain."

"What do you know about Lucy Talbot, apart from that she's blonde?"

"I don't know her personally. We've attended few of the same dinners; I've seen her out at a few clubs. Rather tall, pretty enough. Looking to get advantageously settled but enjoying the looking from what I can tell. Attwood and Gresham . . . I don't know recognize those names. That doesn't necessarily mean much, though—I might know them quite well."

Saffron glared at his wink and grin. "You don't even remember the names of your conquests? Do you mean to give the impression that you're intimately acquainted with half the women in England?"

"As long as it's the attractive half, I don't mind." He winked again. "I could ask 'round my club. That lot would know any girls having fun while up to no good. Probably could help us find the dealer too."

Saffron frowned. "We can't be known to be asking around, Lee. Can you do it without being stupendously obvious?"

"Yes, I can manage not to be stupendously obvious."

"Let me know what you find out," she said briskly, rising from her chair. "When will you go?"

Lee shut the book he'd been slowing turning into a pillow. "I'll ask around tonight, if you like. But chances are I'll have to wait until someone sets up a game of cards or something."

Pleased, she nodded. "Thank you."

"Anything for you, partner."

Chapter 6

Though the fall semester wouldn't begin until October, the month of September meant that University College London was no longer a dull, quiet place. Rather than empty halls greeting Lee when he emerged from the office that afternoon, a pleasant hum of activity echoed on the tiled floors. Professors—for who else could the crusty old men bustling around the place be?—and researchers, looking much like the younger versions of the professors, with varying degrees of style and grooming, were returning from their holidays.

School had been a pleasure for Lee, what with his penchant for science and maths and socialization, so he took in the buzz with increasing good humor as he strode down the hall. There was always something to do at school. When his studies were dull, there was a horde of young men ready to carouse with if he so desired.

Lee had been on campus infrequently before third term finished at the end of June, as he and Everleigh had raced out of the gate to take advantage of the flurry of poisonings at the start of the summer bloom season. He was therefore stopped more than once to inquire if he was a new faculty member or, more often, a student with the incorrect dates for the opening of the fall term. One such exchange led to an invitation to join some of the staff for tea later that afternoon.

A quick dip into the library's medical textbooks answered a lingering question about the toxins in water hemlock dropwort—a poisonous mouthful if he'd ever heard one—and Lee returned to the little office he shared with Everleigh with a spring in his step.

"Exciting news, Everleigh," he declared upon entering the room. The dusty smell of old books and the delicate scent of whatever perfume Everleigh spritzed on each morning wafted over to him, carried on the warm breeze coming from the opened window behind her desk. His partner looked up, a slight frown pinching her face.

In the months they'd worked together, Saffron Everleigh had revealed only two moods: enthusiasm and annoyance. The enthusiasm came out any time she saw anything green, a plant or a drawing of one. The annoyance seemed to be reserved entirely for him. He found it incomprehensibly enjoyable.

His smile graduated to a grin accordingly as he shut the door behind him and automatically shed his suit jacket. The weather had finally cooled to reasonable temperatures after a scorcher of a summer, but Everleigh despised it when he made himself comfortable in the office she so clearly saw as her own. He draped the flax-colored jacket over the back of his chair and sat, tucking his hands back behind his head and sighing with the enjoyment of taunting his partner. Nothing delighted him—and annoyed her—more than tempting her with information. She liked knowing things, and he'd promised something new for her to learn. He actually did have rather exciting news, but he knew her well enough to know that the second he mentioned the murder investigation, she'd have no interest in anything else the rest of the day.

Saffron held out for a full five seconds before setting aside the papers she was examining and asking, with a long-suffering air, "Well, what is it, then?"

Savoring the bite in her tone, he said, "We have been invited to tea."

Wariness followed surprise across her face. "By whom?"

"A little do for all the department members back from the holidays. Fischer-Hays invited us."

"The both of us?" Saffron asked, a note of suspicion in her voice.

Lee waved a hand. "Well, as I was standing there and you were not—"

"You will enjoy it, I suppose," Saffron said, returning her attention to her papers. "Be sure to avoid taking too much sugar. Dr. Miller will likely dive into a lecture about the virtues of sugar cane versus beets that would bore you to death if you let him."

"Why does it sound like you won't be joining me?"

She shuffled a few sheets of paper about. "I have far too much to do. I can't be wasting time with tea."

Good God, it was like she wanted him to tease her. Very well, he would oblige. "First of all, that is sacrilege and I am ashamed to call you a fellow Englishman. Woman. You are already on thin ice because of your inexplicable habit of taking your tea without milk or sugar. Second, you waste time with tea nearly every day. Just last week at Darby's, we spent half an hour waiting when the serving girl forgot about us."

"We were working while we waited."

"Arguing about the correct way to annotate an academic paper is not working; it is prelude to something more exciting." He waggled his eyebrows.

Saffron reddened. "I don't have any interest in your ideas of . . . *that*, nor do I have an interest in teatime with the rest of the staff."

"Whyever not?"

There was a long pause, during which Saffron merely glared at her desk.

At long last, she said, "Very well." She sounded more like she was agreeing to witness an execution than take tea with a bunch of doddering old men. Lee had long since stopped wondering if she had an interest in catching the eye of one of the younger fellows, mostly because she all but seethed when he flirted with her.

When the allotted hour arrived, Lee replaced his suit jacket and straightened his tie. Saffron rose from her desk and followed him out the door.

Beyond, the hall was bright with the indirect light of a sunny day. He had to slow his stride more than once to keep pace with his partner, who seemed determined to take her time with mincing steps down the quiet hall.

They descended to the basement level, where the air became stale and cool. The dim electric lights barely illuminated a narrow corridor sparsely populated by cast-off furniture covered in white sheets and boxes full of the detritus of decades of science. He held out a hand for Everleigh to lead the way. Her shoulders had crept up beneath her ears, and her mouth was turned down into a flat line.

"I say," he murmured as she stepped in front of him, her skirt brushing his leg, "you're acting like I'm walking you to the gallows. It's just tea."

The rumble of male voices grew as they drew closer to the break room at the end of the hall. Lee's heart couldn't help but pick up its pace; he was eager to circulate and figure out who was who.

The small room was papered with out-of-date maps, diagrams, and scientific illustrations, giving Lee the impression they'd stepped into a very dull textbook. It was crowded with fifteen or so men milling around the rectangular table in the center of the room. Its scarred surface was cluttered with the makings of a very informal tea: several earthenware teapots that sported chips here and there, a few plates of uninspiring sandwiches, and a stack of plain teacups and saucers. A poor showing, but Lee wasn't there for the victuals.

A few people near the door shuffled out of the way when they entered, and Lee caught a bit of conversation.

". . . making it difficult for the rest of us now he's in charge," said a portly man with a grandiose mustache decades out of style.

"We knew he would," replied his companion, a man in late middle age with a bulbous red nose. "I protested his advancement to the dean, but it made no difference."

"And now we have to cope with the overbearing misanthrope." The mustachioed fellow's watery blue eyes glanced past Lee to the door, and his lips stretched into a sneer. "And tolerate his little pet."

Curious at the man's ire, Lee turned to see to whom he was referring, but saw only Saffron behind him, standing somewhat timidly just inside the door.

The red-nosed man hummed meaningfully before shuffling over to the table to snatch a sandwich.

Lee sidled over to Saffron, summoning a pleasant smile. "Everleigh, won't you introduce me to your colleagues?"

He expected a cheeky "no," or a very long-suffering "yes," or perhaps an eye roll, but she merely nodded and took a few steps toward the mustachioed man.

"Professor Miller," she said, "may I introduce to you my study partner, Dr. Michael Lee?"

Lee had the distinct impression that, had she not been introducing someone to him, Dr. Miller might have ignored her. His attention floated over her and landed on Lee.

"I have heard little about your . . . study," he said slowly, looking Lee over as if he wasn't certain what to make of him. Considering the man's suit likely originated before the song was sung "God Save the *Queen*," rather than "the King," it might have been Lee's green tie and softly pink shirt beneath his pale gold suit that garnered his scrutiny. Dr. Miller's gaze flicked back to Saffron. "I didn't realize Aster had paired you up with someone. Clever of him, to ensure you could complete it."

Saffron's brows dipped momentarily before smoothing out. Without feeling, she said, "Dr. Aster knew the work would benefit from a medical perspective."

"Indeed," Miller said, equally disinterested.

It didn't surprise Lee that Miller was short with his partner; she had mentioned that Miller was a bit of a wet blanket, and he'd clearly been talking about Aster earlier. "Overbearing misanthrope" was an apt description. He was ice cold and no doubt held the purse strings of his department tightly. And to be fair, Saffron did jump to ensure she followed his directions perfectly. Calling her Aster's pet wasn't wrong.

Lee nodded politely at Dr. Miller and murmured, "Pleasure to meet you," before gently nudging Saffron with his elbow. "Onward, Everleigh."

With every introduction, Lee learned from the painful way the others interacted with Saffron that Dr. Miller was, indeed, a curmudgeon, but the majority of the others were too. Had their cool manners or outright rudeness been confined to the older men, Lee might have understood. A woman joining their ranks would rankle the more traditional lot. But the younger men, too, regarded Everleigh with unfriendly apathy and occasionally outright derision.

"No surprise Aster isn't down here," said a fellow Saffron had designated Clinton McGuire, not bothering to modulate his drawling voice in the midst of the little knot of younger researchers when they approached. He was tall and narrow-shouldered, his amber-brown eyes glittering unpleasantly. "Be sure to give him our love, Miss Everleigh."

Amusement warred with the need not to appear to be an absolute ass to his partner in front of her colleagues.

"My cup has gone dry," said a scrawny man called Silas Gastrell, who was only barely taller than Everleigh. "Be a dear, won't you?" He thrust his cup and saucer toward her.

Saffron blinked, hands jolting up to accept the cup automatically before it hit her chest. Milky dregs sloshed up from the bottom of the cup and dotted her white blouse.

Lee felt the smile die on his lips as the trio of researchers around them tittered. "Oh, I see," he said.

Saffron's face had gone rather blank, but the three researchers looked at him with confusion.

Lifting his voice to a hearty, friendly tone, he said, "I suppose every department has their little welcoming rituals. Cambridge medical was no different. My first year, I was made to believe I had to dispose of my own cadaver after an anatomy lesson, you know." He forced a chuckle. "It's a relief to know the Biology Department here at UCL has not quite so drastic an initiation. But I'm afraid Everleigh is no longer the most recent addition to the researcher pool. I am here temporarily, it is true, but I refuse to slough off my duties as the newest member of the department."

He plucked the cup from Everleigh's hands, with some difficulty as she'd clenched her fingers around it, and marched to the table to pour tea and milk. With an ostentatious bow, he returned the teacup to Gastrell, resisting the urge to splatter it over his shirtfront. "There you are. Don't recommend letting Everleigh fill your cup in the future. We are studying poisonous plants, you know."

Gastrell opened his mouth, then closed it, darting a glance over to McGuire. McGuire and the other researcher, whose name was too long and too Welsh to remember it, were not the only people watching the exchange. Several nearby conversations had halted, and curious eyes turned their way.

Lee smiled pleasantly, and then when no one spoke, he made a show of checking his wristwatch. "Ah, I've neglected the time. Must go," he said cheerily. He quickly shook each man's hand, nodded cordially to Everleigh, and took his leave without another word.

Everleigh found him in the office not five minutes later.

She shut the door none too gently. "Is there a particular reason you dragged me to tea and then promptly fled?" she asked, arms crossing tightly over her tea-stained chest.

"I felt it was a good time to clear out," Lee replied, placing a bookmark in the textbook he'd been perusing. "Dreadful little room, that is. I don't understand why they don't move it to the top floor instead of that musty old basement."

"You felt it was a good time to clear out," Saffron echoed softly, anger tightening her features. "You might have made an excuse for the both of us, so I wasn't subject to—" She cut herself off. That unnaturally smooth mask fell over her features again. She went to her desk and began putting things into her bag.

Lee gusted out an impatient breath. He was really going to have to explain things to her? "Don't be cross, Everleigh. It was for the best I breezed when I did."

She murmured something that sounded suspiciously like, "The best for *you*, maybe."

"It was for the best," he repeated firmly, "for the both of us. I only wanted to go to understand how this department works, which can only benefit you. How would you like for me to accidentally offend your fellow botanists or biologists or entomologists or any other '-ists' that are wandering about?"

"It wouldn't matter," she said, a strangely brittle tone in her voice. "You saw what they were like. They could hardly think worse of me, even if you told Dr. Miller his mustache is a crime against upper lips."

Lee snorted a surprised laugh. "Yes, they are rather a surly lot, aren't they?"

Her blue eyes lifted and met his. There was emotion there, something vulnerable that made his teeth clench. The look barely lasted a second before she was burying things into her bag once again.

Lee sighed with exasperation, attempting to exhale that unpleasant feeling. "Everleigh, had I swept you away with me, what would every last one of those idiots think I was about? The whole lot clearly have some issue with you, and me acting the white knight and shielding you from their rudeness could only encourage their idiocy and stir rumors about what we get up to in here." He waved a hand to indicate the office.

There was a long pause, during which Saffron stared at him and Lee grew increasingly uncomfortable. It was so inelegant, explaining oneself. He knew he was in the right, but she certainly wasn't acting like she knew it.

"Thank you," Saffron said at long last, slowly and warily, as if not trusting the words coming out of her mouth. "I appreciate the consideration."

"My pleasure," he said, a bit sarcastically. He didn't expect her to throw herself at him in gratitude, but a bit more enthusiasm would have been nice. "You might have warned me we were walking into a hornet's nest. I didn't realize biologists were so averse to females in the workplace."

A slight flush rose in her face. "They aren't, as a rule. But . . ." She set down her handbag. "With the recent change in leadership, there has been a great deal of grumbling. About funding, about Aster, about—"

"You?"

"Yes." Any semblance of that unfeeling mask was gone, and his partner looked miserable.

"They don't care for a woman rising through their ranks?"

"Women in general, no. The university college was one of the first in the country to admit women, and has had a number of women as professors and lecturers. But a young woman without an advanced degree is different. Several of the other researchers, even ones not in botany, believe Aster showed me special treatment by promoting me to researcher before my master's was even started."

Lee bit his lip on a laugh. "Because Aster clearly dotes on you."

Saffron gave him a look. "Clearly." She opened her mouth to continue speaking but shook her head and instead leaned over to open a drawer. She began placing things into her handbag.

"So, you just avoid the whole Biology Department?" Lee asked, wondering if he'd perhaps made a mistake in signing on to a half year's worth of work with the North Wing's pariah.

Not looking up, she replied, "Once they realize that Aster treats me with the same cold calculation as he does everyone else, I believe they'll ease up. And when the expedition team returns from Brazil, people will be too distracted to fuss over my promotion." Her fingers fiddled with the edge of a large atlas that stuck out from beneath a stack of files. "Things will be better when they return."

There had to be more to the story. An entire department hating one woman because she got a promotion? But that was what the gossip mill was for. He'd figure it out before long. "Now, may we get onto more important things?"

"Unless it's a new case that requires immediate action, I think—"

"Not a new *poisoning* case. I have an update about the murders."

Pique colored her voice. "What update?"

There, that was better. "I've found out when and where Lucy Talbot and her friends like to go dancing."

"Why is that helpful? They're not likely to discuss a murder while dancing."

Lee rolled his eyes. He'd been counting on a *little* excitement that he'd finally managed to find out something useful after two nights of puttering around his club. "Dope makes people do strange things. Lucy Talbot and the rest go to the Blue Room on Wednesdays to hear the band. Several of the chaps at the club have seen them there."

"How fortunate that tomorrow is Wednesday, then. Shall we go?"

The Blue Room was not the sort of club he imagined Everleigh had ever gone to, not with its reputation for being a place where things were fast and flashy, but he couldn't help but be a little curious what she would make of it. "Absolutely."

"Well, I'll be going then. Tomorrow we will have to put our nose to the grindstone to finish this section. We only have a few weeks until the library will be all but unbearable to work in when the students come back."

"It's unbearable now." And because her eyes were still a bit hollow, he added suggestively, "But yes, have no fear, Everleigh. I will most definitely be ready to work."

She grimaced, snapping her handbag shut. "Right. See you tomorrow."

Pleased, he chuckled as she disappeared through the door. "See you tomorrow."

CHAPTER 7

"You couldn't have made Lee bring another fellow so I could come along?" Elizabeth wriggled her red-tipped fingers over Saffron's shoulder, and Saffron passed her another hairpin. "A group of people is far more convincing than just a couple, you know."

Saffron wasn't paying much attention to her flatmate's constant ribbing as she expertly styled her hair into a faux bob before the mirror at Elizabeth's dressing table. The plan to go to the Blue Room had excited Elizabeth, but adding in mention of the murders had made her practically gleeful until Saffron said she couldn't come along. It was bad enough that Saffron had told her all about the poison bouquets, even if she'd done it because Elizabeth might have known something about the murdered women. Elizabeth was acquainted with all sorts of people, high and low, and she might have known something or someone relevant. But tonight, they needed to be as inconspicuous as possible, and Elizabeth was never that.

She didn't want to admit it, but Saffron was as nervous as she was excited. She didn't want to let Inspector Green down. Her connection to any of Miss Williams's friends would be tenuous, if it existed at all. Most of the young women Saffron had been acquainted with back when she and Elizabeth had first arrived in London had been trying hard to find a husband and hadn't cared a pin about her studies, just as she hadn't been interested in their prospective matches. Elizabeth had stuck with her through the tedious dinners and teas until they stopped being invited, either because Saffron hadn't shown enough interest in society's comings and goings or because Elizabeth's family's sudden lack of standing had become known.

Saffron would have never guessed she'd regret leaving that part of herself behind, not even when her grandparents threatened to cut her off financially when she refused to leave the university, and then when they'd actually done it when she'd taken an assistant researcher position after graduating. But now, with a murderer of the upper class in the picture, Saffron wondered if she should have tried to maintain a few of the bridges into the nobility rather than allow them all to decay.

Her comfort was that Lee was still very much a part of that world and could make even the most starchy of individuals crack a smile. And they could always simply leave the club if things didn't go well.

"I don't see why you bother with all this hair still," Elizabeth said as she brushed out a long brunette lock.

The refrain of *"bob your hair"* was so familiar at this point, Saffron ignored it in favor of pressing Elizabeth's darkest lipstick to her lips.

"Well, what do you think?" Saffron asked, pouting in the mirror at Elizabeth. She'd emphasized her cupid's bow, making her lips appear rounder and plump.

Elizabeth paused in her ministrations to examine her friend with a critical eye. "I think you'd scare the corset right off your grandmother, for one. But you still look like yourself." She opened a drawer and dug around. "This will be just the thing."

"No Vaseline," Saffron warned. "It always makes my eyes feel gummy."

"No Vaseline," Elizabeth said with a long-suffering sigh. "You've no need for it with all those lashes. Close your eyes."

Saffron did so, and when she looked into the mirror again, her blue eyes had taken on a sultry cast that was quite unfamiliar. Gray kohl darkened her eyelids, and, after Elizabeth secured a glittering beaded band around her head, she did not recognize herself. Draped in one of Elizabeth's outrageously bright, silky dressing gowns, she looked like a film star in her boudoir. "Well done, Eliza!"

Elizabeth did an old-fashioned curtsy. Saffron rose and followed her down the hall, then scurried into her bedroom when a knock sounded at the door.

She heard Lee and Elizabeth trading barbs as they made their way down the hall to the parlor and hurriedly threw on a dress that she rarely had the chance to wear. The aubergine silk had been made over at least once since she'd come to London, with added sleeves of nearly matching gauze and its narrow skirt now falling past her knees. She stacked herself with necklaces and buckled her heeled black shoes over black stockings. With one last check in the mirror, where she saw a much darker, more glamorous version of herself, missing only a gasper and a stiff drink in her black-gloved hands. Satisfied with her disguise, she allowed herself a generous spritz of the bottle of Tabac Blond she and Elizabeth shared, and set off down the hall.

Saffron found Lee draped over the armchair in the parlor. His stark black dinner jacket and crisp white shirt were quite at odds with his languorous pose. His golden hair shone in a slick wave; his slightly darker brows furrowed as he read a book of Elizabeth's poetry.

Saffron perched on the arm of the couch, watching his expressions with curiosity. Elizabeth had just brought home that newly printed volume of her poetry, appropriately titled *Hidden Verses*. They had spent an hour debating the title but finally agreed that the poems were so risqué that anyone who had the book would no doubt have to actually hide it.

"Enjoying the poetry?" Saffron asked casually, smoothing her skirt.

"Immensely," Lee said, looking over the top of the small book, green eyes full of mischief. Her cheeks heated slightly at the way his gaze moved over her, taking in her ensemble. "I really should report you, you know."

"For what, reading poetry?" He would never report her for having an indecent publication. He probably had a few of his own.

He shot her a wink. "Ready to go, Arlette?"

Heat rose in her cheeks. "Lee, I'm not Arlette Dejoie."

He cocked a brow. "With that rose poem in there? There was just a little too much anatomical—I mean, botanical—detail in there to

be anyone other than you. 'Calyx fringes framing the dewy bloom?'"
He chuckled over her sputtered denial of owning Elizabeth's nom
de plume. "But come along, let's get inspiration for more of your
naughty rhymes."

The Blue Room was on an average-looking street in an unas-
suming neighborhood in Elephant and Castle in south London. It
was identified by a single, blue-colored lightbulb hanging over a plain
door on the side of a building that looked like it might contain warehouse storage for the closed shops lining the other side of the street.
At another time of day, Saffron guessed no one would have suspected
that one of London's most notorious jazz clubs lurked within its walls,
but by night, the hum of music trailed down the street, snaking
through groups of men and women hovering outside the azure-tinted
door.

A thrill of nerves raced through Saffron as they emerged from the
cab. She was no stranger to night clubs or jazz—not with Elizabeth
as her closest friend—but this place was rumored to be a favorite of
Alice Diamond and her Forty Elephants. Some might argue Saffron
had a taste for danger, what with involving herself in a murder investigation, but she had no desire to cross paths with the all-female gang.

As Lee led Saffron to the door, she considered she could take
some pointers from Alice Diamond; she ruled her roost with an iron
fist. Saffron could do with a bit more iron lately. She'd been abomi-
nably passive with McGuire and his cronies the other day, and she'd
allowed Lee to manage them for her, just like she'd allowed Dr. Maxwell to do before his sabbatical. How would she ever prove herself
in the department if she crumbled or hid at any hint of posturing or
conflict?

Lee murmured something to the large man wearing a long trench
coat and standing just beside the blue door. He must have known the
right thing to say, for the man barely glanced at them before permit-
ting them to enter.

Darkness, alive with raucous sounds of jazz, immediately
engulfed them. Lee guided her by the hand into the densely packed
room. What little light shone from tabletop lamps and occasional
wall sconces was cerulean. The dance floor was invisible beneath the

crush of bodies. The band, a mixture of Black and White men, in blue-stained tuxedoes, whose talent fortunately matched their raging enthusiasm, blazed through a song from the small stage at the front of the room.

Saffron squinted into the crowd, a further mixture of all sorts of people, and caught sight of platinum blonde hair glowing blue. The woman topped her companion by nearly a full head. A thrill chased down Saffron's spine; the woman matched Lee's description of Miss Williams's friend, Lucy Talbot.

Saffron nudged Lee, and he tugged her to him, mouth nearly touching her ear. "What's the plan?"

Finding the friends was supposed to have been much more difficult, so she hadn't quite formed a plan yet. She leaned into him, nose tingling with the citrus spice of his aftershave. "Since you're somewhat acquainted with Miss Talbot, you should try to dance with her. See if you can get her talking about Miss Williams or the cocaine."

"Righto." He straightened up, adjusted his black bow tie, and slipped into the dancing masses. Saffron scanned the faces at the tables, hoping she might recognize someone while equally hoping she'd pass by unnoticed.

A voice close behind her made her jump.

"Excuse me, might I assist you in finding someone?"

Saffron turned and found herself quite close to a man dressed in full evening attire. He was perhaps Lee's height, and well on his way to becoming portly. His rounded face was completely smooth, as if he'd just emerged from his morning toilette, and his thin, fair hair was glossy, slicked to one side. His wholesome appearance was rather at odds with the bawdy atmosphere of the club.

Saffron smiled politely. "No, thank you. I'm just looking for my friend."

"I can perhaps guide you to her."

Taken aback by his insistent manner, Saffron said, "Er, I—that's very kind, but I'll just check the powder room for her. Pardon me."

She did indeed retreat to the powder room, wondering how she might avoid the smooth-faced man and still watch the tables without appearing suspicious.

Just as Saffron resolved to return to the dance floor, the woman believed to be Lucy Talbot entered the small room. She was tall and blonde as promised, with refined features dramatized with bright lipstick and generous rouge. Her brows were two thin arches over large blue eyes. A small, raven-haired woman, with sooty lashes, dark lipstick, and a sparkling emerald dress, followed her, wearing a disgruntled expression.

"If you're going to be such a bore, Caro, you might as well leave," the blonde said over her shoulder as they approached the mirrors. She adjusted the thin straps of her embroidered salmon dress and began digging through her handbag.

Caro, likely Caroline Attwood, Saffron realized with a flare of excitement. Thinking fast, Saffron stepped forward and exclaimed, "Lucy, is that you?"

The blonde looked up at her blankly before breaking into a smile. Lucy dropped what seemed to be a tiny, antique perfume bottle back into her bag. "Why, hello, darling!"

They briefly grasped hands as Saffron said excitedly, "I haven't seen you for an age! What a coincidence! I don't think we've seen each other since that party—do you remember?"

Spidery black lashes fluttered. "But of course!"

Saffron smiled expectantly at Lucy and glanced at her black-bobbed friend, waiting for an introduction before she remembered that Lucy had no idea who she was.

"Sa—Sally Eversby," she said quickly, extending her hand to the girl.

The other woman took it, her hand limp and hot, even through her gloves. She was not a beauty like Lucy, though perhaps with less makeup and less displeasure distorting her delicate features, she might be. "Caroline Attwood," she said flatly.

"How do you do? What a coincidence to see you, Lucy! Do you often come to the Blue Room? I've only just returned to town, and my friend roped me into coming here. Rather dramatic, isn't it?"

Lucy nodded, turning to the mirror and opening her bag once more. She withdrew a tube of lipstick. "Oh yes, we come here quite often. Absolutely the best club for jazz. We love jazz, don't we?" She nudged her friend, who didn't bother to feign enthusiasm.

"You'll have to show me the best spots, then. My mother never let me get out much. I felt like I was wasting away in the country!" Saffron hoped the hint of a country home might provide her an in, and she wasn't disappointed.

Lucy's smile widened. "I absolutely understand, darling. The moment I could, I got out from under my mother too. Now, Sally, my dear, won't you come and sit at our table?"

CHAPTER 8

Saffron followed Lucy and Caroline back out into the moodily lit club to a table set on a low mezzanine that lined the back of the room. The man with the overeager manners sat at the large round table, talking to another young woman.

"This is Sally Eversby, a friend of mine I just bumped into. Sally, this is Percy Edwards, son of the Earl of Laughton," Lucy said in a drawl that carried over the music. "And our dear little friend, Millie. Amelia Gresham."

Amelia Gresham was the plainest of the group, in a gown of indeterminate color and no jewelry but a pair of pearl earrings. Her small eyes and top-heavy lips were bare of cosmetics, and her fair hair was set in drooping marcel waves. She offered only a brief nod to Saffron, but Mr. Edwards seemed delighted to meet her. He stood and offered a little bow. "Miss Eversby, how lovely to put a name to a face."

He offered her a seat, but Saffron realized she should find Lee, who clearly wasn't having any luck dancing with Lucy Talbot. She excused herself and waded into the swaying crowd of dancers. She spotted Lee quickly. He was leaned against a far wall, smoking a cigarette and eying the dancers.

"There you are," he said, blowing smoke to the side as she drew near. "No luck with Lucy. She disappeared just as I was making my way to her."

"I found her," she replied, leaning close. "I've convinced her we're old friends. She must be totally muddled to accept it without a question. I just mentioned a party, and she followed right along and invited me to sit at their table. Come on."

Lee put out his cigarette and followed but pulled her into the crowd and in step with the dancing a moment later.

"I forgot to ask," he said into her hair, "what did you tell them about me?"

"What do you mean?" Saffron asked, confused by the question and his sudden proximity.

"Am I your friend or lover?"

Saffron missed a step, and Lee laughed. "What did you tell them, so I don't ruin the story? Honestly, Everleigh . . ."

"I said we're friends. It leaves it open for you to flirt."

"Righto. Childhood friends, I think. I'll get Miss Talbot dancing, shall I?"

"Yes. I suppose I'll try to dance with the man they're with. Oh, and my name is Sally Eversby."

It was Lee's turn to miss a step. "*Sally Eversby?* I'll never be able to say that with a straight face. Why the false name?"

In all honesty, it had seemed necessary for her protection, both from a potential murderer and for the sake of her reputation. Saffron Everleigh's reputation might have been able to survive one brush with crime, but dancing in a jazz club alongside cocaine users was courting scandal. "It seemed prudent."

They broke away from the crowd and made their way, arm in arm, to the table. Three pairs of eyes followed Lee as they climbed the steps to the mezzanine. The women all sat up a little straighter, Saffron was amused to see.

"This is my friend—" Saffron began, forming a pseudonym for him too, but he broke in, saying, "Dr. Michael Lee—a pleasure."

She elbowed his side subtly. "He was nice enough to bring me dancing."

"Dr. Lee, so good to meet you," Lucy said, extending her gloved hand across the table with a coy curve of her lips. "Won't you both sit down?"

The others introduced themselves. They settled into conversation over fresh drinks. Saffron watched the group for signs that their friend's death was weighing them down or guilting them, or that they were intoxicated with more than just alcohol. They seemed normal enough, if a little disjointed in their interactions with each other. They referred to each other by nicknames, but Percy Edwards was always "Mr. Edwards." They had no other gentlemen with them, though one approached the table to request a dance with Lucy, who politely declined before glancing at Lee. Lucy and Mr. Edwards carried the conversation, but with stops and starts and uncomfortable moments where it seemed they were at odds with who was leading, with Edwards usually taking it in an unexpected, seemingly disconnected direction that made Lucy's smile tighten and her fingers tap on the table. Saffron and Lee tried to ingratiate themselves as much as was prudent. Amelia spent most of her time staring at Lee, and Caroline didn't seem to want to engage with anyone. She sat slightly slumped, idly flipping open and then shut a ring on her finger that revealed a tiny compartment behind a large jewel.

While Lee and Mr. Edwards spoke, Lucy bent over to Saffron. "He is an absolute sheik. Wherever did you find such a delicious man?"

Caroline, next to her, softly scoffed before gulping her drink.

Saffron smiled at her wistfully. "We've known each other since we were children. Our mothers were friends."

"Well, dear, if you wouldn't mind . . ." Lucy looked meaningfully at Saffron, and Caroline's expression soured further.

Saffron laughed. "Do give it a go. I'm always trying to get him to find a decent girl. He's very picky, you know."

Seemingly up for a challenge, Lucy caught Lee's eye. Lee took a long sip of his drink, then asked Lucy to dance.

Mr. Edwards and Amelia had fallen into deep conversation about a new item Mr. Edwards had purchased for a collection of some kind, or so it seemed from the bits Saffron could catch, so she turned to Caroline.

"Have you known Lucy long?" Saffron asked, sipping at her own drink, something sweet and far too strong.

Caroline shrugged. "Ages."

"My oldest friend is Lee, and you can imagine how that goes. He frightens off the men and draws all the attention of the women."

Caroline seemed to soften slightly at that. "I know the feeling. Luce outshines us all, especially with that hair."

"She does seem very confident."

"And Percy can't speak two words without saying something ridiculous," Caroline went on, wrinkling her nose. "He's quite an antidote."

Surprised by her outright negativity, Saffron said brightly, "But isn't it nice to have a group of friends to go through life with?"

The line of Caroline's dark lips dipped at the corners, but at that moment, Mr. Edwards asked if she'd like to dance. She felt the loss at accepting him and leaving Caroline, but she had no choice but to say yes.

They made their way onto the crowded floor. Edwards was slightly offbeat for the entire number. Saffron smiled and pressed onward, wishing she could think of a good question to lead him to start discussing Miss Williams or possibly the cocaine. Nothing occurred to her, so she went to an old standby.

"Jazz is so exhilarating, don't you think?" she commented.

"It's not my favorite, I'm afraid. I can't get a handle on the syncopation!" Mr. Edwards replied breathlessly, pink in the face.

Saffron, herself, was feeling the heat of a hundred dancing bodies in close proximity. Sweat trickled down her spine. "What do you prefer?"

"I enjoy something a bit more classic—you know, Bland and Cowen." He began singing a tune wordlessly, but was immediately cut off by a screaming rip of a trumpet, and the crowd dissolved into the Charleston. Not feeling up to attempting the quick dance with Edwards, Saffron suggested they return to the table.

Rather than sit, Edwards stood near the table almost like a guard, looking quite out of place against the wall of shuffling dancers.

Caroline had disappeared, leaving Amelia alone, hands idly running back and forth over each other.

Saffron settled next to her, fanning her face with a hand. "The band is absolutely fantastic! Lucy said you all come here often."

Amelia slowly turned and settled dull eyes on Saffron. They were a little glazed and bloodshot, evident even through the colored lights. Was it symptomatic of drug use?

Saffron plucked at her black gloves, racking her brain for a way to ask. "Lee always has such energy. I wonder how he can go from working all day in an environment as trying as a hospital, then come here and dance for hours."

Amelia's flat gaze wandered. "Yes, the work of a doctor is challenging."

Her biting tone sparked curiosity in Saffron. "Lee is a laugh, but he does drag me about late in the evening."

Amelia smiled ruefully. "Luce and Caro are much the same."

"I'm sure I haven't half their energy. I'm rather envious," she said, hoping Amelia might mention a helpful curative.

"It's actually late now. I'll have to collect Percy and go home," Amelia said, picking up her handbag.

"Oh, I didn't realize you and Mr. Edwards—"

"He's just my dearest friend. He always escorts me," said Amelia quickly, showing energy for the first time that evening. "Although I rather think I escort him, sometimes. He isn't the most socially adept creature."

Saffron had to agree; he was rather odd. Though Amelia certainly was not a stunning conversationalist either.

Lucy and Lee staggered off the dance floor a moment later, flushed and grinning.

Amelia beckoned to Edwards, saying, "Percy, we must be going."

"Of course, my dear." He bowed to the table, adding to Lee, "I'll be seeing you, Dr. Lee. It was a pleasure, Miss Eversby. I hope to see you again."

Saffron smiled at him, then made her and Lee's apologies as well. They exchanged blue light for the gray of the street and caught a cab.

When they were safely ensconced in the backseat, Saffron said, "What an odd bunch of people! I don't think I got anything useful."

Lee, smiling wickedly, reached into his pocket and pulled out a tiny white packet. "Fortunately, I did."

Saffron gasped. "That's not—who gave it to you?"

"When we were dancing, I told Lucy I wanted something more entertaining than alcohol, and the next thing I know, she's pressing it into my palm."

Saffron dropped her voice so her incredulity couldn't be heard over the trundle of the cab's engine. "You flirt with a girl for two dances, and she's giving you drugs? That is ridiculous."

Lee looked thoughtfully at the packet, a spot of brightness in the dark cab. "I just talked about parties and long hours and feeling so dull. She passed it right over. Now I just need to find out where she gets it from. And Mr. Edwards said he wanted to hear more about my work, wants to take me to lunch." He crossed his arms over his chest as he tried to settle more comfortably into the corner of the seat.

"You win this round of who's the better detective, then," she said irritably.

"Don't be sour, Everleigh," he murmured.

"I am not sour. I just wish I had gotten more out of them. They were just so strange. None of them seemed perturbed that their friend had been murdered. They all have these little nicknames, but there doesn't seem to be much affection between them. Lucy no doubt uses cocaine herself and apparently gives it away freely, and Caroline is clearly jealous of Lucy. Amelia seems to only like Mr. Edwards, and Mr. Edwards is an odd sort of man who may or may not have been attached to Miss Williams. But they could have been strained with one another because their friend was just killed." She shot Lee a glance, only to see in the shifting light of the streets that his eyes were closed. She poked him in the side. "Have you tried the cocaine?"

"Have I *tried* it?" He sat up and glared at her. "Why the bloody hell would I have tried it?"

"To see if it's actually cocaine, of course," Saffron replied, nonplussed at his irritation. "You would know—I suspect you've prescribed it at some point. I take it you didn't, then."

His unexpected temper cooled, but his voice was still clipped. "No, I did not try it. If you're worried about its legitimacy, I have a friend in chemistry at the U who would test it without raising a fuss."

"Shouldn't we take it to Inspector Green? Unless you don't think it's the real thing. I'd hate to waste his time," she said, uncertainty pinching her brow.

"I'll just pop over to the Chemistry Department tomorrow morning and find out. Then you can take it to the inspector."

"If you're sure your friend can be quiet about it, then yes, I suppose."

Saffron allowed their conversation to lapse into silence while she reviewed each word the friends had said. Their mission hadn't been the complete success she'd hoped for, but Lee had accomplished something at least.

Lee's eyes opened, and he frowned. "That's why she kept looking at me like that."

Saffron let out a laugh. "You do realize the whole table was drooling all over you the entire time, Mr. Edwards included."

"No, not in the usual way. Not as though I were the answer to their prayers. Amelia Gresham must have remembered me."

"Miss Gresham? I don't think so."

The cab pulled up to Saffron's building. A half-moon veiled by clouds added a cool wash to the warm lights lining the quiet Chelsea street. Lee opened the door and helped her out, then walked her across the pavement and up the stairs leading to her flat. "No, I'm quite sure she recognized me. She's a nurse. She works at University College Hospital."

"She does?"

"I could be wrong, of course. She looked different without a cap and apron and all that. Still miserable, though."

"But she's friends with Lucy and Caroline and Mr. Edwards. From their conversation, it's clear they're all well-off. Why would she be employed as a nurse?"

Lee shrugged. "I wonder if her pals know. I can't imagine they'd be pleased to learn she works for a living. They don't seem like the sort of people who'd put up with a flat tire like that."

Lips pursing, Saffron mulled this over, wondering what it meant for her admittedly very thin disguise as Sally Eversby. The hospital was steps away from the university. She and Lee were in and out of the hospital several times a month, taking in samples from their poisoning victims to be analyzed, and Lee often consulted doctors there. Amelia hadn't given any indication she'd recognized Saffron, but could she maintain the facade long enough to get information out of Amelia and the others?

Lee paused on the top step, frowning up as if examining the arch over the door. "Unless it's Amelia who is giving Lucy the dope. She could be nicking it from the hospital. I'll ask around after I get the packet tested, shall I?" He leaned a hand the doorjamb, eyes twinkling. "Well, I feel as if we've made a good start."

"You did, at least."

Saffron unlocked the door and considered inviting him in to further discuss the information they'd gathered, but decided against it. It was far too late to ask him to come inside. She cleared her throat, suddenly feeling awkward she'd even considered it. "Thank you for your help this evening, Lee. Goodnight."

"'Night, old thing," he replied over his shoulder, walking down the stairs and back into the waiting cab.

CHAPTER 9

Lee awoke the next morning, glad he hadn't indulged in more than one drink at the Blue Room. He despised hangovers, and his peaceful bedroom, done up in shades of blue and white, was nearly blindingly bright. Sunlight streamed through the wide windows overlooking Cavendish Square Gardens—a feature of his flat he rarely appreciated. He was barely home to enjoy the view.

He rolled over, away from the glare, and his eyes landed on the little white packet he'd left on his bedside table. Any lingering tiredness from the late night evaporated with a thrill of excitement.

If this was how easy it was to be an amateur detective, it was no wonder that Sherlock Holmes had a reputation for such success.

Lee sat up and ran his fingers through the gummy strands of his hair, still thick with Brilliantine from the previous evening. He plucked the little packet up and squinted at it in the harsh morning light.

The packet was plain white, no markings, no seals but a simple line of white wax. Cautiously, he opened it. Within, white powder.

Lee scowled. It was outrageous that this posse was handing out drugs willy-nilly to near strangers.

His father and Uncle Matthias would have a fit. His father had prescribed cocaine for years, but under careful supervision. He'd warned Lee firmly and often about its addictive qualities, not wanting his only son, an admittedly spirited and experimental lad, to be swept up in the torrent of white powder washing through the streets of London when the war began. Once Lee had begun his education, he'd developed his own opinions of the drug, and to his horror, they were in alignment with those of his father and uncle.

Using the engraved lighter he'd dumped onto his bedside table before falling into bed last night, he heated the wax to reseal the packet and replaced it on the table before springing out of bed, eager to do something about this striking development in a case he had no business getting involved in. The notion only made it more impossible to resist.

When he arrived at the university an hour later, a close shave and pressed suit leaving no trace of the late night left on his person, he entered the Chemistry Hall, a nondescript building just across a side street from the North Wing.

Investigating drug dealers and murders was invigorating, similar to the hum of intensity he felt when presented with a new patient. Certainly worth a few more late nights. Especially if Everleigh kept dressing like that, he thought with a smirk. Beneath her layers of cotton, wool, and peevishness, she was rather a looker.

He'd barely taken two steps into the hall when he caught sight of Romesh Datta, a former classmate. As usual, Romesh's too-short shirtsleeves showed a few extra inches of his bronze skin, and his spectacles magnified his brown eyes, giving the impression of perpetual surprise.

"Romesh! How convenient—I was just coming to find you," Lee said, offering his classmate a hand. "I've got something I need you to test, if you have a moment."

Romesh pumped Lee's hand enthusiastically. "Sounds intriguing. I just came out for a spot of air; you remember how ghastly it gets with all the chemicals."

They exchanged looks that cracked into smiles. Lee had managed to get him into a number of scrapes during their years at Cambridge, including one particularly memorable escapade involving mixing several substances that had created a most intriguing and disastrous reaction. Romesh had always been one of the more genuine fellows in Lee's class, always with his nose to the grindstone. Some of their classmates took offense to an Indian in their classes, even if he had been born and raised in England, and Lee took offense to their idiocy. He and Romesh had become friends. It was a happy coincidence they'd ended up at University College at the same time, especially since Lee needed a favor.

They ascended to the upper floors as Romesh chatted happily about his fiancée, and Lee poked fun at his upcoming nuptials. Just before they entered Romesh's office, he came to a stop in the hallway and fished in his pockets, no doubt for a key. "Well, what have you got for me?"

Lee gave him an apologetic grin. "Well, Romesh, I brought you a packet of cocaine."

Romesh dropped the key with a ping. Oversized eyes blinking in confusion behind his spectacles, he sputtered, "But why?"

Lee knelt and retrieved the key, passing it back to Romesh. "It's a long story."

Romesh accepted it, and pushed the door open to his lab. Beakers, stained reference books, and papers cluttered every surface, with glass jars and bottles of various chemicals lining the shelves. Their amber- and blue-tinted containers glowed in the light from the wall of windows.

Lee pointed to them in question, and Romesh heaved a sigh. "I don't open them because I'd have rain pouring onto my experiments when the mechanisms got stuck." He donned his white coat and began clearing a space on the long wooden counter nearest them. "What am I looking for? I'm afraid I don't have the ability to tell you if your latest toy will be satisfactory."

Irate that so many people seemed to think he'd dive headfirst into a pile of white powder, Lee said, "Of course not. A friend of mine asked me to see if it was straight as opposed to some hobnob of stuff."

"Come off it. Your current ladybird wants you to check on cocaine for her, I'd wager. I know you have a taste for the wild side, but I must protest."

"I do mean a friend, Romesh," Lee said. Saffron would be terribly annoyed if he revealed all to his friend, but she also wouldn't have reason to ever talk to Romesh. He knew well that she despised chemistry. He rubbed a hand over his face, deciding on the more convenient option. "My study partner is helping with an investigation and came across the packet. She wants to make sure it's the real thing before she raises the alarm."

Romesh looked up, confusion joining his brows together once more. "Your partner is a woman? And what do you mean an investigation? A police investigation?"

Cringing slightly at his incredulous tone, Lee nodded.

Romesh's eyes bulged, and he dropped the packet onto the table like it'd caught fire. "You've gotten our fingerprints all over it!"

"Relax, old man. You'll give yourself apoplexy. I *am* a doctor, you know. I'm allowed to have it."

"Not to snort or inject yourself, which is exactly what anyone with half a brain will think if they see you carrying it around like that." Romesh shook his head slowly as he added a few drops of a liquid into a dish. "Who is this study partner? Another doctor?"

Lee hesitated, not necessarily wanting to connect Everleigh to the cocaine business now Romesh had had such a poor reaction. But Romesh had been at the university for years now and would likely know all about her and why most of her colleagues seemed to loathe her.

"Saffron Everleigh. She's a botanist in the North Wing," Lee said casually. "Heard of her?"

Romesh's fingers fumbled, and he nearly dropped the glass plate that held a little pile of white powder. "Everleigh? The girl who got rid of Berking?"

That name was vaguely familiar. "Berking is . . .?"

It took ten minutes for Romesh to tell the whole story, one that left Lee increasingly incredulous. Poison in champagne glasses, embezzlement schemes, and his officemate consuming poisons left and right? It was something out of a particularly lurid novel.

Romesh dropped acid onto the plate, and Lee watched it fizz as he considered the tale. So, the whole university thought Everleigh had gotten her revenge on Berking for failing to exchange her favors for advancement in her department. He'd been caught in a funding conspiracy alongside another staff member, supposedly revealed by Everleigh and a fellow called Ashton. Naturally, since Everleigh had been the one to get Berking imprisoned, leaving his position open to Aster, the new department head gave her whatever she wanted.

He rather doubted that was the real story. He knew how the gossip mill worked. There was a kernel of truth in there somewhere, and Lee had to decide if he cared enough to excavate it.

At the conclusion of the improbable story, Romesh showed Lee the results, which he wrote out in block letters on a sheet torn from a notebook. Lee raised his eyebrows at that, to which Romesh said he was disguising his handwriting. According to the analysis, the white powder was indeed cocaine, not cut with bicarb or anything else.

"Thanks, old man. Don't worry—I won't let them arrest you," Lee said, clapping Romesh on the shoulder again and picking up the remaining cocaine, still enclosed in the packet.

"Right. Next time you want a favor, Lee, don't have it be one that could get me fired or arrested."

Lee departed with a grin and the promise of a drink to celebrate his engagement soon. But with each step down to the ground floor and out into the street, his smile faded as he mulled over Romesh's words. Anyone with half a brain *would* assume he was using the drug if it got around that he'd accepted a packet of it off Lucy.

Just as he crossed the street to return to the North Wing, he noticed a vaguely familiar figure crossing Gower Street in the direction of the Quad. Percy Edwards, his fair head topped with a bowler hat. Intrigued, Lee hastened to catch up to him.

"Mr. Edwards!" Lee called, and jogged toward the street.

Edwards turned to him with delighted smile. "I say, Dr. Lee, you're very easy to find. I was just coming to say hello," he said, his smooth face shining with perspiration in the increasingly muggy morning. He made a show of checking the time on his pocket watch, a gaudy piece that looked like something Lee's grandfather would have used. "Would you care to join me for luncheon? I found our brief conversation last night a mere taste of what fascinating insights you must have about your profession."

The promise of an hour in Edwards's unctuous company was not Lee's notion of a good time, but, reminding himself that he was trying to help catch a murderer, he agreed.

"Jolly good! You shall have to tell me of your most thrilling adventures during your training," blustered Edwards as they began the walk back down the street.

Guilt touched his mind as he recalled Everleigh would be awaiting the conclusion of the packet's test as soon as possible, but he would hopefully have something even more substantial to tell her when he returned.

Lee scrubbed his hands over his face and fought off the urge to yawn. One more and it'd crack his jaw. Luncheon with Edwards had stretched into a nearly two-hour affair, with excellent food and wine he really ought to have said no to. Lunch had been hard to enjoy, despite the quality, and not just because Lee had worried every eye that passed over him in the crowded men's club saw that he was dining with someone who hung around at the Blue Room with girls who had a taste for white powder.

Edwards was polite and overly formal, continuing to refer to him as Dr. Lee, though he'd invited Edwards to be informal with his name in hopes of establishing some rapport. Once Edwards was satisfied with Lee's tales of medicine, he spoke of nothing but his collectibles and Amelia Gresham. Lee thought it would be a convenient entrée into discussion of Miss Williams, but it turned out to be Edwards's means of inviting Lee along for an excursion to his familial seat, where he kept his extensive collection of antiques. He'd evidently just acquired an original Carl Benz one-cylinder engine, which Amelia had found "utterly fascinating" on their recent trip to Sussex.

Lee liked motorcars—he had one himself, a sweet little blue thing that practically flew on the rare occasion he got to drive it—but consigning himself to a few hours of driving and then admiring Edwards's dusty collectibles didn't hold much appeal, especially considering Amelia Gresham would be accompanying them. She'd looked half asleep at the Blue Room, not to mention that anyone who was a close friend of Edwards had to be an odd duck. He didn't care if Amelia had recently discovered an interest in Edwards's antiques; Lee wouldn't be sacrificing a full day to boredom.

His cab stopped all too soon at the entry into the Quad, and Lee forced himself from his overfed stupor to pass the driver payment and alight from the vehicle. Across the street, the hospital stood in all its full, hideous glory: a mass of red brick and white stone in a bizarre shape that ensured one got lost every other time one entered. He considered going across to do what he'd promised Everleigh he would—investigate missing stores of drugs—but he'd been gone ages. And the notion of walking around the twisty halls was vastly unpleasant just now.

Lee entered the North Wing and hiked up the stairs as quickly as his overfed stomach allowed. At the office door, he exhaled slowly, preparing for a skewering for being absent for so long, then swung the door open.

Or attempted to, but it was locked. Lee scoffed, digging in his jacket pocket for his keys. Well, if Everleigh herself was going to absent too, then he shouldn't feel so bad. He might even have a bit of a lie down while he digested.

Content he'd avoided the glares of his partner, Lee sat at his desk and rested the back of his head on the top of his well-padded chair. But before his eyes could close, they caught on a piece of paper fluttering on the ceiling over his head.

Lee blinked. There was a note pinned to the ceiling.

He stood on his chair to reach it and saw that it was fastened to the plaster with a hat pin topped with a tiny pearl. He snorted. Everleigh.

The note was brief, written with an edginess that came across in the sharp slashes of black ink. *A report came in at noon: poisoning in Little Gaddesden, three young women found this morning. Their condition is not severe. I would say I hope to see you there, but I'm not counting on it.* —S. Everleigh

A quick consultation of the train timetable left open on Saffron's desk showed she'd only just have arrived there herself. The next train in that direction was not for another forty minutes, and that simply wouldn't do.

Lee gathered his things, a smile forming on his lips. It seemed he would be getting to drive his zippy little motorcar after all.

CHAPTER 10

How any young women lived to see the age of fifteen was beyond Saffron's comprehension. With their inclination to incite violent feelings against themselves with their wretched attitudes, it was incredible they had enough time and energy to get themselves into actual trouble. Yet the three young women sitting before Saffron managed to find significant trouble, all while maintaining their insolent manners.

Saffron sat opposite three girls, ages thirteen, thirteen, and *fourteen*, as the eldest was quick to point out, in a small, shabby parlor, the windows of which were shut against the sun. The oppressive darkness was broken only by a handful of candles about the room. Anything more, Saffron had been told, and the girls complained that the light hurt their eyes.

"And so," Saffron said slowly, scanning the notes she'd just finished writing, "you decided that to answer your quandary, you would eat some of the nightshade berries in Mrs. Hannaford's garden." She said it not as a question, because it wasn't. Upon her arrival at the tiny village train station, the father of one of the girls had collected her and explained that the three young ladies had been found dancing in the garden of the local widow, Mrs. Hannaford, at the crack of dawn. The uncomfortable father had intimated that it was commonly thought among the children of the village that the unsociable widow was, in fact, a witch.

One of the thirteen-year-olds, a plump girl with her red hair coming loose from her sleeping braids, sat forward in her armchair and said earnestly, "Minnie was the one who said we ought to try them."

Minnie, the eldest, with narrow features pinched by irritation, glared at her from the settee she shared with the third girl. "I said I'd heard of witches' brew, Anne, not that I knew how to make it or what it would do."

"Liar!" exclaimed the other girl, Katherine. "You said it would make us fly!"

Saffron sighed, caught between amusement and irritation. They'd been going 'round in circles for the last hour, gaining the merest bit more information with each version of the story. Saffron thought it more likely they were just embarrassed they'd been caught running about their neighbor's garden in their nightgowns. She wasn't entirely confident they'd even been hallucinating, but just convinced the single berry they'd each consumed had affected them. Hours later, they didn't appear symptomatic except for sore eyes and the occasional disappearance to the necessary for unspoken reasons.

Saffron cleared her throat to discourage the girls from springing back into battle. They shifted their scowls to Saffron with startling coordination.

"Witches' brew, I see," Saffron said. That at least made perfect sense; nightshade had long been known as an ingredient in a potion rumored to make a witch's broom fly. "Where did you hear about this witches' brew, and what made you decide to try it?"

Even in the dim light of the candles, Saffron could see color rising in their faces. She made a note of it; flushing was a symptom of nightshade poisoning in addition to being an indicator there was something afoot.

"Did you read of it in a book, perhaps?" Saffron offered, looking from face to embarrassed face. "Or someone mentioned it?"

Anne opened her mouth, but Minnie made a hushing sound, and she snapped it shut once again.

This was getting ridiculous, Saffron thought with another surge of frustration. She couldn't let them maintain their sulky silence. There were other children in the village, and they needed to be protected from whatever foolishness had led these girls to eat the berries. "Look," she began, "I understand that—"

The door swung open behind her. The girls' eyes narrowed against the glare. Saffron spun in her seat and bit back a groan.

Lee was standing in the door, his figure all the more impressive for the smallness of the frame. When he stepped inside and closed the door, his hair and skin glowed in the candlelight, making him look like a Botticelli painting. Saffron glanced at the girls; their mouths were slack. She'd have no hope of maintaining their attention now.

"Well, well," Lee said, removing red driving gloves from his hands with exaggerated slowness, "I hear there's been a poisoning."

Deadly nightshade berries stained gloves. They not only stained gloves, but the purplish red juice had soaked through the thick leather gloves Saffron wore in the field and was likely going to stain her fingertips too.

Saffron paused in her harvest, frowning down at her purple gloves. Could the toxins be absorbed through the skin?

She continued her work in the little garden, recalling a case she'd read about, in which a rose gardener had accidentally poisoned himself with nicotine pesticide spray that had been absorbed through his dampened clothing into his skin. There was a chance that she could be poisoned by—what was in deadly nightshade again? Atropine, she thought—but it was unlikely that such a tiny dosage would have a significant effect. Or would it? But that was in part what the study was meant to find out.

She plucked a few more berries from the bush, looked at them with suspicion, then went to work on the stone bench nearby, removing the seeds to dry and store. She didn't know why Aster had specifically asked for so many seeds, but at least they were plentiful.

The little garden tucked behind the accused Mrs. Hannaford's cottage was overgrown, with shabby hedges and plentiful weeds everywhere except in the neatly tended vegetable patch near the cottage's back door. But the sky was a bright, pearly white, and the air was fresh and cool. It was a pleasant place, despite the neglect.

Anything was preferable to remaining in that dark room with those horrid girls.

She tried to recall if she had ever been so foolish, so contrary. She and Elizabeth had made mischief, sure enough, often sneaking out of their respective houses as girls, usually to wander the ruins on the edge of her family's property and tell ghost stories. In the early mornings, heavy fog would cloak the ruins at the corner of the estate and make the whole thing seem like a grand adventure. And there had been a close call when she'd eaten a berry plucked from something in her father's overcrowded conservatory as a young girl, and of course, she'd consumed another poisonous botanical just months ago, but she at least had had a better reason than wanting to see if it would make her *fly*.

"Finished yet?"

Lee's chipper question snapped her back to reality, the little garden in which she stood, berry juice drying her sticky fingers to her gloves. She set down her scalpel, a tool she'd nabbed from Lee's kit before abandoning him to question the girls when it became apparent she could have sung opera without any of them so much as batting an eyelash. "Nearly. I assume you're here because you've finished with them?"

Lee chuckled, stepping over a low stone wall bracketed with leggy rose bushes.

"I'm here," he said, placing his hands in his pants pockets, "because I received your rather snarky note. I'm glad I came, even if the girls didn't have much need for a doctor."

"Oh, they had need of you all right," Saffron said ruefully. "I suspect they melted into puddles at your feet and told you everything." He ducked his head, hiding a smile. "They did, didn't they?" She let out a disbelieving laugh. "Well, let's hear it then. What's the story?"

"Apparently, the vicar's son has a fondness for penny dreadfuls. He is also, apparently, not half so handsome as I am, though attractive enough that Minnie simply had to get his attention."

"Oh, of course," she said with a sigh. That should have been her first guess. "I suppose we need to speak to the vicar's son now?"

"Already taken care of," Lee reported with a grin. "I told him the way of things."

"And what way is that?"

"If you encourage pretty girls to eat poisonous berries, there won't be any pretty girls left."

Saffron burst out laughing. "And what did he have to say to that?"

Lee shrugged, looking pleased. "He said I made a very good point, thanks for the advice."

"I hope the vicar has a strong constitution."

"He'll have to develop one if those girls keep chasing after his boy."

"I don't recall being quite so determined as a girl."

"I very much doubt a vicar's son would hold so much appeal for a young Saffron Everleigh," Lee replied. "Our victims are more likely to grow into the Lucy Talbots and Caroline Attwoods of the world, wouldn't you say? Catty, you know."

Saffron considered this, uneasiness pushing out her amusement. The young girls did display the same sort of chafing dynamics of the other group and, oddly enough, also chose to indulge in risky substances. She wondered what the older women's inducement was, if not a handsome village boy.

Lee looked about the garden, eyes landing on the berry-studded bush with a gleam of interest. "Ah, our culprit?"

Saffron stood and crossed to the massive bush, glad for a change of subject. "Yes. *Atropa belladonna*, deadly nightshade." Saffron plucked another berry from its star-shaped setting, and handed it to him. "I'd been hoping it was *Solanum nigrum*, which is very similar in appearance and far less poisonous, but the berries are too large and aren't growing in clusters as the other species does. But the girls seemed to come out of it alright anyway."

"Rather pleasant looking, aren't they?" Lee murmured, holding it up. It was shiny and black as a beetle. He nicked the skin of the berry with his teeth. "Ah, it is sweet."

"You can't eat that!"

"I'm not eating it," Lee said easily. His tongue darted over his lips, clearing them of the stain of wine-colored juice before flicking the berry back into the bush. "Besides, you're one to talk. Did you not poison yourself intentionally just a few months ago?"

Drat the rumor mill for doing just the opposite of what she wanted. "That was for an investigation. For *science*."

He gave her a sly smile. "Oh, I know. You and a fellow called Ashton helped solve that poisoning a few months ago. Something about a couple of blackguards stealing from the university?"

Saffron lamented the blush that crept up her face. "That's right."

"This Ashton—I don't believe I've seen him around the U. Should I seek his advice on how to manage you when you're going after murderers?"

"Sorry, he's unavailable. You'll have to find another way to *manage* me."

"Unavailable? Did you poison him once you'd caught the criminals?"

Exasperated, she made to cross her arms, and only realized her mistake when the sticky leather touched her bare arms. She jerked her hands away and scowled at the purple prints dotting her skin. "Alexander Ashton is on the Amazonian expedition. He'll be back in October, if you can suffer that long without his advice."

"Oh. That certainly explains a lot."

Startled, she blurted, "What?"

Lee grinned widely and reached into his pocket. He withdrew a handkerchief. Rather than offering it, he took her by the elbow and began wiping her skin with the soft cotton. "Your atlas, for one thing. Every so often, you open it to a page in Brazil. It sits there on your desk, open, for a day or two, and then you put it away again. He must write to you, then?"

Heat rose through her face. His hands were bare, as were her arms. Him gently cleaning her arm was far too intimate, but worse was his perceptiveness. She tugged her arm out of his grasp.

Unfazed, he folded the soiled handkerchief and replaced it in his pocket. "That would be a 'yes.' So, you've foiled criminals with him, and now he's in Brazil, chopping through jungles with a machete and wrestling jaguars. How enticing."

"If my friend writes to me from a foreign location, it's natural to want to know more about it. And one would become friends with someone who helped one do something important. You and I have become friends working on the study, haven't we?" She wasn't sure about that last bit, but he already had that teasing look she hated.

"Oh, and so much more, Everleigh," Lee crooned.

So much for that. She turned on her heel and returned to the bench, where she tidied up the mess she'd made of the dissected berries.

They stepped over the low wall and down the lane next to Mrs. Hannaford's cottage. Saffron glanced up at the sky, which had darkened from milky white to gray, wondering if they might ask for a ride down the road to the train station. She didn't look forward to waiting on the uncovered platform for the train when it looked like rain. "I suppose we can't ask for—*oh*. What is that doing here?"

A shining blue motorcar was parked on the side of the road opposite a field of turnip greens, utterly out of place.

"That, Everleigh," Lee said, striding up to it and patting the rear lovingly, "is our ride."

CHAPTER 11

When Saffron reached the police station the next morning, prepared to report the findings from the Blue Room to Inspector Green, Sergeant Johnson was at his throne-like seat, directing the incoming traffic to the station.

"I'd like to see Inspector Green, if he has a moment," Saffron told him.

"Sorry, miss, 'e's not here," the sergeant replied.

Saffron was just going to ask when he might be expected back when Sergeant Simpson strode out from one of the halls.

"Sergeant Simpson," she called to him, and he stumbled slightly, narrowly avoiding colliding with another officer. He righted himself and stopped at the desk before her. One of the gold buttons on his navy-blue jacket was coming loose. "Do you know when Inspector Green might be back? I have something rather urgent for him."

"Oh, I'll take it, Miss Everleigh," he said brightly.

As petty as it might be, she wanted to give Inspector Green the packet of cocaine herself. She wouldn't take credit for it, not when it was Lee who'd gotten a hold of it, but she wanted the inspector to know she was doing something of value. She smiled in what she hoped was a charming way. "I would prefer to give it straight to him, if you don't mind. It's quite important."

"I couldn't say when he'll be finished with the latest, er"—he glanced at Sergeant Johnson, who watched their exchange with an amused arched brow—"the latest case. 'Scuse me." He stepped away, making toward the door.

Saffron followed at his heels. "The latest case? He's out on a case now? A murder?"

He looked over his shoulder at her. "Er, well—that is—"

From his panicked reaction, she knew she was on the right track. Suspicion flashed across her mind. "It isn't another bouquet murder, is it?"

"No," he said far too quickly, nearly running into the door. He jerked it opened and pressed his lips together when she followed him and he was forced to hold it open for her. They stepped outside. "No, it is not."

She narrowed her eyes at him, and he gulped. "It *is*," she gasped. "Where? Shall I come with you?"

"C-come with me?" Simpson stammered.

"Yes, right now. I didn't have a chance to examine the other bouquets in person, and that could have been incredibly informative."

"The inspector wouldn't want—"

"He wouldn't want you to cause valuable evidence to disappear because some policeman or maid was careless. Didn't he say the only connection between the first two victims was the flowers?" Inspector Green definitely had not said that, but Saffron was determined to see the crime scene. It seemed immeasurably important to get to see where one of the victims actually lived, especially after meeting Bridget Williams's strange collection of friends had revealed so little about who she'd been. Not to mention, it would undoubtedly be fascinating to see a real crime scene.

Simpson had no reply for her, likely because he made a dash for the bus that had stopped down the street. Saffron followed him, unsure if that made her very stupid or very clever. On the bus, Simpson pressed his mouth shut and refused to give her any answers to her many questions. They alighted in Knightsbridge and made their way into a well-off neighborhood. Saffron trailed Simpson, who was walking so quickly she had to scurry to keep up as they passed high-walled brick walls, tidy gardens, and polished motorcars parked along the clean streets.

They reached a stately house with the front gate open between tall stone walls. Several police officers milled about in the front garden.

Simpson attempted to disappear into the house, possibly hoping that one of the other policemen would stop Saffron from entering, but they let her by. Saffron suspected it was because they'd arrived together, not because they didn't notice her, for there were several curious faces following her progress inside.

The large townhouse was decorated in a fussy, outdated style, with several shades of pink coating each room. A surprisingly nauseating combination of dusty potpourri and fresh bread scented the air. A handful of servants flitted about, pale faces creased with lines of worry, adding to the dense atmosphere.

Simpson looked over his shoulder at her, his uncertain frown almost comical from beneath his custodian's helmet. She smiled reassuringly at him.

"Simpson," called a familiar dry voice from above.

Simpson jogged up the stairs, Saffron falling slightly behind. She'd reached the top a moment after Simpson disappeared into a doorway in the middle of the corridor.

She'd taken but one step when Inspector Green emerged from the same room. He looked like a black and white photograph slipped between the pages of a fashion magazine, arrestingly bland amid so much lurid color.

"Miss Everleigh?" His nostrils were slightly flared and his lips thin and white, clearly his version of indignation or anger.

She swallowed, unprepared for his ire. She reached into her handbag and passed him the small white packet.

He slowly turned the packet over, some of the tension easing from his face and replaced by his usual watchfulness. Saffron released a quiet breath of relief.

"Where did you get this from?" he asked.

"Dr. Lee and I met Miss Williams's friends at the Blue Room, a jazz club in Elephant and Castle, and Lucy Talbot gave it to Dr. Lee. We've had it tested, and it is cocaine."

He considered her, ultimately ending whatever assessment he'd been carrying out with a minute sigh. "You do recall I said you didn't need to befriend those people?"

"Yes, but it worked out that way anyway," Saffron said. "We learned something else. A Mr. Percy Edwards was with the ladies. They appear to be quite close, and he wasn't on the list you gave me."

That seemed to mean something to the inspector. His eyes were still on her, but she suspected he wasn't seeing her at all, but reviewing some clue in his mind. She used the momentary lapse in attention to inch forward to get a glimpse of the scene just beyond the doorway.

The door led to a lavish bedroom. The furniture was inspired by the Orient, all black lacquered wood that stood out from the busy floral pattern of the wallpaper. Several large windows let in bright morning light. A small writing desk was tucked between two of the windows, and in the center of the room stood a round table, over which was splayed an armful of flowers.

Saffron's chest constricted with something that might have been excitement—or just as easily dread. This *was* another bouquet murder; a length of black ribbon was visible from where she stood, the same as the other two. It was at once gratifying and horrifying that she'd been right.

She stepped forward, past the inspector who had drawn out his notebook, and into the room.

At the snap of an angry voice from the other side of the room, Saffron swung around, startled. She'd been so absorbed with the flowers that she hadn't realized that there were other people in the room. Or rather, two other people and a body.

She stared at the dead woman on the bed, and horribly, terrifyingly—she stared back.

The sensation that gripped her was unmistakable: she was going to be sick. Her gorge rising, she stumbled from the room, eyes burning with the gruesome image of the woman on a bed soaked in blood.

She heard someone issue some sharp words but was in too desperate need of a private place to heave up her breakfast to pay any mind. Fortunately, the bathroom was steps away. She hurled herself inside and lost the contents of her stomach into the sink.

When there was nothing left to retch, Saffron bit her lip on a groan and turned to the door to see Inspector Green was standing just outside. He was good enough not to comment as he offered his handkerchief.

"I-I should not—" Saffron pressed the handkerchief to her mouth, inhaling the comforting scent of clean laundry. "I should not have come."

Inspector Green made a dismissive sound in his throat. "As much as I do not care for you coming uninvited to a crime scene, perhaps it is a good thing you did."

Saffron looked at him through a haze of moisture that might have been tears.

He regarded her without reprehension, the slight softness in his eyes easing the harshness of his next words. "Perhaps it will remind you that this is not an adventure or scientific experiment."

Properly chastened, she crushed the handkerchief in her hand. "You're right. I take it very seriously, Inspector, I assure you." There was no way not to—not after seeing a person in such a state. It was one thing to imagine murder and quite another to see a bed painted red with blood and unseeing eyes in a gray face. "I'll be on my way, then." She stepped into the hall, where Simpson was hovering, anxiety plain on his face. "And, Inspector, it wasn't Sergeant Simpson's fault. I made a pest of myself, and he had no way to avoid me."

Her testimony served only to make Simpson twitch. She made for the stairs, feeling utterly wretched.

"Miss Everleigh." She paused, and found Inspector Green with a somewhat pained expression. "Perhaps you might return later. Once the coroner has completed his business." He nodded to the bedroom, where no doubt the man she'd seen prodding the dead woman with appalling interest was still working.

"H-here?" Saffron swallowed. Her curiosity had fled her along with her breakfast; she had absolutely no desire to be in this house.

"You might accompany Simpson to examine the exterior of the house for footprints or disturbed plants, or to see if there is a florist nearby and get a list of the flowers that were sold in the past few days," he continued. "By the time you're done, I'll be ready to allow you to examine the bouquet."

Simpson looked at him with disappointment akin to a puppy losing a fallen tidbit from the dinner table, but Saffron perked up. She could be useful in that regard, at least.

It was half past one when Saffron and Simpson returned. Now that the windows were closed, the cloying odor of roses seemed to fill the entire downstairs of the house. It was quiet at least, with most of the policemen gone.

The inspector was in the dining room, evidently finishing interviewing the household staff. A round woman in a white cap and black dress was just getting up from the table.

They waited in the parlor for him to finish. Saffron and the young sergeant gratefully accepted the tea a maid brought for them.

When the inspector came into the room, Simpson immediately regaled him with a detailed report of all they'd seen. Saffron thought it sounded much more interesting and official when Simpson explained it. To her, it had been along the lines of combing a garden or field during a case study—tedious work that made her back hurt. This time, however, she'd earned a crick in her neck from all the time they'd spent looking up at the ivy climbing near the dead woman's bedroom windows.

They'd found nothing unusual. None of the vines had been broken to indicate someone had climbed it. *Hedera helix* was a hardy plant, but it could not stand up to the weight of a full-grown man or woman without a few tendrils snapping. No footprints in the moist dirt of the garden. No fabric conveniently caught on rosebush thorns. No shady characters had bought unusual bouquets from either of the two florists close to the townhouse.

Inspector Green took it all in without batting an eyelash. "The flowers are still upstairs." He regarded Saffron warily.

She gave him a nod she hoped reflected far more confidence than she felt. "I can manage."

They trooped upstairs, Saffron taking gulps of the too-sweet air to steady herself. Alexander popped into her mind, face relaxed, with his chest moving slowly with each deep, even breath. She'd playfully requested instruction in his meditation technique, the one that helped him overcome his symptoms of shell shock from his time in the trenches of Fromelles. Although Saffron didn't think she could realistically sit down on the floor without shoes or stockings whenever she needed to calm her mind, she had enjoyed the demonstration immensely, though not for entirely educational purposes.

There had been something intensely intimate about the experience, sitting across from one another on the floor, knee to knee, the silence around them heavy with the pleasant anticipation that had filled the two weeks of their time together before his departure. He'd allowed her a glimpse of vulnerability, not just in words but in action. Remembering it now, the crescents of dark lashes on his cheeks, his chest expanding with each slow breath, helped her feel a fraction better about entering the room where she'd seen a bloodied corpse.

She stepped into the room after the policemen, careful to not immediately look at the bed. The flowers were just before her on the small, round table, so she fixed her attention on them, putting her back to the canopied bed.

"Peony and hydrangea, common garden fare." She drew closer, squinting down at the center of the fallen bouquet. Beneath the fluff of white peony and blue hydrangea splayed on the table were threads of linear leaves. Saffron blinked down at them, hardly believing they were what they were. She carefully pinched off a few of them, holding them close to her nose.

"Rosemary," she murmured. The next words came automatically. "For remembrance."

The combination of the long-remembered words of Ophelia just before her death and the horrible scene she'd witnessed just hours ago in this very spot proved to be too much for her. Her knees went wobbly, and she started from the room.

In the hall, she pressed her back to the wall and shut her eyes, only to open them again when blood-soaked images flooded her mind's eye.

Simpson tentatively poked his head around the corner. "Miss Everleigh?"

"I'm all right. It was just—it's rather a lot," Saffron said weakly. The message the rosemary proclaimed was clear without the floriography book to translate: the killer wanted the dead woman to remember something—likely whatever sin she'd committed that fueled the rage leading to her murder. Saffron wasn't sure why that so unnerved her.

Simpson joined her in the hall. "It is. I lost my lunch my first time."

That made her feel better, even as it riled her empty stomach. There was a heavy sliding sound from within the room, but she found she had no curiosity for what the inspector was moving about.

They remained in the hallway for another minute or two before Saffron had made up her mind that she would return inside. She'd been the one to force her way into this house, and she would do what she'd come to do.

The inspector had opened the window, allowing in a breeze that carried away the heavy scent of dried roses and the lingering tang of blood and cleaning products.

Back at the table with the flowers, Saffron used the end of her pen to nudge aside a handful of stems to get a better look at several tall sprigs that were utterly unrecognizable. The prickly green stems were laden with blue blossoms, pink stamens sticking out like so many thin tongues from the petals. The plant tickled her mind with near recognition, but she couldn't put a finger on the name.

Miniature magnifying glass in hand, she knelt beside the table. The flowers were unruly in their clusters, with thick, curling cymes coiled beneath the initial opened blooms. The whorl of immature buds curled like a scorpion's tail. That impression was furthered by the generous coating of stinging trichomes on everything but the petals themselves.

This wild-looking plant didn't belong in an elegant flower arrangement. Its inclusion made her uneasy, but she couldn't decide if it was simply because she didn't want to tell Inspector Green she didn't know what it was. She made a quick but thorough sketch of it in her notebook, resolving to consult a wildflower guidebook the moment she had an opportunity.

Simpson rocked on his heels, face bright with curiosity. "Are any of them poisonous?"

"Most plants are, Sergeant, if you eat the right amount of the wrong part of them." She hesitated, the blue flowers drawing her eye once again. "And I can't say for certain, but I'm fairly sure that no one should touch this blue one without gloves."

"Ah." Simpson smothered a smile. "Donovan already found that out. Itchy hands."

Inspector Green asked, "You'll be able to decode the flowers?"

"Yes, I will," Saffron said. Hopefully their interpretations would provide a meaningful clue as to why this woman was killed and who might have done it. Her eyes trailed over to the bed, now bare and blessedly stainless. "May I ask what happened to the victim?"

To her surprise, Inspector Green said, "At eight o'clock this morning, September thirteenth, a report was received from a housekeeper that her mistress was dead. We sent a man over, and he reported back a body." Saffron suppressed a shiver, and the inspector nodded solemnly. "Yes, a particularly gruesome way to die. She'd been stabbed in the back. Just once, but there was a good deal of blood, as you saw. We'll hear more after the postmortem."

"Strangled, suffocated, and now stabbed. And the only connection is the flowers?" Saffron asked, bewildered. "But surely there must be some other connection. Acquaintances or tradesmen they patronize . . . something."

"The ribbon is just the same as the last two," Simpson put in, rocking on his heels again and looking to his superior for confirmation. "That's how I knew it was the same culprit."

Inspector Green gave him a mildly quelling stare. "We can't say that with any certainty. But the ribbon does appear to be the same. Black velvet, high-quality stuff."

Saffron returned her attention to the bouquet. The black ribbon that she'd noticed before trailed off the edge of the table. She picked up her magnifier once more and examined the ends of the ribbon. It was cut neatly, though she thought she saw the barest hint of ruddy orange on the tip, as if the blade had been rusted. She pointed it out to the inspector.

"A good find." She wished he'd say something more about his plans for the evidence, like seeing if the other ribbons had rust on them, but he merely continued his report. "None of the maids recalled a delivery of flowers. The responding police officer ran into the table, knocked the vase over."

Now she'd conquered the bed, Saffron examined the rest of the room. She wandered through the fussy space. It was just like the rest of the house, brightly decorated with bric-a-brac covering every gleaming surface.

"Who was she?" Saffron asked softly, pausing on a portrait of a young boy in a gold frame on the dressing table.

"Mrs. Audrey Keller, forty-seven years old. Widowed during the war. Mr. Arnold Keller was new money, but respectable. I'll be looking into where exactly that new money comes from. Two children, a sixteen-year-old daughter who recently died of a fever and a twelve-year-old son who is away at school."

Surprised, Saffron looked around the room for signs of mourning. "When did the daughter die?"

Inspector Green examined his notes. "Three weeks ago."

It had been years and years since black coverings for windows and lamps or other signs of mourning were considered a social requirement, but it was strange there was no sign of a recent death in the family. She moved to the wardrobe, next to the dressing table. Within, a dozen expensive outfits, most of which came from Allard, a well-known fashion house. There were several outfits of darker, more somber materials, suitable for a woman grieving the loss of a child.

"Publicly, she was mourning. But here . . ." Saffron drifted to the dressing table, almost touching her glove to the picture of the young boy. "Her son is here, but not the daughter."

Inspector Green came next to her, humming slightly. "An important observation." He bent to record it in his notebook. "We need to discuss your evidence."

Saffron explained about going dancing and ingratiating herself to Lucy Talbot, and told him about Lee's involvement. The inspector echoed Saffron's shock that Lee had so easily gotten hands on the drugs. Saffron shrugged. "He's quite convincing, especially to silly young women."

Over the inspector's shoulder, Simpson grinned. Inspector Green asked, "And this fellow, Percy Edwards. I've seen that name before. It was on a calling card at Miss Williams's home."

"He's friends with the women, so I expect he was at least acquainted with Miss Williams too."

"A particular friend, maybe?"

"I don't think so," she replied slowly. Edwards was no doubt good friends with Amelia but hadn't seem at all upset, like one might expect of someone whose paramour had recently been killed. But really, she didn't know much about him apart from his interest in old-fashioned things. She gasped with belated realization. "Inspector! Mr. Edwards did mention he has some sort of antique collection, and he named some older composers as his favorites. His interest might stray far enough back to be knowledgeable about floriography!"

"It's possible that this fellow is involved, then."

Now she'd said it all, it felt like she'd barely discovered anything. Edwards's identity and interest in old-fashioned things were not evidence. "I was thinking to go back to the Blue Room. Miss Williams's friends must know something about her mysterious romantic partner."

The inspector frowned slightly. "Any whiff of trouble and you remove yourself from the situation. Let me know if you find out something, and please do not accept more of these packets. You may be consulting on this case, but I can't do anything if you're caught with cocaine. You or Dr. Lee."

Her heart swelled. He wasn't telling her to stay out of it. In fact, he was almost giving her permission. "I truly am sorry for barging in here earlier. And . . . thank you for trusting me. I'm happy I can help."

He gave her a curt nod, likely holding back more warnings about the seriousness of the investigation, and Saffron set off, ready to delve back into the mysterious world of floriography.

Inspector Green was right. This experience, however horrific, had put her firmly into the right mind to help solve these murders. It had been stupid to think that this was some sort of exciting adventure. There were lives at stake.

The thought brought nausea rushing to the surface once again. She stopped, just outside Mrs. Keller's house, and leaned against the tall stone wall. She forced herself to slowly breathe in the fresh air until it receded. She would long be haunted by what she'd seen. But at least she had someone close at hand who could commiserate with a close encounter with death. She wondered what her partner would make of the news of yet another murder.

CHAPTER 12

The case in his pocket tapped Lee's chest as he climbed the stairs of the North Wing. He was certain he was about to be mercilessly mocked, if not outright scolded, when he reached the office. He'd absented himself from the office without telling Everleigh he'd be gone *again*, just when they had significant work to do on the nightshade study. He'd been gone for hours, much longer than anticipated.

Perhaps he'd be lucky, and she'd still in be in the pleasant mood from the previous day. She'd actually smiled at him, not in exasperation or even as a result of a silly joke he'd made, at least twice on their way back to town. Lee had little doubt that riding in a motorcar with the roof detached rather than being stuffed like a sardine in a grimy train compartment had improved her mood a good deal.

Lee released a sigh at the top of the stairs. The light glowed from behind the frosted pane and the light sounds of his partner's rapid typing emanated from the office.

Saffron barely lifted her eyes from the typewriter when he stepped through the door. Her mouth tightened, pinching the rosebud color from her unrouged lips. Indeed, she was rather pale all over.

"Made good progress?" he asked.

"Yes," she replied curtly.

He held her gaze, her expression slightly caustic, with mouth flattened and eyebrows lifted, and his with a smile threatening. But he thought of nothing else to say.

He went to his chair. Everleigh had already gone back to her typing. He slipped the slim leather case out of his breast pocket and set it on his desk, eying it like it might bite. The case and its contents, certainly not. His partner, however, would likely milk it for all it was worth.

He drew a file toward him. The text was as blurry as it always was, and his immediate reaction was to hunch over the papers and squint, but he stopped himself. Glancing at Everleigh, who was as clear as she always was from across the room, he opened the case and quickly hinged over his ears the pair of gold eyeglasses within.

Immediately, the words before him sharpened to perfection, and the woman across the room went blurry. He didn't need to see her to know she wasn't looking at him, though, and he was annoyed to find he was slightly put out.

An hour passed, during which Lee read his text and found his temples didn't throb with the effort of squinting, and Everleigh maintained her silence.

The novelty of seeing clearly for the first time in years wore off around the same time that Saffron's clattering on the typewriter ended.

He removed his glasses and slipped them into his breast pocket when she stood and took her handbag from a drawer.

Fully aware he was tempting a tongue-lashing, he asked, "You're leaving?"

"I've done my work," she said with a pointed look.

"I'll get mine done," Lee muttered.

"Oh, I'm sure," she replied, tone taking a sharp turn toward waspish.

He put on the most irritatingly syrupy voice he knew and asked, "Are you going to explain to me what I've done wrong?"

She jerked her bag up on her shoulder, glaring at him. "Nothing. I was apparently wrong to assume that you would be available to discuss things today." She was across the room, snatching her coat from the rack by the door, then slamming the door before he could puzzle out what exactly they were meant to discuss.

After a minute of staring at the door, he decided that Inspector Green had given her a hard time about the cocaine that morning, and he ought to have asked about it. Then again, maybe she was just hungry. Everleigh's mood always took a turn for the worst when she was peckish.

That thought in mind, he eyed her desk, contemplating digging into the drawers for her stash of biscuits. He sidled over, half expecting her to burst through the door. Her notebook sat atop the ever-present stack of books, open to a page covered with a great deal of scratched-out writing.

Curious, he held the notebook close to his face to make it out, then recalled he had no need to squint any longer, thanks to the eyeglasses he'd wasted the morning obtaining. He drew them out of his pocket and slipped them on. He read:

Bouquet Three, stabbed:

Unbidden, Lee's hand jerked. A third bouquet meant someone else had died. Stabbed, apparently. Saffron must have heard about it when she went to give the inspector the drugs. He rushed through the rest, struggling to make out the notes she'd made.

Bouquet Three, stabbed:
Peony, white—shame, anger, ostentation
Hydrangea, blue—heartlessness, boasting, coldness
Rosemary—remembrance

Then came a series of blotted out words. Even with the assistance of the glasses, they were hard to understand, but Lee made out *Coventry bells*, and *bugleweed*. That made little sense to him, but if he'd learned anything about botany over the course of the last few weeks, it was that plants had most deucedly ridiculous names.

Another such ridiculous moniker was etched in the corner of the paper—monkshood. That rang a bell, actually. Aconite, one of the plants Everleigh had introduced him to in their first week working together, was called monkshood, along with a number of other silly names. Beneath the word was the melodramatic phrase *"a deadly foe is near."*

Lee set down the paper, a finger meditatively stroking his chin. Why had she placed that in the corner rather than listed it with the other plants?

He flipped back in the notebook until he found her notes on the other bouquets. Aconite was listed among the second bouquet, Birdie Williams's. Apparently, a deadly foe lurked near Birdie before her death. Considering she'd been murdered, that was hardly illuminating.

He set the notebook back where he'd found it, humming. Had Everleigh's frustration come from the flowers rather than his absence? She had been taking their lack of progress in the case rather hard . . .

He let out a sigh, irritated that he apparently cared so much about her feelings. She wasn't here to be prickly, so he ought not to care. His gaze landed on an unaddressed envelope sitting a few inches from the bouquet's interpretation. Casting another wary glance at the door, he picked it up.

Curiosity easily overtook his qualms about her privacy. After all, as with the notes on the third bouquet, it was likely to be relevant to him too. That and she was being a proper bother right now, and snubbing his nose at her helped alleviate his annoyance.

He immediately saw that the papers didn't relate at all to their work, or the poisoned bouquets.

It was a letter addressed to Alexander, who must be Alexander Ashton. It was dated that day. Lee snorted; he hadn't been the only dewdropper today. He was about to replace it when his own name caught his eye toward the bottom of a page, and he again gave into curiosity once again. He sunk into Everleigh's cushioned chair and began to read.

August 31, 1923

Dear Alexander,

I hope this letter finds you well and returned safely to Macapá. I put off responding since you said you would be wandering the jungle for some weeks, though now I worry this letter might miss you altogether. Or you might read it on the ship back to England.

I'm most impressed that you've made so much progress on the specimen list. I'm sure you've already considered this, but have a care in their transportation. It's unlikely that the hull of a ship, lacking in light and air circulation, would be that much different from their normal growing conditions, but it is essential to provide moisture and warmth. That could easily be accomplished by providing water in dishes nearby, which evaporate to provide some humidity, but you will need to arrange something for the warmth. Dried seeds, of course, are also acceptable for the plants that provide them, though that is of course not preferable if I'm to finish this new study with any speed. Your notes contain details of which plants might be handled which way.

I'm relieved to hear of Trumont's recovery. I heard a rather different version of the story of how he was bitten from Dr. Feinstein, and I have to say it was rather foolish of him to pick up any snake, even if he thought it was a new species to be christened Oxybelis trumonti. *I wonder if the other name floating around the North Wing has made its way across the ocean to him—*Oxybelis stultus? *Maybe don't pass that bit of gossip on to him.*

Lee snickered at that. Foolish snake indeed. He spared a moment of curiosity for the way she so casually mentioned the gossip mill, as if she wasn't its frequent target.

It was most entertaining to see the photograph of the team. You fit the part of an explorer perfectly, though I barely recognized you with a beard. You were right—the bandage did give me pause until I looked up what a jaguarundi is. You were apparently swatted at by a large cat. However will you recover?

Lee stared at Everleigh's looping handwriting. Was she *flirting* with him on paper?

My work is progressing well. Dr. Lee and I have passed the halfway point in our study, and I have new wind in my sails after Inspector Green asked me to consult on one of his cases. Fear not—it's flowers this time. You can understand why I won't include many details here,

*as the case is ongoing, but suffice it to say it is most intriguing. I eagerly
anticipate telling you how I solved it.*

Lee rolled his eyes. *She* was solving it, was she? He huffed, then
wondered at her cavalier tone. The case was quite exciting, but she'd
just learned of another murder. Seemed rather odd that she didn't
mention the three dead bodies they were trying to account for.

*I hope you're enjoying yourself and being careful. It would be a
pity to take away the jaguarundi's title as the most dangerous creature
you have encountered. I look forward to hearing of your adventures
in person soon.*

Yours,

Saffron Everleigh

P.S. *You may rest easy about potentially dangerous mangoes. Man-
gifera indica only grows on the Indian subcontinent.*

Lee replaced the letter in its envelope, puzzling over the postscript.
The letter surprised him. It was neither soppy and romantic nor
exclusively businesslike. It offered information, but not entire truths.
And it was rather annoying that she could so easily be playful with
this Ashton—through a letter, to boot—but refused to joke with him.
Lee speculated how Ashton felt. Lee certainly wouldn't have kept up
a correspondence in the midst of an exciting expedition for just a
friend.

He began on his work, insisting that he didn't mind at all that
Everleigh hadn't written more than a few words about him. They
were with each other all day, every day, and had been for nearly four
months. Surely, he deserved more than a passing mention. After a
few minutes, he wondered why he was still thinking about Alexander
Ashton at all.

❦

The words on Lee's list of toxins in *Atropa belladonna*—the wretch had
actually made good progress the previous day—swam before Saffron's

unfocused eyes. She blinked, and the letters comprising atropine, hyoscyamine, and scopolamine arranged themselves in their proper order.

She'd barely slept that night, too haunted by visions of flowers and the fatalities they proceeded. After staggering awake, she'd decided she needed to make some progress in the case, but all her exhausted mind could come up with was revisiting the flowers. Mrs. Keller had done something that someone felt she should be ashamed of. And they'd punished her for it by stabbing her in the back. Stabbing in the back indicated betrayal. Perhaps that was the meaning of the unidentified wildflower from Mrs. Keller's bouquet. She'd searched through her own wildflower guidebook and found nothing resembling the mysterious cutting.

She was just contemplating swallowing her pride and asking some of the other botanists about it when Lee banged through the office door, immediately tossing his hat onto the couch. His eyes gleamed with excitement.

"A boon for you, Everleigh," he said, coming to lean on her desk. "Edwards has invited us to a party."

Attending a party was the last thing she wanted to do at that moment, but she reminded herself that it was in the service of finding a killer. She could cope, even if she became more and more uncertain with every detail Lee shared of his plan.

Mostly because there was not much of a plan. She was used to investigating, both in her work and in her sparse experience with crime, within environments where she had some measure of control. The university's greenhouses—and even the fields and gardens she'd searched—were her bread and butter. The Blue Room had been uncomfortable, but certainly not unfamiliar. This was little more than a vague extension of an invitation that Edwards had received from an "old friend" who would "be delighted" to meet any of Edwards's associates.

But she couldn't *not* agree to go. Another body had been discovered, another woman murdered. Saffron had *seen* her, cold and dead in her own bed. They had yet to learn anything about Miss Williams or how she might be connected to Mrs. Sullivan or Mrs. Keller.

Inspector Green hadn't mentioned any progress in discovering who might be responsible for the murders. This would be an opportunity to question a great deal of people who might have known any of the three women. Saffron didn't have a choice but to dress herself up as Sally Eversby once again and hope she and Lee learned something useful.

CHAPTER 13

September

Saffron's noble connections had accustomed her to the glittering fanfare and expensive tastes of the wealthy, but it had not prepared her for the absolute decadence of the dwelling she and Lee arrived at the following Friday.

The house seemed to be more windows than brick, with light pouring from every window, illuminating the fragrant gardens and etching the ground with a thousand little rectangles of light. The sounds of laughter and music floated on the soft night air. Its location in Hampstead afforded the property some privacy, being just outside London proper.

Had her life taken the path her grandparents would have preferred, Saffron would have been accustomed to such idyllic prospects. As it was, she was wary. She'd known Mr. Edwards must have connections, being the heir to an earl, but this house suggested something loftier than she'd expected.

Saffron cast Lee a look that said, *What have you gotten us into now?* before accepting his arm and starting up the stairs. He was clad in flawless black, which provided a lively contrast with his gold hair and green eyes. Saffron didn't match him. She was also wearing black, but it was heavy; the handkerchief points of her dress pointing to the floor, the borrowed sparkling bandeau across her forehead dripping with jet beads at her temples. Her generous application of kohl and dark lipstick made her features more prominent but weighed down her pale, powdered face.

Looking at the crowd within the impressive house's walls, she was glad for her disguise, however thin it might be. All around her, she saw faces she vaguely knew. If the grand house itself wasn't clue enough, the people within it were. Elegantly dressed and expensively perfumed, they spoke with upper-crust drawls and roamed with polished ennui. She was among the peerage that had once discarded her, just as she'd discarded it.

Lee took her by her gloved hand and tugged her through the crush of bodies. The room, lovely with its cheerful, rose-colored wallpaper and elegant furnishings, was warm and hazy with cigarette smoke, despite the multitude of windows flung wide. Saffron kept her face turned away as they passed a handful of men laughing together near the doorway into the next room. She was quite sure she'd danced with two of the guffawing men at the last ball she'd attended before exiting the social scene. She didn't need to be recognized and risk her suspects realizing she'd given them a false name.

The next room was a vast parlor that would likely be gorgeous in the morning. Windows embellished with sky-blue glass reached to the ceiling, punctuating lemon-yellow-papered walls. More blue accented the space, along with gleaming dark wood furniture that was currently buried beneath platters of food and drink.

The elegance of the room had distracted her momentarily from the outrageous behavior of those occupying it. Two women sat atop a piano, singing along to the music, loudly and poorly, while a man lying on the bench guzzled liquor straight from the bottle. Couples cluttered the open space around the piano, doing indecent approximations of dancing. In fact, more than one couple was acting amorously. She even caught a few homogenous pairings, drawing daringly close or furtively exchanging a kiss. That other version of herself might have fainted at the sight of it, had Elizabeth's literary circles that Saffron occasionally attended not been so open to unconventional sorts.

Even so, she couldn't help but gawk. She'd thought she'd seen wild parties—but this was extreme. It was not yet ten in the evening, and the tone of the room was somewhat frenetic.

Someone bumped her back, and she stumbled. Lee swooped an arm around her. "Steady on, old thing." He pushed them through still more people toward one corner of the room.

"Miss Eversby!" came Mr. Edwards's cry as he extended a hand toward her. He made to kiss it when she placed her hand in his, his lips not quite brushing her glove. He beamed at her, perspiration dotting his brow. "How do you do?"

Saffron replied in kind with a smile. She found his overzealous manners bemusing. He was highly polished in his blindingly white shirt and tails, his silk lapels as shiny as his forehead.

"What a sensational party," she said. "I'm not sure whether to thank you for inviting us to tag along or ask you what new civilization you've discovered."

Edwards chuckled, but his expression tensed slightly. "These gatherings are always the stuff of legend. They crop up rather suddenly and are swept away with equal speed."

Over his words came a screech of furniture over hardwood floors. People were making more room for dancing, apparently. She glanced at Lee, who caught her eye and winked. His duty was to find Lucy Talbot again and see what she might reveal. Saffron's task was to discover the identity of Miss Williams's paramour. They would both attempt to see if anyone knew anything of Mrs. Keller or Mrs. Sullivan.

"Have you seen Miss Gresham or Miss Attwood?" she asked, leaning in close to be heard over the music.

"Miss Gresham stepped outside for some fresh air," he answered. "And I have not yet seen Miss Attwood or Miss Talbot. They might be lost in the crowd."

She didn't see Edwards's face as he spoke, but Saffron thought there was a touch of impatience in his words. She shot him a smile. "I might require some fresh air myself. I didn't expect it to be quite such a crush."

Edwards swept an arm toward the French doors a few steps away. "I will fetch you a drink."

Saffron gave him an appreciative nod and made her way outside. The cool air was pleasant after the feverish energy inside.

She couldn't help but be reminded of escaping a party in a similar fashion months ago, and suddenly longed for the company of the man she'd escaped it with. What would Alexander think of all this? Would he be as entertained with the case as Lee was, or be wary of the dangers Saffron was courting? She hadn't mentioned any of those dangers in her most recent letter, not wanting to worry him, but she couldn't help but think he'd be an asset in this investigation. He was always so sure of himself, always so steady.

She caught sight of Amelia, standing at the end of the terrace in conversation with a man, the pair washed in yellow light by a window directly before them. Amelia was fiddling with her gloves, which, Saffron saw as she approached, were a bit shabbier than her own. She and Elizabeth shared their gloves, and this pair had seen quite a few outings but were in decent enough shape. Amelia's were a bit off-color and frayed. The way she rubbed her hands together somewhat self-consciously wasn't likely to help their condition.

The man swung around at Saffron's approach, his toothy grin widening as he looked her up and down without pretense. "Good evening," he said.

Saffron murmured a "Good evening," in reply, making it clear by focusing on Amelia that she'd come to speak to her.

Unfortunately, Amelia didn't look happy to see her. "Miss Eversby?"

"Hello." Saffron sidled past the man, to Amelia's side. "Mr. Edwards mentioned I would find you here. It is rather overstimulating inside, is it not?"

The man's gaze flicked between them, and when Amelia made no move to introduce him to Saffron, he bowed slightly with an annoyed expression and strode down the terrace and back into the house.

Amelia turned to watch him go, a frown creasing her features and catching shadows deep under her eyes. It reminded Saffron of Lee's conviction that Amelia was an overworked nurse, and she decided to pursue that avenue first. Commiserating over one's experiences as a woman in the sciences was usually a bonding experience. If she could get Amelia to confide in her about her work, she might confide in her about something else.

Saffron affected a sigh and leaned against the stone rail. "I like a party as much as the next girl, but I find myself exhausted by coming and going so late in the evening. I'm studying at the University College, you know," she said, adding a hint of pride into her voice.

Amelia's eyebrows rose. "You are?" She glanced to the French doors, then added, "What do you study?"

"Medicine." That would explain her presence at the hospital if Amelia had ever noticed it.

"Like your friend," Amelia said without much interest.

"I find it one of the most noble professions. So many lives were saved thanks to dedicated doctors and nurses during the war. And so many continue to require care, of course." Amelia said nothing, merely rubbed her hands together again, not looking at her. "Nurses, in particular, are rather undervalued, don't you think?"

Amelia's pale eyes flickered to her, but she straightened up with a smile directed over Saffron's shoulder. "Thank you, Percy."

Edwards was approaching them, two drinks in hand. Saffron accepted hers and took a small sip of the cloudy yellow liquid, to show her thanks. The punch was more alcohol than juice, cementing Saffron's decision to sip it only to be personable.

"I was just telling Miss Gresham about my studies," Saffron said to Edwards. "It can be exhausting, spending all day on campus touting around my textbooks, then going on an outing with Lee." Neither Edwards nor Amelia made an effort to engage with that line of conversation, so Saffron added, "He insists, you know. How he is so full of energy, I can't imagine. His work is so very challenging."

The words nearly stuck in her throat. Lee would be delighted if he heard her waxing poetic about his challenging, noble profession.

"Yes, a doctor's work is *so* hard," Amelia muttered, taking a long drink from her glass.

That was the first spirited thing Saffron had heard from Amelia, but she didn't have the chance to pursue it, as Edwards cleared his throat.

He was smiling, but his teeth seemed to be clenched together. It put to mind someone who had a very bad itch but couldn't permit themselves to scratch it. "What field are you engaged in, Miss Eversby?"

"Medicine," she replied, glancing at Amelia. She was gazing morosely through the windows into the room. "I hope that I can follow in the footsteps of a number of my friends, like Lee, who provide such an essential service."

Edwards nodded enthusiastically, and his cheeks were flushed somewhat. "Oh yes. Absolutely. An essential service, indeed." Saffron opened her mouth to make a connection between service to the community and the charities Mrs. Sullivan had been involved in, but Edwards barreled on, saying, "Miss Eversby, would do you me the honor of a dance? I daresay I enjoyed dancing with you at the Blue Room and would love to repeat the pleasure."

Taken aback by the abrupt shift, Saffron merely nodded before Edwards swept her away with her hand on his arm.

CHAPTER 14

"Is everything all right, Miss Eversby?" Edwards asked, a solicitous concern on his face. They'd stopped dancing a few moments ago and now stood with Amelia in the same corner of the yellow-papered room with the piano. It was just as raucous as before, and they had to speak loudly to be heard.

Saffron came up with an appropriate response for why she'd just been frowning as she gazed around the room, searching for Lee. "I've just been admiring the house, as much of it as I can see. Would it be terribly gauche for me to ask who owns it?"

Edwards, who was already pink from the warmth of the room, went pinker. "I apologize most profusely! My manners have been carried away, it seems. This is the home of a dear friend of mine, Lord Vale."

Lord Vale was not a name known to her, unfortunately, but Sally Eversby wasn't likely to know all the peers in the country anyway.

"Gerald Harrington is his name. He's been the Viscount Vale for less than a year," Amelia offered. "He doesn't limit himself to his own circles like many of his peers, though. He's very engaged with politics, as well as many other interests. He enjoys modern design. His townhouse in London is the same. Very bright and airy."

Saffron said, "I see," if only to fill the suddenly awkward space between Amelia and Edwards. Edwards's smooth face had creased into a thoughtful frown at Amelia's words, and she hadn't noticed, merely looking with idle curiosity into the crowd.

Amelia straightened up, a smile blooming on her face. Edwards caught the change too and turned to the man who'd just come from a group of people parting for him like the sea parted for Moses.

"Ah," Edwards said, somewhat sullenly, "here he is now."

Lord Vale's hair was inky black, his skin untanned olive, and he wore a dinner jacket that was tailored perfectly to his stocky form. He was perhaps a few inches shorter than Edwards, but his manner gave him a presence that most simply didn't have, no matter their stature. His gravitas didn't match the sort of party he was hosting, where, in one corner, a man was now attempting to knock an empty liquor bottle off a woman's outstretched hand with wooden lawn bowling balls, and a lewd French song was being sung in another.

He approached with a broad smile, eyes sweeping over them in a carefully measured way. He held out a hand to Edwards, but his first words were directed toward Saffron and Amelia.

"New friends and old," he rumbled, his rich voice pitched to be heard despite the noise. "Welcome."

Amelia took a half step toward him to offer her hand, which he kissed. She was much prettier with her cheeks rounded and pink. "Sally Eversby, this is Lord Vale," she said, nodding to Saffron.

It was not much by way of an introduction, especially for a viscount, and Saffron did her best to look a bit flustered. She'd met her fair share of lords and ladies, even a duke or two, but these people didn't know that. "How do you do?"

He replied in kind, and Amelia added, "Sally is our new friend." She spoke much more familiarly than Saffron would have expected.

Edwards took a half step closer to Amelia. "We met at the Blue Room just last week."

"Fast friends, indeed," Lord Vale said, turning his gaze onto Saffron. He was not a noticeably handsome man, with a heavy brow and a slight blockiness to his jaw, but his eyes, a kaleidoscope of blue, green, and brown, drew her in. "Any friends of Mr. Edwards or Amelia are friends of mine. You are welcome."

Saffron noted he referred to the other two in the same way their little group of friends did. "Thank you, my lord. I did not mean to come uninvited—"

Lord Vale chuckled. "Half the room would have to be cleared if I cared about such conventions. As I said, friends of friends are welcome."

"Thank you. Your home is exceptionally beautiful," Saffron said. It was the appropriate thing to say, and it was true.

"You are too kind. My father was one of the first to give the old heave-ho to the ancient manse in Mayfair and had this place built to give the family a bit of breathing room away from the smog of town."

"It is lovely." Her words were overtaken by Edwards rushing to agree verbosely and Amelia adding her own quieter agreement.

To Amelia, Vale said, "I was sorry to miss you the other day."

Her cheeks heated faintly. "I was sorry to miss you too. But I had promised Mr. Edwards that I would go with him to Sussex. He added another Benz dial to his collection, and I wanted to see it."

"I didn't realize you'd come to share Mr. Edwards's fascination for original objects," Vale replied.

Amelia smiled prettily. "I can appreciate finely made things."

Saffron glanced between the pair, trying to determine if this was a flirtation. Edwards, too, was frowning between them as he flexed his hands at his side. He looked like he was trying to figure out the same thing, or he'd already figured it out and wasn't pleased with his conclusion.

Another man came behind Lord Vale and murmured in his ear. A moment later, Vale said, "You must excuse me—a matter I must attend to. Miss Eversby, a pleasure. Do enjoy the party. Amelia." He touched his lips to her hand. To Edwards, he gave a brief nod and then disappeared.

A moment later, Edwards had excused himself in the direction that Vale had gone, and Saffron was left with Amelia.

In search of something to say, Saffron asked, "Have you known Lord Vale long?"

"I've known Lord Vale since we were children." Her smile faded somewhat. "I met Percy when I came to London after the war. Mr. Edwards, that is. He prefers the formality."

She could see she was losing Amelia's interest from the way she was glancing about, likely hoping for an excuse to leave the conversation.

Not for the first time, Saffron lamented the impossibility of finding ways to ask sticky questions when one had absolutely no excuse to do so. At the university, she'd had reasons to ask her colleagues questions related to the poisoning of Mrs. Henry. It would draw suspicion if she started asking direct questions about Miss Williams and her drug use, or her boyfriend, or her connections to two other murdered women. She had no excuse now but nosiness, and that simply wouldn't do.

Bolstering her courage, Saffron said, "I don't suppose you or your friends are involved in any sort of charity work? There is so much need in London, you know, and I should like to be of assistance to others."

With a look of surprise, Amelia turned back to her. "I was under the impression that you were very busy with your studies. But I suppose I misunderstood your comments from earlier. I might be able to introduce you to a few people who are involved in charities. There are several here who like to play at savior and would know organizations you might join."

Saffron's face burned at her mistake and Amelia's stinging implication. "That would be lovely, thank you. But perhaps in a moment, after I've greeted Miss Attwood. I haven't yet seen her."

"Caro likes to play cards," Amelia said, her voice dropping back down into a lower, wearier register. Her shoulders seemed to hunch forward slightly as she nodded to a doorway. "You'll likely find her in there. But be warned: she'll take the gloves right off your hands if you're not careful."

Uncertain what to make of that comment, Saffron gave her a smile and followed her directions into the next room.

🌿

Progress in search of Lucy Talbot was slow. Every few steps, Lee was stopped by a simpering smile or a friendly clap on the back.

It was off-putting, Lee thought as he shook the hand of a thickset older man with whom he'd apparently attended a house party ages ago, that he only vaguely remembered most of these people. He'd lived rather fast during his university years, and it showed in how few he could name or place in his hazy memories of that time. He was doubly glad he'd tamed himself a smidge in recent years.

He made for the windows, hoping to catch a breeze in what looked to be a smoking room. The walls were a dark plum, and a good many of the comfortable-looking armchairs were filled with more than one occupant each. Just as a hint of cooler air met his face, he spotted the telltale peroxide blonde he'd been searching for.

He was by her side in a moment, in the next room over, a sort of morning room decorated with a dizzying wallpaper of brightly colored birds. "Miss Talbot," he said, unable to murmur her name with warm silk in his voice, like he would have otherwise. She was surrounded by a rowdy crowd next to a table stacked with bottles. "A pleasure to see you again."

"Dr. Lee!" Lucy Talbot squealed, fluttering her lashes. "How divine!"

There was little use for further pleasantries with her collection of admirers now glaring at him, so Lee simply took her proffered hand before tugging her away, into the quieter smoking room.

"I hope you don't mind," Lee said. "Me snatching you away from your devotees."

"Not at all," she said with a laugh. "They're bores. They can only speak a lot of nonsense about stocks and interest rates and complaints about their work. Hearing about a man's work is so frightfully dull."

"Sounds dreadful," Lee said honestly. He helped Lucy up to sit on the windowsill, maintaining one hand on her hip.

"Oh!" she said, her lips actually forming an O, her eyes going wide. They were red around the edges. "I have such admiration for you, Dr. Lee. I just mean that the others are so . . . plebian, you know."

He stroked a thumb over the silk of her white gown at her waist. "I see. Well, let's talk about you rather than the dull commoners. That's a decidedly more fascinating subject."

He should have known better. Through the next ten minutes, he listened to an exquisitely boring treatise on topics that would have otherwise been enjoyably scandalous gossip. According to Lucy, her life had been one trial after another; when her stuffy father died, his heir had removed Lucy and her mother from their comfortable home.

Her mother had then married a horrid man who soon also died but left her mother a pile of money. Since then, Lee understood, she and her mother had enjoyed traveling about, and from the dubious hints that Lucy kept dropping about the "amusing" company her mother kept, the older woman was enjoying her life as a wealthy merry widow. Lucy had somehow managed to make the whole diatribe an absolute snore.

"Mama couldn't be convinced to come to town," she said with a sigh. "She's very popular in Bath, but I'm afraid she's been the subject of cruel gossip. Many in London turn their noses up at her. I think they're jealous, truly."

Lee let her prattle on, only half listening. Everleigh was nowhere in sight, but he hoped she was making better progress than he was. Thus far, all he'd heard were a lot of reasons why Lucy seemed desperate for something to take her mind off how unfair and unsatisfying she found her life.

From their position by the open window, Lee could see a band of young men stumbling over to the massive fountain in the middle of a formal garden beyond the patio. From the looks of things, they meant to take a swim, and from their drunken laughing, they were likely to need rescuing before one of them ended up drowned.

His eyes slid back to the chattering woman next to him, an idea forming. "Lucy, darling, you don't have to keep on such a brave face for me, you know."

Lucy stopped mid-sentence, blinking. "Whatever do you mean?"

He cupped her bare shoulder and squeezed with comforting pressure. "I know you've been through an ordeal. Your friend was killed just a few weeks ago, wasn't she?"

Lucy's blue eyes widened almost comically. "You heard about Birdie?"

"Birdie? Is that Miss Williams?"

"Oh yes, she was my dearest friend. I can't believe . . ." Her lashes fluttered, as if blinking away tears, though her eyes remained dry. She sniffed loudly and pulled a handkerchief from her handbag. "I can't believe what happened to her."

"She was murdered," Lee said gently, not quite a question.

She nodded, blonde bob swinging. "It was dreadful."

From beyond the window came a splash, followed by a chorus of laughter. Lee sighed. He'd be doing chest compressions on some blue-lipped sot before long.

Recalling himself to his task, he asked, "What happened?"

"I don't know," Lucy said somewhat plaintively, patting her nose with her handkerchief. Lee had noticed she did that an awful lot. "The wretched policeman who is investigating wouldn't tell me anything more than that she'd been murdered in her home."

She leaned into him, and he allowed her to. "Tell me about it."

"I was just getting ready to go out to meet Caro for lunch, and the inspector and his little minion arrived on my doorstep and insisted on coming inside. He forced me to sit down and tell him all about the past few weeks, what I had been doing and who I'd been seeing. And how was I to remember all that at the drop of a hat?"

Lee clenched his jaw, too tempted to insist she tell him the same things.

"Then he asked all these questions about my friendship with Birdie. He kept saying that I'd argued with her! A little spat between the best of friends is meaningless," she said with a pout. "I simply didn't want her making a foolish choice like she always did! Reaching for things she could never have. I didn't want her wasting her time, you see."

Lee nodded as if he had the least bit idea of what she was talking about, and patted her hand. "Watching out for your friends is admirable. Did you tell the inspector what she was trying to do? Perhaps she put herself in danger."

But Lucy ignored his question, saying, "It *is* admirable. You might do the same, Dr. Lee. Your friend is rather cozy with Percy, isn't she?" Lucy inched toward him on the windowsill, her legs pressing against his thighs.

Lee followed her gaze to where he could just see Everleigh talking to Edwards in the main hall. They didn't seem particularly engaged with each other. "*We* are rather cozy," he replied.

Her answering smile was as blinding as her hair. "Yes, but we might actually get some enjoyment out of it." She twined her arms about his neck, the heel of one of her shoes on the back of his thigh, nudging him closer. The full-body contact might have been enjoyable if the woman wasn't so blasted annoying. "Percy has been hung up on Amelia for an age, you know. He tolerates me and Caro, but he *obsesses* over Amelia. Thinks he's some sort of protector, barely lets anyone get near her, even if he can't be bothered to do anything more to get her attention."

That was interesting. Lee had easily picked up on his attentiveness toward Amelia Gresham but hadn't noticed any overt pining. "Has he never tried to pursue her?"

"No, but if he keeps on scaring off all the other gents, he won't have to make an effort, will he? She is frightfully dull to look at, but she's still managed to get a few admirers. She'll have to marry eventually, and if Percy is the only one left, she'll be stuck with him." She hummed and drew him still closer. He could see his reflection in her overly dilated pupils. "Enough about Percy and Millie. They're both dreadful bores—even when Percy's had a little tickle."

"Why not branch out to more exciting friendships, then?" Lee asked.

Lucy pouted, then did a little wiggle until she was practically climbing him. They really ought to go somewhere more private if she was going to do *that*. "Because, darling, without Percy, I'll never get to go anywhere exciting. Can't make a match if you're never invited out, and Percy gets all sorts of invitations."

That was a callous but practical way to go about things, Lee thought. Her mother was no longer considered good *ton*, to use an old-fashioned term, and so she needed Percy to keep a foot in the door and land herself a husband. No wonder she didn't want to waste time with the plebians, as she'd called them.

Her hot breath in his ear brought to mind sick patients, but he managed not to shudder. "I see."

"I'm so glad you do," she whispered, lips on his earlobe. "Simply can't miss a Vale party, you know, even if I do have to thank Percy for letting me tag along."

"A Vale party?" The familiarity of the phrase pricked his mind.

"Yes, darling." Lucy nuzzled his neck with a happy sigh. "Somehow Millie and Percy are friends with him. Lord Vale knows how to throw the very best parties, don't you think?"

Despite the heat of the room, despite the woman attempting to endanger the little that remained of his virtue where they sat on the windowsill, Lee went ice cold.

His uncle's voice, pronouncing harsh warnings about a young lord's maneuverings and manipulations, rang out in Lee's mind.

This was Lord Vale's party. Lord Vale's house. It was time to leave.

CHAPTER 15

Amelia was right. Saffron hadn't watched Caroline's game of vingt-et-un for more than five minutes before Caroline had bluffed her way into winning ten pounds. After that, the stakes only increased, along with Caroline's pile of winnings.

It finally broke up thirty minutes later, after a heated duel over an entire summer house between two of the players. The rest got up and left behind their table for others nearby, or left the smoky room altogether. Caroline rose from her seat, depositing coins, bills, and promissory notes into her beaded handbag and smoothing down her dress. It was a peculiar shade of silvery green that reminded Saffron of Dr. Maxwell's prized Japanese painted fern. She looked rather festive in the midst of the rich reds of the card room.

A lanky man with brown hair so saturated with oil that it looked wet to the touch sidled up to Caroline. He offered her a cigarette, but she shook her head. Shrugging, he stuck it into his mouth and lit it.

"Where is Miss Williams these days?" the oily man asked with an exaggerated glance around, as if she might materialize. "She was always a laugh. I'd rather lose money to her than to you, even if she'd just use the funds for dope." His smile, partially clouded by a puff of smoke, was pure slime.

From her position, Saffron could see Caroline go rigid. Color crept up her neck to her pale cheeks.

Saffron wanted to hear more about Miss Williams's reputation, but she recognized an opportunity to gain Caroline's trust through an intervention. Stumbling forward, she caught the man's shoulder. She leaned into him and slopped her drink down his front. She blinked at him as if unaware of what she'd done.

"Gah!" the man exclaimed, jumping back. He flicked liquid from the front of his jacket and swore, glaring at Saffron. "You stupid cow!"

He stalked away, his curses lost the moment he passed through the door into the main hall.

"That was a horrid thing to say," Saffron said, frowning after him.

"Calling a woman a cow? I've heard worse." Caroline made to move away.

"No, what he said about Miss Williams. What a nasty rumor to spread." Caroline's eyes leaped to hers, momentarily wide with surprise. Saffron smiled gently. "I heard about how you all were friends with her and that she died. I'm so sorry."

Caroline stared at her for a few more seconds before looking away, busying herself with her handbag. "Kind of you. Sally Eversby, wasn't it?"

Saffron nodded and inched closer. "I suppose it isn't public knowledge yet. Ought I not to have said anything?"

"No, it's—I prefer it. I prefer that people know. Then they wouldn't say damned nonsense about her without thinking twice." Caroline slid a cigarette between her dark painted lips and lit it, hand shaking around her silver lighter. "Perhaps if we spoke more often about Birdie, we'd remember. We wouldn't just go on as things were before, as if she hadn't just been *murdered*." She seemed to be speaking more to herself than Saffron.

"She was murdered?" Saffron whispered, drawing closer to Caroline. *Birdie* was clearly a nickname for Bridget Williams. "Good God, how?"

"I don't know," she snapped, then drew deeply from her cigarette. With smoke pouring from her lips, she muttered, "But I wish I did."

The malice Saffron had seen in Caroline at the Blue Room made a reappearance in the dark glitter of her eyes.

It was slightly alarming, but Caroline—*someone*—was finally speaking about Miss Williams, and she had to see what she could find out. "What sort of person was she?"

Caroline's thinly penciled brows rose, the spite fading. "Birdie?" She took a puff and glared in the direction of the rude man. "She was sweet, sometimes. Liked to have a laugh, liked to sing. That's why we started calling her Birdie. She sang along to anything loud enough to make the alley cats howl."

Saffron smiled at the small measure of warmth in Caroline's words. "She sounds lovely."

"She is. Was." Her tone had gone hard, almost dismissive, but she had already revealed her affection for Birdie. She was likely pushing aside her sadness, something Saffron had watched both her grandparents do time and time again.

Caroline mashed her cigarette into the crystal dish on the card table behind her, and when her back was turned, she fiddled with a thick ring she wore. The jeweled top flipped open, and Caroline brought the hand bearing it to her face. She sniffed.

Startled, Saffron took a half step back and glanced around. Caroline had just inhaled what had to be cocaine in the middle of the party, in full view of half a dozen people. She ought not to be surprised by that, considering what she knew of the friends and the tenor of the party, but she found herself shocked, nonetheless.

Caroline patted her nose with a handkerchief from her handbag, then withdrew long, pearl-colored gloves and tugged them up her arms. She turned around, still sniffling, and seemed surprised to see Saffron was still standing there.

Her mind blank, Saffron blurted the question she'd been about to ask before the ring had opened. "Did she enjoy charity work?"

Caroline blinked. "Charity work?" She sniffed again, pressing the back of a finger to her nose before shaking her head, a rueful smile on her dark lips. "The only charity Birdie ever considered was dancing with a less than handsome man. And even that was only out of the need for the barest social graces. Birdie had little tolerance for the rules of society." Caroline's lip curled. "Ironic, given . . . Well."

"She was friends with Miss Talbot and Mr. Edwards and Miss Gresham too?" Saffron asked, hoping to keep her talking.

"She's friends with all of them, but she's closest to me—or she was." Her expression shuttered, and she murmured, "Excuse me," before she made her way from the room.

Saffron watched her go, wondering if she ought to go after to offer a shoulder to cry on, when someone behind her called, "Saffron Everleigh, is that you?"

The voice was high and loose, likely because the woman proclaiming her real name loudly enough for half the room to hear was clearly very drunk. She and the man she clung to swaggered into the room, both unsteady on their feet.

Saffron gave her best confused but politely smiling expression. "Beg pardon?"

"It has been an absolute age, darling!" crowed the woman. Her high forehead, overlarge teeth, and generous lips were unfortunately familiar.

"Helen Crawford, how good it is to see you again." She couldn't muster much more enthusiasm than a tight smile. She'd never been close to Helen, though Elizabeth had been counted among her friends until it became widely known that the Hale family had lost their fortune. Helen's invitations to teas and luncheons had stopped almost immediately when rumors started to go around. The man propping her up grinned toothily at her. "And Jeremy Straits. How do you do?"

Jeremy's head bobbled in a vigorous nod. "Just ducky, my dear."

Helen patted his arm, which was around her waist, fondly. "Jeremy asked me to marry him, you know."

"Oh, how lovely. Congratulations," Saffron said, her smile pinching her cheeks. Had they not been careless with her name, she might have asked them if they knew anything of the murder victims, but as it was, she was keen for an excuse to escape.

"That was two years ago." Jeremy frowned at her. "Been married almost six months, silly girl."

"Haven't seen her for five," grumbled Helen before brightening up. "Where have you been, Saffron? Last I heard, you were returning to Ellington to rusticate. Terribly dull to be there all this time."

Panic flashed through her, hot and strong. They were speaking of this all so loudly, so obviously. Someone was bound to hear and—

"But what a way to come back into society!" said Jeremy with a laugh. "And so much better, for so many of the old crowd flock to Vale's good times. Can't help it—they all want the ear of the man.

Says he'll stomp out those trumped-up socialists come election day."
He hiccupped, then patted a fist on his chest as if he might belch.
"Chesham is here somewhere—you remember him, don't you?"
Jeremy spun to the open door, dragging Helen with him. He bel-
lowed, "I say, Tolly, go find Chesham! You'll never guess who I've
just found!"

The card room was the last place Lee would have expected to find
Saffron, but there she was, looking nervous as anything, speaking to a
couple who were clearly three sheets to the wind.

Saffron jumped when Lee touched her shoulder.

"Come along and have a dance, Sally girl," Lee said, gritting his
teeth in a smile. The last thing he wanted to do was make nice with
still more boiled party guests.

Her eyes wide with what Lee imagined was desperation, she
wrapped her hand around his arm. "Absolutely. Let's go now." She
squeezed his arm.

"Sally?" snorted the man. The woman giggled. "I always thought
your name was a daft choice for someone of your father's station—"

"But *Sally*?" The woman laughed again. "You could have come
up with something better, darling."

Saffron merely smiled in a pained way and threatened to cut off
circulation to his fingers.

"Darling," Lee said, squeezing her against him. "I know it's lovely
to catch up with friends, but I simply must have you in my arms.
Immediately."

He didn't wait for her or the others to reply before he was marching her from the card room. He half expected Saffron to struggle, but
she went willingly to the drawing room crowded with other pairs
making their way sloppily across the floor.

It was both too loud and too risky to have the conversation Lee
needed to have with his partner. She held herself so stiffly that anyone
halfway sober would realize something was the matter. Given what
he'd just learned, they needed to look the part of snozzled party guests
until they could take their leave. He murmured a joke in her ear.

Saffron managed a laugh and relaxed in his arms infinitesimally. They danced three numbers before Lee felt they'd sufficiently sold their appearance of having a good time.

He'd spotted Edwards in the corner of the room with Amelia and kept an eye on him as they rotated about the room. Lee made a show of realizing the time, then led Saffron over to bid Edwards and Amelia good night.

"If you see Miss Talbot, please give her my particular regrets," Lee said, lying through his teeth. He'd shaken her off when she tried to lure him into the library.

Edwards nodded somberly. "I will, Dr. Lee. I wonder if I could inconvenience you for a moment before you go."

Lee reminded himself to be sanguine. "'Fraid not, old boy. Must get this one to bed at a reasonable hour." He tilted his head to Saffron.

"But of course," Edwards murmured. "I will call on you soon, then. It was terribly good to see you and Miss Eversby again. Goodnight."

Lee was glad Edwards didn't make their goodbyes into the drawn-out affair he'd dreaded. Waiting to leave had put him on edge, and Saffron's odd tension only tightened his nerves further.

As they wove through the debauched crowd, Lee kept a lookout for their host. Discovering that Lord Vale was friendly with the odd little group he'd been investigating had turned this evening from a harmless adventure into a potentially life-ruining disaster. It was one thing to go dancing at the Blue Room but another to allow his name to be attached to Edwards and the rest in such a public way, where Lord Vale might make something of it.

After the heat and stink of cigarettes, sweat, and a hundred heavy eaux de parfum, the night air was blissfully cool and sweet. Lee wasn't much for pacing, but just at that moment he felt like he might need to take up the habit right there on the tiled porch as they awaited the cab a footman inside had called for them.

Not yet, he reminded himself. He could not hit the roof yet.

Saffron must have noticed his buzz of uneasy energy, because she squeezed his hand gently. "What a do! I don't know when I last had such a good time."

"Nor me," he replied, too much cheer in his voice. He cleared his throat and drew her a few steps down the gravel drive. "Quite a party. Hope you don't mind being out so late. I know you have assignments to finish." The nonsense statement was his way of reminding her that they might be observed even here.

With a small smile, she said, "Of course not."

Some of his nerves relaxed. She was keeping her head, even when he thought he might lose his.

Only when they finally climbed into the cab five minutes later, and he had opened a window to let out the reek of pub that still clung to the driver, did Lee relax. But not completely, not when Saffron looked at him with those blue eyes shining with expectation.

"Well?" she asked when he didn't launch into what he'd learned.

An unfamiliar weight pressed on him, making him unconsciously rub at the tense muscles of his neck. "Well, old thing," he said, wondering just how much his partner would hate him for what he was about to say. "I'm bowing out. I'm off the case."

CHAPTER 16

Saffron didn't speak to Lee after he made his little announcement. Rather than poke at him, trying to determine what had happened during Lord Vale's party that made him proclaim he was going to have nothing to do with any of it, she swallowed down her questions and burgeoning hurt feelings and simply listened to him explain what he'd learned from Lucy Talbot.

It was not much, which only served to make her angrier. She kept a tight lid on that frustration, however. She was tempted to complain to Elizabeth when she reached the flat that night, but she found that something like embarrassment held her back from confessing all.

Had she been so wrong about Lee? Had she been foolish to all but invite him to help her and rely on his assistance in her investigation? For that's exactly what she'd allowed herself to do: rely on Lee. Now the rug had been pulled out from beneath her, and she was left with nothing more than a pretended connection to one suspect and notes about flowers.

She kept it all to herself and failed miserably to distract herself by helping Elizabeth clean the flat Saturday morning. Another mistake, if she was being honest, and one that Elizabeth didn't fail to point out when Saffron dusted the mantle wrong. How, precisely, one dusted incorrectly, she still didn't know.

In the end, she settled for what she'd done in her miniscule amounts of spare time, flipping through the stack of worn wildflower guidebooks she'd compiled in order to discover the identity of the strange blue wildflower in Mrs. Keller's bouquet. She'd gone over all of the bouquets and their interpretations again, integrating what she'd learned of the victims with their meanings, and all she'd come up with was that Bridget Williams's love of singing could have been the reason that her killer included tuberose, suggesting "a sweet voice" in addition to "dangerous pleasures."

If she could only clarify the meanings of Mrs. Keller's bouquet to the same extent. The message seemed clear enough without knowing what the final flower meant, that a shameful, heartless action had been avenged, but she couldn't help but hope it would somehow offer a key clue to solving all three murders. The killer had plainly known Birdie Williams well enough to point to her love of singing, perhaps there was a similar clue in the mystery flower.

She'd gone through two of the six books in the stack and had seen nothing resembling the scorpion curl of the blue flower clusters. It reminded her of forget-me-nots, one species of which was sometimes called scorpion grass for the curling cymes of its blooms, same as the mystery flower, but apart from that similarity and the fact both boasted blue petals, she had found nothing else that came close.

Curled on the couch next to the radiator as rain pattered on the window, she opened the next guidebook and stared at the name inked inside the cover: *A. Maxwell.*

She sighed, flipping away from her mentor's messy scrawl.

She hadn't seen or spoken to Dr. Maxwell since he'd closed up his office in May. She'd written once to give a birthday greeting to him at the start of June, but no doubt her letter had been misplaced in his chaotic home study, and she'd therefore received no reply. It wasn't as if she would have confided in Maxwell about Lee or the investigation, but he might have perked her up with an amusing tale or strange specimen he'd come across. She missed him and wasn't sure when, or if, he was coming back to the university.

And of course, there was that pesky and persistent doubt that a certain murderous former department head had planted in her mind about her father and his work. She'd told herself to ask Dr. Maxwell about it before he departed, but she couldn't bring herself to upset his weakened nerves further. And frankly, she'd had enough to deal with without wondering if she even really knew who Thomas Ever-leigh had been, as a man or a scientist, if he'd been doing work to strengthen the toxins in dangerous plants. There was only one application she could imagine for such work, and it was not one she liked to contemplate. It was easier to tuck it all away into a dark corner of her mind, where she might pretend the implications of such work during the years leading to a horrific war did not exist. She'd let Dr. Maxwell escape to the seaside without asking about her father's unpublished materials and what their intention might have been.

She forcibly turned the page in the guidebook, wishing it was as easy to be rid of her feelings.

She blinked at the page's illustration and nearly dropped the book.

It was the strange wildflower from the bouquet, at last revealed to be viper's bugloss. She ran a finger over the image, her fingers imaging the stinging hairs where the paint barely rippled on the stems. Viper's bugloss! She *had* seen it before, along the sides of roads and ditches out in the countryside. She might have even passed by it this summer when she was scouting in fields. And blast it, *Echium vulgare* came from the same family as forget-me-nots. She should have tugged on that thread when it occurred to her.

She lunged across the couch to her discarded flower dictionary. Anticipation tripping through her, it faltered when she reached the "B" page, and she saw it defined bugloss as "falsehood."

She let out a disappointed huff. Not enormously helpful.

She tapped on the page of the dictionary, thinking. The murderer might have used a number of other flowers to communicate the same thing: yellow lily, dogsbane, even manchineel tree, all of which were also dangerous to varying degrees. It was important, somehow, that viper's bugloss had been chosen, and not something else. Was it because of its irritating properties, its name, mere convenience, or something else?

She had a new piece of the puzzle—a tiny piece, but something— and she was determined to collect more, with or without help from Lee.

❧

That afternoon, Saffron went to the police station. Neither Inspector Green nor Simpson were available, not surprising considering it was a Saturday, but she was gratified when the sergeant she spoke to gave her the information she requested about Mrs. Sullivan without a fuss. She thanked him and then went on her way.

She boarded a bus to Blackfriars, down the river, and walked down the cobblestone street to the offices of *The Times*. The entire printing house square and its immediate surroundings were steeped with the dry scents of paper and tobacco from the nearby factory. Though the press itself was quiet, the offices were not. The news waited for no man and certainly did not rest on the weekend.

After passing through a warehouse full of paper-strewn desks occupied by frantically typing men and women, the reception-ist deposited Saffron in a long, narrow room with a low ceiling and gave her the briefest introduction to the organization system. Crates and file cabinets stood in long rows and contained newspapers and an assortment of notes, receipts, and other miscellany.

It turned out that examining newspapers was very much like examining textbooks. Dusty, tedious, and at times rewarding.

Saffron began with her scant information about Mrs. Sullivan. Her husband was a wealthy railway magnate, and she'd been involved in many charities, a list of which the sergeant had provided. She gathered armfuls of newspapers from a filing cabinet close to the front of the room and settled at a rickety desk someone had shoved between a dusty stack of periodicals and an unmarked cabinet.

She scouted through a few years' worth of news, searching out news of railways, Camden Railway, in particular, and its founder. She found a few mentions, but only one that showed any promise.

In 1921, Mrs. Sullivan and her husband had been photographed at a railway opening ceremony in Swindon. The article mentioned that Mrs. Sullivan was involved in an organization for orphans, with a location in Swindon, which the couple also visited. Saffron made note of the orphanage's name and the charity it was associated with: the Organization for the Advancement of Parentless Children.

There, that was something, Saffron thought, making note of it in her as-yet blank notebook page. The Organization for the

Advancement of Parentless Children was not on the list of hospital committees and educational boards that Mr. Sullivan had provided the police. Perhaps Mrs. Sullivan had had a dreadful row with someone at the charity, dropped her patronage, and she had been killed because of it.

She nibbled on the end of her pen, frowning. That was a bit far-fetched, even for her. But the charities seemed to be a good bet, given the allusions to wealth and greed in Mrs. Sullivan's bouquets. She'd thought the key would be to discover the common denominator between the victims, but perhaps it was more important to solve the mystery of one victim at a time.

Saffron found one more mention of the strangled woman in the newspapers, in the society section. She'd kept her eyes peeled for the other suspects and victims but found none apart from Lord Vale, whose name leaped off the page at her often, but only when she scanned political and economic reports. For a man with such social tastes, he was largely off the social map. Lee's uncle was mentioned often too. She forcefully ignored his name, for every time she saw Matthias Lee, she wanted to look up and point it out to the man who should have been sitting across from her, slogging through old papers too.

She wrinkled her nose at the thought. He ought not to have agreed to do anything to do with the investigation if he was just going to drop it, and her, like a hot potato.

A few feet away, the door opened with an ominous creak. Saffron looked up.

Elizabeth entered the room with curiosity on her carefully made-up face. When her eyes alighted on Saffron, she grinned. "There you are, darling!"

"What are you doing here?" Saffron asked.

Elizabeth sent her a sly smile as she set her handbag down atop a stack of Saffron's newspapers. "Well, I thought I might come and lend a hand. I feel rather left out, you know, with you running all over while I molder away at home. I, too, crave adventure."

Saffron snorted a laugh; Elizabeth went out most evenings, whether on a date or to her literary salon, where one was more likely to drink or smoke something exotic than discuss poetry and philosophy. "Yes, you clearly need to liven up your life with dusty old newspapers."

Elizabeth looked with suspicion at the top of the nearest waist-high cabinet before withdrawing a handkerchief from her handbag and wiping the surface off. She wrinkled her nose at the filthy handkerchief before perching on top. "Well, perhaps a search into the bowels of *The Times* is not the thrilling feat I imagined it, but you could certainly use help. You'll be here hours, otherwise."

Saffron had no qualms taking up Elizabeth on her offer of help. She'd been at it nearly an hour and had nothing to show for it but that note about the charity for orphaned children, and smudges covering her fingers.

If not for the decidedly industrial atmosphere, they might have been spending a drowsy Saturday afternoon together in their flat. Elizabeth hummed "When My Baby Smiles at Me" as she flipped through the pages.

She soon reported that, in the newspapers from the last three months, Edwards was mentioned once, Lucy Talbot three times—but nothing more than alluding to their being among the guests at certain events or parties. Caroline Attwood was not commented upon, nor was Amelia Gresham.

Saffron pressed on with her own stack, all dated well before the murders took place. Her eyes flew over newsprint, only snagging on grim words related to the search.

Near the bottom of her stack of papers, 1919 gave way to 1918, and reporting about the war shifted from past to present. She recognized some of the headlines: reports of bombings of German railways, destroyers being sunk, and brave efforts of soldiers in Italy. Like most, she'd clung to any source of information that might offer hope that the war would soon end, and had read each edition cover to cover. When the end finally did come, Saffron found that newspapers more often than not reminded her of dark, frantic moments when she scanned headlines for news good or bad, and so rarely read them.

A heavy sigh gusted from her lips as she forced herself to continue; 1918 became 1917, and Saffron was nearly ready to give up when another name caught her eye.

Samuel Gresham, age forty-seven, died April 25, at his home . . . If the Samuel Gresham who was survived by a daughter named Amelia was the father of the sullen nurse spending time in seedy jazz clubs, it would certainly explain a lot.

Amelia's father had died quite suddenly, it seemed. Given Amelia's connections, one would expect that they would have had funds enough to last a while. Saffron guessed those funds had finally run out, and now Amelia was left to work for a living. Given the two sisters and wife John Gresham had left behind, Amelia might be supporting them too.

It was strange how Amelia clung to her status in the upper class when it would have been much easier to step into the middle class, where there would be less pressure to keep up appearances. It would have been one thing had she shown a passion for nursing and been willing to work despite her friends' opinions, but Saffron didn't think they knew anything about it. Amelia didn't even seem to really enjoy their company anyway. She seemed to almost scorn the wealthy at Vale's party. She'd referred to those participating in charities as "saviors," and she'd noted with enthusiasm that Vale had interests outside of the peerage.

But she was likely letting her own experiences color her understanding of Amelia. She'd given up her connections with little regret, but she couldn't expect others would do the same so willingly.

Her eyes ran over the slightly smudged script of the obituary again, paying attention to the wording. It was similar to the one her uncle had received years ago, bland and suspiciously short on details.

Her father's brother had ended his life shortly after he returned from his deployment. His death had not been something spoken of even in hushed tones in Ellington, not like her father's death, which had been extensively mourned just months before. The family had attributed Uncle John's death to heavy drinking and a muddled head. She'd been an adolescent at the time, sheltered from most of the talk, but her cousin, John Junior, had told it to her plainly after the funeral: his father had killed himself. Had Amelia's father suffered the same?

"Absolutely no conjecture about the deaths being related," Elizabeth said, interrupting Saffron's macabre thoughts. She set down her paper and poked it with one of her red varnished nails, right on a small headline proclaiming a murder in Kensington. "No mention of the bouquets. That's odd, isn't it?"

Saffron considered. "The murders did take place relatively close together, but without the flowers to link them, I suppose they seem unconnected. Inspector Green only decided the flowers were important well after the first two took place."

"I suppose," Elizabeth said slowly, removing her finger from the paper and curling it around a strand of her sandy bob, "that they really might not be related. A mad man might have just walked down the street one day, seen one of the victims, and decided to kill her. They might be no more connected than I am to anyone visiting the same market for groceries."

Saffron straightened up, a rush of intuition sparking through her. Elizabeth might have little in common with the other shoppers at their nearest market, true, but they *did* shop alongside one another. "Eliza! You are brilliant!"

Elizabeth broke into a smile. "Aren't I just! Each of the victims was rather high in step, didn't you? And where do all fine ladies with clams rattling in their pockets go?"

CHAPTER 17

"I don't suppose we can just go to Harrods and call it a day?" Saffron asked hopefully.

New Bond Street was crowded with motorcars and trams, and the pavement was no different. She and Elizabeth were buffeted by pairs of women in elegant suits and dresses, chatting gaily beneath hats of all shapes, sizes, and colors. The shop windows displayed more finery, anything from evening gowns to delicately heeled shoes, to handbags and shawls, and tailors proclaiming their quality in curling gold letters over their doors.

Elizabeth shot her a withering look. "If you want to learn absolutely nothing, then by all means, toodle off to Harrods. But these were women of quality, Saff, or at least they were attempting to look like it. None of them were titled, but all had the funds to create a wardrobe that suggested they might be, if I understand correctly. The dresses in Mrs. Keller's wardrobe were made by Allard, correct?"

Saffron nodded, though the motion was lost as she and Elizabeth hopped up on the curb to avoid a cab rushing around the corner.

"So, we go to the House of Allard, see if we can sniff out if any of the other ladies shopped there. Could be a very telling connection between the three women. And a seamstress is likely to overhear a good deal of information about her employers," Elizabeth said sagely.

They set off down the road, arm in arm. Saffron asked, "What about the other shops?"

"Well, there are at least a dozen likely places they might have gone. Allard is merely the first on the list."

"Reville?" Saffron suggested. It was a name she was familiar with from her mother's more fashionable days.

"They're over in Hanover Square. And Reville and Rossiter is fashion for the more conservative crowd. A girl like Birdie was likely to go somewhere exciting and new. Patou, or Lanvin, if she could afford it. Allard keeps up with the times, but without alienating older clients. The other victims might have shopped there. Let's try there first."

A hush fell around them as the doors of the House of Allard closed on the busy street at their backs. With the sudden quiet and infusion of scent, it was as if they'd entered a sacred space.

A few mannequins, costumed in lavish styles, greeted them as they stepped into the warmly lit foyer. The dwindling rush of air from the street stirred the gowns, making it seem as if the mannequins, startled at the intrusion, had frozen mid-step.

It was odd, Saffron considered as she and Elizabeth stepped across the marble tiled floor and into a refined parlor with more posing mannequins, how one could suddenly become utterly gauche and painfully unkempt just by passing through a set of doors. On the street, Saffron's ready-made suit, purchased for a few precious pounds, and blouse, made over once with a large lace collar, were perfectly serviceable, if uninspiring. But in the hallowed halls of Fashion, she felt quite the leper. She gazed at the nearest dress with equal parts admiration and wariness. It was a little too reminiscent of something Marie Antoinette might have worn, with fabric flaring away from the body at the hips but cut down to suit the more modern sensibilities of 1923.

"*Bienvenue, mesdames,*" a raspy feminine voice said.

Saffron and Elizabeth turned as one to the side of the shop where a doorway framed a young woman with a waif-like figure.

"Welcome to Maison d'Allard." She came forward with a small smile. Her accent was barely there French, and therefore very chic. It matched her effortless ensemble of a knitted jumper and tennis skirt in a daring geometric print. She was perhaps their age, though her regal expression and perfectly lovely face rendered her ageless. "How may I assist you today?"

Though her slumberous dark eyes did not stray from theirs, Saffron got the impression she'd taken note of their outfits and already had made a judgment about them.

Elizabeth, unaware or more likely uncaring, launched into a verbose story about their journey to London, to be dressed by world-famous designers, after inheriting a good deal of money from a deceased aunt. Had Saffron not known it was fiction, she might have believed Elizabeth's wide-eyed naivety. Perhaps Elizabeth was a better actor than she'd given her credit for.

The woman, Honorine, who introduced herself as one of the house models, seemed pleased to assist them. They sat together in a cozy corner of the salon for a terribly long time, discussing at length what styles would be most appropriate for their body types, coloring, and current social calendar. Saffron could barely maintain her composure. Clothing was all well and good, but they had a reason for visiting, and it wasn't to listen to Honorine wax on about the new sportswear line that Allard himself had designed with "feminine motion" in mind.

When Honorine excused herself to retrieve fabric samples, Saffron leaned over to Elizabeth and hissed, "Are you planning on asking any relevant questions, or are we supposed to sit here for three hours while she declares again and again that she has the perfect slimming corset for you?"

Elizabeth sent her a sardonic smile. "If she mentions it one more time, I'm likely to tell her I'm using all my inheritance to go on a slimming holiday to a spa somewhere." She blew out a breath, adjusting a pin in her bob. "One must grease the gear if it is to turn smoothly. If I babble on, she'll get used to the idea of conversation and hopefully reveal something useful."

Saffron might not have believed in the method had it not worked twenty minutes later.

"My dear grandmamma was in *such* a state when I told her my cousin and I would be coming to town for new clothes," Elizabeth said with an expansive sigh. "She was terrified that something dreadful would happen to us."

After showing them the fabric samples, Honorine had brought them back to a private room, where Saffron and Elizabeth were bid to undress down to their camiknicks and stockings in order to be measured.

Honorine was not participating in the measuring, but had stayed to keep them company as Saffron and Elizabeth's limbs were moved about like dolls by two other women. She nodded, lips pursed. "Indeed, my own family worries for me. City life can be dangerous, especially for young women."

"It was all to do with that article in the papers," Elizabeth went on. "A woman murdered in her home, right in the middle of a good neighborhood. What was her name, darling?" She directed this question to Saffron.

"Kelson," Saffron murmured. "No, Keller, I believe."

"Ah!" Honorine's handsome face lit with recognition. "But I know of this! She was a customer of ours, a very loyal client."

Agog, Elizabeth breathed, "Was she?"

Saffron nearly choked on a laugh at the terribly overblown reaction but schooled herself.

"But that is life," Honorine said quickly, darting a glance between them. She put on a consoling smile. "The uncertainties of fate mean we must live our life while we still may, no?"

"That is exactly right." Elizabeth nodded firmly. "I've told my cousin as much many times. And that Mrs. Keller, she must have been the kind of woman one might expect to meet an untimely end."

Honorine's head reared back. *"Excusez-moi?* What can you mean by this? Maison d'Allard has a sterling reputation. We do not serve—"

Saffron was about to intercede and make an excuse, but Elizabeth gasped loudly and rushed off the step, nearly knocking over her seamstress, to take Honorine's hand. It was a strange sight, Elizabeth in her art silk camiknickers and stockings towering over the exquisitely arrayed Honorine. "Oh, but I didn't mean to cause offense! I beg your pardon, Mademoiselle Honorine. I simply meant that dangerous women might have a taste for fine things as well. In fact, a dangerous woman is usually the one best dressed!"

The French woman looked startled by Elizabeth's candor. "I suppose you are right. But Madame Keller was no such woman. She was not interested in fashion or even fine materials. She came here on the recommendation of a friend. They came here together for each of her fittings, and her friend made nearly all the choices for her, you know."

Saffron's heart sped up, and her muscles tensed as if she, too, needed to clutch Honorine's hand in anticipation. Who could the friend be? One of the suspects, or another of the victims? She fought to keep her voice even as she said, "What a friend, to do such a thing for her. She was a client also, I suppose."

"Oh yes," Honorine said, extracting her hand gently from Elizabeth's. "A very good friend and a very good client."

It was a challenge for Saffron to keep from bursting out, asking for her name. "But she must have been crushed to learn of her friend's sudden death."

"Indeed," Honorine said. "But Madame Halton-Smythe was good enough to assure us of her continued patronage . . ."

To Saffron's disappointment, the conversation returned to clothing. Halton-Smythe was a name with very old, conservative roots, and the current matriarch was the daughter of a friend of Saffron's grandmother. She'd pass the name on to the Inspector, but she didn't expect anything to come of it.

The afternoon was now nearly gone, and the determined energy with which she'd set out that morning faded into resigned disappointment. She'd gotten so little information for what felt like a great deal of effort. Then again, searching through newspapers and holding up one's arms to be measured was not quite so athletic a feat as crawling around in a garden.

She was about to recall an urgent appointment that would require their immediate departure when a low murmur of French began somewhere near her ankles, where the seamstresses were perched.

Saffron's French was abysmal, but she could understand well enough what the seamstresses murmured to each other as Elizabeth and Honorine chattered on about more pleasant things over their heads.

"The woman deserved it," mumbled the one with blonde hair cut in a pencil-straight bob.

"You cannot say such things," hissed the other girl, with black waves. "You cannot speak ill of the dead like that."

"I will speak ill of that old hag," replied the blonde in an undertone. She nudged herself closer to the dark-haired girl on the pretense of measuring Saffron's other ankle, as Elizabeth had not returned to finish her measurements. "She brought her daughter to tears, you remember? Just because she had gained an inch since her last fitting."

"I could not forget! The way that sad creature sobbed when her mother finally let her alone. A horrible way to ruin what should have been a treat for the girl, her first tea dresses from a proper fashion house."

"And saying the girl was shaming her family—as if her tantrum did not do just that!" The blonde tsked dismissively before glancing up at Saffron. Finding Saffron was looking at her, she flashed her a bright smile that contradicted their dark conversation, and said in accented English, "Extend your leg, if you please."

Saffron did so and attempted to ignore the ticklish feeling of the woman's tape creeping up her leg as she attempted to follow the rest of their murmurs. But the seamstresses soon scurried off to a back room.

When, at long last, they departed the House of Allard, with promises to return to finalize their selections for wardrobes that would never exist, Saffron told Elizabeth it was time to return home.

"It's not like we're getting much information anyway," she told Elizabeth when they'd gained the street. "We learned what I already knew, that Mrs. Keller was a customer, and she wasn't particularly fashionable. Her wardrobe told me as much. And the bit of gossip just revealed that she didn't like her daughter particularly well." She released a sigh. Mrs. Keller had been harsh to her daughter, a daughter she did not seem to have truly mourned, and her flowers spoke of heartlessness. Perhaps it was related.

"Very well," Elizabeth said, straightening her shoulders and smiling determinedly. "I will do the investigating for you. I'll see to the rest of the shops, and I will gloat terribly over supper when I reveal who the villain is."

On the tram back to Chelsea, Saffron pondered the flowers once again. Mrs. Sullivan had been involved in numerous charities, and her flowers alluded to money. Birdie Williams had used cocaine, and her flowers warned of dangerous pleasures. Saffron would find out about what exactly Mrs. Keller ought to have been ashamed, whether it was connected to her treatment of her deceased daughter or something else, and see if it got her any closer to finding out who'd killed her.

CHAPTER 18

It was one thing, being summoned to your supervisor's office, but Lee found it was quite another to be summoned to the man's home. It was eleven o'clock in the evening, a time at which Lee might have expected Dr. Aster to be long since gone to rest in his crypt—for the man was as cool and creepy as any ghoul. It was strange to enter into the home of a man who seemed to exist solely behind a desk.

Lee chuckled to himself as he pressed the ringer outside the modest home. All Hallow's Eve, though it was still weeks away, was evidently on his mind. Perhaps it was the chilled fog that clouded the streets that evening. More likely it was the vague and ominous telephone call requesting his immediate presence.

A young maid led him straight back through the house. It was dark inside, with only a sconce here and there to light the way. She knocked softly twice on a door at the end of the hall, then opened it.

Lee found himself on the threshold of a study. A cheerful fire danced in the hearth, and a pair of uncomfortable-looking chairs sat before a desk that might have been the exact copy of the one Dr. Aster occupied at the university.

The man himself did not stand, but merely beckoned to Lee wordlessly. Dr. Aster was thin and wiry, always arrayed so neatly it was nearly militaristic, but the shadows catching on the crevices of the deep wrinkles of his face lent him a phantasmal air.

Lee stepped forward, fighting off a nervous grin at the fact that he wouldn't actually be seeing the leader of the Botany Department beyond what was visible above the desk. Had he ever actually seen proof the man had anything other than a torso, arms, and head?

The generous nightcap he'd sloshed back before departing his flat was clearly having more of an effect than he'd anticipated.

"Please have a seat," Aster said formally. Lee sat, withholding a wince. The leather seat might have been a slab of rock, it was so cold and unforgiving.

"I confess myself intrigued," Lee said, looking around the room. It was all a little unoriginal for a botany professor: thick texts stamped with gilt letters, and a handful of framed botanical illustrations, mostly of leaves, decorated the shelves. "I didn't take you for the cloak-and-dagger sort, Dr. Aster, but I'm game for it if you are."

The sour cast to Aster's expression gave Lee some small bit of satisfaction. "'Cloak-and-dagger' is an exaggeration. There is simply a business matter that requires immediate attention."

"Business?" Lee repeated with a lifted brow.

"Indeed." Aster folded his hands on the desk before him, a move that he might have patented for how often Lee had seen him do it. "You see, Dr. Lee, although my department is concerned with scientific investigation, it is, in the end, a business, as is the university as a whole."

"Science for the sake of science is out of date, is it?"

"Are you in the medical profession solely to learn about the human body?"

Lee's lips twitched in surprise at the implied insult, though he didn't think Aster meant it to be insulting. It was the truth, anyway. The elder Dr. Lee had said in no uncertain terms that Lee would earn his living respectably or never see a penny of their family's significant wealth. "I suppose not."

Aster's gray-eyed gaze did not waver from his face. "While I have enjoyed my career, there has always been a need to consider the value that others place on my work. My predecessor had every interest in financial gain, but his scope was limited to his own. That meant that my department did not establish itself as a destination for brilliant, disciplined minds. A number of well-known scientists declined joining the staff of University College because of Dr. Berking." His sour expression returned. "That will not be the case for much longer."

"You must have some grand plans, then."

"I do. I believe you are already aware of one. A partnership between the hospital and the Botany Department might have originated with me, Dr. Lee, but the incentive for it came from elsewhere, a place that values the information that you and Miss Everleigh have been gathering."

Lee had no opportunity to pry into that enigmatic statement, for the sounds of feminine voices and footsteps drew his attention to the door opening behind him.

The maid stepped back to reveal his partner. Her dark coat obscured her dress, but her heavily made-up face and flashy jewelry made it obvious that Aster had not roused Saffron from a modest repose. And damn it all—it *was* Wednesday, the night to go dancing at the Blue Room.

Irritation tightened his shoulders. Had she been with the suspects? Without him?

It truly wasn't that surprising; it had been more than a week since they had exchanged more than a few terse words about their work. She'd been darting in and out of the office, occasionally for hours at a time, clearly still investigating. But he didn't like it all the same.

He scanned her appearance for signs of harm or intoxication. Kohl lined her eyes, and rouge topped her cheeks—unnecessary, since he could tell she was blushing—and the area around her mouth was red, as if she'd been heartily kissed.

That thought made his stomach swoop uncomfortably, though it dissipated when he noticed how anxious she looked as she tightened her overcoat around herself.

Saffron Everleigh had shown up to her department head's home looking halfway to being an utter tart. She would *hate* that. Her lips were reddened and pouting likely because she'd tried to scrub off her lipstick when she got word to come straight here.

Dr. Aster's cold voice cut through his thoughts. "Miss Everleigh, I was given to understand that you understood the importance of discretion in the matter of the work you are currently pursuing."

Wincing, Saffron said, "I do, sir, but—"

"But *I* told her," came a woman's alto voice, brash and unapologetic, "that she wasn't going anywhere alone at this time of night.

I don't trust any department head at that school of yours for a moment."

Lee bit his lip on a delighted grin. Elizabeth Hale stood behind Saffron, dolled up even more than Saffron was. Her single-buttoned coat did nothing to hide the generous curves that rounded her body, nor the glittering, salmon-colored gown beneath it. Her bobbed, dark blonde hair was still decorated with a feather and rhinestone frippery that he worried might give Aster heart palpitations.

Lee glanced at the professor, absolutely breathless to see how he would respond.

The only reaction Aster gave was a slight narrowing of his eyes, making them almost disappear into a roadmap of wrinkles. "I'm afraid I have not had the pleasure of an introduction."

Lee might just have heart palpitations himself. This was better than Christmas.

"Dr. Aster, this is Miss Elizabeth Hale, my flatmate," Saffron said hurriedly, glancing between them. Elizabeth did nothing but bare her teeth in a dangerous smile. "Dr. Aster, I apologize for my appearance and for arriving with my friend—"

"You will do no such thing!" Elizabeth marched to Saffron's side, wafting perfume into the room. With her heels, she topped Saffron by a good five inches. "Being summoned at this hour is *outrageous*. I work for a government minister, and I've never been dragged out of my house this late. I don't care if he's the king himself!"

Saffron sighed. "Elizabeth, really—"

"*Saffron*, really." Elizabeth turned once more to Aster, the beads of her earrings swinging like medieval flails. "Dr. Aster, with all due respect"—Lee withheld a snort at so sarcastic a platitude—"I do not feel it is appropriate that you have called Saffron to your home at all, let alone at this time of night, given the complete moral corruption of the man who held this job before you. The man that no one but Dr. Maxwell seemed to realize was absolute scum. You must see how a woman made to withstand foul behavior from a superior might interpret it poorly for you to require her to come here—with another male colleague, no less—in the middle of the night."

Lee's eyes swung back to Aster, who blinked once.

"Elizabeth," hissed Saffron as she angled her body in front of her friend in a poor attempt to stem the tide of Elizabeth's barely contained tirade. Her face was as pink as a rose, and Lee suddenly understood that she wasn't just embarrassed by Elizabeth's words. It seemed the rumors about Dr. Berking were not as exaggerated as he'd imagined. His nightcap churned in his stomach at the realization.

Ignoring Saffron entirely, Elizabeth said, "I will be staying here, in this room, until your business is completed." She lifted her chin, her wide, deeply red mouth set in an implacable line.

A cheery pop of the fire threatened to utterly ruin the promising tense silence in the room.

"While I cannot appreciate the mode of this . . . complaint," Aster said, sounding as if he were picking his way through a conversational mine field, "I can appreciate its contents."

"Good," Elizabeth said loftily. "I'll just sit over here." She strode over and patted the window seat at the far end of the room, which was clearly well within earshot. "And occupy myself with . . . this!" She snatched a book from the shelf that looked violently boring, and held it up with a little smile of victory. She then perched on the windowsill, crossing her legs and unintentionally putting on display a good bit of stockinged leg and a pair of well-loved dancing shoes.

Lee rolled his lips together to prevent a laugh escaping. Aster appeared uninterested, ready to proceed with whatever business he'd gathered them for, but Saffron looked a bit lost. Her eyes strayed to Lee's, and for a moment he thought he saw some emotion in them before she turned back to Aster.

"A seat, if you please, Miss Everleigh," Aster said. He folded his hands once more. "I have a new case for you. It requires the utmost delicacy, for it relates to Mr. Howard Caywood."

Saffron perked up. "Caywood, sir? Would that be the same Caywood that donated the new wing of the Anatomy building?"

"The very same."

Lee, who felt no need for the deference Saffron was compelled to show Aster, let out an exasperated sigh. "If they've the money to donate an entire wing to the university, surely they have access to all kinds of doctors at any hour of day or night. Why do we need to be deprived of our rest because some donor ate something funny from the garden?"

Aster's eyes bored into him. "Because, Dr. Lee, when we are told that one of the few donors that support the work we do at the university might be the victim of poisoning, we ensure that his concerns are treated with the utmost care. So that he might, in turn, ensure that we are allowed to continue said work."

Lee supported his heavy head with his fist. "Why did he not go to his own doctors if he was worried about a poisoning?"

Saffron was looking resolutely at Aster, making clear her stance on this subject by ignoring Lee.

"It is not for us to ask." Aster retrieved a piece of paper from a desk drawer and drew a pen from the stand before him. Slowly, he wrote something on the paper, then looked up at the pair of them, with steely eyes glittering. "It is for you to act and report back as necessary. You're to go to the Caywood residence tomorrow. Be the very essence of professionalism"—he gave Saffron a significant look—"and attend to whatever it is that has Mr. Caywood telephoning my private residence so late in the evening."

Lee wanted to laugh at the sourness that had returned to Aster's face, but the old man spoke once again. "This is not just an opportunity to establish yourselves among the people who hold power over your careers, but also my own," he said softly. "Do not ruin it."

CHAPTER 19

Despite their late night the previous evening, Saffron and Elizabeth were up with the sun the next morning. Saffron dressed better than usual, since Dr. Aster had made it clear that the university's—and his—reputations were on the line. She dug out the fine gray wool suit with decorative seams along the thin lapels that she'd purchased upon her promotion and worn only once; an airy white blouse; and her mother's pearl earrings tucked under her coiled hair. She felt prepared to face the day—or she would after a cup of coffee.

Elizabeth hadn't found out anything useful at the other fashion houses. Saffron hadn't learned anything helpful at the meeting of the Organization for the Advancement of Parentless Children she'd attended in order to learn more about Mrs. Sullivan, nor did she hear anything of import when she'd gone to tea with Amelia Gresham two days ago. The woman was as cold as a marble statue, even when Saffron mentioned how sorry she was to hear of Birdie's death. She'd merely blinked, thanked her for her concern, and sipped her tea.

Saffron was utterly put out that her plans to question Birdie's friends about possible interest in flowers and floriography during their weekly visit to the Blue Room had come to nothing. She was loath to ask Lee anything about a young woman dying of fever, but could think of no way to learn anything about Mrs. Keller and her daughter's death.

She felt as though she was utterly failing in this investigation. There were far too many threads of possibility, as well as suspects and motives and opportunity, and she had a firm hold on none of them. Continuing on getting to know Birdie Williams's friends seemed her only viable course of action, and so she felt she must pursue it if she was to find out anything useful. She was annoyed that her day would now undoubtedly be occupied with the Caywoods and whatever mysterious ailment they were suffering, but she was intrigued by the vague information provided by Dr. Aster.

Elizabeth, as usual, was sitting at the kitchen table wrapped in her favorite scarlet dressing gown, halfway through her own breakfast when Saffron arrived in the room. Forgoing the fried eggs and tomatoes on the little kitchen table, Saffron settled for toast and a cup of coffee with milk and sugar.

"That was unnecessary," Saffron said. Elizabeth's barely there eyebrows rose over the morning paper. "Last night. You shouting at Dr. Aster."

"Darling"—Elizabeth returned her attention to the newspaper and turned the page—"if I was shouting, you would have known it. I said what needed to be said. And it all turned out fine. You received your mysterious briefing, and we went on our merry way."

"And now I have to face Dr. Aster and apologize—"

"You will not be apologizing to anyone," Elizabeth said, snapping the paper closed. "As I said last night, it was outrageous for him to telephone and force you to his house in the middle of the bloody night!"

"You know this study business is a little unorthodox."

"*I* know that there are cretinous wretches in every corner of the city, and Dr. Aster didn't consider for a moment that you might not be safe at that time of night, nor what his actions implied when he knows full well what Berking did to you. They ought to know you're not one to be trifled with. Not on campus, and not in the middle of the night."

"It wasn't the middle of the night. It wasn't even midnight."

"He telephoned as we were walking out the door, and that was exactly ten o'clock. Not only that, but we wasted scads of money getting to Peckham and back. If you'd just be willing to take the Tube—"

"You know it gives me the shivers."

Rolling her eyes, Elizabeth splashed more coffee into her own cup. "You dig things out of the ground all the time. I don't see why traveling in a nice, comfortable train beneath it should be so different."

Saffron shuddered at the thought. "I think you're cross because you didn't get to meet the suspects." She drained her cup and took it to the sink, giving it a quick rinse. "We were both foiled in that. Now I'm off to Mayfair."

"Best of luck," Elizabeth said, rising from her chair. She wafted over to her, dressing gown fluttering, and pecked her on the cheek. "Can't wait to hear what this is all about."

"I don't know, Eliza . . ." Saffron frowned and steepled her fingers. "I assured Dr. Aster that I would be professional."

The journey from Chelsea to Mayfair was brief, as only several miles separated the neighborhoods, but the differences were plain as day. Where Chelsea had a cozy, lived-in feeling to it, Mayfair was austere. Even with a brilliantly blue sky, a rarity in London at the open of autumn, it was somber. Perhaps it was the buildings, tall and imposing and impeccably maintained, with the gravitas that came from being the wealthiest neighborhood in London.

Anxiety roiled in her middle when she reached the house number she was looking for. She'd done this a dozen times, she told herself. Interviewing a wealthy family would be little different from a poor one. She rang the bell.

The glossy black door was opened by a middle-aged man in tidy butler's black and white. She offered her name and her card and was admitted.

Her impressions of the foyer were brief and expected: tasteful, expensive, and old-fashioned. The butler led her into a parlor done in shades of lavender, where she found Lee and an older woman Saffron guessed was Mrs. Caywood. She was perhaps forty-five or fifty years of age, with wheat-colored hair and small, dark eyes set in a soft face.

"Ah, Everleigh," Lee said, rising. "Allow me to introduce you to Mrs. Caywood. She is our patient for the day."

Mrs. Caywood offered Saffron a stiff nod. She did not rise or offer her hand. She was wearing gloves, the lightweight cotton sort Saffron herself usually wore during summer. She murmured, "How do you do?"

Saffron replied in kind, and at Mrs. Caywood's gesture of invitation, she settled herself in the cushioned chair next to the couch on which the older woman and Lee sat.

The quiet, luxurious room brought to mind the hours Saffron had wasted with her grandmother and her friends. Under normal circumstances, in such a social setting, Saffron would usually remain quiet until Mrs. Caywood addressed her, and then only converse over matters deemed acceptable for polite company. But she was there to help this woman, and so she spoke up. "I am sorry to be making your acquaintance under such circumstances, Mrs. Caywood. May I inquire as to how Dr. Lee and I may assist you?"

This polite inquiry earned her a withering look. "As I have already explained to your colleague," Mrs. Caywood said in a cross, nasally voice, "there is little with which I feel either of you may help me. I do not understand why my husband believed he needed to parade my private matters in front of a pair of schoolchildren." She harumphed and looked determinedly toward the window.

Saffron found her eye drawn to Lee's, unconsciously searching out his reaction. A polite smile was plastered onto his face.

Well, this was off to a promising start. Raising her brows at him, she tilted her head slightly in question toward Mrs. Caywood. His lips flattened momentarily in silent answer. Saffron took that to mean that the application of his trademark charm had gotten him nowhere.

"I understand it is most uncomfortable to share one's personal matters with strangers," Saffron said in a soothing voice. "I am sure Mr. Caywood thought only to provide you relief for whatever ails you in the quickest manner possible."

"I very much doubt," Mrs. Caywood said, turning a jaundiced eye on her, "that you will provide superior medical advice than my own physician."

"And what did your physician recommend?" Lee asked.

"That is none of your business," Mrs. Caywood said sharply. She shifted herself a few inches farther away from him, landing on nearly the edge of the chintz sofa. Its loud floral pattern clashed with her demure seafoam-green dress.

"If it would be possible to examine the affected area . . ."

"If that is what will put to an end such indignant questions, then yes." Mrs. Caywood plucked the cotton gloves from her fingers.

Saffron swallowed a gasp at the sight of Mrs. Caywood's hands. They were covered in red blisters and welts that seemed to teem beneath the taut, angry skin.

Mrs. Caywood's expression was informative as Lee leaned closer to examine her hands. She was watchful, her dark eyes locked on Lee's face. Was she fearful of him examining her? Or perhaps worried she was about to hear the condition of her hands was worse than she'd imagined? It eased Saffron's annoyance at the prickly woman; she must have been in a great deal of pain.

"I am very sorry you've been so afflicted," Saffron said softly, offering her an apologetic smile. "It must pain you terribly."

"It does." Mrs. Caywood sniffed, looking away from her hands. They twitched awkwardly, almost as if she wished she could scratch the reddened skin.

That was at least a proper answer, so Saffron asked carefully, "Has anything given you relief since it began?"

"Cool water," Mrs. Caywood replied, "but one cannot sit and soak one's hands all day."

"A burn does usually benefit from cool water," Saffron said, stating her guess as to the older woman's affliction.

"A burn does not appear out of nowhere," Mrs. Caywood cried plaintively. Her cheeks had gone nearly as red as her hands.

Well, that was something, Saffron thought, glancing at Lee. He was discreetly jotting down something in his notebook, set in his lap.

"How galling," murmured Saffron, pulling a sympathetic face. "And to have coped with this for so long already without answers . . ."

The older woman pouted. "It has been only a day, but it feels as if it's been weeks."

They continued on in this way, in the rhythm of complaint and sympathy as Saffron drew answers from Mrs. Caywood about how she'd spent the last few days. Ideas formed in Saffron's mind as she recalled her scarce knowledge of plants that caused burnlike dermatological conditions, only to have her ideas squashed by Mrs. Caywood's answers. She hadn't roamed the countryside or cut flowers from her own garden. She'd attended an outdoor luncheon, where she'd touched nothing unusual, rested in the afternoon, then had had to cancel plans to attend a dinner because her hands had already been burning. She'd spent yesterday in her bedroom, soaking her hands and visiting with her physician. She'd tried no new foods, perfumes, soaps, or anything else.

At last Lee managed to extract an answer himself.

"But of course, I have no allergies," Mrs. Caywood told him, bridling slightly at his question. "I am not like the soft young people of today, too delicate to eat a simple meal without complaining over headaches and stomachaches and all sorts of nonsense." She shot them both a beady look, as if silently challenging them to complain about the tea that had been rolled in moments before by a maid.

"Indeed," Lee said soothingly. "I see it in my line of work constantly, Mrs. Caywood. People these days certainly do play up their delicate constitutions."

Saffron rolled her lips together, keeping her eyes fixed on the tea tray rather than him. She was still upset with him, and she could not laugh at his subtle barb, however well deserved.

"Yes, well." Mrs. Caywood shifted in her seat once more, uneasily looking to the tea tray.

Saffron realized the woman would be unable to perform her duties as hostess, and offered to serve the tea herself, which Mrs. Caywood accepted with stiff gratitude.

Saffron quickly went through the motions, setting the strainer in a rose-patterned teacup before pouring the amber tea over it. A luxurious scent rose with the steam, full with the heaviness of black tea and something playful and delicate.

She doctored the tea to Mrs. Caywood's liking, then passed Lee a cup with a dash of milk and just a touch of sugar, as he preferred. For her own she took neither, the better to enjoy the flavors. There was more to it than the bergamot usually added to Earl Grey tea.

"This is delicious," Saffron said between sips. "What a delightful blend!"

"Thank you. I make it myself." Mrs. Caywood winced as she struggled to pick up her own cup.

Surprised, Saffron asked, "Might I ask what is your recipe?"

With reluctance, Mrs. Caywood replied, "A little bit of everything. My rather eccentric great aunt died last year and left to me a grove of citrus trees, of all things. Lemons, oranges, limes, kumquats, bergamot, and everything else—all in hundreds of terracotta pots. I thought it would be pleasant, having such trees, but when the fruit ripens, it is all we can do to keep bushels of the stuff from rotting in the pantry. My cook has made variations of citrus *everything* for weeks. She's only now finished off the lemons and limes. The bergamots have come up ripe, but there is so little to be done with it. The fruit is all but inedible, so there's been a great deal of marmalade."

"And tea," Saffron said.

"Yes, the tea was my idea," Mrs. Caywood said, some of her irritation giving way to pride. Her cheeks lifted into almost a smile. "I thought to myself, 'What use is this ugly fruit?'—like lumpy lemons the size of oranges—and then I recalled that bergamot is used in tea. I even helped my housekeeper and the maids prepare it, you know. Just the day before, I was elbow-deep in fruit."

She went on, something about using the dried peels of the other fruit, but Saffron's mind had stalled. Mrs. Caywood might think she had done nothing unusual in the last few days, but peeling citrus fruit could not be an activity she typically engaged in. But she was clearly not allergic to citrus if she'd been eating foods flavored with them for weeks without a reaction.

"I beg your pardon, Mrs. Caywood," Lee said, interrupting her description of experimenting with the blend of the tea, "but did you wear gloves while you experimented with the peels?"

Mrs. Caywood blinked, any enthusiasm she'd exhibited for her creative endeavor slipping away. "Why on earth would I wear gloves?" Her lips pursed. "My tale of woe has taken up quite enough of your time. If that is all?"

They took their leave before Saffron managed to ask anything further.

Outside, Lee patted his hat onto his head with a gusty sigh. "I don't know what the devil Aster was thinking, wasting our whole morning like that. Do you think we ought to just go back inside and tell her what caused the burns, or make her wait a day or two?"

Saffron's mouth fell open. He knew what the problem was? They hadn't done any research or run any tests or anything! How could he possibly know from a thirty-second examination of her hands and the scant information Mrs. Caywood had parted with?

Lee raised a brow at her in question.

Flustered, Saffron looked toward the street, snapping her mouth shut.

He stepped up next to her, murmuring, "Quite right." He lifted his hand to hail a cab, which pulled up almost immediately.

Unwilling to be squashed in a cab with Lee just then, Saffron began, "I've a few things to do—"

"We are going to lunch." He took her arm and firmly guided her toward the stopped car. "And don't bother with any nonsense about us wasting time when we have work to do!"

Right on cue, her stomach growled. "Fine."

Lee smirked at her and helped her into the back seat.

CHAPTER 20

"Did you choose this place for the name alone?" Saffron asked as they alighted from the cab.

The glass window was covered in golden lettering, proclaiming the restaurant within was called "The Grove." Lee grinned in response, opening the door with a gallant bow.

The bustling café's black-and-white-checkered floor, shining black tables, and gilt light fixtures made it just a touch glamorous, and the windows allowed in streams of sunlight. Some sort of citrus trees, recognizable by the shapes of the dark, glossy leaves and the faint fruity smell, dotted the space in stoneware pots and gave it the impression of a stylish picnic spot.

"Well," Lee said, putting aside his menu as the server drifted away from their table a few minutes later. His lips were set in an amused smile.

His easiness irritated her, but more than that, he apparently had already solved the case, and she was clueless. "Well, what?"

"Mrs. Caywood was certainly a wet blanket, wasn't she? I'm rather of a mind to give her the run-around." He sipped from his water glass. "But I suppose you're in favor of going back straightaway to explain about the bergamot."

The bergamot? Her mind struggled to connect what he clearly thought was obvious. "Of course, I think we ought to tell her sooner rather than later," she hedged, furiously thinking.

Obviously, the bergamot was the cause of the burns. But Mrs. Caywood wasn't allergic to bergamot; she'd been drinking the stuff in her tea for years. What made the difference?

Lee leaned back in his chair. "I'm rather surprised Aster didn't simply solve this little mystery himself. I'm sure if he'd known the facts, he'd have spotted it too. But perhaps his specialty doesn't include citrus fruit." He canted his head thoughtfully. "What does he specialize in?"

"He taught leaf morphology before he was made head of the department."

"No wonder he's as dry as three-day-old biscuits," Lee mused. "I suppose he might have heard about phytophotodermatitis. I imagine the botanically minded are often the victims of it themselves."

Understanding struck her, and Saffron gasped out a little "Oh!" before she could suppress it. She attempted to disguise it with a strange hiccupping cough that had Lee leaning over the table toward her with his brows furrowed.

He urged her to take a drink of water. "Steady on."

"I'm fine," Saffron said with a false cough. She sipped water, feeling utterly idiotic. She'd been the one to tell Lee about phytophotodermatitis months ago, when they'd encountered hemlock in Aldershot. The sap of some species within the Apiaceae family, such as the wildflower Queen Ann's lace, when in contact with skin that was then exposed to sunlight, developed a skin irritation. When severe, it caused itching, burning blisters just like those on Mrs. Caywood's hands.

Frustration flooded her. She'd known some plants caused burns, but how Lee could have connected *bergamot*, of all things, to those plants was beyond her, and that itself was infuriating.

She gritted her teeth as the waiter returned to their table to serve them their lunches. When he was gone, she said, "While I am glad that the conclusion was not difficult to arrive at, I have to think that more than a single consultation—and a very brief one at that—is needed before we approach Mrs. Caywood with a diagnosis and treatment plan."

"I hardly think Mrs. Caywood would tolerate another visit," Lee replied before taking a bite of his sandwich.

"You didn't even take any samples," Saffron said. "How can you say with any certainty that it is phytophotodermatitis?"

His reply was obnoxiously placating. "Because it looks precisely like the records of the condition I found after you told me about the nasty plants that cause it."

Momentarily taken aback that he'd taken the trouble to research the condition, Saffron hurriedly took a bite of her own food. She scarcely paid it any attention, as Lee continued on.

"Mrs. Caywood is about as likely to give me a tissue sample as she is a kiss. I've no hope of getting anywhere near her hands again, unless it's with an ointment her own doctor approves of. This is an easy one, Everleigh. We go back to the townhouse, tell the woman she ought to wear gloves and avoid sunlight if she touches bergamot peels or juice, and get back to our real work."

"We cannot just barge in there and throw out a simple solution that hasn't been researched," Saffron shot back.

"What research needs to be done?" Lee replied, exasperation tightening his features.

"How do you even know that bergamots contain the chemicals that react with sunlight to cause burns?"

Lee tilted his head, confusion on his face. "That actor was scarred from wearing some cologne made with bergamot oil when he was on holiday in Italy. You know the one—it was in the papers three or four years ago. And as I said, I looked it up when you told me about it. Honestly, Everleigh, you do know other people read newspapers and textbooks, don't you? You're not the only one who takes their work seriously."

Frustration ignited into fury. "Thus far, all you've done is insist that a film star's cologne is enough evidence to go to a highly regarded member of the university's community and—"

"Oh, give it a rest." Lee sighed, an obnoxiously superior look on his face. "I know that you love being Aster's pet scientist, Everleigh, but this is ridiculous. He sent us there for one reason: we're meant to show the might of his rather unimportant department. Who gives a damn about that?"

Leaning forward, she kept her voice low, but her anger made her voice harsh. "I do, Lee, because I have to. You might be able to waltz into any room and use your name and your charm to get whatever you want, but the rest of us have to play by other people's rules to get a foot in the door, even of an *unimportant* department." She might have stopped at the flush that rose in his cheeks, but she didn't. "I'm going to do right by Mrs. Caywood and Dr. Aster and get some evidence of her diagnosis, rather than making light of this assignment and suggesting abandoning it altogether." Before she could think better of it, she added. "But I suppose it's no different from the bouquets matter. Are you planning on walking out on our study too?"

He regarded her coldly. "Maybe I should."

Saffron opened and shut her mouth, so completely frustrated she simply had no words.

She stood, dipping into her purse and smacking a few coins next to her half-finished plate. Before Lee had even risen from the table, she was storming away.

Luckily, the tram was at its stop just one shop down. Saffron leaped onto the back of it just as its jerked away from the curb. She glanced behind her and saw Lee standing just outside the door to the Grove, his white napkin still in his hand. He looked furious.

Good, she thought. Let him be as confused and upset as she was.

⚘

By the time she had situated herself in the library, surrounded by comforting piles of her most frequently used books, Saffron had come to several conclusions.

The first was that she really must eat more for breakfast because a bit of toast and coffee was not enough to bulwark her against the day, and made her more susceptible to feeling overwrought.

Second was that she'd been wrong. About storming out on Lee, and about why she was angry with him to begin with. What he'd said about Aster was right: he very likely did see this as an opportunity to show off the scientists he had at his beck and call. And Mrs. Caywood was really quite unpleasant to deal with. But Saffron knew she was also right: Lee cared nothing for Aster's opinion, and whether or not Aster looked favorably on him had little bearing on his future career. But for Saffron, it was everything.

Ruminating on all of this made her feel better, but staring down at illustrations of citrus trees hadn't done much more than confirm that bergamots were truly less than beautiful fruit.

For all that he was a vain, overconfident flirt with the penchant for saying the exact right thing to irritate her, Lee managed to push her thinking in the direction that more often than not led to their shared success. This case notwithstanding, he was good at his practice and took care to become better. He had the sort of impatient zeal for their work that she saw in herself. He might have looked like the worst sort of rake on the outside, with that golden hair and a smile people sighed over, but on the inside, she thought they were rather more alike than either of them realized. They'd come to have the sort of partnership she'd always imagined in a colleague—someone with whom to share ideas and work toward a common goal.

Right now, she was making no progress toward that common goal. She wasn't sure they even shared a common goal anymore. What if she had scared him off by acting like the exact kind of idiot he so despised?

Uncertainty clawed at her until she shut her book and hurried from the library.

He was not in the office. The hospital was her next best guess.

She clattered down the stairs of the North Wing and strode across the bustling Quad. The day was fine as ever. Bright afternoon sunshine cooled with a brisk breeze kicked up a stray paper or two as she walked over the oval of pavement and passed between the twin gate houses. The hospital, which she had always thought was mightily ugly, stood like a great, pointy cacophony of red brick and white stone across the street. She marched straight up to the entrance framed by white and red stripes. The scent of antiseptic immediately made her sneeze as she pushed the door open.

"Oh, God bless you," said a passing nurse. She paused and took a better look at Saffron, allowing Saffron in turn to see her pretty, youthful face framed by a white cap over red hair. "Miss Everleigh! How do you do?"

"Oh, hello, Nurse Linsdale. I'm in search of Dr. Lee, as usual."

The hope on the nurse's face told her that she hadn't seen Lee yet that day; otherwise, she was likely to be blushing. Saffron had watched him flirt up a storm with most of the nurses they'd seen over the course of their work, this one included.

"I haven't seen him, sorry," said the nurse somewhat plaintively. "I've just come on duty, myself. But if I do, I'll tell him you're looking for him." She bustled off in a swirl of white.

It took Saffron fifteen minutes of wandering the white-washed halls and passing through curiously arched tiled passages to find Lee. He was in a lonely lab on one of the lower levels, nestled among storage closets and defunct examination rooms. The room was cramped and lit with four too bright examination lights standing around the center counter.

Rather than entertaining an adoring nurse, Lee was frowning down into a microscope.

Her curiosity immediately piqued, she asked, "What is it?"

He startled, looking up at her from behind his gold-rimmed glasses. She'd been contemplating the perfect comment to make about his new eyeglasses but had decided it miffed him more that she pretended not to notice. A wry smile spread over his face when he realized it was her, and seeing it, her heart stuttered.

After months of being impervious to Lee's appeal, she hadn't expected to find him attractive as he leaned over a microscope in a gloomy laboratory, wearing spectacles.

She cleared her throat, determined to ignore that disturbing thought.

He removed his glasses and tucked them into his pocket. "I'm looking at a sample that one of the dermatologists had stashed in his office. It's just burned tissue, mind you—nothing like the evidence you so dramatically insisted on—but still." His expression turned speculative. "Are you likely to run away from me again? Because I would prefer you didn't. I've found little helpful information confirming my diagnosis here, so we'll have to find a way to rub on together without starting another fire."

She waited a beat for the inevitable joke about rubbing along, but it didn't come. "No, I won't run off again," she said with a sigh.

"Good" was his only reply.

They stood awkwardly before Lee cleared his throat. "The dermatologist had never seen phytophotodermatitis before, but he mentioned a fellow, over at St. George's in Hyde Park Corner, who might know something useful. I could pop over there tomorrow if we don't find anything helpful in the library."

A strange sort of relief overtook her, knowing that Lee was willing to bury the unwieldy hatchet she'd thrown earlier and go about finishing Mrs. Caywood's case the right way. "Good idea."

They looked at each other for a moment before Lee said, "Well, let's go, then."

Everleigh's quiet presence in the hospital corridor next to him, which usually gave Lee a measure of comfort because he didn't have to chat and flirt unless he wanted to, only served to escalate the headache that was already banging around his skull like an overenthusiastic jazz drummer.

It was bad enough that he'd essentially wasted most of the day on a case that should have been finished in ten minutes, but the way Saffron now spoke with him, with only the earnest and somewhat uneasy need to cooperate, was maddening. It was reminiscent of their earliest days of partnership, when he'd poke and prod her to see how to break down her impenetrable wall of icy professionalism. They'd finally gotten past it, and then he'd managed to snap it right back into place between them, just as tall and cold as ever.

It was bloody irritating.

She'd made him feel like an utter git during that tragic lunch. He'd known he was in the wrong, suggesting sloughing off Mrs. Caywood's care. Worse, he had bowed out of her investigation without an explanation. That was not well done of him, especially when he knew what it meant to her to help Inspector Green on the case. He ought to have just explained the why of it earlier, rather than let it fester like one of Mrs. Caywood's ulcerations.

He was just opening his mouth to finally address his decision to cut out of the bouquet business when a low voice rumbled through the hallway. He quickly caught Saffron's hand and tucked it into the crook of his elbow. "And these," he said loudly, "are the older labs and the storage rooms for medicines. I doubt you'll have much cause to come down here, of course, but you must know where they are."

Saffron was already tugging her hand away from him with a glare, but he squeezed it in place just as Lord Vale came around the corner.

An unpleasant chill raced down Lee's spine as Lord Vale took them in, then smiled in recognition at Saffron. "Miss Eversby, what a surprise."

"Oh, it is, my lord," Saffron said with a smile. "And Miss Gresham, how you do you?"

With surprise, Lee looked more closely at the woman at Lord Vale's side, cloaked in nurse's white. It was Amelia Gresham, looking rather like a somber ghost.

His attention snapped back to Everleigh when she said brightly, "Lord Vale, are you acquainted with my friend, Dr. Michael Lee?"

They shook hands briefly. Vale was his height but had a chest like a barrel with shoulders to match. His hazel eyes searched his face, then he smiled. "I know that name. You're the Baron Carmichael's son, aren't you?"

"His nephew," Lee said with a poor attempt at returning his smile. "Miss Gresham, always a pleasure."

"Ah, but of course." Vale smiled at Amelia. "I believe Edwards mentioned he'd met with a doctor recently. I'd thought it was for advice, but—"

"You've found him!" came a cheerful, feminine voice from behind Lee, interrupting whatever Vale was saying. They turned to see one of Lee's favorite nurses coming down the hall with an armful of files. Her cheeks blushed dark enough to match her ruddy hair. "I knew you would, Miss Everleigh. How do you do, Dr. Lee?"

A bolt of panic seized Lee, and his hand tightened reflexively on Saffron's hand. He didn't dare look at Vale to see if he'd caught Saffron's real name. "Good day, Nurse Linsdale."

There was a moment of awkwardness where the nurse glanced between the four of them, lingering on Amelia, before she smiled brightly and said, "Well, I must be going."

She scurried down the hall, and Lee took advantage of the opportunity. "'Fraid we must be off as well. I've just ducked out to give Miss Eversby a tour here."

"We won't keep you, of course," Vale said. "But allow me to extend an invitation. We—that is, Amelia and I and a few friends, including Mr. Edwards—are going out to the Blue Room tomorrow night. Would you be good enough to join us, both of you?"

That was abso-bloody-lutely the last thing Lee wanted to do, but he had no choice. One didn't say no to Lord Vale. That was the entire problem.

He glanced at Saffron, who was looking at him with a confused smile pasted on her face. How the hell was he going to explain this? "That'd be a laugh, thank you. We'll see you there."

CHAPTER 21

Lord Vale and Amelia's appearance had caused whatever fragile truce she and Lee had just managed to construct to crumple, and Saffron found herself clenching her jaw to prevent herself launching into questions the minute they stepped onto Gower Street.

She said not a word, however, for Lee seemed even more on edge than she was. Wordlessly, they crossed the street and fell in step mounting the stairs to the Wilkins Building, not needing to say aloud that they required the library.

The fall semester had not yet begun, but it seemed as if every corner of the campus had already shrunken. Saffron didn't recall it ever feeling so crowded before the students flooded the campus. The skylight in the domed ceiling of the Flaxman Gallery filtered dusty light down on the small room buzzing with low conversations. Moving through the double glass-paned doors of the vestibule into the library only muted the noise so it droned in the background. She paused for a moment within the doors to get her bearings—Mrs. Caywood's burns had been chased from her mind by Amelia and Lord Vale—but she was immediately knocked into, causing her to bump into Lee.

An apology came to her lips automatically, but as she turned to give it, she saw an unpleasantly familiar face.

"McGuire," she said with resignation.

The biologist's copper-eyed gaze flicked up and down her body, a sneer pulling at his features. "Miss Everleigh. I guess you forgot this isn't your personal playground. Other people are walking here."

Saffron lifted a brow. During her studies, McGuire had taken offense that her father was heir to a viscountcy and concluded she'd only been admitted because of that—a reminder that was not welcome since she'd just lambasted Lee for using his own family name to make his way in the world. That was the ammunition McGuire used against her to split her up from her previous boyfriend, Archie. He'd always been unpleasant to her, but her promotion to researcher had only stoked his ire to outright animosity. She'd put up with his behavior for years, worried that confronting him would lead to alienation within their small university circle. But she'd had more than her share of dealing with irascible men lately. "And you think I should apologize that you walked into me?"

McGuire's chest puffed up a bit, mouth opening, but Lee cut in smoothly, saying, "I seem to remember you. You're a researcher here, aren't you?" His voice dripped with unimpressed arrogance.

A tired sigh escaped Saffron's lips. She'd introduced them already, weeks ago. "Dr. Michael Lee, this is—"

McGuire smirked. "Oh, I remember. Half the North Wing has bets placed on who will walk in on the pair of you in that cozy little office—"

"Preparing for our study to be published?" drawled Lee. A glance at him told her that the smile on his lips was purely for show. His eyes were cold.

Nothing good could come from this. Already, those sitting at tables or browsing bookshelves were watching them, no doubt wondering why the trio spoke at full volume in the library. Saffron cleared her throat and attempted to look neutral. "Yes, I suppose someone without a publication to his name would be very interested to learn how others manage to get so much accomplished. I would be happy to explain it to you, McGuire."

He leaned forward and whispered, "Anytime."

Anger flared hot within her. Saffron merely stared balefully at McGuire until he shrugged and sauntered off, down the long row of tables lining the center hall.

Saffron released her breath slowly, battling the urge to shelter in her office. Or a washroom. Or the nearest storage closet. She'd been dreading the return of students and staff to the campus for a reason, and this was it. It was exhausting, donning her mental armor every time she entered the North Wing, the library—anywhere on campus. She'd been somewhat insulated, working alone with Lee the majority of the summer, and she'd been caught unawares. Now she felt foolish as well as angry.

If she stood there any longer, she would only draw further attention. She marched to the medical section, Lee behind her. Interest in their little conflict soon evaporated into a renewed hush.

They paused at the far end of a row of shelves, in the blue light of an arched window.

Lee immediately began pulling books down. He stared at one, then reached into his pocket for his spectacles.

Those blasted eyeglasses and his rapier wit against McGuire were a dangerously attractive combination. She summoned her indignation and asked in a near whisper, "Why did you accept Vale's invitation if you mean to be finished with this?"

Lee let out a sigh, looking up at the ceiling. "Because it was Lord Vale who invited us. He's not exactly someone one says 'no' to."

Saffron wasn't sure what to make of that statement. She shrugged it off. "Well, then. I suppose we need a plan."

He leaned forward, taking off his glasses and fixing her with a sharp glare. "There doesn't need to be a plan apart from us going to the club and dancing. I mean it, Everleigh. I'm done, and that's flat. And you ought to be too. You saw how wild Vale's party got, and we left before things got really out of hand. People messing about with drugs aren't exactly stable people."

She crossed her arms. "As far as I can tell, only Caroline and Lucy 'mess about with drugs.'"

"Then you're more clueless than I thought." Saffron jerked back, stung by his cold tone. He took a half step forward, invading her space and further dropping his voice. "*All* of them are using except perhaps Amelia Gresham. They all show the symptoms. Lucy Talbot could keep an entire shop in business with how many hankies she uses. Caroline Attwood's eyes practically glow red in the dark. Edwards is paranoid and has now twice needled me for medical advice, for

God's sake. And Lord Vale is friendly enough with Amelia Gresham to wander the hospital halls with her? He's a man with a great deal of influence. I can't be seen to be associating with people who snort more dope than air."

That was the reason why Lee had dropped out of the case? He was worried for his reputation? Another wave of frustration made her low words clipped. "You might have told me that, rather than leaving me to wonder—" She cut herself off, exhaling harshly. "You don't have to go to the Blue Room at all. I'll make an excuse for you."

"And let you go alone?" Lee let out an unamused huff and took a step away from her. "I don't think so."

Saffron straightened her shoulders to hide the little sprout of hope attempting to poke up through the layers of her irritation. "Fine. But don't get in my way."

The air was thick with smoke and vibrating with the rhythm of the band. The Blue Room seemed even darker and less welcoming than last time. Perhaps it was because Lee knew what—or rather, who— was waiting for them within.

He'd barely noted what Everleigh was wearing when she'd stepped from her flat and into the cab, but when her coat came off minutes ago, he'd been thrown off balance anew. She was wearing the sort of dress designed for torturing well-meaning men, with a back that dipped so low that Lee could count her vertebrae as she sat in the chair he'd pulled out for her at Edwards's table. With her dark hair gathered up around the base of her neck, there was an awful lot of very appealing skin on display, all stained blue in the endless cerulean sea of the club.

They sat and immediately fell into conversation. Lord Vale sat between Amelia and Edwards, the former smiling winsomely at the viscount, and the latter looking glum. Caroline's pinched face suggested she'd rather be anywhere but there, and Lucy was so giddy that Lee was quite sure she was already floating in the clouds.

There were drinks and chatter, and had it not been for his being overly aware of the man across the table from him, Lee might have believed this was just a normal evening out.

Before long, partners broke off to dance. Lee was obliged to ask Caroline after Vale claimed Lucy, and Edwards offered Saffron his hand.

Caroline had little to say. She scowled in the direction of Amelia and Vale, clearly not pleased that the plain woman had gotten the attention of the lord.

Saffron and Edwards, on the other hand, seemed to be having a lively chat. Lee watched them over Caroline's shoulder with growing irritation. She'd ignored him most of the day as they combed through what must have been every book on campus that mentioned burns. They'd rubbed on well enough when Mrs. Caywood was their topic of conversation, but she'd refused to engage about the murder investigation, and she cut him off entirely when he'd tried to explain again about Lord Vale.

His annoyance only grew when they returned to the table for another round of drinks sometime later, and Saffron managed to sit next to Vale. She was clearly doing her best to charm him. The lord's gaze lingered on her slender shoulders and arms, making Lee's skin feel too tight. Her flirting must have worked, for moments later she was in his arms on the dance floor.

It was a mixed blessing when the other ladies made their way to the powder room. The usual jovial attitude he'd come to expect from Edwards was diminished this evening, and Lee couldn't help but wonder why. Lee invited him outside for a smoke, and they left the stifling crowd for the chilly street.

The bite of the cool air was enough to cut down on the effects of the drinks he'd tossed back out of anxiety. He pulled out his cigarette case, and Edwards retrieved a cigar from his jacket pocket. They smoked in silence for a few minutes, watching the steady stream of people on the pavement and the occasional motorcar billowing exhaust in the street. The low clouds overhead glowed dull gold, reflecting the lights from the city. Usually, the city at night energized him with the notion of endless possibilities. Tonight, there was just one possibility on his mind, and it filled him with dread.

Lee flicked ash from his cigarette unnecessarily and cleared his throat. "I'm surprised to see Lord Vale here. Not a grand enough sort of place for him, I would think."

"Indeed."

"I don't think I like him dancing with Miss Eversby," Lee went on quietly. "I've heard some things about Vale—seems like not the right type of chap for her. Maybe a little too . . . worldly, you know."

Edwards glanced at him, unease tightening his brow. "I know exactly what you mean. He's been getting rather friendly with Amelia, and I can't approve. He was involved with Miss Williams, you know."

Lee dropped his cigarette on the ground and immediately lit another, the taste acrid in his throat. "The murdered girl?"

Edwards scuffed his foot on the ground absently. "I suppose one of the ladies told you. Yes, she was murdered." His voice went taut. "Miss Williams was engaging, but she had strong opinions. I think that is why we made such good friends in the beginning; we understood what it was to feel things deeply." Lee would have never thought of Edwards as a man of strong anything, certainly not great passion, but he was clearly feeling something now. His shoulders were hunched, his lips downturned. It was a departure from his usual starch.

Edwards looked up at Lee, grief cutting into his smooth features. "Just before she died, I went to speak with her. We met in the park near her home, a public place where I was certain she wouldn't make a scene. I'd forgotten what she was like when she had . . . imbibed. She was unsteady, agitated. But I was frustrated myself. I was angry before I'd even opened my mouth to speak." Lee felt as if he was missing something, like Edwards was having the conversation in his head at double speed, and Lee only heard half of it. "But . . . I was the last to see her alive, Dr. Lee. I was the last, and we argued bitterly. You cannot imagine how that weighs on me."

Lee made an empathetic noise. He didn't need to know any of this, and he really ought not to *want* to know, but after weeks of working with Everleigh to piece together the puzzle, it was impossible to simply cut off his curiosity when someone was finally laying out information.

Edwards pressed his palm on his forehead. "I feel it keenly. I cannot cease thinking about it, in truth. And there are . . . other thoughts, that I cannot seem to be rid of." He dropped his hand and looked earnestly at Lee. "If I could ask of you a medical opinion, Dr. Lee?"

Warily, Lee nodded.

"There are times . . ." Edwards lifted the cigar, the end heavy with ash, to his lips, but let it go unsmoked. After a long pause, during which Lee finished yet another gaspar and lit one more, he asked, "What is the current thinking regarding temporary unawareness?"

"Unawareness? A loss of consciousness?"

"Perhaps it would be better described as . . . as finding oneself in a different location from the one last remembered."

Lee rocked back on his heels, uncertain of how to proceed. Edwards was not his patient, but the man was clearly unnerved. "And this happened after one . . . imbibed certain narcotics?"

Edwards's already thin lips narrowed to a grim line. "No."

"Did you serve, Edwards?"

"My father made arrangements with Mr. Law, and I became one of his secretaries for a short period of time."

Lee nodded, mulling it over. A position with the chancellor of the treasury would have kept Edwards far from the trauma of the war. Without drugs or shell shock as a quick cause to point to, he had little to offer off the cuff. He cleared his throat. "Medically, there are any number of reasons for such a loss of awareness, as you termed it. One would require a thorough examination to determine a cause."

"But there is no . . ." Edwards shifted on his feet, looking around somewhat helplessly. "There is nothing one might do to prevent it?"

"Are you unwell, Edwards?" Lee asked, taking a step nearer. His face was pale on the side not colored by the blue light of the door.

"No, no. I am well, thank you," Edwards said. "My own troubles pale in comparison to what Amelia must cope with, and poor Miss Williams . . ."

"I am sorry, my friend," Lee murmured. The question came out before he thought better of it. "What did you argue about, that last time you saw her?"

"I . . ." He let out a breath, shaking his head. "Miss Williams . . . she sought something that was not wise. She had developed a tolerance for the"—he cleared his throat, and Lee took it that he meant cocaine—"and was after something stronger. I warned her that was a foolish path that could only lead to her demise. She didn't care for my interference. She told me she no longer desired my friendship." He frowned down at his cigar, more than half ash, tapped it off, and then took a puff. His tone turned brittle. "Now Lord Vale has been most interested in Amelia. She mentioned he insisted on taking her to lunch after his party, after he'd danced attendance on her half the night. Not a month after Miss Williams was brutally killed. She's been cheered by his continuing attentions. I am not cheered by them."

"Why not? If a man like Vale can abide her working as a nurse—"

Edwards's face lost its smoothness and his voice its unctuous quality. "What do you know about that?"

Taken aback, Lee said, "I often visit the University College Hospital in the course of my work. I've met her there before. Miss Eversby and I saw her there the other day, in fact. With Lord Vale."

Edwards's face darkened further, and he took a step toward Lee. Haloed in cool blue light, he was almost menacing. "Why would a man like Lord Vale be interested in a nurse? What benefit would a nurse be to a man like that?"

The answer came readily enough: a nurse in a hospital would have access to all manner of chemicals that might be interesting to a man with a taste for it, like Vale. He was surprised Edwards had spoken of Lord Vale's habit, but the man was agitated. He might have forgotten the danger of speaking so freely of Vale's business. Lee had known people who'd been ruined for less. "I see."

"You can understand my concern, then. I want to see Amelia settled, secure, and happy. I don't want her *used*, only to be discarded." He shook his head with disgust, then pressed his hand against his forehead as if in pain. "I have already rid of her of several upstart young men seeking to tempt her into degrading matches. I have no means of discouraging this connection to Lord Vale. They are old friends, not to mention Lord Vale has significant pull in many directions."

This was an opportunity, Lee realized with leaden certainty. This confirmation of Vale's connection to both the drugs and Miss Williams had to be significant. But if Lee pursued this, word might get back to Vale that he was nosing around. If he told Saffron, that would only lead to *her* nosing around, and he had no doubt Vale would learn of it. Both of them would suffer, he was certain.

But if he did nothing, was he aiding a murderer avoid justice?

Still undecided, Lee asked, "Have you warned Miss Gresham? Or told Vale to leave off?"

"I wasn't sure about his interest until he invited himself along this evening." Edwards shook his head slowly. "If his eyes are set on Amelia, I'm not sure what there is to be done about it."

Lee nodded again, a meaningless gesture. It was nothing more than he already knew. It was the reason he'd tried to distance himself from this business, only to be roped back in by the very man he was hoping to avoid. Vale was powerful, and Lee couldn't afford to bring his reputation, and that of his family, into Gerald Harrington's line of fire. Vale could use this entire venture as leverage against Lee himself or, worse, against his uncle. He occupied a high office that Vale could use to his and his party's advantage. For as ruthless as Uncle Matt could be, he cared for him. He'd plucked him out of trouble when his own father wouldn't, and he owed him a great deal.

They lingered without speaking for another minute as Lee finished his cigarette. The smoke did nothing to calm his nerves; if anything, his thoughts were swirling even faster and more urgently than before. Action was needed, Lee decided. But what action that was, he hadn't a damn clue.

CHAPTER 22

Attempting to speak to Lord Vale in the midst of the swaying crowd proved to be entirely inefficient. Saffron could barely hear him and could think of no way to bring up Birdie or the cocaine. They merely danced together, Vale occasionally offering her a smile that could have been of true enjoyment or politeness—she had no way of knowing.

By the time she and the viscount returned to the table, her head was throbbing with music and frustration. Caroline was just standing, her feet a little unsteady.

"Enjoying yourself?" she asked sharply. But when Saffron looked at her in surprise, she saw it was Vale she was glaring at, not her.

"Yes, thank you," Vale said blandly.

Caroline practically snarled, "You ought to be ashamed of yourself."

Vale lifted a brow. "I'm afraid I don't know what you're talking about, Miss Attwood. But you look unwell. Perhaps someone might accompany you outside for some fresh air?"

Saffron jumped at the opportunity. "That is a good idea, my lord. Caroline, let's just nip outside, shall we?"

Caroline didn't protest as Saffron looped their arms together and led her away. Rather than outside, where Saffron was sure Lee and Edwards were, she led Caroline to the ladies' room. Caroline was shaking badly and burning hot.

"Are you all right?" Saffron asked her when they'd passed beyond the reach of the blaring music and arrived in the mirrored room.

"No," she spat. "No, I am not all right." She paced, her whole body trembling. "But I have to be here, don't I? I have to be here and act like everything is fine, like it's *fine* that *he* is here, worming his way into Millie's skirts just like he did with Birdie. And Birdie is gone and he doesn't care, and I'm the only one who cares!" A sudden sob left her gasping. "I'm the only one who cares that she's dead! She kept us all together, and now she's gone—Oh! Lucy is probably *glad* she's gone. She hated that Birdie outdid her. And Percy has always hated how spirited she was." Her face screwed up, and she put on a hoity-toity voice. "Inappropriate. Undignified."

Saffron's heart stuttered at her careless words, her mouth opening to ask what exactly she meant, but Caroline was truly working herself up into a state. Her face was flushed, and her forehead glistened with sweat. Her words were running together, like her mouth couldn't form them to keep pace with her brain.

"*I* liked Birdie. I miss her. She cared about more than a good time. She cared about *me*. And I can't say anything because that horrible bastard is so *important*, and my father would be furious if I offended him. But he doesn't care either. He doesn't care that I'm here." She dissolved into wretched sobs.

Saffron just stared as Caroline folded in on herself, sliding down the wall to sit on the filthy floor. Alarm overwhelmed Saffron's sympathy as she put together what Caroline had just said. Vale had gotten into Birdie's skirts. Vale was Birdie's secret boyfriend. Vale, who had hosted a large party just weeks after his lover's death and who was out in the club, escorting another woman and acting as if nothing was wrong.

"Will you be all right, Caro?" Saffron asked. Her voice sounded strange to her ears, almost strangled.

Caroline's tears subsided. She looked up at Saffron, her face streaked with running mascara. "I'm wretched, aren't I? Weeping on the floor of this horrid place." She scrambled to her feet, her hands clawing at the wall to keep her balance. "I'm not going to do it anymore. I'm not staying here anymore. Tell them—tell them I'm finished with it!"

She ripped a ring from her finger, the one with the jewel hiding a compartment, and flung it at the mirror. It rapped against the mirror, cracking it, and fell to the ground.

Caroline glared at it before stomping off, her movements jerky with fury. She flung open the door and disappeared into the indigo haze beyond.

It took Saffron a few heartbeats to hurry after her.

The club was a labyrinth of dark figures. Caroline was gone, but there was someone else she needed to find. Saffron lifted up onto the tips of her toes to seek out Lee's sleek blond hair. She needed to tell him what she'd learned, that he was right to be worried about Vale. She hadn't felt this buzz of anxiety since the last time she'd found a vital clue and sought out Alexander. Oh, how she wished Alexander could be here! She would at least not feel like she was alone and drowning in a waterless ocean of blue.

The crowd parted slightly before her, and she saw Lee. He was walking side by side with Edwards, both looking rather grim. Saffron bolted forward and latched onto Lee's arm. "A dance?"

"Of course," Lee replied, immediately leading her out onto the floor. A hand slid around her waist and another reached up to take her hand.

"What," he murmured into her ear, "is the matter? You're shaking like a leaf."

"Vale was Birdie's lover," she whispered back. "Caroline broke down into hysterics and told me. And how angry she is that he's paying attention to Amelia now."

"Is Caroline all right? She wasn't having spasms or unable to breathe, was she?"

It hadn't even occurred to Saffron that Caroline might have been seriously unwell. Guilt welled in her, eased only when she recalled how Caroline had somewhat pulled herself together. "No, she was just ranting and raving. Crying. But she stood up and walked out of her own accord."

Lee was silent for a long time, guiding their steps smartly through the other dancers.

"What did you speak to Edwards about?" she asked him, pressing her lips to his ear. His hand tightened where it rested on her back.

"Edwards doesn't care for Vale's attentions to Miss Gresham. Seems to think he's up to no good," he replied.

Her eyes went wide over his shoulder as he explained Edwards's suspicions. Saffron scanned the room as they rotated, and sure enough, Vale and Amelia were dancing again just a few feet away. "I suppose that might be why he's so interested in her of a sudden. Why else would a wealthy, influential lord pay Amelia any mind?"

"Heartless," Lee murmured. "There are any number of reasons that a man of his station would be interested in a woman who is . . . er . . . not of his station."

"I got the impression that Miss Gresham has fallen on hard times."

"So Edwards said."

Saffron attempted to read him in the shifting blue light; he was talking like he was still investigating. "Should we trust what Edwards says? He's not the most reliable witness, is he?"

Lee managed to shrug through a turn.

They finished the song in each other's arms, and then another, slower one started up. Amelia and Vale still danced together, and with the slightly calmer music, they appeared to be in conversation. Saffron had half a mind to guide Lee in that direction on the chance they might be able to overhear something. But would Lee sense what she was trying to do and resist it?

Not for the first time, she wondered if she was being unfair to her partner. Lord Vale was not all he appeared to be where Birdie Williams was concerned, so it seemed there might be something to fear from him after all. She didn't agree that one's reputation was worth letting a murderer go free, but she appreciated that his concern was not just for himself but also his family.

About Lee and his family, too, she'd been unjust. She'd accused him of using his family name and connections to make his way in his profession, but hadn't she done the same? She might not have bandied about the Everleigh name or their standing to get into university or be taken on as a researcher, but she'd taken pride in her father's accomplishments and had certainly never distanced herself from him.

She let out a sigh, something Lee must have noticed with his arms about her.

"Troubles?" he asked, breath tickling her ear.

"I feel I owe you an apology," she told him. "As much as it pains me to admit, I think I was rather unfair to you the other day at the Grove."

"Running out on a fellow in the middle of lunch is certainly an offense worth an apology," he replied with a touch of dry humor.

"Well, that too. But I mean that I said some things that I"—she blew out a breath—"regret."

"I am all ears."

Admitting her wrongs without having to look at him was better than face-to-face. Body to body was only slightly less uncomfortable; he was holding her rather close. She cleared her throat. "I apologize for suggesting that your successes resulted from your family connections."

"And my excessive charm." She could hear the grin in his voice.

"And your very sparse charm," she said, unable to keep humor from her own voice. "I was upset that you'd so easily captured my own faults, needing Aster to think well of me. In reality, I've benefitted from my own family connections at the university."

"What family connections?"

Saffron leaned away from him, nonplussed by the surprise on his face. "I thought you were up on all the U's gossip. My father rather famously chose botany over a viscountcy. Or he would have, had he not died in the war."

The blue lights washed away the color of Lee's face, making his sudden stillness all the more eerie just as the music picked up. "What viscountcy?"

"My grandfather is the Lord Easting, of Ellington in Bedford. It's not a large one or anything, but—"

"Your grandfather is *Lord Easting*?" Lee blinked. "Uncle Matt is friends with him. They go shooting together."

The music came to a head, trumpets blaring and drums crashing. Standing still as they were, they were going to get run into. From the corner of her eye, Saffron saw Edwards interrupt Vale and Amelia's dance. Amelia looked stricken. A moment later, Vale and Edwards were disappearing into the crowd.

In a decisive flash, Saffron snatched Lee's hand and dragged him to the side of the dance floor, following them. Saffron came up short,

Lee knocking into her, when she lost track of the two men, but the slick sheen of Edwards's hair emerged in the crowd, and she hastened after him.

Outside, sharp air chilled her sweat-dampened skin, and she craned her neck around, searching the clusters of people smoking and talking. Lee had started speaking, no doubt to ask her what she was about, when she saw a pair of dark forms slip around a corner.

She dashed forward, her heels clicking a rapid tattoo on the pavement. Lee followed her, bumping into her back again when she stopped, suddenly, at the edge of the building. She ignored his hands on her shoulders, like hot brands on her cold skin, and glanced around. The side street was empty. Had she missed them somehow?

Determined, Saffron began down the street. Lee caught her arm, and she opened her mouth to object, but he only tucked her arm under his, planting her hand on his arm. The lines of his mouth and brow were tight.

There was movement in front of them, and she was swirled around. Before she knew it, her back was pressed to bitingly cold brick and Lee's face was inches from her own. There were footsteps and male voices, just beyond the little alley Lee had pulled her into. And they were growing closer.

Her eyes locked with Lee's, and from the trepidation she saw in them, she realized what a very stupid plan this was. She was going to pretend she and Lee had just *happened* upon the very place Edwards and Vale were arguing? For the voices most certainly were theirs, low and cutting, and so close—

Lee's eyes shot to the street, then to her. Then to her lips.

Pounding heart in her throat, the voices nearly clear now they'd drawn so close, Saffron nodded once.

Lee's arm wrapped around her shoulder, his other at her waist. Then his lips crushed hers.

They were enthusiastic, all the more to make it convincing and perhaps embarrass anyone from looking too closely at who was lingering in an alley behind the jazz club. There were tongues and teeth and roaming hands, but Saffron tried desperately to listen even as the embrace teased away more and more of her attention.

From the way their voices' volume remained the same, they'd stopped somewhere near the other side of the wall, not two feet from where she was pinned between Lee and the cool brick wall.

"I won't abide it," Edwards was saying.

"Abide it?" Vale let out a soft laugh. "I don't think it's up to you."

"And what of Miss Williams?"

There was a pause, and Lee's lips stilled on hers, leaving them in breathless silence.

Vale's reply was quiet and devoid of any humor. "Don't talk to me about Birdie. Not when I know—"

There was a scuffle, and Lee's arms closed even more tightly around her. Harsh words were spoken, too quiet to hear, and then another scuffle. One pair of feet moved off at a steady pace.

Saffron broke away from Lee and dared to peek over his shoulder to the street beyond. Edwards stood alone in the middle of the street. Abruptly, he ducked his head into his hands, and Saffron could see him clutching his temples. After a moment, a hesitant voice said his name, and he jerked up, dropping his hands. A small blonde figure came tentatively forward and cautiously took his hand, almost as if she was fearful that Edwards would lash out at her. Amelia led Edwards away.

Saffron recalled where she was, and she relaxed her grip on Lee's waist, which she hadn't even realized she'd been clutching. She was breathing hard. She bit her lip, unsure of what she'd just witnessed and what had just happened between her and Lee.

CHAPTER 23

"I've changed my mind."

Lee's breath was warm on her cold shoulder and neck. Unwillingly, she turned to look at him. He looked utterly serious. "What?"

"I want to help with the investigation again."

"Why?" She hadn't meant to sound so breathless, but his arms were still tight around her, and it was hard not to feel the intensity of his green-eyed stare. He looked almost lit up from within, so full of fervor that she couldn't help but stare back.

"Because you were right, and I was wrong."

"I don't know what you mean," she whispered back, throat tight. His words were affecting, even as they confused her.

"You have just as much to lose as I do, but you're doing this anyway. I was a bloody coward." His tongue skated over his lips, and her eyes were drawn to his mouth. His lips were full and red from their frenzied embrace.

She found it hard to comprehend his words, especially when they were still pressed against one another. "You were afraid? Of what?"

"I don't even know," Lee murmured. His eyes didn't meet hers. They were focused on her lips.

Uncertainty warred with something that felt suspiciously like desire. Her heartbeat was still fast and hard in her chest. She managed to say, "Edwards?"

"What about him?"

"Are you afraid of Edwards?"

"Not at all."

"Lucy Talbot?"

Lee chuckled, and she felt it all the way to her toes. Her fingers tightened in his jacket involuntarily. "She should frighten me," he conceded.

"Lord Vale, then?"

Lee let out a sigh, surprising her by resting his forehead against her own. "He does frighten me. He ought to scare you too, Everleigh." He drew back, dropping his arm from about her shoulder. Cold air met her bare skin. "Despite his wild reputation, the man is influential. I can't . . . I can't afford to give him offense. And neither can you. Not without risking our family's good names."

Saffron shivered, as much from the temperature as a rush of apprehension. "You keep saying you need to protect your name with Vale. What do you mean?"

"He knows who I am," Lee said, brows knitting. "Knows who I'm nephew to. Vale knows I've been lingering with the likes of Edwards and Lucy. I'm a doctor, Saffron. Who would trust a doctor who spends his evenings swishing around in the bottom of a bottle or flying as high as a kite on dope? And I . . . I owe my uncle too much to allow myself to be a liability." He swallowed audibly, his handsome face taking on an earnestness that made Saffron's already unsettled stomach turn. "He took me in when my parents found themselves too distressed to cope with me. There was a . . . family tragedy. He ensured I didn't spend my childhood locked in a gloomy nursery. He provided me with what any young boy reeling from loss needs."

"What is that?"

Lee's lips quirked into a sardonic smile. "Someone to shout at. Someone who wouldn't wallop my arse when I intentionally broke an invaluable sixteenth-century urn." He huffed a laugh and shifted so his shoulder braced against the wall. "Uncle Matt shouted right back at me. Made me sweep up the broken urn but never mentioned it again. Tossed me in the lake a time or two when he felt I needed to cool my temper."

As bittersweet as those memories were, Saffron wanted to know why his uncle had found them necessary. "But what happened? What happened to your family?"

"I had a brother," Lee said. "A year younger than me. We were thick as thieves. I would bring books to his bedside and read to him. We'd build little boats to float in the bathwater, since he was too ill to go out to send them off down the river.

"He was born with a congenital defect of his heart. Succumbed to pneumonia when he was five, despite my father's best efforts." His focus strayed to a distant point over her shoulder. "You can't imagine how completely our household fell apart. My mother didn't leave her bed, and my father refused to leave the offices of his practice. They were senseless to anything but their own failings and pain, which left me in the company of servants who didn't know what to do with a little boy who mourned the loss by destroying everything he could get his hands on." Lee cleared his throat, gaze sharpening as it fell on her face once more. "My parents eventually came 'round, but my uncle gave me something precious, rescuing me from all that. It would be a bad show to allow myself to get caught up in something nasty that Vale could use to pin him down into doing his bidding."

"Blackmail," Saffron murmured, finally comprehending.

"If you want to put it so inelegantly." His momentary humor disappeared. "And he might do the same to you, Everleigh. If he catches wind of who you really are, he could make sure word gets 'round, make things difficult for you—and your family."

"My grandfather would haul me back to Bedford," she said to herself. If her grandfather caught wind of Saffron threatening the Everleigh name by getting mixed up with murder and drugs, he wouldn't stand for it. Everything she'd worked to create for herself in London was at risk. She'd known it was a possibility, but she'd counted on her grandfather discovering her activities *after* the mystery was solved, when she could manage how her involvement was seen. She'd learned a thing or two from her first go-around with crime, but evidently not enough.

Even as a new fear rose in her chest, renewed determination steeled her. Three women had been brutally killed. There was every chance there would be another. It was not an option to do nothing to help prevent it.

With a deep breath to steady the thrumming of her heart, she lifted her eyes to Lee's. "Vale is very likely involved in all this."

"Almost certainly. I suppose we'll just have to tread carefully."

Relief washed over her. "You're right. We'll—"

Lee kissed her, hand coming up to the back of her neck and holding her to him for a long moment before Saffron pushed him away.

"W-what was that for?" she stammered.

"That was because you said I was right." Then he kissed her again, this time more gently.

He lured her into deepening the kiss with a playful nip of teeth, the tightening of his arm about her waist. It was a heated contrast to the cold brick pressed against her side, but she barely noticed the bite of it through the thin silk of her dress.

Lee was the one to end it this time, and Saffron was left blinking at him dumbly as he said, "And that was because you're stupidly brave, and I can't help but admire it."

With that, he maneuvered her arm around his, and they made their way back into the Blue Room to make their excuses to the others. Saffron scarcely registered their departure, too busy thinking about what Lee had said.

She wasn't sure she was brave, but she certainly was stupid.

The next morning dawned cold, with the somber gray shades of an autumn morning peering through the curtains. The night had not been restful, and Saffron was ashamed to say that she hadn't been tossing and turning solely because of the concerns about Lord Vale.

Somewhere around three in the morning, Saffron decided that she'd been caught off guard by Lee kissing her. They'd spent months in close company with one another. He was irritating and smug, *and* intelligent, clever, and handsome. He'd shared with her a painful truth she'd never imagined lurked behind that glossy exterior. And she was ashamed to say she'd been a little tempted by the way he'd taunted her with a daring caress on her back, a matching one with his tongue.

But in the cool light of early morning, her capitulation seemed even worse. Why had she allowed him to kiss her like that? Why had she kissed him back at all?

She suppressed a groan and buried her head in her arms, forehead pressed against the kitchen table. She'd retreated into the kitchen somewhere around five that morning for a cup of tea.

The whole thing had felt like a game. First, a kiss to disguise themselves, like a farce in a play. The second kiss had been little more than a comic device too, something to shock her and amuse Lee. But the last one, when she'd kissed him back . . .

They'd been unwilling colleagues. Their barbs had turned to teasing, and then teasing had bloomed into hesitant respect, then friendship. Was it merely a natural progression, this step toward romance? Did friendship and an attraction to occasional thoughtfulness and gold-rimmed eyeglasses make for real affection?

But that last kiss hadn't been an earnest expression of affection. No, that was what she and Alexander had shared in that rose garden—something that felt at once so long ago it might have been years, but also an immediate memory for all the times she'd replayed it in her mind. Saffron had imagined it as a promise of more when he returned. What would he have thought of another man kissing her in a dingy alley behind a jazz club?

As if that wasn't enough to make her feel awful, she'd rather fossilize in bed forever than face Lee and the impending jokes about her finally yielding after months of frivolous flirtation.

"All right, darling, tell me everything."

Saffron did groan, then. Elizabeth bustled over to the stove to light it and refill the kettle, wrapped in her thickest and ugliest dressing gown of quilted pink. "Come, come, let's have it all."

"Lord Vale was at the Blue Room, as promised," Saffron said heavily. "Vale was Birdie Williams's paramour but now is trying to seduce Amelia Gresham. Edwards implied that Vale suffers some kind of addiction, like the rest of them. So Lee thinks it's because of Amelia's access to the hospital's supply of drugs. Edwards is evidently having some sort of amnesiac episodes, and he isn't at all happy about Vale and Amelia. He interrupted their dance. Lee and I followed them outside to overhear their quarrel, but we didn't hear much. We were really rather . . . um . . . occupied," she finished lamely.

Slowly, Elizabeth turned away from the stove to look at her. "You were *occupied*?"

"We had to disguise ourselves," she said miserably, avoiding her eyes. "By . . . er . . . necking."

Elizabeth hummed and began shifting pots and pans around.

Saffron was unnerved by the silence. Elizabeth always had something to say, but she'd moved on to slicing bread without a word. Saffron anxiously awaited her response. Was she disappointed? Angry? "I don't know what to do about it. Alexander will be back soon."

Elizabeth gave her an evaluating look, as if Saffron were trying on a new dress. "Lee is an attractive man, Saff. You've become friendly. He is also an outrageous flirt, as we all know. Alexander *has* been gone for ages. And"—she raised an eyebrow—"you two hadn't exactly worked anything out between you before he left. Maybe by design?"

Saffron frowned. Yes, all of that was true. Alexander's letters made it clear he still held her in some regard, but he hadn't *said* anything. He'd kissed her before leaving, but what did that mean? She didn't feel like the lack of clarity absolved her, though. She still cared a great deal for Alexander.

"I wonder if perhaps the agitation you are so clearly feeling stems more from worries about Alexander, or from guilt that you enjoyed necking with Lee," Elizabeth said in far too light a tone. She set down eggs and toast before her.

Saffron frowned down at the steaming plate. "This whole thing is ridiculous."

"It is, really. You, with two men salivating over you, and me, with only the impossibly dry Colin Smith to keep me company." Elizabeth shook her head and brought a pot of coffee to the table. "Utterly ridiculous. I swear, he grows duller by the day, even as he lurks at my elbow."

Saffron offered her a feeble smile. Colin Smith was the new leading man of Elizabeth's work complaints. He was the worst of her boss's private secretaries and had apparently taken a determined fancy to her. "You do talk about him often."

"And you go on about Lee, I promise you," Elizabeth retorted without any ire. "Let us focus on something more weighty. What is to be done about the case? Lord Vale appears to be a suspect, doesn't he?"

"I suppose he is," Saffron allowed. "Not like we needed any more of those. Amelia has secrets to hide, Edwards and Caroline are increasingly unstable, and Vale was her lover. The only person I'm sure didn't kill Birdie or the others is Lucy Talbot."

"Still, darling, you're making progress. You were supposed to find out who Birdie Williams's sweetheart was, and you've done that."

"It only took me two months," Saffron grumbled.

"None of that," Elizabeth said sharply. "Don't put yourself down. You did something the police couldn't do."

Saffron forced herself to mull that over on her walk to catch the bus to the university. Elizabeth was right. She had at long last discovered that important piece of information, even if it felt like the smallest sliver of a larger mosaic that remained stubbornly inscrutable.

CHAPTER 24

The bus ride gave her plenty of time to dread Lee's reaction to what had happened between them in the alley. The steps up to the office were simultaneously burdened with anticipation of his teasing yet lightened by it.

She paused outside the door, biting her lip. She was being utterly juvenile.

The moment she stepped into the room, she saw that Lee was reading a file at her desk, shining oxfords propped on the corner, his spectacles low on his nose. At the sound of the door opening, he looked up, and his lips tilted into a smirk as he slowly slipped his glasses from his nose. He touched one of the hooks to his bottom lip, like some particularly seductive illustration out of *La Moda Maschile*.

He stared at her for a full five seconds before saying, "Everleigh, did you really put off coming inside just because we necked a bit last night? I could see your shadow in the window pane, you know."

And just like that, any flutters of expectation fled, and she was left with the indignation he so often ignited within her. "Are you ready to go see Mrs. Caywood or not?"

"Everleigh, there's no need to be embarrassed. I'm certainly not," he crooned, teeth nibbling on the hook of his eyeglasses. "We'll just talk it through in excruciating detail. Everything's jake, old thing."

"Everything is *not* jake, Lee." She stomped over to the desk and shoved his feet from the top. His grin only grew as his feet hit the floor. "I'm going to see Mrs. Caywood, and then I'm going to speak with Inspector Green. Come if you can manage to stop flirting for longer than thirty seconds."

🙥🙧

Mrs. Caywood, for all her hostility, managed to be appreciative of Lee's diagnosis and their recommendations for treatment and prevention of future instances of phytophotodermatitis. Saffron had left the townhouse with a sense of accomplishment that slowly soured to anxiety as the cab drew near the police station.

She had succeeded, more or less, to put from her mind her intimate look at Mrs. Keller's death, but approaching the police station, her hands began to sweat within her gloves. The recollections of the last time she'd seen Inspector Green made her stomach twist dangerously.

Lee helped her from the cab, then tucked her hand under his arm and patted it genially. "You look a little green around the gills."

"I . . ." She couldn't help but hold his arm a little tighter. "I followed Simpson to the crime scene of the last bouquet murder. I saw Mrs. Keller's body."

"Ah," Lee said quietly. "She was stabbed, wasn't she?"

"Yes."

"And it was dreadful?"

Her insides did a queasy tumble. "Yes."

Lee slowed his steps, coming to pause on the dirty pavement. With great sobriety, he leaned just a bit closer. "Did you upchuck, Everleigh?"

Saffron swatted his shoulder. "That was very rude."

"You did. You absolutely did." He grinned. "Come off it— anyone might spew when confronted with a bloody mess—a literal bloody mess."

"Are you saying that you've vomited in the line of duty?"

Lee laughed. "It sounds so noble when you put it like that."

"I suppose it does. I'll take it that *you* did too."

Saffron walked arm in arm with Lee into the police station and found it just a bit easier to not think of the horrible things she'd witnessed.

They were quickly settled in Inspector Green's office. Saffron explained what they'd seen and conjectured from the previous evening, and then they submitted to the inspector's follow-up questions. She was rather surprised at how seriously Lee replied. He only made one joke and wilted under Inspector Green's answering blank look.

A knock came at the door, followed by Simpson pushing it open without leave from the inspector. He bounded inside with an armful of files and an eager expression. "Inspector, I—oh, drat. Sorry, sir."

With the merest hint of exasperation, Inspector Green said, "It's all right, Simpson. Come in."

He brightened and hastily stepped inside, kicking the door with his booted toe to close it. It slammed shut, making them all wince. "I was just reading over the reports about the poison bouquets again—"

"Would that be when you were meant to be completing your paperwork?" Inspector Green asked mildly.

"Yes, sir," Simpson said, his color rising further. "But I did finish! I just wanted to look it over again because I heard some of the fellows down the pub talking about the worst complaints they've gotten the last few months—"

"Ah." Inspector Green's lips lifted into something like a smile. "The bellyachers. I used to keep a record of the worst offenses when I was fresh on the force myself."

Simpson was agog, mouth open. He probably thought of Inspector Green like Saffron did—forever middle-aged and serious.

"Well, Sergeant?" prompted the inspector.

"Er, well, sir, they mentioned something about a toff complaining about flowers. Prank flowers, sir, ones that gave her a rash on her face and hands. She called the station herself to say she wanted to make an official complaint."

Saffron turned fully toward him. "Who was it?"

"It was Mrs. Sullivan."

"Erin Sullivan, the first victim," said Inspector Green, flicking his notebook open. Saffron retrieved her own notebook to recall what plant might have given her the rash. "Why didn't I hear about this?"

"They didn't make a report, sir. Just rolled their eyes and moved on. Said it was just flowers and she had an allergy. I got their notes, though," Simpson said, shifting his armful of files to hold up one file.

"I am going to assume," Inspector Green said, voice suddenly cold, "that you kept to our agreement."

Simpson audibly gulped. "Of course, sir! Not one word about the bouquet killer or the bluebell butcher or Jack the Florist or—"

Lee stifled a laugh, and Saffron bit her lip.

Undaunted, though his face was flaming, Simpson passed the inspector the file. "But sir—Mrs. Sullivan received the flowers two days before she was killed."

Inspector Green took it, frowning slightly. "Two days before?"

"Why is that important?" asked Lee, glancing between Saffron and the inspector, who was flipping through his notes.

"What about Miss Williams and Mrs. Keller?" she asked.

"The flowers were on Miss Williams's doorstep the morning she was found dead," Inspector Green said, not looking up from his notes.

"And Mrs. Keller's bouquet appeared in her room. None of the maids or the housekeeper or anyone had seen it before," concluded Simpson. He was practically vibrating with energy.

"What does that mean?" Lee asked, eyes bouncing between the two policemen.

"The killer sent the flowers as a warning the first time?" Simpson sounded uncertain.

"But left them *after* Miss Williams had been killed, and probably brought them to Mrs. Keller's house himself, since none of the household recalled them being delivered," said the inspector.

"Why warn the first, but not the second and third?" Saffron asked.

"It might have been a warning. Might have been a threat. Some of Mrs. Sullivan's jewels went missing, suggesting there was some kind of financial motivation in addition to a personal one. Mrs. Sullivan might have owed the murderer money, and she refused to pay." He leaned his forearms against the table, looking at Saffron. "Or it could relate to the recent discovery that the hospital committee on which Mrs. Sullivan sat as treasurer is short several hundred pounds. We've been looking into it."

"What hospital?" Lee asked.

"St. Thomas's."

Lee chuckled. "Looks like I'll be taking Miss Dennis to supper again."

Inspector Green gave Saffron a questioning look. Saffron opened her mouth to explain that Miss Dennis had utility beyond being Lee's evening entertainment, considering she belonged to that same committee, but she recalled another connection. "Where did Mrs. Keller's daughter receive treatment before she died? Was it St. Thomas's?"

Inspector Green flipped through his notes. "I can find out. Another possible connection."

"There was something else, sir." Simpson passed a paper to the inspector. "I looked at the lists of callers each of the housekeepers gave us. Telephone calls, visitors, deliveries. And I saw this"—he pointed to something on the paper, and Saffron craned her neck to see what it was—"on Miss Williams's list. Percy Edwards," he added for Saffron and Lee's benefit. "He left a card the day of her murder."

"He told me he visited her and that they argued," Lee said. "But he told me he met her in a park, not at her home. He would not have left a calling card."

Inspector Green hummed and added a note to his notebook. Saffron wondered what his plan was for clarifying that information, or if it was important enough to look into. Edwards had told Lee he occasionally lost track of where he was. Perhaps his memory was muddled. Lee had mentioned cocaine might have that effect on some users.

When Inspector Green spoke, it was in a carefully measured tone. "I suppose you would be interested to learn that Lord Vale is invested in Camden Railways, Mr. Sullivan's company." Saffron blinked, gratified that he'd told them. The inspector continued, saying, "I appreciate your assistance, Miss Everleigh, Dr. Lee. I hope this means your involvement is at its end?"

Saffron considered lying, saying that she and Lee would keep their noses out of it from now on. But Inspector Green had showed her so much more trust than she'd ever expected, and it would be wrong to betray that.

Clearing her throat, she straightened up in her seat and looked him square in the eye. "We've built relationships with these people, Inspector. It would be suspicious if we disappeared from their circle now. Especially when I expect you may have more questions for them."

He held her gaze, but she could practically see his mind working. His mouth took a decidedly unhappy angle. "I take your point."

Squashing excitement, she added, "We will maintain our friend–ships, and you might call on us to see if there is another specific piece of information you require."

He said no more, but Saffron took that as tacit approval. Or at least not disapproval.

They exited the police station into a fine mist dampening the pavement. Despite the turn in the weather, they began walking in the direction of the university. Saffron wanted a few blocks to clear her head. Lee, too, seemed lost in thought, and they walked arm in arm in silence.

Inspector Green thought she and Lee ought to be finished with the case, and perhaps they ought to be. But she felt far from done.

CHAPTER 25

October

The telephone's *brrring* jolted Saffron upright with a gasp, eyes blinking in the darkness. She lifted her small clock from her bedside table and squinted at the face—nearly one in the morning.

She stood, tugging on the comforting warmth of her dressing gown, and padded into the hall to quickly lift the receiver from the hook.

She was about to whisper a greeting to the operator when Elizabeth's door crashed open.

"*Who*"—she took a step out into the hall to reveal a wrathful face framed by pinned curls and a lacy boudoir cap—"is ringing us up? Now?"

"I don't know yet. Go back to bed."

Elizabeth turned on her heel and slammed her door shut, with grumblings of leaving the telephone off the hook from now on.

At the operator's word, Saffron agreed to accept the call.

"Everleigh, is that you?"

Lee's voice brought Saffron's eyes fully open. "What on earth are you doing, calling so late!" she scolded mildly before catching herself. Nothing could be worse than letting Elizabeth know that Lee had woken them up. "Whatever is the matter?"

"Just got back from dinner." He sounded almost breathless. "Had to tell you what I learned."

A swooping pang tugged on her stomach. He was just now getting back from dinner and dancing with Miss Dennis? She supposed she should be gratified that he'd wanted to ring her rather than go to bed, or that he'd returned home at all. She shoved that wayward thought aside. "What did Miss Dennis say about the hospital committee?"

"Well," he began with relish, "Miss Dennis—Lisa—is not a regular member of the St. Thomas Ladies' Committee, but she was well acquainted with the demise of Mrs. Sullivan and the shocking disappearance of a great deal of funds from the committee's pot. But— get this, Everleigh—Mrs. Sullivan's was not the only familiar name I heard tonight. Guess who was also on the Ladies' Council?"

Considering any one of their female suspects or victims could have been involved, and Saffron's bare feet were going cold despite the carpet on the floor, Saffron was in no mood to guess. "Who?"

"Amelia Gresham!" Lee crowed.

Saffron held the receiver away from her ear for a moment, his shout making her ears ring. She barely had a moment to process her surprise at hearing Amelia was tangled up with one of the other murder victims, for Lee was prattling on already.

"And the rumor is that Amelia Gresham, the administration's choice to bridge the gap between their staff and the committee, and Mrs. Sullivan did not get along, but Lisa didn't deign to share any details of what the origin of their disagreement was. But Amelia worked there and knew Mrs. Sullivan, Everleigh, and they didn't get on. That is stunning! *Amelia!* The bloody well last person I'd ever think would take after Jack the Ripper."

From the broad and verbose way Lee was going on, Saffron deduced that he was not entirely sober. His next comment cemented that conclusion.

"I have a brilliant idea. I am going to search Amelia's flat. I can easily get a key—I'll just nick it from her handbag during her shift and—"

"You will do no such thing!" Saffron protested in a whisper. She glanced down the hall to Elizabeth's door. "Lee, there is no call for breaking into Amelia Gresham's home. What exactly do you think you'll find over a month after the last murder?"

He scoffed into the telephone. "We've talked to the suspects until our ears bled. We've gotten nowhere! And you haven't had any luck finding Caroline Attwood."

It was true, Saffron hadn't had any luck with Caroline following her dramatic revelations at the Blue Room the last week. Saffron had gone 'round to her home, a swanky place in Belgravia not far from Birdie's address, to see what more she would be willing to say about Birdie and her death, but found the place had been shut up. Saffron had even knocked on the door of the next place over and was told by an overly friendly maid that Miss Attwood had traveled to an exclusive spa in France to convalesce after she took ill with a nasty cold. That sounded suspicious to Saffron and Lee. She obviously was recovering from her addiction rather than a head cold, if she'd gone to France at all. Saffron had reported it to Inspector Green, and they'd heard nothing more.

Lee groaned. "We've been sitting on our hands for days. I finally have a perfectly good scheme to find more clues. I'll start with Amelia's place and see what I can dig up."

"You'll see what you can dig up?" Saffron arched a brow, though he could not see it. "What, no gardening jokes?"

"I am trying," Lee said with great dignity, "to catch a murderer, Everleigh. This is not the time for botanical humor. I shall formulate a brilliant plan, and you shall be so very impressed that you cannot help but maul me again. I am very much looking forward to it. Now, tuck yourself up in your bed and go to sleep, old thing."

Biting her lip on a laugh, she rang off and did just what Lee had said, though it took her a while to fall asleep. That had been the closest they'd come to speaking about the alley and the kisses they'd shared. She wasn't sure what it meant that neither of them had brought it up in the week since it had occurred, but she certainly wouldn't be the one to broach the subject.

Lee did, indeed, have a plan the following Monday, and despite the fact Saffron was not at all convinced Lee should be breaking into anyone's flat, she had to admit that his scheme was not entirely ludicrous.

When Lee had last spoken to Edwards, he'd mentioned Amelia had made a date to go to the theater with Lord Vale the following week. Lee would tell Edwards that he'd promised Sally Eversby a night out that same evening, then pretend he'd been asked to assist in some sort of fictional medical procedure at the last minute and was obliged to ask Edwards to take his place.

It went exactly as Lee said. When he reported back the day before the outing, he said it'd been too easy to convince Edwards a trip to the theater was the perfect opportunity to keep an eye on Amelia and Vale. It was also the perfect opportunity for Saffron to further question Edwards, and perhaps Vale and Amelia too.

Saffron found herself on Mr. Edwards's arm as they made their way through a murky Saturday evening in Covent Garden, where they shuffled along in a stream of umbrellas into the theater. The weather had nosedived into proper autumnal gloom, and Saffron shivered beneath her thick coat.

Ahead, the theater glowed, golden and wonderfully elegant. Saffron felt like a moth drawn to a flame, lured in by the promise of warmth within the theater's beautifully decadent walls.

Saffron had not seen a performance at the Theatre Royal since before the extensive renovations done the last few years, so each new feature caught her eye as they passed through the doors and into the glowing foyer. Lush carpet padded their feet through the entrance hall and up the stairs that took her and Edwards past plasterwork and classical paintings in elaborate gold frames. Saffron glanced over the railing at the colorful, well-dressed parade of humanity. The smell of rainy mildew mixed with a hundred scents far more pleasant: hair oil and eau de cologne, floral perfumes, starch, and something vaguely dusty and papery that reminded her of the library.

The swell of the audience tittering happily greeted them as they entered the auditorium. Red velvet rows lined the space, an auditorium covered in so many golden curlicues that she wondered if the palace of Versailles had noticed some had gone missing.

Here in the brightly lit theater, surrounded by laughter and chatter, Saffron felt she might be just another person in the crowd eager for amusement rather than for a chance to interview murder suspects.

But the reminder was never far from her mind as Edwards escorted her to their seats and settled next to her.

Saffron didn't mind that Edwards seemed slightly more subdued than usual. He nodded to a few people who waved at him, but seemed largely content to sit quietly with her before the curtain rose. It allowed her to keep a distance from anyone who might recognize her, even if she was disguised with heavy kohl, a lavishly decorated bandeau, and a red dress borrowed from Elizabeth's fashionable friend, Esther.

A quick scan of the private boxes above showed that Lord Vale and Amelia were in attendance, talking with their heads together and looking very much like a couple.

Edwards followed her gaze. "I suppose I should be happy to see them together."

"Lord Vale is your friend," Saffron said. "As is Amelia. It would be a good match for her, would it not?"

Mr. Edwards offered her a tight smile as his response. Upon closer inspection, his cheeks bore a slight flush, and lines bracketed his mouth.

"Are you quite all right, Mr. Edwards?" she asked.

"I suffer from the occasional migraine," he said with a slight grimace. "The weather changing so swiftly to chilled rain usually induces one. And my usual physician is occupied, you see." He nodded to Vale and Amelia's box. "Amelia is good enough to provide the occasional remedy for me. I've been missing her ministrations."

A flourish of music and the darkening of the lights announced the play's opening.

With her mind on the mission Lee was at that moment undertaking, and her own impending plans, Saffron found she couldn't concentrate on the whirl of song and color on the stage. Somewhere in the rainy night, Lee was creeping into Amelia's flat. She didn't think it was likely he'd be caught; from the information Lee had retrieved from the hospital records, her neighborhood was clinging to respectability by the fingernails. There wasn't likely to be a doorman barring his entry to the building, nor a maid in the flat.

Still, her mind rolled through numerous horrible outcomes that involved her partner landing in a grimy jail cell or on the wet pavement with a broken neck from falling out a window.

Next to her, Edwards shifted, round face lifting briefly to the box where Amelia and Lord Vale sat. Vale was another objective for the evening, one she hadn't discussed with Lee. It was essential she find a way to have a private conversation with him. She was confident she could come off as a clueless, adoring woman fawning over him and get a bit of information about his relationship with Birdie. She'd established Sally Eversby as being a bit empty-headed when they'd danced together at the Blue Room. She'd flirted her way into information before; she could do it again, if only she got the chance.

At the interval, Saffron and Edwards followed the crowd toward the lobby. Wreaths of gold surrounded the lamps above them, illuminating a classical scene painted on the ceiling. Colorful gowns were punctuated with severe black, blocking the wallpapered walls and polished floors.

"If you'll excuse me," Saffron murmured with an embarrassed smile. She nodded toward the ladies' room.

Edwards immediately released her arm, and she darted through the crowd and into the powder room. When she emerged, she saw that Edwards was speaking to two other men at one side of the hall.

That problem suitably addressed, Saffron made her way to the grand stairs that led to the private boxes. She needed to avoid Amelia if she wanted to try to maintain her friendship with her. Surely, she'd be offended if Saffron was obviously trying to get a private audience with Vale.

At the top, she moved quickly over the plush carpet. It was much quieter and cooler up here, where only a few patrons dotted the lavish hall.

Curtains rippled as she passed, counting the boxes as she went. Just . . . one . . . more.

Amelia emerged from behind a red swath of fabric, looking radiant and relaxed for the first time since Saffron had met her. Not wanting to be spotted, Saffron slipped through the nearest set of curtains. She turned and found herself staring at a surprised older couple who looked at her expectantly.

"Er—" Saffron tried to look confused. "I beg your pardon— wrong box." She hurriedly slipped back through the curtain and into the walkway alongside the boxes. The violet-clad back of Amelia Gresham was disappearing down the stairs. Saffron had taken no more than a step forward when she bumped headlong into someone.

"Excuse me," a pleasantly deep voice said, and a strong set of hands set her aright before she toppled over.

"Lord Vale!" Saffron gasped, delighted and alarmed at the ease with which she'd found her query.

He took a step back. His heavy brow lifted over those colorful eyes, a smile growing on his lips. "Miss Eversby, I beg your pardon. Is this your box?"

"No, I stepped in there by accident. I saw that you and Miss Gresham were up here and wanted to say hello."

"I'm afraid you just missed her."

"I know," Saffron replied, smiling back coyly.

Vale chuckled quietly. "And now I suppose you have me to yourself."

"How ideal," Saffron murmured. "I wonder if I can ask something rather indelicate."

A thick eyebrow lifted, but Vale still looked neutrally agreeable. "This is an intriguing way to begin a conversation."

He turned slightly and offered his arm. She fell in step with him. Though her arm barely rested on his, she could tell he was powerfully built. Her nerves reignited.

"I was wondering," Saffron said as they reached the red velvet curtains of Vale's box, "how Amelia is holding up."

Lord Vale paused with his brow slightly furrowed. "I'm not sure what you mean."

"After Miss Williams's murder," Saffron said somewhat bluntly.

He frowned more deeply. "She's doing as well as one would expect. It's never easy to cope with the sudden loss of a friend."

"Of course," Saffron said, "but it's a loss for her other friends too. Miss Talbot and Mr. Edwards. They all seem to be recovering their spirits well enough. Only Miss Attwood seems to be affected still."

"Miss Williams counted Miss Attwood as a dear friend. As for the others, the path to closure is never straightforward."

Saffron smiled slightly, though her frustration was increasing. He was very skilled at vague politeness; it must be a great asset for him as a politician. Hoping he might usher her into his box to continue their conversation, she placed a hand on his arm and leaned into him slightly. "And you? How are you coping?"

Vale patted her hand and detached it gently but firmly. "Miss Williams was a special woman. Her loss is challenging for all who knew her." His expression lost some of its warmth. "Hopefully, the police will soon catch the madman who killed her, and she can be at peace. Now, shall I escort you back to your seat, Miss Eversby? Interval is nearly through, I should think."

Internally kicking herself, Saffron agreed politely. They stepped back through the curtains, and Vale made a few general comments about the show, Saffron agreeing while racking her brain for inspiration.

"I had heard . . ." She began, trying to keep her nerve. She forced more lightness into her voice. "I had heard that Miss Williams was a rather good friend of yours, Lord Vale. A particular friend, in fact. I think that sort of friendship is not . . . unique?" Lord Vale slowed his steps. "I don't suggest such a friend can be replaced, but one can't expect healing to happen alone. Perhaps Amelia is helping your heart mend."

Lord Vale guided their steps a few paces more until they were to the side of the next flight of stairs, just past where they would be visible to passersby. "I wonder at a woman such as yourself being overly concerned with notions of replacement," Vale said quietly, his hand firmly on her elbow, "since you appear to have replaced someone I've recently learned a great deal about. Sally Eversby sounds an awful lot like Saffron Everleigh, doesn't it?"

CHAPTER 26

Breaking into someone's home shouldn't have been as easy as it was, Lee thought as the door to Amelia Gresham's flat swung open. All he'd had to do was sneak into the room where the nurses stored their things, nick Amelia's keys from her handbag, and have each copied. He'd paid the locksmith triple rate to get it done within a few hours, and had replaced her keys into her handbag with no one the wiser. He'd let himself right into the building, the address of which he'd found in the hospital's records, and only fumbled for a moment to find the right key to open the door to the flat. He'd needlessly dressed in a black jumper and trousers, making himself look rather like an informal pall bearer.

And now he stood on the threshold, a familiar sense of ripe anticipation pumping through his body.

It dampened somewhat as he took in the slatternly flat. It was downright depressing to see how Amelia lived. The windows in the small sitting room had no curtains, and in the hazy light of the infrequent streetlamps below, he saw there was the bare minimum of furniture and creature comforts. An ancient table with two chairs occupied one side of the room, and a desk, tidy but stacked with papers, stood before one of the windows.

Lee began with the desk. He retrieved his torch from his pocket and flicked it on to scan the piles of documents. There was none of the usual flotsam of loose scraps of notes one might expect, but carefully organized papers. More than anything else, he found loan applications. Some were complete, some rejected already, and some were blank or half completed. Small, tidy script filled lines with Amelia's details, painting a sorry picture of her life. Lee felt a pang of sympathy for her. Saffron had been right—she really was barely hanging on.

He looked deeper into the piles, in a stack of correspondence, for the source of her impoverishment. Near the top there was a letter dated the thirty-first of May. It was a terse missive asking when more funds might be expected. The only way Lee knew it was not from a bill collector was the mention of younger sisters in need of new dresses, and because it was signed "Your loving mother."

A calendar hung above the desk, marking Amelia's hospital shifts with the times. There were a handful of other symbols and initials that Lee couldn't make heads nor tails of. He flipped back a few months, to July, when the first murders took place. Similar symbols haunted the little squares, but no convenient key was handy to reveal their meaning, nor were there easily interpretable initials like BW for Bridget Williams. STT became UCH, marking the shift between when Amelia moved from St. Thomas's to University College Hospital, in the middle of May. He hadn't yet investigated the gossip around St. Thomas's about Amelia's departure. Had she been dismissed because of her disagreements with Mrs. Sullivan, or had she quit?

Impatient to move on, he opened the first of three doors leading off the short hallway from the sitting room.

A tiny bathroom was behind the first door, spotless but utterly miserable to behold in its ancient fixtures and cracked tiles. He glanced through the medicine cabinet, finding only a single pack of headache powder among the usual female toiletries. A small tin sat among the hairpins and nearly empty box of face powder, the same salve that Lee himself used when his hands grew dry and chapped in the colder months from religious handwashing.

The next door was a closet, empty of anything but a pair of sensible shoes that were worn so thoroughly they nearly fell apart in Lee's hands, and a woman's coat that was still serviceable but ugly as sin. He prodded the floorboards and the walls of the closet, idly wondering if people actually did hide things in secret compartments, but found none.

Humming unhappily, Lee closed the closet door and looked to the last one. He supposed it would be too much to ask that this room reveal bloodstained gloves or something.

He crept into the final room but was unable to find a light switch or lamp. His torch cut swaths in the darkness, revealing with every sweep another piece of the puzzle that was Amelia Gresham.

Where every inch of the other rooms spoke of strict pragmatism, even asceticism, in their extreme plainness, Amelia's bedroom was a riot of *things*. It was crowded with so many objects that Lee wondered how Amelia managed to find her way to the small bed to sleep. That bed was thick with quilts, which made sense since her fireplace was blocked.

Furniture was shoved along the walls; two desks, a dressing table far too large for the size of the bedroom, and an armoire that looked, with its flaking gold embellishments, like it could have belonged to Marie Antoinette. An elegant, old-fashioned lamp; a massive Chinese urn; and a handful of large paintings in gilt frames took up the rest of the space.

Various objects of interest sat upon every possible surface. It looked like a pawn shop he'd visited with an unfortunate friend who'd been had at poker, though without the layer of dust and desperation. Lee swept his gaze over the room around again, striking that last one. There was an awful lot of desperation in this flat.

These objects must have been from her family home, he concluded as he carefully made his way through the maze. She was saving them, perhaps out of sentimentality or because she was selling them off piecemeal to support herself and her family. Either that, or Edwards lavished antique gifts upon Amelia, and she kept them all rather than selling them. Lee made a mental note to return to the desk to search for evidence of a bank account or perhaps a ledger of some kind.

Lee threw open the wardrobe, half expecting moth-eaten furs to come toppling out.

A collection of sad clothing, showing proof of secondhand use in the poor stitchwork at the fitting seams, hung within. The only decent thing was a white nurse's uniform, still smelling of bleach. He pushed a few items aside and found a hanger wrapped in heavy cloth. Curious, he unwrapped it and found two evening dresses within. Like the other clothing, it was clear they were secondhand garments, a little faded from washing, and their details no longer in style. He examined the first one, deciding that was the dress she'd worn at Vale's party. The other dress was suitable for going out but so uninspiring he couldn't recall if he'd ever seen Amelia wear it. There was another hanger, probably for whatever Amelia had worn to the theater.

The cloth covering dragged heavily at the bottom when he attempted to shove it aside. He bent, praying he wouldn't find a rodent of some kind using the covering as a hammock, as he blindly reached to the bottom. His fingers closed on something, and he lifted it out. It was a little leather pouch that revealed a few cheap sparkles, the stones far too large to be real. He deposited the pouch at the bottom and rewrapped the dresses. His nose tingled from the nurse uniform's astringent scent as he pushed deeper into the wardrobe.

Tucked in the corner was a maid's uniform, prim black, with a fresh white apron and cap pinned to the hanger.

Lee took a step back, switching his torch to the other hand and frowning at the maid getup. It made sense, in a sad sort of way. Amelia was no doubt preparing for the inevitable moment when her finances gave out. She'd likely grown up with a horde of servants, and so she'd know how they were meant to act, and nursing would have taught her cleaning and stitching and such. She was clearly the practical sort, and she wouldn't want to wait until she was out of coin to purchase a suitable uniform. No doubt Amelia planned to work nights at the hospital, then don her maid's uniform during the day. It'd be hard to find employment as a maid, though, when so many of the upper class were cutting down on their expenses these days.

"Well, that's bloody depressing," he muttered to himself, closing the wardrobe.

He picked his way to the bedside table and extracted one thing at a time so as not to misplace any of the many objects inside. More letters and documents, including a newspaper clipping of an obituary column, soft with age. Foreboding crept over Lee, wondering if he'd found evidence she'd kept mementos of the murders, only for it to wash away at recognition of the Gresham name. Samuel Gresham, her father. Lee tucked the newspaper clipping back into its place.

He glanced at his wristwatch, saw the hour had grown late, and reached deeper into the drawer. He needed to finish his snooping and make his way to Saffron's flat. It wasn't part of the plan, but Edwards and Vale were both at that theater, and he didn't want to wait to make sure she was all right.

He dug farther into the drawer and brought out a slender object. A folding frame of black leather, revealing a family portrait of three young children and a handsome couple. It was sad what had happened to Amelia's family, and he didn't care to dwell on it, considering she was a murder suspect. He shoved them back into the drawer, irritated with himself. Give him a scalpel and he could cut someone open without blinking. But show him someone's inner life, and he was as sappy as one of Everleigh's precious plants.

Lee sunk onto the bed with a sigh, needing a moment to think. What more was there to find? The question was answered when he realized he was sitting on something too lumpy to be explained by the numerous quilts atop the bed. He shoved them aside and found a handbag. Glee sparked through him. Of course! Amelia hadn't taken her usual handbag.

The little brown thing was as ugly and wrinkled as his uncle's favorite bulldog. He delved inside and withdrew a tube of lipstick that had the merest nub of color left, a handful of bus tickets and Underground stubs, a black case the size of his hand, and a palm-sized booklet. The dark blue cover was familiar. He opened it and found a license for Amelia Jane Gresham to drive an automobile.

"Now why does a London-bound nurse need to drive?" he murmured.

Plenty of women could drive; indeed, some of the old battle-ax nurses he'd worked with during his residency had driven ambulances on the front during the war and often told hair-raising tales to intimidate young doctors. But Amelia, according to her license, was two years his junior, and he'd been half a year shy of eighteen when the war ended, much to his shameful relief. Amelia would have been far too young.

From the ticket stubs, she clearly didn't use the license in the city. The only reason he could think that she could drive was because Edwards had a motorcar, and they often went to and from his family home together for his antique collection. Perhaps she'd gotten bored of being the passenger and decided to learn for herself.

Lee replaced the license in the handbag and looked to the little black case. He flicked the ornate silver latch to open it.

Brass and glass gleamed in a bed of faded purple cloth. The shapes were familiar to him; he could assemble them in his sleep. The parts of the old-fashioned syringe were likely an antique, given their delicate engravings, but were well maintained. The needle attachments nestled in the case's lid looked brand-new.

He'd been convinced that Amelia was alone, in her crowd, in her abstention from drugs, but he was clearly wrong. This had to be for cocaine or morphia or something similarly nasty. There was nothing within the case or the handbag indicating what exactly she used it for.

His gaze swept the shadowed room once more, frustration growing. There were no signs of interests in floriography, no indications of a relationship with anyone apart from her needy mother, let alone any of the victims. All he'd found were confirmations of a miserable life.

"I hope you're having better luck than I am, Everleigh," he muttered, and shoved those sad clues back into the handbag.

CHAPTER 27

Lord Vale's hazel eyes bored into Saffron's. His deep voice was thoughtful as he told her, "I met a young man at a party once. Must have been a year or two ago, but I remember his drunken story. It sounded to me like the blue-eyed harlot he was mustering the courage to attempt to win back was a bluestocking who'd abandoned her place in the peerage. Apparently, this girl who'd tossed him over was looking to follow in her father's footsteps and become a botanist, of all things. He seemed quite crushed that he wouldn't be marrying into the family of a viscount."

Her throat suddenly very dry, Saffron searched for some confidence. "Would that have been Archie Drummond? Did he really call me a harlot?"

Lord Vale laughed, the sound reverberating in his chest and down her arm, where he still held her. "He did, most distastefully. I believe the friend who'd invited him to the party was rather embarrassed he was insulting you so openly, and carted him off for a dose of cold water."

Saffron stepped back slightly, and he let her slide away. "How nice to know I have some defenders somewhere."

Vale nodded politely at a passing couple returning late to their box. His eyes came back to rest on her with an arched brow. "I think there must be quite a story to you becoming Miss Eversby." His face was pleasantly arranged, but his jaw was squared off with tension. "Why do you want to know about my connection to Bridget Williams?"

Saffron shuffled her feet, suddenly feeling exposed, though they were tucked into the corner of the hall. "If you know who I am, then you must know that I was involved in a crime in the spring. A horrid affair. I was almost killed, myself. Since then, I . . . I suppose I've become a little obsessed. I don't . . ." She grasped for words and turned her face from his, not needing to feign distress as the image of Mrs. Keller's corpse burst to life in her mind's eye. "I don't understand how someone can take someone's life like that. It's just morbid curiosity, I'm afraid. It seems heartless of me to be asking you about it when you lost someone you cared for. I'm sorry."

After a long, indecipherable moment, Vale said, "I've heard of that matter at the university. I'm sure it was very traumatic." He didn't sound at all convinced.

"It was." She needed to extricate herself from this situation before she damned herself further. "I'm sorry for harassing you when I should have left you alone to grieve."

With a wry smile, Vale stepped forward and gently took her hands, clasped together before her. "I'm sure the trauma of nearly being killed was not the only thing that stuck with you about your experience. You could have befriended Mr. Edwards and Miss Gresham without feigning being a student, without changing your name." The pressure on her hands increased. "I assure you, mourning my friend is none of your concern. But if it ends your intrusive curiosity, I will say this. Birdie wasn't a songbird, but a hawk. She chased higher highs until something sent her plummeting down. She'd been in one of those lows for a few days before she died. If you're looking for the responsible party, my guess is that it would be whoever caused that low. She was unsettled and wouldn't tell me why. Perhaps it was Caroline, again bothering her about me requiring all her spare time. She is a possessive creature, as you saw." He exhaled, emotion lurking in his hard-eyed gaze. "But I cannot fault her for that, for I am not a reasonable man when it comes to matters of the heart either. I love quickly and with great passion."

Startled by this admission, related without much feeling but for the anger implied by the continuing pressure on her hands, Saffron made to remove herself from his grasp. His grip only tightened painfully around her wrists.

"Birdie knew this," Vale went on, ignoring her struggle. "I warned her of it when we took up. I thought she understood, but I was mistaken. Our relationship came to a swift end just before her death when I saw she'd been receiving tokens from another man. I went to her home, intending to help alleviate her recent low mood, and saw a ragamuffin of a girl leaving flowers on her doorstep. I am a jealous man, and I do not tolerate the women I have an understanding with sharing their favors with others. Such situations raise my temper, which can be terrible."

A hint of that temper shone through in the renewed hotness of his glare. "Rather than cause a scene at Birdie's home, I went to my own. My household can attest to how I spent the next several days until I learned of Birdie's death. If you fear that I killed Birdie in a jealous rage, they will attest to the destruction of several of my townhome's rooms and the depletion of my liquor stores. I was too busy destroying the remnants of my regard for her to destroy her myself."

Too shocked by his admission to check herself, Saffron blurted, "But how can you take an interest in Miss Gresham, then? It is known to all that Mr. Edwards is her closest friend. How could you tolerate them spending time together, if you are so possessive?"

Lord Vale removed the viselike grip on hers wrists. Her fingers tingled as blood flow returned. "I have known them both for some time. Amelia is well aware of my nature and has never faulted me for it. She is a clever girl. She knows being seen at my side is good for her prospects. As for Percy . . ." His lips twisted into a grimace of a smile. "He is harmless. And if he was going to declare an interest in her, he would have done so long ago."

"All this being said," he continued, taking half a step back and smoothing a hand over his shirtfront unnecessarily, "my relationship with Miss Williams or Miss Gresham is no more your business than it is mine who your friends are, what clubs you frequent, and what men you spend time with in back alleys. Such things ought to be private, but if you see fit to make my private matters public, you may be assured I will respond in kind. It would be unfortunate for Viscount Easting to hear rumors of your extracurriculars, don't you think?"

Saffron stared at him and flinched when Vale suddenly pivoted and laughed. The pleasant sound was utterly at odds with his threat.

"Ah, Edwards! I suppose you've come to collect your companion. We bumped into each other, and I'm afraid I've rather monopolized her. Interval must be well over."

"How silly of me," Saffron said, slipping past Vale toward Edwards.

He wore an odd expression, standing on the top stair just a few feet away, but she was grateful to see him, nonetheless. She took his proffered arm before turning back to Vale. "I will take into consideration what you said, Lord Vale. Good evening."

She escaped with Edwards down the stairs. He didn't question her and indeed didn't speak but to make excuses to the people in their row as they reclaimed their seats. Saffron racked her brain for the right thing to say but came up with nothing. She sat next to Edwards in silence, paying no more attention to the action on stage the second half of the play than she did the first.

Saffron was not surprised that Edwards did not insist on escorting her back to her flat after the show ended. She almost felt guilty leaving him alone when he looked so pale and unwell. He lifted a gloved hand from beneath an umbrella, looking somber as her cab pulled away from the curb.

Her own head began to ache as the driver navigated the wet streets toward Chelsea. Hopefully, she could telephone Lee to exchange information quickly, and she could be in bed with a foot warmer and a cup of hot tea within the hour. The weather had turned dismal, and the wet chill sank into her bones.

She was shivering by the time she stepped out of the cab, in front of her flat. The street was quiet, as was usual for the late hour, but it made her uneasy. Something about the misting rain and the chill of the air . . .

A hand clasped around her shoulder, and she yelped. Automatically, she swung her handbag at the person accosting her.

"Quit that, Everleigh, or I swear—"

She let out a gasp and threw herself at Lee, wrapping her arms about him and pressing her face to his shoulder. "Hells bells, Lee, you gave me the fright of my life."

He held her away from himself, giving her a quizzical once-over. "What happened?"

"Let's go up," Saffron said, teeth chattering. "My feet are going to freeze."

It was risky, taking Lee up to her flat, but Mrs. Gladstone, her landlady, always said she slept like the dead when it rained, so Saffron had to hope Lee's presence would go unnoticed.

"Eliza?" Saffron called softly when they stepped inside. There was no answer. "She must still be out," she said as they removed their damp coats.

"Who's the lucky fellow?" Lee asked.

She led him down the hall into the parlor. She flicked on the lights, illuminating the comfortable room. It dispelled a small measure of her unease to see her home untouched by the evening's drama. "She's at a poets' meeting tonight, I believe. She'll either be along shortly, or she'll be out far too late and come home smelling like Cuban cigars or Indian curries." She immediately cranked the radiator on and rubbed her gloved hands over her bare arms. Her skin was pebbled, and she was trembling.

Lee was before her in an instant, rubbing his hands along her arms vigorously. Pearls of moisture glinted in his hair as he looked down at her. "You're shaking like my great-aunt Lucinda's pathetic little terrier."

"I thought you were meant to be charming," she replied sourly.

"Who says I'm not?" He winked. "Now, tell me what's gotten you so worked up. I thought you'd blacken my eye right there on the street."

Saffron quickly explained what had happened with Vale. Lee's hands slowed their path on her arms until they were clasped about her bruised wrists. He let out a groan when she told him what Vale had said about her grandfather.

Fingers pinching the bridge of his nose, he said, "Good Lord, Everleigh. That is precisely why I told you *not* to—"

"I know," Saffron said impatiently. "Anything you tell me I've already thought of myself. Approaching him was foolish."

"And dangerous," Lee added. "He might be the murderer."

She looked at him, matching his serious gaze. "He might be the murderer. He admitted he's volatile when jealous. He's financially connected to Mrs. Sullivan and had a relationship with Birdie. Given his Hampstead house is in the country, he could have access to the sorts of plants that were included in the bouquets, or at least has the money to ensure access and silence."

"That's quite cynical," Lee said. "I think I rather like that shade of pessimism on you. It's very similar to when you're cross, which I find—"

"It will very soon be my mood if you don't get on with it and tell me about what you found at Amelia's flat."

He meandered over to the couch and, explained what he had found, noting the letter asking for money, the driver's license, and the syringe. "It's a pity Edwards is ailing, I wanted to needle him— apologies for the poor joke—tomorrow for some more information about Amelia's family. If she's in as desperate a situation as it appears, she could have been the one to take the jewels from Mrs. Sullivan." His countenance went blank, then he threw his head back onto the cushions, one hand scrubbing over his face. "The jewels! Blast! Amelia had jewels in her room, tucked up with her dresses. I thought they were paste, but they could have been real."

Saffron frowned. "But surely the inspector would have seen them when her flat was searched after Birdie's death."

Lee shook his head. "They don't actually search a place unless they have reason to. They have to have a warrant for that sort of thing."

"Well, maybe this would give them a reason to," Saffron said hopefully.

"What, and tell them that I broke into her flat and might have found jewels?" Lee snorted. "No, old thing, this is not something we can tell him about."

With a sigh, Saffron admitted he was right. There was no way the inspector would ever let her consult again if he thought she was back to her old ways of breaking and entering. At least she hadn't been the one to do it this time.

"Maybe you could ask him for a description of the things that went missing and see if they match what you saw."

"I barely glanced at them."

"Still . . ."

The radiator's soft pings were the only sound in the room, and beyond there was the shush of rain as the weather turned to a downpour. Saffron reached up to remove the bandeau from across her forehead; the pressure of the pins holding it in place was worsening her headache. There was definitely something strange going on between Amelia, Edwards, and Lord Vale. But the question was, did it directly relate to the poison bouquets, or was it simply a romantic tangle?

She looked up to find Lee looking at her. His golden hair was darkened and tousled from the rain, and the smile he gave her was softer than usual. Butterflies fluttered inconveniently in her middle.

Should she mention what had happened in the alley? She'd expected his jokes, and hadn't been disappointed, but she found herself curiously wishing he'd bring it up in a more serious way. But perhaps it had been a lark for him. Something about the way he looked at her now, though, with something more than amusement, made her suspect—hope?—that that wasn't the case.

She was still debating when a knock came at the door.

Lee's eyes met hers, and he must have seen the thrill of fear that raced through her at the possibility of who was knocking at this hour, given the activities they'd been engaged in, for he got to his feet and was down the hall in a flash. Saffron was hot on his heels.

He tiptoed toward the door and pushed the metal plate that backed the doorknocker, to reveal a sliver of the hallway beyond. He turned back to her with a frown, mouthing, "Don't know him."

Bracing herself on Lee's shoulder, she peered around him to see into the hall.

A tall man with dark hair stood just before the door.

Saffron swallowed a gasp and threw the door open, rushing heedlessly into the arms of Alexander Ashton.

Chapter 28

"Alexander! What are you doing here?" Smiling from ear to ear, Saffron pulled him by the arm into the flat and closed the door on the cold air creeping inside. "When did you get back?"

"Not an hour ago." He removed a rain-soaked leather satchel from his shoulder and placed it on the floor. She tugged his wet coat from his shoulders, which were broader than she remembered.

"But you must be exhausted!" Saffron said, taking him in. His olive skin was golden from the equatorial sun, and his damp black hair curled around his ears. He was dressed informally in a dark blue jumper with rough trousers and boots, a cap he'd already removed in his hands. "What are you doing here?"

Alexander's dark eyes moved down her body, still clad in her red evening gown from the theater, and then shifted behind her, where she'd just remembered Lee was still standing.

"Oh, I'm sorry. Alexander Ashton, this is Dr. Michael Lee." She stepped back, pressing herself against the hall wall to allow them space to greet each other.

Lee stepped forward, hand extended and jaunty smile in place. "Pleased to meet you. Everleigh has tried very hard not to tell me a thing about you."

Alexander shook his hand. "Dr. Lee. You must be Saffron's research partner."

"Yes, we've been working together these past few months. I'm the medical side of things, she does the plant bit. And the investigation, too. Trying to solve a couple of murders requires many hands, evidently." Lee grinned, but his eyes flicked between her and Alexander as if sensing his quip hadn't landed well.

Alexander straightened, his gaze falling heavily on Saffron.

She smiled nervously, unsure of the source of the mounting tension making the little hall suddenly feel far too small for the three of them. She cleared her throat, hands running up and down her cold arms. "Let's not just stand here. Shall I make tea, or—?"

"I think you would rather catch up with the intrepid explorer, Everleigh." Lee turned his smile on her, but there was something edgy about the set of his jaw. "I'll see you on Monday. Or tomorrow, if you'd rather discuss what happened this evening further."

Saffron said something, she didn't know exactly what, but a moment later Lee had donned his hat and coat and was out the door.

There was a long silence, one Saffron almost wished would hold because, in each second that passed, it felt like something ominous was building between her and the man standing at her back.

"What did he mean about murders?"

Saffron released her breath, pressing a hand to her diaphragm as if that would diminish her jittering nerves. She turned around, pasting a bright smile on her face. "Did you want tea, Alexander? Or food? I should think you're famished. Elizabeth likely has left something in—"

"Saffron." His voice saying her name was at once so welcome and so alarming with the warning in his tone. "Murders? What did he mean?"

Saffron attempted to walk around him, to lead him out of the cool hall to the parlor, or even to the kitchen, simply to have something to do other than address his question.

Alexander blocked her way. Looming over her, he seemed less like the neatness-obsessed academic she'd known and more like the untamed explorer Elizabeth had tried to convince her Alexander truly was.

"I wrote to you about the case I'm working on for Inspector Green." She forced her chin up. She hadn't lied, and she genuinely felt she couldn't have explained it in a letter, but that didn't stop her heart from pounding at the sight of Alexander's jaw tightening.

"You said it was flowers," he said, his tone careful not to reveal any of the thunder evident in his eyes.

"That's how it started. Can we please not stand here like this?"

He stepped aside, and she quickly made her way down the hall and into the parlor, where she retreated to the radiator. Alexander stopped at the mantle, his eyes flicking over the same silver-framed portraits of her and Elizabeth's families they'd once discussed. They seemed to irritate him, his nostrils flaring.

He turned to her, like a dark, expectant shadow.

"Do you not want anything? Or maybe just—"

"You're stalling."

"Only because you're acting like you spent the last few months pacing a cage rather than doing experiments in a jungle," she shot back, annoyed. What was making him act this way? "Perhaps we should speak tomorrow, instead."

"I don't want to speak tomorrow. I came straight here when we disembarked because I wanted to see you."

She smiled tremulously. "I'm glad you did. Why are you back so early? I thought you weren't meant to return until October twenty-first."

"Dr. Henry," Alexander said, the corners of his lips lifting. "No one knows for certain, but there were wagers he changed our plans because he didn't care to be away from Mrs. Henry any longer."

Dr. Henry and his wife had had a tumultuous relationship, resolving their differences only after Mrs. Henry had been poisoned and in a coma for two weeks, and Dr. Henry had been a top suspect for the poisoning. Now it seemed they were devoted to each other.

Imagining the strapping history professor pining after his wife made Saffron grin. "How will they settle their wagers?"

"I don't know." He abandoned the mantle, drawing close enough that she could smell the scent of rain and sea on him. She gazed up at him, lost in the rush of relief and excitement that Alexander Ashton was standing in her flat after so long missing him, when the warmth in his expression faded.

"Tell me about the murders, Saffron."

Disappointed, she looked away, rubbing her hands over her arms again.

"I'm assuming they have something to do with why you're dressed like that."

"Like what?" Saffron glanced down at herself, face burning when she recalled she was dolled up like Sally Eversby. "Oh. Yes. I've been . . . not myself. Pretending to be someone else, for the investigation."

She hurriedly explained about the bouquets, the murders, and finally, what she and Lee had been attempting to do. Saffron tried to ignore how his eyes flashed with each mention of Lee. Alexander finding him at her flat so late, when she was dressed like this, was unfortunate. He'd think there was something between her and Lee. Worse, there might be.

"And Inspector Green has been . . . encouraging this?" Alexander asked, showing exasperation for the first time.

"Not precisely. But Lee and I have been able to give him information about the relationships between Miss Williams's friends, and we've discovered things about some of the other victims and even provided the inspector a sample of the cocaine—"

"You've been messing about with cocaine?" Alexander started, his hands coming from his pockets and fisting at his sides. "Cocaine?"

She was too surprised by his harsh tone to manage more than a nod.

"Excuse me."

Confused, she asked, "What?"

But he was already striding from the room.

"Alexander, please wait!" She rushed down the hall after him, her heels' rapid tattoo muffled by the thin carpet, and caught his arm as he bent to snatch up his pack. "Please, I don't know why you're so upset."

His eyes were fathomless when he turned to her. "I don't like you putting yourself at risk with this investigation. I don't like that Inspector Green and Dr. Lee are allowing you to endanger yourself with murderers and drug pushers and God knows what else. I don't like that you don't see the problem with any of this." He dropped his pack. "You almost *died*, Saffron. You were almost killed by Berking and Blake just a few months ago. Why are you putting yourself in the same situation again?"

"Why did you agree to go off and explore a jungle?" The indignant question slipped from her lips. "You almost died, same as me. But you went to the Amazon, which is full of dangers, without a second thought." She took another step toward him, placing herself between him and the door and lowering her voice. "I'm doing something important, helping the inspector. He doesn't have access to the people and places that Lee and I do."

At Lee's name, Alexander's glower deepened, and he looked away, nostrils flaring.

"You don't need to be jealous," Saffron said. Actually, a treacherous little voice in her head whispered, he did have cause.

"I'm not jealous of the man who's pushed you into danger," Alexander said harshly. "Danger involving things you've no way to understand. I've seen what cocaine does to people. I've known doctors who abuse their access to cocaine and morphine and everything else, Saffron. Some of them were *my* doctors, my brother's doctors, men addicted to the same chemicals they pushed on us."

Saffron went still at the break in his voice, the startling admission. She suddenly felt like she'd waded out into water much too deep.

They stood staring at each other, their too-quick breaths loud in the narrow space. Distantly, a clock chime rang out twelve times.

She dropped her gaze, feeling as if her body weighed a hundred stone. "I'm glad you've arrived back safely." She moved away from the door, desiring only to escape his disconcerting anger.

Alexander stepped forward, his body once again blocking her path. Saffron looked up into his eyes, hard and determined, before he took her in his arms and kissed her.

Surprise froze her into place, and confusion kept her there. Why was he kissing her when he was so angry? How had their reunion been so ruined?

He broke away, dropping his hands from her with obvious dissatisfaction, his face already turning away from hers. Seeing his disappointment stoked her own. She didn't want this to be how they left things.

Before he could move away, she lifted onto her toes and brought her hand up to his cheek. A hint of beard was rough against her palm.

He went still, the dark depths of his eyes unreadable.

"I care for you, Saffron," he murmured. "I don't want something to happen to you."

He cupped her jaw in his hands, and his mouth slanted over hers, firmer and more certain. Her hands dropped to his waist, fingers tangling in the thick weave of his jumper. She mused for a moment that he could probably feel her racing pulse, then all thought slid from her mind when a strong arm coiled around her and pressed her against him.

Before long, they were wrapped around each other, their embrace growing tighter even as their kisses went loose and fierce.

The scrape of a key in the lock brought Saffron back to herself. She stepped unsteadily back from Alexander, hands pressing against her burning face.

The door swung open, nearly smacking into Alexander's shoulder.

Elizabeth blinked at him, only a few inches shorter than him in her tallest pair of heels. She squinted at him, then at the door. "Is this the wrong flat?"

Saffron hurried forward, nudging Alexander out of the way. She caught a strong whiff of spirits and almost choked. "Good Lord, Eliza, what have you been doing?"

"After the readings, Jarle brought out his most recent batch of plum wine. Vile, it was, but didn't it packa da wallop?" She snorted with laughter.

Saffron sighed, shooting Alexander an apologetic look. "Elizabeth, in your drunken state, I'm afraid you didn't notice that Alexander is back."

"Alexander?" Elizabeth's slur became an exclamation as she rounded on him with a fatuous grin. "Alexander Ashton! Marvelous. Welcome back, darling."

"Thank you." Alexander's lips twitched. He said to Saffron, "I suppose I'll see you later."

"Tomorrow?" Saffron wanted to make sure things were all right between them as soon as possible, but Elizabeth was an incorrigible drunk and required management.

Even now, she was toddling away, using a hand against the wall to guide her unsteady steps.

Alexander picked up Saffron's hand and pressed his lips to it, his warm breath washing over her chilled skin. "If you like."

"Saff!" called Elizabeth. Saffron gave Alexander an exasperated smile. "Saffron, are you going to tell him about Lee? I wouldn't, darling. No man likes his girl being petted by another fellow. Now where's the bloody—" Something crashed to the floor in the kitchen, but Saffron didn't even wince.

Alexander had gone utterly motionless, her hand still in his. It lasted only a moment before he dropped it and reached for his coat.

He was out the door before Saffron had even opened her mouth. She darted out the door and down the hall to the stairs, following his dark figure as he descended.

"Alexander, wait," she hissed, unwilling to call out when her landlady's flat was on the other side of the wall.

He'd reached the bottom. She dashed forward, half falling down the steps. She caught herself on the banister, breathing hard. *Wait.*

The lamp hanging from the ceiling swung from their rapid descent, casting twisting shadows over Alexander as he halted and rounded on her. His face was a storm of tension, his implacable mask gone.

"I'm sorry, Alexander, that wasn't—"

"Was it true?" he asked bluntly.

"Well, in a way," Saffron said sheepishly, caught off guard by his abruptness.

There was a beat of silence during which Saffron couldn't meet his eyes.

"Did he—has he done something?"

Alarmed at the sudden anger in his voice, she looked up. The shadows on his face churned. Struggling to come up with an explanation, she said, "No, no, we just—"

"You just what?" he spat.

Her throat tightened at his cold expression. "It wasn't on purpose," she whispered. "And you were gone. When you left, neither of us said anything—"

"I see," Alexander said flatly. "Goodnight."

He walked away, down the steps and into the rainstorm beyond.

CHAPTER 29

As if his evening needed another unpleasant intrusion, the cold rain trickling down Lee's neck was jarring each time a new rivulet found its way under his collar. Saffron's street was too quiet to have any cabs running along it, so he'd had to walk ten minutes to even see one, let alone an empty one. Each sloshing step was provoking, reminding him of the cozy scene he'd left behind. Everleigh, reunited with her pal Ashton.

The skinny, bespeckled man he'd envisioned was nothing like the hulking fellow who'd been standing in Everleigh's door. He looked more like a dock worker than a man of science. Indeed, of the two of them, Lee was the scrawny one with eyeglasses. The thought rankled.

When he'd finally clambered into a cab, soaked through and steaming with irritation, he'd finally been able to admit to himself that he was jealous. It was a novel experience and one that he didn't care for. It wasn't as if he'd spent a lot of time mulling over his feelings for his partner—hell, he'd kissed her on a whim and had been pleasantly surprised that she'd kissed him back at all. He hadn't known what to make of it, truthfully. But it had been like lighting a fire, a fire that had only been fanned by the reappearance of Alexander Ashton.

He dashed from the cab into his building, shoes squealing obnoxiously on the polished tile until he reached the little rug placed just before the lifts.

"Dr. Lee," said the porter, "you had a call, sir."

"Who from?" Lee asked without enthusiasm. He needed a drink.

"A Mr. Edwards, sir."

Sighing, Lee dragged himself to the desk. "Did he leave a message, Holmstead?"

"He did." The older man, with skin so dark as to appear like ink over creased parchment and hair a fine, snowy white, was rigid and upright as a steel pole. He passed him the folded paper with dignified aplomb. "If I might say, Dr. Lee, the gentleman sounded unsettled. I encouraged him to contact immediate medical services rather than wait for yours."

Lee paused in his search for his reading glasses. "Why?"

"He was quite upset," he intoned.

As Holmstead was as unflappable as the starchiest of English butlers, Lee took this to mean that Edwards was one step away from being stark raving mad. Lee quickly retrieved his glasses and read over the message, noting the time. It had been less than half an hour ago.

With a sigh, Lee tucked the little paper and his glasses into his pocket.

Going back out in the increasingly dismal weather was the last thing Lee wanted to do. No, he thought grimly to himself as his cab pulled away from the curb once more—the driver had been delighted to see him again—going out in this weather to see *Edwards* was the last thing he wanted to do. But his conscious prickled at leaving him languishing, not to mention Saffron would never forgive him if he didn't follow up on whatever grand emergency Edwards was having, and so off he went.

He reached Edwards's townhouse—or rather, his father's—minutes before midnight. He was admitted into the eerily quiet home and led to a study, where the butler announced him and disappeared on silent feet.

The room could have been an exact replica of his own father's study. Heavy mahogany furniture was interspersed among ornately framed paintings and dark-colored carpets, a rather exact impression of 1885. The impression was rendered sinister by the sole illumination, the flickering flames in the hearth.

Edwards's weak voice startled him. "Dr. Lee." He was barely visible from where he sat in a winged armchair before the fire.

Lee hurried to his side. "What's the matter, old boy?" Lee's physician's instincts came to life at the sight of Edwards's pained expression. He automatically pushed up the sleeve of Edwards's red silk smoking jacket to take his pulse. His skin was hot to the touch.

"Migraine," he mumbled. "Dreadful."

"You ought to lie down," said Lee, looking about for a couch. There was one across the room. The proximity to the fire, though low, would probably make his head and fever worse. He helped Edwards to his feet. "You might have mentioned you suffered migraines when you asked me about losing time. Feeling like your head is boiling can certainly make you forget."

He gently arranged Edwards horizontally on the couch. He looked for his medical bag at his feet, cursing when he recalled he hadn't bothered to retrieve it from his flat.

"Stupid," Edwards mumbled. "Shouldn't have said it. So angry."

Lee went still. "Who was angry?"

"She looked . . . like I was nothing. Nothing."

Lee leaned over Edwards, examining his face. His flush was visible even in the low light. "Who was angry with you, Edwards?"

"'Melia." He shifted restlessly. "I said things . . ."

"What did you say?"

"Vale's up t'no good. Bad sort. Get her . . . to trouble." He was growing agitated, his slurred voice growing louder. "Can't help her. Won't let me." He clamped his mouth shut, nostrils flaring with each breath.

"Calm yourself, Edwards. Do you have ergotamine tablets?"

Edwards's arm flailed, then flailed again. Lee realized he was being directed to a sideboard, where sat a little black leather case.

Lee's fingers paused as he went to open it. The silver latch was familiar. No, not familiar. Exactly the same design as the one he'd seen just hours ago at Amelia's flat.

Lee opened the case, moving aside a few packets of powder to find that there was a matching antique brass syringe. It appeared it was a matching set, likely a gift from Edwards to Amelia. All but one of the little white packets were clearly labeled Askit, a combination of pain medication and caffeine that Edwards could have bought at any druggist's. A quick dab on the tongue revealed the powders were, in fact, what the label proclaimed.

The final packet contained ergotamine tablets, a newer medication that ought to dull his symptoms. If Edwards experienced acute attacks like this one often, it was little wonder that he'd carry around a case like this. Lee wondered if it was originally for recreation or for medical use. Just because there was not currently cocaine stored within didn't mean it wasn't also used for that purpose.

A moan from Edwards brought Lee back to the present situation. He retrieved a glass of water from the tray sitting next to the armchair and brought Edwards an ergotamine tablet. Lee helped him swallow it and resettled him on the couch.

Edwards groaned, still caught in the throes of pain and mumbling about Amelia and Vale. He was exhausted and was letting himself unravel now Lee was there to take care of him. He'd seen it before, people holding themselves together until help arrived.

"Why do you think Vale is up to no good?" Guilt touched his mind at questioning Edwards when he was clearly not himself.

"Lying," he whispered. He blinked his eyes open, only to grimace and shut them quickly again. "Lying 'bout 'Melia. Said *she* wanted him—" He gagged, jerking upright. Lee braced him immediately, looking about for a basin, but Edwards managed not to vomit.

Lee eased him back down and got up to look for something to keep handy just in case Edwards needed it. After seeing nothing convenient but a vase that was likely the value of Lee's motorcar, he rang the bell to ask a footman.

He promptly produced a porcelain tub, and Lee found Vale was still on Edwards's lips when he returned to his side.

"Wretch," he was saying. "Scandals and . . . schemes . . ."

"Why do you abide him, then?" Lee wondered out loud.

"Birdie. Birdie said . . . Her fault. God damn her. Making threats. 'Melia." He groaned before rolling onto his side, facing the cushions. "Send her flowers," he mumbled. "Send them all flowers."

Lee's blood ran cold. Carefully he stood, and keeping his voice low, said, "Send flowers? To whom?"

Edwards's head lolled toward him, and Lee held his breath. But Edwards's eyes were closed, his mouth agape. He was asleep.

Lee bolted.

If Saffron dreaded getting out of bed that morning, it was nothing to the extremely vocal reluctance that Elizabeth expressed.

"Just bring it here," Elizabeth groaned into one of her many pillows. "Please, Saff, I will die without it."

Saffron rolled her eyes from Elizabeth's doorway. "I have the cup right here. If you want coffee, you'll have to come and get it. And make something to eat, unless you want to torture yourself with my burnt toast."

"I'm going to kill you, you know," Elizabeth replied, not moving.

"You'd be caught right away. Inspector Green will find you out before you can even dig a proper hole in the garden for my body," Saffron said. She made a show of inhaling the fragrance of the strong black coffee in the cup. "Mmm, perhaps I shall drink this myself."

Elizabeth sat up, groaned and clutched at her head, and fell back into her nest of brightly colored pillows. "You are the very devil."

"No, *you* are the very devil. Do you have any idea what you said last night?"

Elizabeth's one visible makeup-smudged eye opened, and she asked warily, "What did I say to whom, and when? And where?"

"Last night," Saffron said, coming to sit on the bed, "you waltzed into our flat, interrupting a quite wonderful moment between me and Alexander—who I have not seen for five months—that might have gone on for quite a bit longer had you not blabbed about Lee *petting* me."

Elizabeth was still and silent for so long that Saffron thought she might have fallen back asleep.

But she slowly rose on her elbows, head hanging and mop of hair covering her face. "Do you hate me now?"

"No," Saffron said, sniffing. "But I'm quite angry. You are a wretched drunk, and I believe you owe me a great favor now."

"Might I make it up to you when I don't feel as if the flu is making a return?" Elizabeth asked, her chin tilting to give Saffron a sweet smile through her unruly sandy waves. She resembled a raccoon trying to cajole its way into the good graces of the owner of the garbage bin she'd just overturned.

"We shall see," Saffron replied primly, giving her the cup of coffee.

Elizabeth sat up gingerly, and they settled side by side while she gulped it down. The morning was cold, so Saffron snuggled into the blankets.

After a few quiet minutes, Elizabeth said, "That was a dreadful thing for me to do, darling. I'm terribly sorry."

"It was awful. I wish I could just erase all of yesterday and do it over again."

"Would you go back to Lee kissing you and erase that too?"

"Is that your way of figuring out which man I prefer?"

Elizabeth shrugged, nightgown slipping low on her shoulder.

"After last night, and the things Alexander said . . ." Saffron heaved a sigh as heavy as her heart.

"What did he say?"

She related what had happened the previous evening, from Vale threatening her at the theater to Alexander showing up. "I don't know what to think. He seemed so condemning, but I can't dismiss it out of hand because his experience was legitimate. Who knows what sort of things his doctors might have done if they'd been indulging with the medications at their disposal? And he mentioned his brother . . ." That had caused her heart to ache more than anything. He'd only ever mentioned his older brother to her once before, but it had been clear Alexander loved him a great deal.

"Just because someone has as a negative experience with one sort of person doesn't give them the right to claim every single one is bad. Alexander ought to know that," Elizabeth said. She set the coffee cup down on her bedside table with a clink and rolled on her side, to burrow into the blankets next to Saffron. "I thought Lee was very much against the abuse of drugs."

Lee had taken great offense when she'd asked if he'd tried the drugs Lucy had given him. "I don't know how to explain it to Alexander. That Lee isn't like that, and . . . everything else."

"Bosh," said Elizabeth, very firmly for someone who still resembled a fuzzy little creature in their den. "You don't owe him any explanation. He didn't make his intentions known upon his departure, Saff. Nor did he proclaim love in his letters. Neither did you. He oughtn't have had expectations coming back." Elizabeth rolled over, getting unsteadily to her feet. She pressed a hand against her head, pursing her lips. She looked a bit like a well-loved doll, colors faded and limbs loose. "I'm more concerned with him sweeping in and declaring you ought not to do things. Not very modern, is it?"

Saffron agreed, a heavier sense of melancholy settling over her.

They padded into the kitchen, where Elizabeth almost immediately chivvied Saffron away from the stove.

The doorbell rang out, and Elizabeth swore. "Who invented those things?"

"I'll just see who that is, tormenting us at the unholy hour of"—Saffron glanced at the clock—"seven thirty in the morning."

She tightened her flannel dressing gown around herself, and with no little amount of mingled hope and trepidation, considering who had been behind the door last time, peered outside.

Cautiously, she opened the door just a crack. "Lee? What are you doing here so early?"

"I saw Edwards last night."

That was enough for Saffron to open the door the rest of the way and shepherd him into the entry. "Stay here," she said with a warning glance before returning to the kitchen.

Elizabeth gave her a scornful look when she announced their caller. "It is *unseemly*," she hissed. "I am in my dressing gown, Saff. Not the pretty one. This is something that old spinsters wear because they haven't anyone to keep them warm."

"Your dressing gown is at least something from this decade," she whispered back. She gestured down at her faded blue flannel and thick knit socks. "Not to mention these!" She pointed to the waves still in pins around her face.

It was the work of five minutes to put herself to rights and join Lee in the sitting room. Elizabeth, naturally, took much longer, insisting that insisted she couldn't cope with Lee until she'd eaten breakfast, and left Saffron alone with him. He was perfectly dressed for a casual weekend morning in a thick tan jumper and brown slacks, but his eyes were shadowed, his mouth held in a taut half smile.

"Pleasant evening?" he asked as she settled on the couch next to him.

"Not particularly."

"I'm afraid I have little sympathy for you. I had the pleasure of attending Edwards's sickbed after I left here."

"He was looking poorly when I left him at the theater. I hope it wasn't serious."

"Nothing life-threatening, though he was in quite a state. But I did hear some interesting things that I thought were worth interrupting your day of rest for."

Elizabeth bustled in with a tray of coffee and a rack of toast. "Michael, how do you do this fine, *early* morning?"

"Quite well, thank you," Lee said easily. He'd long since adapted to Elizabeth's ribbing about his preference for being called by his surname. "I daresay you'd like to hear the latest about the bouquet business."

"I would, thank you," she said, seating herself in the chair next to Saffron's.

"Ah, but what a pity." Lee cast a forlorn eye over the tray. "Haven't you any jam for the toast?"

"What a pity," Elizabeth replied with an equally exaggerated expression. "We have only the kind Saffron made with her delightful little samples."

Lee grinned at her parry and raised his cup of coffee in salute. "Edwards had a migraine, the sort that keeps people in bed for days."

"And Amelia usually provides him a remedy, but she's been too busy with Lord Vale," Saffron put in.

"Which," Lee continued with a raised brow, "if I am correctly interpreting the mumbling of a man half mad with pain, is actually because *Amelia* craves Vale's attention, and not the other way 'round."

Saffron looked at him with surprise. "But at the Blue Room Edwards said Vale was courting her quite insistently."

"He's already proven himself to be a rather unreliable witness."

Elizabeth said, "Lee, you were in Amelia's flat. Were there flowers and things?"

"Believe it or not, Elizabeth, I might actually have noticed if there was a stock of poisonous flowers sitting around."

Elizabeth gave Saffron a look. "Lord preserve us from the obtuse minds of men." Then, while Saffron was suppressing a laugh, she said slowly to Lee, "I know you prefer to woo women in alleys behind jazz clubs—"

"For heaven's sake, Eliza," groaned Saffron.

"—but most men with any sense of courtesy give ladies flowers, sweets, or other tokens of their affections. Did you see anything like that in Amelia's flat?"

Lee's brows dipped, though clearly not in reaction to her attempt to scold him. "No, there was nothing like that. Every room but her bedroom was as bare as a hospital ward, and everything inside was old enough to be one of Edwards's collectibles."

"But that makes sense," Saffron said, brain still piecing things together. "Vale told me last night he was a passionate man"—she ignored Elizabeth's snort and Lee's arched brow—"and that he was prone to violent jealousy. If he was serious about Amelia, he wouldn't likely court a girl without sending her gifts to remind her of him. He isn't serious about Amelia, thus no gifts."

"So, Amelia is pursing Vale." Elizabeth tutted. "And here I was admiring her for taking up a profession. She's simply biding her time until she can land a wealthy husband to save her and her family, isn't she?"

Saffron recalled the questions about Amelia that had plagued her for weeks, answered so easily by Elizabeth. Of course that was why Amelia was trying to stay in her wealthy circles. She was trying to do what so many of their peers aimed to do: marry well. It was surprising how disappointing that was. "It's rather cold-blooded of her to immediately attempt to snatch up Vale so soon after his last lover, her *friend*, was murdered."

Elizabeth shot her a look that told her she ought to know better.

"Edwards also said something that I swear made my blood ice right over in my veins." Lee looked at the woman darkly before saying carefully, "'*Send her flowers, send them all flowers.*'"

Elizabeth swore soundly, and Saffron felt the blood drain from her face. Her voice was a whisper. "Edwards sent the flowers?"

"I don't know," Lee admitted. "But what else could that mean? He said something about Birdie making threats and using Amelia. That's an easy connection—Birdie wanted something stronger, and Amelia has access to drugs. We all know that Edwards cares far too much for Amelia, even if he won't pursue her himself. And honestly, Everleigh, I could believe it. I could believe he'd killed Birdie for Amelia's sake. He has these moments, you know." Lee seemed to struggle for words, something Saffron had never seen before. He was truly rattled, it seemed. "He hides this other side of himself, something his polite exterior can't quite cover all the time. Like he could just snap at any moment."

"Like Jekyll and Hyde," murmured Elizabeth.

No one spoke for a moment, each no doubt contemplating the implications.

Elizabeth rose to her feet, clearing her throat and looking pointedly at the tray. "Ah, it seems all the coffee is gone."

An utter lie, of course, but Elizabeth had evidently decided that was enough talk about crimes and excused herself to make another pot.

"I believe that is my cue," Lee said dryly.

"For what?"

"To coax out of you what your true feelings for me are, of course."

Alarmed, Saffron's eyes snapped back to Lee, who was snickering. She rolled her eyes. "You're even worse than she is."

"I am, and one day Elizabeth will realize it, and she'll be terribly disappointed." He crossed his leg casually, a smile still playing at his lips. "But in all seriousness, Everleigh, I hadn't realized there was something between you and Ashton. I might have tread more carefully if I had. Poaching is simply not the thing."

She had no idea what to say to that. She had tried to tease out her feelings all night, and the most progress she'd gotten was through Elizabeth's question about her regretting Lee kissing her. She didn't, but looking at him now, she wasn't sure she wanted to go down that path with Lee. He was all charm, with just a touch of professionalism when it was necessary. She didn't think she could cope with his flirtatious nature, always wondering if he was being serious when those green eyes twinkled. But they did get on well when they cooperated, and disagreeing with him was usually just as fun . . .

"Well," he said somewhat sardonically, "I suppose you not rushing to contradict me suggests whatever it is might not be as serious as it looked."

After last night, she wasn't sure if Alexander would want to pursue her any longer. And the more she considered their confrontation, the more she wasn't sure she wanted that either. Elizabeth was right, it wasn't good form to show up and immediately start questioning her choices. "I don't really want to talk about it."

Lee hummed noncommittally, and she fidgeted under his scrutiny. He seemed to decide not to press the issue. "What shall we do with Edwards's mysterious mumblings, then?"

"The inspector needs to be informed, obviously," Elizabeth said, entering the room with suspiciously good timing. She'd doubtless been lurking outside the door, the snoop. She set the tray down and perched on the arm of Saffron's side of the couch.

"Agreed. I doubt Edwards will be capable of more than rolling over in bed today, so we can wait 'til tomorrow." Lee patted his legs once before getting to his feet. He pecked Elizabeth on the cheek, earning him another scowl, then pressed a kiss onto Saffron's with jarring gentleness and a ticklish hint of a laugh in her ear. "We'll make a plan of attack at the office, Everleigh. Always a pleasure, Elizabeth."

Saffron's face was warm with a blush as Lee glided out the door. At the sound of the front door closing down the hall, Elizabeth cackled.

"Oh darling," she said between laughs, "you are in trouble."

CHAPTER 30

Saffron shoved her keys into the office door, jerking it open with uncharacteristic roughness. Her thoughts were a spinning cyclone of confounding contradictions. Edwards seemed to have admitted to sending the bouquets, and Lee believed he might be unhinged enough to kill. But Vale, who'd known him for years, called him harmless, while he himself seemed full of dark feelings toward Birdie. Who was right? Between those questions and the debacle between her and Alexander, she'd done far too much thinking in the last twenty-four hours.

She was full of impatient energy. She wasn't sure work would provide her an outlet, as most of the instigators of their case study opportunities had tapered off with the cooler, wetter weather. She'd rather not spend the day cooped up with Lee in her office when she knew Alexander was just down the hall. The floriography dictionary was a heavy weight in her handbag, tempting her to hide in the library with it so she might check over the meanings of the bouquets again to see if she'd missed something.

She hadn't even slipped her coat from her shoulders when there came a knock on the door. She merely turned around to open it.

Alexander stood before her in a gray suit and green tie. Had his black hair not remained unfashionably long and his skin not glowed with a tan, Saffron could have placed that moment back several months ago, before he'd left. Except there was no small smile lingering in the corners of his lips, as it had before. He looked as intimidating as she'd thought him before they'd become . . . whatever it was they'd been.

There was a gaggle of students chatting loudly in the hall, so she knew there was no chance of a semiprivate conversation with Alexander standing in the door. But she didn't particularly want to speak with him, not with his hot words of suspicion and anger lingering in her mind.

The reminder stiffened her spine and brought a dismissal to her lips, but the look Alexander gave her brought her up short. His shoulders were tense and his lips were downturned, lips she'd refamiliarized herself with just a few days ago.

Saffron realized she'd been staring at him. "Come in," was the reply she finally gave, and she was proud of her self-assured tone. She stepped away, and he followed.

"I share this office with Lee," Saffron said, following Alexander's gaze to Lee's messy desk in the corner of the room. Her desk was only marginally better. She felt a perverse pleasure in the notion that the disarray would bother Alexander.

If it did bother him, he didn't reveal it. He stopped at the side of the rumpled couch. They had spent hours on that couch when it still had belonged to Dr. Maxwell, researching and talking and decidedly not doing the things that Saffron had really wanted to do with him before he'd left.

"Yes?" she prompted.

"Will you come with me for a moment?"

Saffron blinked. She'd been expecting either an apology or a surly comment. "Where?"

"The greenhouses."

Neither his expression nor his voice gave anything away, but Saffron thought perhaps the location itself did. The air in that place had always been thick with more than just humidity and the scent of blooms when she shared it with him.

"Why?" Her voice was softer than before.

Alexander didn't reply, just went to the door and opened it, tilting his head in invitation.

A damp breeze blew across the faces of the stone buildings as Saffron and Alexander exited the North Wing from the east entrance to Gordon Street. Nine in the morning found the side street much quieter than the bustle of Gower Street. The gentle scattering of colorful leaves across the pavement, the only movement.

Neither of them spoke on the brief walk to the fenced-in green filling the block. Was he still angry? Would he apologize—or should she? She wished he'd just say what he was going to say and be done with it.

Alexander flicked open the gate and held it open for her to walk inside. Five glass buildings stood side by side within. Lit with milky light, their condensation-clouded walls revealed hints of green and the fanning shapes of leaves.

They stepped inside the humid air of the first greenhouse, closing the door quickly on the morning chill. The building was overcrowded with verdure. It'd been so long since Saffron had been to visit, she thought with a small pang, that some of the plants were unrecognizable. Then she realized that the plants *were* strangers to her.

"These are the specimens I brought from Brazil," Alexander said from behind her.

"But this . . ." She gazed around, seeing for the first time a hundred leaves and flowers she'd only ever seen as ink on paper. They were beautiful, a mosaic of green and pink and white and a hundred other hues, sitting in small pots and vials of water.

"Oh my," she breathed.

"I did manage to find all of them, though a few had to be transported as seeds."

"It's more than I could have hoped for," Saffron said, turning back to him with a smile that hurt her cheeks.

They stood looking at each other for a moment. Saffron's smile faded along with her enthusiasm as she recalled their disagreement. Well, if he wasn't going to bring it up and settle things between them, she would. She couldn't stand the tension. "Can we talk about what happened the other night?"

Alexander's eyes wandered away from hers. "I've said what I needed to say."

"Well, I haven't," she said, stepping forward. "You seem to be under the impression that I'm thoughtlessly flinging myself into danger, that I'm running headlong into cocaine-fueled parties with dope-fiend murders. You think that I'm being foolish, irresponsible." He hadn't said it in so many words, but Saffron knew he was thinking of how she'd impetuously chased ideas when they'd worked together before. "I know that I made stupid choices when I was trying to save Dr. Maxwell. I know that my decisions were not always thought through and that I . . . In truth, I should have left things to Inspector Green, rather than sneak around myself."

Alexander started to say something, but Saffron didn't give him the chance to get it out. "You said before that I seemed to have a talent for investigation. I don't know that's true, but I do know that I have something to offer in that regard. I—" She stopped, swallowing down the tightness in her throat and forcing her chin up. She wasn't going to shrink when she'd only just begun to feel like she might be blooming. "I am intelligent and observant. I have developed knowledge and skills that might be used for more than just writing papers or books. Inspector Green came to me for help. He didn't want me to type something for him or fetch him a cup of tea or . . . something less savory. You can't imagine how that felt, for him to ask me to use whatever measure of expertise I have in my field. This investigation is an opportunity to be viewed as a professional. Especially after dealing with that *wretch* Berking," she concluded bitterly. Speaking all these painful truths felt like turning over the compost pile and finding a great deal of unpleasant rot and worms. But just like compost, it was important not to leave it undisturbed.

Alexander's color was a little high, whether from agitation or from the warmth of the greenhouse. "I have never doubted your intelligence, nor your abilities. You—you are exceptional, in every way." Her heart swelled, but when Alexander rubbed a hand over his jaw, giving her a hard look, that overfull heart sunk quickly. "But I don't want you to put yourself in that kind of danger again."

It was on the tip of her tongue to say it didn't matter what he wanted her to do or not do, but she couldn't dismiss his concerns out of hand. Tracking down a murderer could not be angled as safe, not when the face of Mrs. Keller and her blood-soaked bed still haunted her dreams.

"What Lee and I are doing—" The muscles in Alexander's jaw fluttered with tension. Annoyed, she said, "Stop that. Lee is only helping with the investigation because he thinks it's a lark, messing about in police business." Saffron regretted the words immediately, that they made Lee seem so shallow and immature.

He looked slightly pained. "Didn't something happen between you?"

Saffron turned away, at a loss. She didn't want to talk about that, not when she wasn't sure how she felt about it. But Alexander had the sort of look that she'd seen him give unorganized microscope slides. He wouldn't let it go. "Something did," she said finally, "a few weeks ago."

"And?"

"And what?" Saffron asked, frustration flaring. "What does it matter?"

His eyes went hot, and he stepped closer. "It matters because I thought about you every day when I was away."

"And I thought about you too. But," she said, trying not to be too affected by his intensity, "I didn't know what either of us would want when you returned."

Alexander held her gaze. "You seemed to know what you wanted the other night."

"I thought so too." Her heart was aching, but she still had a job to do. The victims deserved justice. And the person who killed them deserved to be punished. "I know what I want now. I want to finish what I started and help Inspector Green catch this person before he does more harm."

It was as if a shutter had closed behind Alexander's eyes. "Does Dr. Aster know that you've taken up as a detective again?"

"What?"

"Does he know that you're running around after cocaine users and getting cozy with your study partner?"

Saffron's mouth fell open, face heating. "That's not at all what's happening! And why would Aster need to know?"

"He might not like that his employees are splitting their time for such disreputable pursuits." He said the words coldly, without the humor Saffron desperately wished to see in his expression. Eyes that had burned moments ago were now flat black. It was as if a stranger stood before her, rather than the man she'd longed for.

Fighting the lump in her throat, she managed to ask the question that was the only logical conclusion to draw. "You're going to tell Aster?"

"I don't want to," he said immediately. "I don't want to get you into trouble. But I will if it means you'll be safe."

"Safe from what, exactly?" Saffron demanded. "You keep saying it isn't safe, but you have no idea what I've actually been doing. You haven't given me the chance to explain—"

"I know you're chasing after a murderer again. I know what you're like when you go after some clue."

"That was months ago, Alexander. *Months*. I've learned. I've changed."

The muscle in Alexander's jaw pulsed again. "You've changed?"

For the second time, she steeled herself. "Yes. But I'm not going to change my mind about this. It's too important. I hope—" Her breath left her in a helpless gust. She didn't know what exactly she wanted Alexander to do or say. It seemed ridiculous to imagine him going back to how he was before, when he'd searched out clues all on his own and spoke to her with the easy camaraderie that had pleased her so much. "I hope you'll reconsider speaking to Dr. Aster."

His answer was his immediate departure, brushing aside hanging leaves and leaving them agitated in his wake.

Saffron hadn't intended to bypass the North Wing, but she couldn't stomach going to the office and pretending to Lee that nothing was wrong. He'd notice she was upset, and he'd wiggle it out of her, and then she would likely have to address the unspoken something between them. Instead, she'd marched along the rear of the Quad and found herself glaring at the Euston Square bus stop.

The small war memorial, a marble obelisk with four military servicemen immortalized in bronze at its corners, stood at the center of the round drive. She'd gazed up at that memorial daily, since it was built, and thought of her father, her first sweetheart, and, for the past six months, Alexander. She'd imagined the sacrifices they'd made in order to do what was right. She'd imagined herself along the same lines the past few months, sacrificing her comfort and, at times, safety, to help others.

To think that Alexander meant to take the chance, the *choice* to do that, away from her made her teeth grind together.

A familiar voice calling her name from the other side of the street pulled her out of her contemplation, and his arrival ensured complete distraction from her current woes.

CHAPTER 31

The door of the greenhouse slammed shut behind Alexander, jarring him almost as much as the rush of chill morning air that accosted him. It didn't cool the anger pulsing through his body, however.

During long months slogging through muddy shores, pushing past massive leaves concealing any number of dangers, and putting up with the antics of his bored colleagues, it had been memories of a dark-haired woman in blue smiling at him in the dark that had kept him productive and tolerant. When fever had overtaken him for two weeks, slivers of her smile had swum before his vision, providing him comfort. When a specimen on a certain botanist's list sent him trekking into caiman-infested waters, where a moment's inattention might mean losing a chunk of an arm or leg, it was the anticipation of presenting a strangely shaped plant to the woman who'd sent him after it that gave him the courage to wade into those shady waters.

Every one of those damned plants were the words he'd never managed to write in his letters or say to her before he left.

But he would not think about that now. Nor would he think about how Saffron had spent all that time tracking down a person who'd killed not just one woman, but several. And he definitely would not think about the man who'd been at her side all the while, provoking her to pursue that madness.

Without conscious effort, he'd made his way back to the North Wing. The morning foot traffic had peaked and fallen in the brief minutes he'd spent with Saffron in the greenhouses, and now the campus had fallen into its mid-morning hush. He made his way up the stairs, noting absently at the top that he'd rather continue up and up and up, allowing his body to take over to soothe his agitated mind.

He'd always found exercise a good relief from the anxiety the war had left him with. The hours of rowing and walking he'd done in Brazil had only honed his body into a machine that craved exertion more than ever. His life at the university was far too sedentary. He would have to find a way to ease himself back into life on campus.

As Alexander had gone straight to Saffron's office upon his arrival that morning, his office was still blanketed in white dust sheets. He tugged the first off his bookcase and folded it neatly, absently wondering if he could manage to convince the caretaker of the North Wing to come and run a mop through the room.

When the sheets were stacked tidily on the edge of the desk and his window was open to clear some of the dust from the air, Alexander settled himself in his desk chair and took in the empty room. A sense of heaviness fell over him. His last memories of this place were of Saffron sitting opposite him, her nose buried in his notes as she frantically checked her specimen list for the sixth time.

"I've changed."

He stared at the vacant chair, fists tightening atop his desk. In some respects, he hoped to God Saffron had changed. The moment she'd mentioned cocaine, his first thought was that she'd tried it herself, just like she'd done with the xolotl vine, and he'd nearly lost his temper right then and there.

But it had been that same woman, the one who'd willingly consumed a dangerous substance for the sake of her mentor, that had occupied his thoughts for the past five months.

And now he had nothing to do but fall prey to those months of expectations now utterly collapsed. Because of him.

Alexander considered his prewar self to be a bit of a wayward boy. Growing up in a household with an older brother who made trouble at every opportunity, he'd taken to acting in whatever way rocked the boat the least. He'd gone to university because his father had insisted upon it, and he'd chosen University College because it was the school his father wanted him to attend. He'd gone to classes, made friends, and done the things he was supposed to do, simply because they were easy and he'd wanted to do *something*. It had been easy, too, to enlist when his brother did, when all his friends also were doing it.

After his battlefield injury sent him home, he'd drifted for two years, struggling to make sense of the new ways his body and mind functioned. His flashes of violent, muddy fields and his friends' deaths filled him with fear, and that fear more often than not led to anger. Anger for the casualty war had made of his old self, that stupid boy rushing headlong into danger. Anger for the loss of a future he'd never much wanted, the loss of innocence and a sense of security, the loss of friends and family. The conviction that he'd never heal, never be the man he was before, that no one would want him—not his family nor friends, not a woman—kept him isolated and on edge. Each time his hand shook so badly he dropped a beaker, or the sound of a book slamming sent him sliding back to the battlefield, was proof he'd never recover. A chance encounter with a professor who'd practiced Tibetan meditation, with its measured breathing and rigid poses, saved him from drowning in himself. It had calmed his mind and transformed that anger into something that could be productive.

He'd spent the years since honing that skill and accepting that anger and fear would always be a part of his life. Once he'd regained some sense of himself, his new self, those fears had faded into the background. He was not whole, but he was someone his younger self could have admired. Driven, purposeful, in control. He'd never been those things before.

But something about Saffron Everleigh threatened to undo that control. That was why he'd practically shouted at her. That was why he'd threatened to tell Aster. That was why the idea of her with that golden-haired idiot—

Alexander breathed out, slowly, though his nose. That was entirely the wrong pattern of thought to keep his temper cool.

Forcing himself up from his empty desk, he retrieved a fresh blotter from the cabinet and set about putting the rest of his office to rights. He'd never had much in here—too hard to keep things tidy if shelves and cabinets were overflowing—and so it took less than ten minutes to accomplish.

He blew out a frustrated breath, looking around the room. Cunningham, the Biology Department head, had said he hadn't needed to come in until next week, but being at the university was the best excuse he'd had to see Saffron.

This was not at all how he'd wanted things to go. He'd had a plan, but just like the foolish boy from years ago, he'd let his impulsiveness get the better of him. Now that plan was so far from what had actually happened, he didn't know how he could possibly salvage it.

Apologizing was a start. He shouldn't have been so surprised that Saffron had been so adamant about the investigation. She'd wanted to save Dr. Maxwell originally and had managed to clear his name. She'd never said it, but he was sure she'd kept investigating because she'd hoped Berking was guilty of more than harassing her. He didn't understand why Saffron was so determined now. He somehow didn't think it was solely for the validation that she got from Inspector Green.

Still, if studying the world through a microscope had taught him anything, it was that what he didn't know or understand could fill the Atlantic Ocean ten times over. He needed to keep his head and listen to her explain what this was all about.

He emerged from his office and headed down the hall. Saffron's new office was a few doors farther down the hall, and it gave his heart a twinge to see her name set in the brass plate, "S. Everleigh."

But it wasn't S. Everleigh who opened the door.

"Ashton," Dr. Lee said pleasantly, the same knowing smirk he'd had at Saffron's flat on his face. He was the handsome sort, the kind that likely got his way without any more effort than a smile. "What can I do for you?"

"I need to speak to Miss Everleigh."

"She isn't here at present," he replied, leaning on the doorframe. Behind him, a fine wool coat was hung on the coat stand. Saffron's lavender coat was missing.

"Right," muttered Alexander. He would check the library.

"Come in, if you have a moment," Lee said. "I'd love to hear more about the fellow Everleigh solved her first crime with."

The smugness in his voice grated, and Alexander considered making excuses, but he found he wanted that same knowledge about the man in front of him. Lee, as Saffron called him, had evidently become more important than her letters suggested.

Warily, he entered the room. Lee offered him a seat on the worn couch, a familiar piece of furniture Saffron had inherited from Dr. Maxwell. The room was a mess, but he ignored it and focused instead on the doctor, who now lounged in the chair at his desk. It was shoved into a corner, something that pleased him now that he'd noticed it.

Lee leaned his chin on his fist, still smiling. "So, the Amazon, eh?"

Alexander nodded. It wasn't really a question.

"What'd you get up to over there?"

The vagueness of the question was irritating. "Quite a lot. What do you and Saffron 'get up to' with your study?"

Lee obliged him with a description of their work, concluding with their most recent case with the Caywoods.

Discomfort bubbled under Alexander's skin like hot wax. Nothing he said, not even detailed descriptions of their research and lab work that suggested Lee knew what he was about, made Alexander feel better in the least, considering the man saw fit to encourage her to chase after murderers and drug users. "You never worry that she might be in dangerous situations?"

"Everleigh? No, not much can be a danger to her in a field or garden. I'd be more afraid *of* her than for her, what with all that knowledge of toxins lurking in her head."

"Your work takes you beyond gardens and fields. Jazz clubs, for example."

Lee took it in stride, unfazed by his accusatory tone. "Everleigh is surprisingly multifaceted. At home with dirt up to her knees or twirling around the Blue Room."

"The Blue Room?" Alexander repeated before he could school himself. "That's no place for someone like Saffron."

A faint smile still sketched on his features, Lee drawled, "What sort of person is she, then?"

Saffron's words echoed in his mind again. *"I've changed."*
Unnerved, he ignored Lee's question. "The Blue Room is not a repu-
table place."

"Well, you can't always solve murders in polite tea shops, can
you? But I suppose you know that. I don't see what the difference
is between what you did before and what Everleigh and I are doing
now. Someone is out doing god-awful things, Ashton. You expect us
to just let that go?"

"I expect most people have a notion of self-preservation."

Lee chuckled, shaking his head. "Not Everleigh." His eyes glittered
green as he eyed Alexander again. "Can you cope with that?"

Alexander didn't answer, embarrassed that Lee seemed to see
straight through his pretenses. How could Saffron have become
friends with someone like him, let alone anything more?

"Look, Ashton," Lee said, straightening up and touching his tie,
as if worried the perfect knot was out of place, "you seem a decent
fellow. Everleigh seems to think so, anyway. You traversed the Brazil-
ian rainforest and no doubt came back wanting nothing more than
the girl you'd been thinking of. I understand." His lips tipped up, and
a surprisingly strong urge to remove that smile from his face rose in
Alexander. "But I also understand Everleigh. For all that she appears
to be a dedicated little scholar, she's got a mind of her own. You knew
that already. I daresay it was even attractive to you. I was surprised
to find it irresistible myself. But whatever is between you won't last if
you're in a huff because she's doing as she likes."

Alexander withheld the litany of unhelpful and far too revealing
protests poised to erupt at Lee's words. "Thank you for the advice," he
said, keeping his voice as level as possible. "Allow me to offer some of
my own. Don't pursue this case further. It'll only come off worse for you
when it eventually gets around to Dr. Aster."

Lee's brows dipped momentarily before arching high. "You're
going to *tell* him?" He let out a laugh. "By all means, Ashton, clear
the way for me. Put the final nail in the coffin of your chances with
Everleigh." He chuckled again, shaking his head.

Incensed, Alexander began, "If you think that letting her run
around—"

"This is getting tiresome," Lee interrupted. He rose to his feet, and Alexander matched him. Looking serious for the first time, Lee said, "I don't *let* Everleigh do anything. I don't command her. If anything, she is *my* leader. It's her investigation—it's her case. I even bowed out for a while, only for her to convince me that I was being a damned coward." Color appeared high on his cheeks. "We are both risking quite a lot for the sake of justice. And if you think tattling on her will change her mind, then you don't know her at all."

Alexander could think of no retort. He took a last look at Saffron's desk before leaving the room without another word, feeling like he'd made nothing but mistakes since they'd been in that rose garden together.

CHAPTER 32

Saffron didn't ask any questions on the brief journey to the police station. Sergeant Simpson practically came out of his skin when she tried to do so after they'd settled on the bus. Admittedly, public transportation was not ideal place to learn details of a new crime within earshot of a young mother with her two small children and an old man who looked like a stiff breeze might knock him over.

Upon their arrival, Simpson immediately hustled her back to the inspector's office. The first thing Saffron saw was a colorful bouquet on Inspector Green's desk.

Her breath caught. Another bouquet meant another death. Who had been killed—and who had done the killing?

She opened her mouth to ask the silent inspector what had happened, but a woman's voice asked, "Miss Eversby?"

Amelia Gresham sat, pale-faced and still wearing her nurse's uniform beneath her shabby coat, in one of the chairs. Saffron hadn't even noticed her.

Saffron bit her lip, glancing between the two police officers. Simpson looked a bit panicked, but Inspector Green said, "Miss Gresham, I believe you've met our consultant, Miss Saffron Everleigh."

Amelia's eyes went wide, and Saffron cleared her throat, unsure of how she felt about being revealed in such a way. There was nothing for it. "I apologize for the subterfuge, Miss Gresham. It was necessary for the investigation, I assure you."

"So, you are not a medical student," Amelia said slowly, looking her up and down.

"No, I am not," Saffron admitted, "I am a botanist at University College. I study poisonous plants."

Surprise flared in her eyes but cooled quickly. "And I suppose Dr. Lee . . .?"

"You knew him as a doctor before the investigation, and that is not a lie. We were working together on another matter when Inspector Green asked me to consult." Saffron paused, unsure what the inspector wanted known about the poison bouquets and their relationship to the other murders.

"Miss Gresham brought the flowers here when she found them on her doorstep just now," Inspector Green said evenly, apparently satisfied that Miss Gresham was not going to react poorly to Saffron's deception.

"I knew that Birdie had received a bouquet too, when she was killed. Inspector Green asked me if I knew who might have sent them," Amelia said. "I know nothing has come of the investigation yet, but I got a feeling from these flowers. A wrong feeling. I felt afraid just looking at them."

"Who do you think sent them?" asked Saffron. She was intrigued by Amelia's reaction; Saffron had never taken her for the sort reliant on emotion or intuition. Lord Vale was at the forefront of Saffron's mind, and she wondered if their odd courtship was coming to a head in the wrong direction, and Amelia had been marked as his next victim.

"I . . . I don't know. But I suppose it was Birdie's killer, wasn't it?" Amelia's gloves stretched taut against her knuckles, matching the tension in her voice. "But I don't understand why. I haven't done anything to anyone."

Inspector Green said somberly, "The motivation is not clear yet, Miss Gresham. Sergeant Simpson will finish taking your statement, if you'll go with him."

She stood and left the room with Simpson, casting Saffron a final, uneasy look before the door shut behind them.

Saffron exhaled loudly, turning to the inspector. "What do you make of that?"

"I was about to ask you the same thing."

The bouquet was in a vase, chipped along the top but quality crystal. Saffron raised a gloved finger to it, tracing a carved panel.

"It's been in Evidence for years, and we wanted to keep the flowers as fresh as possible." Inspector Green's fingers tapped along the desk's surface. "Note that there is no ribbon this time."

Saffron set her things down and peered at the blooms. There was no black velvet ribbon. What did that mean?

She prepared her notebook and the floriography book, still in her handbag, for reference. With her magnifier in hand, she made quick work of the bouquet.

There was a stalk of prickly viper's bugloss, the same strange blue wildflower from Mrs. Keller's bouquet, but also golden chrysanthemums, tall rudbeckias with dark cones for centers, and delicate white anemones. Crumpled orange marigold blooms and blue violets were tucked along the rim of the vase, wilted and sad as they could not reach the water pooled below.

Saffron spared a moment to contemplate that; how long ago had this bouquet been assembled, if Amelia had only just received it and already the flowers were wilting? None of them were unusual; they were all likely to be found among autumn gardens. But there were so many different species, indicating access to a large garden set up for both summer and fall blooms. Lord Vale's home would provide such means, but Edwards had admitted to Lee that he had sent flowers, or at least he'd said so in a less than conscious state. Where would he have gotten them?

Carefully, Saffron removed several stems from the vase and examined the cuts on the end. Unlike the flowers given to Mrs. Keller, they were cut rough and uneven. Ragged fibers split off in some places. The damaged xylem would disrupt water absorption, therefore resulting in more wilted flowers. Perhaps that partially accounted for the state of the shorter flowers. That suggested, along with the lack of ribbon, that the bouquet had been made in haste sometime in the last day.

Head swimming with details, some of which she knew were unimportant but which crowded her mind nonetheless, Saffron began analyzing the blooms.

Her hand was shaking when she put her pen down and passed the notebook to the inspector. He did not speak for a long time.

"A heart left to desolation. Friendship. Falsehood. Desertion. Pain," he read.

"I can think of only one person who would send Amelia Gresham flowers that spoke of friendship, abandonment, and pain," Saffron said softly.

Inspector Green nodded slowly. "Percy Edwards."

Saffron emerged from the station into the tenebrous afternoon a few minutes later. The wind that had blown new clouds to cover the sky agitated debris along the street.

Inspector Green's renewed admonition for discretion and caution still rang in her ears. Saffron didn't need the reminder. She was utterly shaken.

It made perfect sense that Edwards was the murderer, but rather than revulsion at his acts of violence, she felt a strange empathy for him. He was an odd man, but that didn't necessitate him being a villain. He seemed to have only one friend, and he'd threatened her with his poison bouquet, just like the others. Would he have killed her had Amelia not brought the bouquet to the attention of the police?

Lost in her thoughts, Saffron began slowly down the street.

"Miss . . . Everleigh?"

Saffron turned to see Amelia standing just behind her, framed in a shop's doorway. Her gloved hands were in fists at her side, her face drawn.

Guilt ate at her. "Hello, Miss Gresham."

"I didn't know you're working for the police."

"I'm sorry to have lied to you." Saffron offered an apologetic smile. "I just wanted to help."

She took a halting step forward. "I knew," she whispered. "I knew it was Percy. I knew it." Her words came out in a rush. "His little eccentricities were always odd, but he's been acting so . . . *strange* lately. He's always been quick to anger, but his temper has been volatile ever since Lord Vale showed an interest in me. But I've never felt anything but friendship for Percy, and I thought he felt the same, but now—"

Saffron put a comforting hand on her shoulder, alarmed at Amelia's rapid unraveling. But if she'd found out her closest friend was a murderer and might have planned to kill her, Saffron would have been even more hysterical than Amelia. Elizabeth would make a formidable villain. "It's all right. You're safe now. Inspector Green will likely take Mr. Edwards in for questioning soon, and they will find the evidence needed to arrest him."

She nodded distractedly, wringing her hands. "Yes. But I . . . I'm sorry to ask when you've done so much, but would you mind walking with me to the bus stop?" She gestured down the street. "I can't afford a cab back to my flat, and I don't feel safe."

"Of course. I ought to head that way myself."

They set off together. The street took on a malevolent air in light of Amelia's comments, and Saffron didn't blame Amelia for walking shoulder to shoulder with her. A storm was brewing overhead, the sky darkening with each minute. Every passing stranger might have been an enemy, every rush of damp wind sounded like a whispered threat.

"Which bus do you take?" Saffron asked, if only to make some distracting conversation.

"The twenty-nine," Amelia said. Her hand came around Saffron's arm. She shot her a nervous smile. "It's really quite frightful out here, isn't it?"

"It is, rather," Saffron replied. "I heard you argued with Mr. Edwards recently. Do you believe that might be why he sent you the flowers? Was it a serious conflict?"

"It was," Amelia said, her voice thick with emotion, though her face was blank. "He objects to Lord Vale's interest in me. He's always been the possessive sort. I believe that is why . . . I believe that is why he attacked Birdie." She paused, looking bleak. "He killed her, Miss Everleigh. He killed Birdie because she wanted more than just him and our little group. She wanted to marry Gerald, and he killed her. Now I'm to meet the same fate, all because I do not choose *him*." She buried her face in her hands.

Saffron had barely a moment to puzzle over her confusing statement of Edwards's motives, for Amelia looked up from her hands and gasped.

She took a step backward, face blanching. "Percy?"

Saffron started, searching for what Amelia was staring at. In the midst of the foot traffic on the busy street, there was a man standing at the next corner, wearing a derby hat low against the wind. Saffron squinted to make out his face in the growing gloom, but Amelia was tugging Saffron away, whispering, "No, no, no—he'll kill me. He'll know I talked to the police—"

Before Saffron could reassure her, or redirect them back to the police station, Amelia had pulled her back down the street. She craned her neck, trying to see if it was Edwards and if he was following them, but Amelia yanked her into an alley between two shops. Her grasp was like a vice. Saffron stumbled after her, through discarded boxes, and felt her stockings catch and her skin break on their rough surfaces.

"Amelia, wait—" she began, but Amelia let out a little scream from before her.

"No," she moaned, backing away so her back pressed Saffron's front. "No, Percy, *please.*"

Before them was another figure stepping from the deeper shadows, this time unmistakably Edwards.

Frantic, Amelia scrambled around Saffron and was babbling about their friendship and begging for his mercy.

"Amelia, *run.*" The words came from Saffron's mouth just as her brain processed what was happening. She might be able to reason with him long enough for Amelia to get away. "Run—go!"

To her relief, Amelia did. She darted around Saffron, ran through the refuse of the alley, and disappeared into the street. Edwards had advanced on her, now standing only an arm's length away. His hat was low over his brow, but it was undeniably him. Saffron held up her hands in a pacifying gesture, saying, "Mr. Edwards, please, let's—"

Things went dark in a burst of pain.

CHAPTER 33

The library was quiet and nearly empty, cleared of students in search of more lively pleasures. The greenhouses were dark, seemingly full of nothing but flora and were locked, besides. Like a Peeping Tom, Lee had pressed his face against the foggy glass panes, looking for a glimpse of his partner.

Frustrated, Lee turned up his coat collar against the damp evening chill and strode to the North Wing. Rather than pace the empty office, he paced the empty hall.

The last he'd seen of Saffron, she'd been agreeing with Elizabeth that the police needed to know of Edward's admission. When he'd arrived at the U that morning and she wasn't in the office, he'd assumed she was reporting to Inspector Green. He'd been a little irked that she'd gone without him when he was the one who had heard Edwards's ramblings firsthand. Then a few hours became more, the tempestuous afternoon passed, and twilight was upon the city, without word from her. The telephone call to her flat hadn't connected, and he didn't know where exactly Elizabeth worked to try to reach her.

Speaking to the inspector would not have taken hours upon hours. However urgent the investigation, she'd never simply cast their work aside. She was more afraid of Aster than she was of the murderer, he reckoned.

It was that chilling thought that had him pacing the length of the silent North Wing, thinking furiously. He was a man of science, but instinct had saved lives at his hands before. He couldn't discount the unease prickling the hairs on the back of his neck.

He would go to her flat and see if she was there, or wait there until she turned up. Or until his nerves got the better of him and he went to the police station.

He reached the end of the hall and, turning on his heel, noticed a tall, dark-haired figure just rounding the corner from the stairwell.

"Ashton!" Lee called, jogging down the hall.

He caught him as he was about to open an office door. Alexander turned, with arms crossed over his chest. His shirtsleeves were rolled up, a large scar mottling the skin on his right arm. "What?"

Had he not been distracted, he might have been curious enough to subtly examine the scar. "I was just wondering if you've seen Everleigh."

"I haven't seen her since this morning."

"What time?"

"Just before you and I spoke."

"She was here?"

"Yes." He gave Lee a withering look. "Why?"

"I'd assumed that she'd just gone down to the police station to tell Inspector Green a new bit of evidence I'd found, but that wouldn't have taken the whole day. We have a deadline, one she wouldn't want to miss." Alexander didn't reply, further irking him. "Well?"

He raised a brow. "I couldn't say. I know nothing about the investigation."

"But you worked Saffron on an investigation before. If she's missing, that's cause for concern, isn't it?"

He seemed to consider this. "Most likely."

This was a strange contrast to the irate man he'd argued with just that morning. "Good Lord, Ashton, at least act like you have some hot blood in those veins. Everleigh is *missing*. In the midst of a *murder investigation*." He paused, waiting for some reaction, his temper spiking when there came none. "Damn it all, don't you care?"

Next he knew, he was being shoved against the wall, a hand gripping his lapel and Ashton's face inches from his own. Ashton's eyes flashed black, his voice low and fierce. "Of course, I care. That's the whole reason we argued—that's the reason she isn't here. I told her to stop." He exhaled, loosening his grip on Lee's lapels. "She didn't care for it. She probably went after one of the suspects to prove me wrong." He stepped away.

Lee smoothed his suit front, adrenaline sending his blood pumping loudly in his ears. He was glad Ashton hadn't hit him; he'd never been good in a fight. He could see Saffron doing exactly as Ashton had said: tearing off to solve the mystery, to prove him wrong. But where would that have taken her?

Alexander frowned. "How do you know she's not just avoiding this?"

"Avoiding what?" Lee said absently, plotting how to get to the police station fastest.

"The two of us," Alexander replied with an eyebrow raised.

"The two—" Lee's mind caught up to his implication. "Ah, that. If she wanted to avoid awkwardness, she would have suggested we meet elsewhere. *I* didn't tell her off, so she has no cause to avoid me." He began walking swiftly back to the office. He could hear Ashton trailing him. He flung the door open and snatched his coat from the stand. "I know she went to the police station, so that's where I'll go first. If she turns up here, do a favor and telephone Inspector Green so I might get your message and not spend the whole night combing the city for her." He locked the door and made his way toward the stairs.

Alexander muttered something before saying louder, "I'm coming with you."

Lee paused at the top of the stairs. "You are? Who says?"

"Saffron is missing after reporting information to the police about a murderer. You're the one who thinks this needs to be taken seriously. Are you saying you don't want me to come with you?"

"Well, when you put it like that . . ." Lee shrugged. "Righto. You don't have a gun or something, do you?" Alexander, who'd started back toward his office, shot daggers at him over his shoulder. "I'm joking!"

Unfortunately, he most definitely wasn't.

~ ❧ ~

Traffic was dire, and by the time Lee and Alexander had reached the police station, it was well-nigh six o'clock. Lee and Alexander alighted from their cab, Lee shoved a few quid at the driver to stay put in case they needed to dash off again, and they entered the police station. The cramped space was bustling with dark uniforms, one of which detached himself from the masses the moment they came through the door.

"Dr. Lee," Simpson said, rushing over to them. Simpson extended his hand to Alexander. "And Mr. Ashton! Good to see you again, sir."

"And you, Sergeant," Alexander replied, looking somewhat amused.

Lee, impatient with their pleasantries, stated, "Miss Everleigh is missing. Last we knew, she was coming here."

Simpson's boyish face went slack for a moment before he said, "Well, yes, I found her at the university. I brought her here to examine the new bouquet."

"What new bouquet?" Lee repeated sharply.

"Miss Gresham brought one in this morning," he stammered, looking as if he immediately regretted answering.

"Miss Gresham received one?" Lee swore. "Miss Everleigh examined the bouquet, and then what?"

"I-I don't know, I took Miss Gresham's statement, she used the telephone, and then I was told to help with paperwork—"

Alexander turned to the older sergeant at the desk, who had a newspaper spread before him. "Did you see Miss Everleigh pass through here this afternoon? Dark haired, wearing a light purple coat and matching hat?"

The jovial man nodded, oblivious to the tenor of the conversation he'd just been pulled into. "I did, indeed. A few hours ago."

"Any chance she said where she was going?" Lee asked.

"No," he replied, then squinted up at the ceiling. "Went in the same direction as the other young lady."

"Miss Amelia Gresham?" Simpson asked, sounding uncharacteristically critical.

"Yes, Simpson," came the other sergeant's sighing reply. "Saw 'em talking in the reflection of the boot shop window."

"So, she left, just after Miss Gresham did, and they spoke outside," Lee summarized, mind working frantically. If Amelia had found Saffron, that meant that Saffron might be in danger from whoever had targeted Amelia. "Who sent the flowers, Simpson?"

The young man looked supremely uncomfortable, his round blue eyes darting between him and Ashton and his face pinkening. "I can't say."

Lee released a frustrated breath. "What did the flowers mean?"

Simpson gulped. "I can't say."

Considering Edwards had all but admitted to him that he'd been the one to send them, and therefore was the murderer, Lee supposed he didn't need to know. "Where is Edwards?"

"Inspector Green is with a judge now, trying to get a warrant to search his home," Simpson said anxiously.

An answer bloomed in Lee's mind, and once it came to him, it felt completely obvious. "Edwards houses his antique collection at his father's manor, but the place is shut up. Nobody lives there. He's got a big empty house somewhere in Sussex, just waiting for him to stash a kidnapped woman in." Lee looked at Alexander and Simpson in turn, wishing they would go ahead and agree so they could get cracking.

Simpson look strained, eyes darting all over behind them. "But the inspector isn't here. No one here is familiar with the case."

"You're familiar with it," Lee said. "Tell us the direction to Edwards's house."

"But I—I can't just give you information."

Lee grinned, inspiration coming once again. "Sergeant, you can do one better."

Chapter 34

Before she opened her eyes, Saffron observed several things. The first was that her head felt like a bell that'd been rung too many times. The second was that she was moving. She spent the next several moments deciding if it was a train or a motorcar she was in before the abrupt change of direction informed her it was indeed a motorcar. Once that was decided, she strove to remember where she was going. She blinked, only to find darkness veiled her vision. She tried to lift her arms to rub at her eyes, but she couldn't pry them apart at her wrists.

That was when she began to panic. She struggled against her bonds, kicking out around her. The motorcar slowed and came to a stop, motor still running. Her heart thundered in her chest.

The door next to her feet opened with a snap of cold air, and she kicked out as fiercely as she could. She made contact with the driver and heard a grunt, which was quickly followed by a sharp blow to her hip. Saffron cried out in surprise and pain.

"It's not enough that you've betrayed me, Miss Everleigh? You'll resort to violence too?"

Edwards? Saffron remembered in a rush, her head spinning with the flood of recollection. Amelia, the alley. Edwards must have taken her. "Mr. Edwards? Please! Please let me go," Saffron called to him.

"I can't," he said, his voice tight. The door slammed at Saffron's feet.

"Mr. Edwards, please—" Saffron cried out over the sound of the engine revving.

The car began moving again. He didn't reply to her pleas, and eventually Saffron stopped calling out. Her aching head dulled her senses. She drifted in and out of awareness, imagining voices, only to jolt awake and find her face still covered and the motorcar still moving. Eventually, pain and exhaustion gave away to unconsciousness.

Cool, crisp air cut through her coat and infiltrated the cover on her face. Saffron found herself being dragged from the motorcar. It was very quiet, apart from a cacophony of footsteps on the gravel beneath their feet. She had no idea where they were, nor how long they'd been driving for. She knew only that little light entered the pinholes of the fabric over her face, and therefore it was possibly evening.

The jingle and scrape of keys told her Edwards was taking her into a building. It was nearly as cold within, and a musty, unused scent met her nostrils. She felt light-headed.

"I need to sit," she said faintly.

Edwards took her by the arm and marched her over carpet and hardwood floors, her stumbling footsteps echoing as they went. Finally, he shoved her down onto something that felt like a couch.

"Stay," he ordered.

She swallowed a wave of nausea and leaned back in the cushions. She struggled to remove the bindings on her wrists, which served only to make her arms and wrists sore and her head throb.

But Edwards was returning, his footsteps slow and heavy. He crossed the room and dropped hard somethings on the floor. After some shuffling, there came the scrape and catch of a match. The subsequent crackle of wood was almost comforting.

"Mr. Edwards," Saffron began tentatively, "could you please take this off my face? I'm certain my head is bleeding." It was the truth. Since becoming upright, it did feel as if a trickle had traveled from the back of her head down her neck.

A moment later, Edwards tore the cover from her head. She shivered at his touch when he moved her partially unpinned hair aside. Saffron caught sight of red smeared across the rough burlap sack he now held. The whirring of her faculties came to a standstill. She was bleeding. Someone had abducted her, and her head was bleeding. This was real.

Amelia knew Edwards had come after her, and she would go to the police. She repeated the thought until it became a desperate litany that silenced all other thoughts.

Edwards built up the fire for a long time, his back to Saffron. Heat gradually seeped through the room, eventually reaching Saffron and awakening her frozen senses as Edwards disappeared into a darkened doorway.

Amelia had escaped. She would have immediately gone to the police station. Inspector Green would figure out what Edwards had done and find her. That meant that escaping, however tempting a prospect, might not be the best idea if it meant she would not be here when he arrived. Edwards hadn't made clear his intentions yet. He'd bashed her over the head and bound her, yes, but he hadn't killed her when he had every opportunity. She didn't know if he could be reasoned with, but she had to at least try to stall whatever his plans for her were until Inspector Green had the chance to track her down.

Edwards returned. He paced about the carpet before the hearth, his shadowed face agitated and his movements a little too loose.

Saffron bit her lip. If she spoke, would he calm down or become more upset? She glanced to the door on the far side of the room, then across the room to another closed door. She chanced a glance behind her but saw only dim paintings, their golden frames glinting in the firelight. When she turned back, she saw Edwards was leaning on the mantle, his face in shadow and eyes dark with something that made her skin crawl.

With spine-shivering quiet, he said, "You've betrayed me, Miss Everleigh."

Saffron flinched at his use of her name.

"Oh yes, Miss *Everleigh*," he said, his cool tone igniting into anger. "I know you've been helping the police. You were there today, no doubt making more false claims. You probably went to see if you could put the final nail in my coffin."

Saffron flinched at the rising anger in his voice. "I wasn't. I was there to convince them of your innocence."

"More lies," he hissed, rising from his seat. He began to pace again.

"Mr. Edwards, I never betrayed you," Saffron said in a small voice. "I only wanted to help. I want to help Amelia too." This was a risk, but a risk that might give her enough time to be found. "I wanted to help the inspector find a murderer. We know Lord Vale killed Miss Williams."

She watched him for signs he might believe her. He merely stared at her, chest still heaving. She pressed on. "Lee was concerned when he heard you describe Lord Vale's interest in Amelia. We went straight to the inspector, to tell him that his people must watch her, to make sure that Vale didn't get to her like he got to Miss Williams. I could never live with myself if I let something happen to her," she said, her voice gaining strength. Edwards didn't respond. She wished his face wasn't submerged in shadow—it was making it impossible to read him. "Mr. Edwards—Percy— please, I know it looks black for me, but you must understand. Lee and I only wanted to prevent more murders from happening, to protect Amelia and—"

"Enough," Edwards murmured, and then, "Enough! Enough of this!"

Saffron jumped, her head throbbing terribly. He groaned and grasped his skull with such violence Saffron wondered if he'd do himself harm.

Stillness settled slowly, its glaring silence spreading like a chill fog.

"Why, why, Miss Everleigh, do you insist on lying?" His voice was quiet, head still buried in his hands. "Why can none of you tell the truth? Just admit—just admit you sought to cast my Amelia into suspicion. They are always trying to harm her, use her, always trying to frame her for terrible crimes that would cost her everything—" His grip went slack, and he lifted his face, voice growing louder. "That foul woman would send her to prison with her accusations. What did she need the money for? I told her exactly what I thought of her treachery."

Saffron struggled to keep up, but the mention of accusations and money brought to mind one person. "Mrs. Sullivan? Erin Sullivan?"

Edwards's hands dropped, revealing a snarl. "She would have thrown Amelia into prison with her own hands, and I couldn't stand for it."

Chills racked Saffron. How on earth was she supposed to pretend at believing in Edwards's innocence when he'd all but admitted he'd murdered one of the victims?

With difficultly, she swallowed. "What about Miss Williams?"

He shook his head slowly, but the motion seemed to pain him. He pressed his hands to his head again, a groan escaping his lips.

Somewhere in the house, there was a sound. It was nothing more than quiet scratch, but Edwards went still and raised his eyes to her. "Do not move."

Saffron didn't obey. She needed to be away from Edwards before he lost whatever remained of his sanity.

The moment the door closed behind him; Saffron was on her feet. She was unsteady with her hands still bound, and her stomach roiled in protest at her sudden movement, but she leaned on the edge of the sofa for support and forced her feet to move. With difficulty, she managed to turn the handle of the door Edwards hadn't gone through and opened it with a creak.

The corridor beyond was dark, with moonlight filtering through half-covered windows. With a shoulder on the wall to keep her upright, she moved into the darkness.

There was another parlor lined with large windows, revealing a terrace. White cloths masked the furniture, and Saffron had the absurd idea to simply crawl beneath one to hide. With her head aching and her legs weak, it was tempting.

A door creaked behind her.

Saffron stumbled forward, knowing what was coming.

Edwards burst into the room, making an animalistic sound as he grabbed her arm. "You'll not find what you're looking for in here." He jerked her forward. "Allow me to show you."

She stumbled after him. He led her through the silent house, his rage entirely at odds with the spectral elegance of the rooms they passed through. He shoved her into a room comprised mostly of windows and French doors. His movements were wide and brash, almost as if he was having as much trouble balancing as she was.

Edwards dragged her to the other side of the room, to a glass door. He shoved her to the ground and flung open the door. The panels of the door cracked at the impact of hitting the wall. He breathed deeply. "The flowers, Miss Everleigh—your expertise."

He lit an old-fashioned oil lamp sitting on the nearest table. His face was utterly unrecognizable. The odd, gentle Edwards was gone, replaced by a man descending into mania before her eyes. His hair hung in every direction, his eyes flitting around. He'd removed his coat, and one shirtsleeve sleeve flapped from the loss of a cufflink.

Saffron struggled to sit up. She was terribly afraid now, unsure if she would last another minute, let alone the hours it would take for the police to catch up to them.

Edwards wrenched her to her feet and forced her through the doorway. The freezing air was fraught with such a strong combinations of smells that Saffron swooned. It stank of rotting flowers.

His voice came rushed and harsh as he roved around the space. He'd brought them to a conservatory, lit by the moon through grimy glass walls. "I have always had an affinity for times long past. Eras of glory and beauty. Ours is a generation tortured and profligate, but in the ages before us, there was delicacy and nobility." He picked up a pair of shears. The rusted blades flashed dully in the lamplight. For a terrible moment, Saffron imagined him plunging them into her heart.

"You no doubt know, every flower has a meaning, and every bouquet a message. I sent my messages clearly. Betrayal, treachery— they came back to those who wrought them."

"You sent the flowers," Saffron said, if only to keep him talking. He had a weapon now, and her hands were tied up behind her.

Edwards zigzagged around the room, snipping at bushes and flower stalks. Saffron looked about desperately, praying for a knife or a blade, a shard of broken pot that she could use to sever her binding and protect herself. The room was filled with mangled shrubs with withered leaves and shelves lined with vases overflowing with spent blooms fuzzy with mold. She worked at the rope again, trying to free herself.

"Buttercup for avarice," Edwards ranted. "Foxglove, insincerity. Nettle for the cruelest betrayal. Shame, remembrance, falsehood—"

He wasn't listing the flowers he was cutting, but the bouquets he'd already sent, Saffron realized.

"From my own hands, they were forced to confront their crimes. And they received justice. I am glad I don't remember."

Tears of fear sprung into Saffron's eyes. He didn't remember murdering three women? How long had he been so far gone? Her wrists burned and her joints protested as she strained against the coarse rope. She managed to get to her feet just as Edwards slowly turned toward her, wrapping a black ribbon around the base of ruined blooms.

"Now, courtesy states I must give this to you with my right hand, so as to not cause offense." His smile was vacant as he presented her with the bouquet. His hands were now steady. "Tell me, Miss Everleigh, what is the message I'm sending to you?"

CHAPTER 35

Alexander found himself squashed in Lee's motorcar with Sergeant Simpson, barreling down the dark road out of town. He'd been surprised, then annoyed, that Lee owned his own vehicle, and then his feelings took a decidedly anxious turn when he realized that Lee drove like the devil himself.

The night grew clearer and colder the farther away from London they went. Simpson shone his torch intermittently on a map, providing Lee directions. The sergeant's objections to accompanying them had lasted only as long as it took for Lee to imply he would be responsible should Saffron die at Edwards's hands.

Alexander stared out into the black night, trying not to think about that possibility. An occasional pair of headlights snapped by, leaving streaks of light imprinted on his eyes.

Fortunately, the house was only two hours away, and Lee clearly thought that with a police officer in the car, he could fudge the speed limit.

Alexander flexed his freezing hands. "What's the plan?"

"You go to the front of the house and cause a distraction," Lee said, not removing his eyes from the road. "Simpson will enter through one side of the house, and I the other, and we search until we find Everleigh or confirm she isn't there."

Simpson cleared his throat before Alexander could voice his irritation at being relegated to being a distraction. "No, sir, we can't break in. Not unless we know Miss Everleigh is inside and in mortal peril." He sounded like he was reading from a handbook.

"What qualifies as mortal peril?" Lee asked with tone of tempered annoyance.

"We know she's in dire straits."

It occurred to Alexander, not for the first time, that they might have made a mistake in bringing so young an officer. He was more likely to knock something over than help. "Unless we can actually see she's in danger or hear her begging for mercy, we can't go inside?"

"Yes, Mr. Ashton."

Alexander glanced at Lee. In the light of an oncoming headlight, Lee caught his eye before saying, "Right, on to the next idea."

By the time they reached the house, they'd decided that Simpson would go to the front door and occupy whoever answered it, hopefully Edwards, long enough for Lee and Alexander to check the windows to see if they caught sight of Saffron or anyone else in "mortal peril." Simpson didn't like this plan, but Alexander and Lee had been adamant. It was unnecessary to say aloud that this would get Simpson out of the way so they could get inside Edwards's house without his insistence on the law.

Upon seeing the first glimpse of the massive, dark house, outlined in the rising half-moon's glow, Alexander had to agree with Lee that if ever a criminal needed the perfect location for hiding someone, this would be it. They'd passed nothing but farmland and woods for miles, and the place looked as if it'd been deserted a long time. The headlights revealed weeds poking through the gravel path leading to the front door, and the trees and hedges looked straggly.

Lee turned off the headlights and eased the motorcar toward the nearest tree, parking just behind it to provide them some cover. Simpson, squaring his shoulders, marched to the front of the house.

The rainstorm that had soaked the city had left this county untouched, and the air was crisp with impending frost. There was not a breath of wind to disturb the neglected landscape surrounding the house, nothing to cover their movements as Alexander and Lee darted around either side of the building.

Peering through the windows revealed nothing more than drawn curtains or the pale shapes of covered furniture. Alexander's hands and feet were growing numb, an uncomfortable sensation that reminded him of long days and nights spent with only a muddy uniform and a thin blanket for comfort. He couldn't help recalling it as he darted from window to window; scouting had been another adventure he'd enjoyed until it had nearly gotten him killed.

It wasn't until Alexander had his face inches from the glass of a window near the back corner of the house that he saw flickering light radiating from an interior room. His stomach plummeted at the sight. Did that mean Lee was right, and Saffron was there?

Hoping for a better angle, he went to the next window but saw no hint of the light. He made his way around the corner and spotted Lee peering into the back wall of a glass structure at the center of the long rear of the house. Careful of disturbing the gravel, he jogged along the grass next to the path and crept up to Lee.

Lee jumped and swore when he tapped him on the shoulder. "Good Lord, Ashton, warn a man! See anything?"

"A light inside." He gestured in that direction.

Their whispered argument about who would check to see if Simpson had seen Edwards was brief, ending with Alexander losing. Lee's point, "The jig would be up in a moment if Edwards caught sight of me," was the deciding factor.

Nerves tingling, Alexander took off around the house to find Simpson.

A distant noise reverberated through the house.

Edwards froze, with the decayed flowers inches from Saffron's face. The repeated sound sent him barreling from the room.

Saffron held her breath until the sounds of his steps disappeared, hardly daring to believe her good fortune. She went to the table, where the shears lay next to the lamp. She struggled onto tiptoes to reach them with her bound hands and managed to get them. She held the blades open in one hand and rubbed her wrist against it. She winced as the blade broke skin. After a few moments, her hands were free. She returned cautiously to the sunroom, where a pair of French doors allowed in thick beams of moonlight.

If that was Inspector Green or another police officer at the door, it would be better to find the front of the house and see if there was a way to intercept them. She made for the doors, but her hand froze on the handle. She could go outside, into the freezing night. But if there was no one helpful at the front, she would be trapped outside. She didn't know the land and had no clue as to where she was. Edwards would no doubt catch her quickly, especially given her head injury.

She needed to make her way to the front of the house or find a hiding place and wait until it was light enough to find her way outside.

Praying for luck, she crept down a corridor, keeping in the shadows. A clock chimed distantly as she padded through room after room, all silent and still.

Her ears strained for the sound of Edwards's footsteps. She anticipated his figure in each doorway. She blinked hard when she was sure she saw a shadow flit past a window. Perhaps her head injury was more serious than she'd thought.

Indeed, when she reached a parlor with a fire burning in a small hearth, Saffron was sure her mind was failing her. How had she gone full circle to find the parlor she'd be held in? But it wasn't the same room; it was lined with shelves of objects, and none of the furniture was covered in dust sheets.

She started at movement in the doorway and stared when she saw who stood before her. Relief threatened to destabilize her knees, even as fear tightened her throat.

"What are you doing here?" she managed to ask. "You can't be here. Edwards has gone completely mad!"

Lee rubbed his gloved hands together as he evaluated the rear of the house under the halved orb of the moon poised high in the sky. He'd already checked the locks on each door and window along his side of the house and the rear, but he'd forgotten to ask Ashton if he'd done the same on the east side. He'd seen light within. That was cause enough for Lee to get inside, and hang the consequences.

He began nudging windows and doors on Ashton's side. None gave way to his prodding.

Lee returned to the glassed conservatory. Ashton was nowhere to be seen, so Lee idly pressed his nose to the glass for another look.

His breath caught.

A lamp, nearly hidden from view by the heaps of plants within, was burning low on a table. It had definitely not been there when he'd last peered inside.

Heart pounding, he poked at all the windows. A single cracked pane about shoulder-high wiggled when pushed on. He groaned with the effort of prying open the large window using only a few fingers. Open it did, however, but a large bush stood in front of it, thorns long enough to see their malicious points through the glass.

Withholding an impatient sigh, Lee took one last look for Simpson and Alexander before working the window wider. With an effort that made him wish he'd taken up an activity more athletic than dancing, he hoisted himself up and got a leg inside. When a distant sound met his ears, he scrambled through and dropped to the floor.

He was off balance, wavering enough to receive several sharp pokes from the bush. Swearing under his breath, he scanned what he could see of the room. The stink of the place was horrible, like a hundred bottles of ancient perfume had smashed.

Somewhere nearby, a clock chimed. The lamp's sallow glow shone off a pair of garden shears crusted with red along the edges. Lee's nose wrinkled at the rust, but at least he'd have a weapon. Beggars couldn't be choosers.

Just as he began to creep forward, a voice made him stop dead. Obscured by the leaves of the thorny bush, Lee crouched down and listened.

CHAPTER 36

S affron stared at Amelia.

"I know," Amelia said sadly, coming into the room and closing the door carefully behind her. "I know Percy has lost his mind. That's why I'm here."

"But you got away. What did the police say when you told them what happened? Are they here too?"

"I don't know," Amelia said almost distractedly. She wore no hat or gloves, only her coat. Her hair was in disarray, and her eyes were weary. "I only knew I couldn't leave you to him."

"We have to get away," Saffron said, ignoring that noble but foolish statement. "He'll come looking for me. We have to hide or get to the front door; someone rang the bell." She took Amelia's hand and pulled her in the direction she'd come.

Amelia followed, but slowly. After passing through two rooms, Saffron remembered the telephone.

"Do you know if this house has a telephone?" she whispered to Amelia as they passed into the breakfast room.

"No, Percy wouldn't allow it," she replied in hushed tones. "You know how he dotes on the past. He wouldn't stand for a telephone here."

"But you've been here." They were in Edwards's family house, she realized. "You've been here many times."

"Of course," Amelia said, frowning. "That's how I knew where to come. I was sure Percy would bring you here."

That should have been a relief, but it only deepened her unease. Sussex was hours from London. "How did you get here?"

"I drove."

Hope pushed out Saffron's disquiet. "Then you can drive us away!"

"I left the motorcar around the side, this way." She took Saffron's hand once again and pulled her toward a door.

An indistinct howl came from one end of the house. Edwards must have found her missing.

Fear swept through Saffron, her throat constricting and her hands going damp with sweat. They brushed uncomfortably along the rough texture of Amelia's hand. They were more than rough; they were bumpy and peeling.

Alarm flashed through her in a hot wave, and she jerked her hand away.

Amelia stopped, surprise written on her face. They stood facing each other in the dining room, which was lined with partially curtained windows that opened to the moonlit terrace.

Saffron stared at her, making painfully slow sense of the facts laid out before her. Amelia's hands were irritated. They'd *been* irritated, she realized, recalling the way Amelia frequently twisted and patted and rubbed her hands, moving just like Mrs. Caywood had, resisting scratching at her blistered hands.

Many of the flowers included in the poison bouquets caused irritation if touched. Foxglove, buttercup, nettle. Amelia's bouquet contained viper's bugloss with its prickles and anemone with sap that could burn the skin. If Amelia had had contact with those plants without taking proper precautions, her hands would be bumpy, burned, and blistered.

Just like they were now. Just like they had been for months.

Amelia's concerned frown smoothed as the last piece clicked in Saffron's mind, as if she'd watched it fall into place. "You've figured it out, then."

Saffron backed away. "You should have worn gloves."

She advanced on her, slowly and carefully. Saffron rounded the long table, placing it between herself and the woman she had only just realized was not a victim at all.

"Amelia."

Saffron and Amelia both started at the softly breathed name. Edwards loomed in the doorway.

"Who was at the door, Percy?" Amelia asked carefully. She backed away from him as he lurched forward, drawing closer to Saffron.

"Police," said Edwards.

Saffron's heart leaped.

"And you sent them away?" Amelia asked.

Edwards nodded, his dazed eyes on Saffron. "I can't let you get away."

Their heads jerked in unison toward a distant noise like breaking pottery. In Saffron's moment of inattention, Amelia's hand closed around her arm.

"Percy, go see what that is. Use your revolver if you need to," Amelia ordered.

Saffron tried to jerk away, but Edwards had drawn a gleaming black gun from his pocket, and she went still. Defeat threatened to sink into Saffron's battered body. What was she going to do?

※

"Blast," Lee whispered, rubbing his bruised knee and glaring down at the inconveniently placed potted tree. It was now rolling around, spilling dirt onto the parquet floors of what must be a sunroom. Lee had no hope of putting it back in place; the pot was shattered. Edwards had likely heard and would come to investigate.

Perhaps it would draw him away from hunting down Saffron. That had been what Edwards had been muttering about when he came to the conservatory not five minutes before. He'd mumbled something about her escaping, before storming out again. Lee had been equal parts relieved and horrified, for it meant that while Everleigh had gotten away, Edwards *had* abducted her and meant her harm.

The swaths of white cloth provided ample hiding places, so Lee darted across the room to the largest and crouched down. The shears weighed heavily in his pocket, and he slipped a hand to the warmed metal.

If it came down to it, would he be able to actually harm Edwards?

The question hung in the moonlit air for thirty seconds before Edwards burst into the room. He rushed to the fallen tree and glared down at it before rounding on the room.

"Where are you?" he snarled. "Where are you? No, not you. Amelia has her."

Lee's grip on the shears tightened. Amelia was here and had Saffron? Damn it all, he didn't know if he could trust a word out of Edwards's mouth.

Edwards began ripping sheets from the furniture, and Lee raised himself on his haunches, unsure what was about to happen and entirely certain he wasn't ready for it. His heart was pounding so loudly he barely heard the swish and snap of the next-to-last cover being whipped off the table just beside him.

Edwards's footsteps paused before him, and Lee popped to his feet, shears tucked behind his back.

Edwards blinked. "Dr. Lee?" There was a gun held loosely in his hand.

By God, he could have been shot, surprising the man like that. A belated wave of panicked heat washed over Lee at the realization.

Edwards wasn't entirely lucid. He was still blinking as if he didn't quite understand who stood before him.

Lee attempted a congenial smile, but his face felt waxy. "Yes, old man, I've been terribly concerned about you so I—"

"Don't bother." Edwards's confusion melted into anger. "Don't bother with your lies. I know them all." He lifted the gun.

Lee raised the hand not holding the shears. "You don't, Edwards. You don't know the truth," Lee said, hoping his voice sounded confident, though he had no idea what he was saying.

"I know it all. Miss Everleigh showed your hand, I'm afraid. You both have been helping the police."

Shaking hands aimed the gun at Lee's heart, which threatened to pound right out of his chest. Lee had to get the gun out of his hands, and preferably into his own. How the hell he was to do that, he hadn't a clue.

CHAPTER 37

From behind a hedge near the front door, Alexander had listened to the far too short exchange between Edwards and Simpson. Simpson had evidently waited a long time to ring the bell, probably working up his nerve, so Alexander caught the end of their brief conversation. As the door closed, Alexander cursed Simpson's lack of skill stalling Edwards.

Hoping Lee would have found something by now, Alexander began working his way toward the back of the house, going around the west side this time. He cleared the first corner and was creeping along when he heard a tiny sound. It was so slight that he thought he'd imagined it, but he stopped, nonetheless. He was at the top of a set of stairs hidden behind a waist-tall hedge. He looked around and listened again. Another faint rattle came from the bottom of the stairs.

Alexander immediately began down the steps. He reached for the handle, bracing himself for whatever might be inside.

The door swung open on silent hinges.

Faint moonlight illuminated only a slender rectangle on the floor, showing rodent tracks in the dust. Alexander crept inside, keeping his arms lifted and hands close to his face. He wasn't going to be caught completely unaware in the dark. It took a few moments for his eyes to adjust to the deep gloom, and he had the notion he was in a vast kitchen. He heard nothing but an echoing drip and his own breath.

He felt along the edge of a wall, then another, until he found stairs. The kitchen was below stairs, and these would take him up to the ground floor. At least there would be light coming through the windows up there. He could hear something in the passage, beyond the slight scuff of his shoes on dusty wood steps.

At the top of the pitch-black stairs, he found a door, through which came muffled voices. His heart stopped when he recognized a feminine voice. He went through the door.

It led to a small room, unfortunately identically encased in darkness, but for a feeble line of light on the floor. He held his breath and listened.

The cold voice of a woman spoke. "Percy, go see what that is."

Alexander only momentarily puzzled over the presence of another woman. He'd heard so little about this case, but he guessed it was Amelia Gresham, who'd received a bouquet and had spoken to Saffron outside the police station. Amelia was in league with Edwards, it seemed.

At the mention of a gun, Alexander had his hands pressed on the door, ready to shove it open and face whatever waited on the other side.

He let out a slow breath, hands curling to fists. That would not help Saffron. She could be hurt if bullets started flying. He inhaled deeply, taking in the sweet, musty smell of the little room. There was motion from the outer room, then silence. Saffron and Amelia must have left.

Cautiously, he slid his hands over the door for the handle but found nothing but smooth wood. He pressed the door, found it gave, and pushed it open an inch.

The sliver of room he saw held nothing but the corner of a table draped in white.

He crept to each of the two doors, one held no sounds, but the other had the echoes of footsteps. Saffron was resisting, he guessed, from the scuffling and a feminine grunt of pain. He quickened his pace down the corridor.

He caught sight of two figures passing into a room ahead. Alexander scanned his surroundings and saw nothing to use as a weapon.

He inhaled and exhaled slowly, concentrating on the oxygen in his lungs. He could do this. He'd not come all this way—

A gunshot pierced the stillness of the house.

Alexander threw himself against the nearest wall. His breath went hot and tight in his chest. It came out in little pants while he tried to master himself.

He blinked away fire and blood and dirt raining down and forced his frozen brain to function. A gunshot. Edwards had a gun. Simpson also had a gun. Either Simpson or Edwards had fired inside the house. His right hand shook badly as he braced himself against the wall to get to his feet.

Saffron was not two rooms away, but one of the others might be bleeding out even now.

Hating the choices laid out before him, he took one last look at the door Saffron had disappeared into and started off in the direction of the gunshot.

The sharp snap of the gunshot must have shocked Amelia into releasing her bruising grip on Saffron's arm. Saffron darted deeper into the small parlor Amelia had led them to. It was the same parlor in which she'd found Amelia, the one with shelves lined with shining antiques, Saffron now saw. The room was the only one that looked lived in.

Amelia lunged for Saffron, teeth bared. When Saffron dodged her and put the short couch between them, Amelia came up short and looked about her. She took up a small leather case lying on the small table on her end of the couch, and with surprising coolness, she unlatched it and flipped it open.

Saffron's stomach lurched at the sight of a syringe lying atop velvet lining.

"I brought this for Percy," Amelia said softly, picking up a vial of clear liquid sitting next to the case. "He needed more encouragement to finish this. It's a mixture of chemicals that I've found give me the result I need. He's never been strong-willed, but . . ." She dipped the syringe's needle into the vial and drew the plunger down. She smiled slightly. "I doubt you'll have much luck fleeing with this in your veins."

"What is that?" Saffron asked, eyes looking desperately at the door. Why had she run into the room rather than out of it at the sound of the gunshot?

"It began with scopolamine," Amelia said.

A flash of recognition distracted Saffron from escape schemes. That was one of the toxins in deadly nightshade. Lee had written about its effects for their report, but she couldn't recall what it did.

As if reading her mind, Amelia said, "It's effective in reducing the nausea brought on by Percy's migraines. On the continent, they've been experimenting with giving it to mothers during childbirth. It makes them forget the horrors of it. It made Percy forgetful too. And curiously biddable." Her smile thinned, and she shoved the sofa with her hip, jerking it toward the wall, blocking Saffron's path to the door. "I am very curious to see how my solution affects you. This is calibrated for a man Percy's size, so will it simply slow you down, or might it be a fatal dose?"

A rush of hot panic flooded Saffron's body, and she stumbled back. "You drugged Edwards and told him to kill those women. Mrs. Sullivan wanted to blame you for the missing committee funds, and Birdie threatened you when you wouldn't give her drugs from the hospital. You made him kill them."

Surprise flashed in Amelia's eyes before she canted her head. "You certainly do know a lot, but you haven't quite gotten it yet."

"*You?*" The shock of the only other explanation nearly robbed Saffron of speech. "*You* killed them. And you framed Edwards with the bouquets."

"They were his idea. He sent the first to Mrs. Sullivan when she threatened telling the police I'd taken the committee's money. Then the night I killed her, Birdie saw me in the maid uniform I wore to sneak inside. She found it funny, the idea I'd taken up as a maid, said she couldn't wait to hear what the others made of it. I let her leave, but only just."

But she'd still murdered her, two days later. "Did you tell Percy she'd seen you? Is that what they really argued about just before you killed her?"

"I told Percy that Birdie decided to reveal my other secrets if I didn't help her find some new drug to play with. Percy knew that word getting out about my profession, let alone the truth of my father's suicide, would have utterly ruined my reputation." Her lip curled. "As if Percy hadn't ruined it himself many times over. He was a panting puppy, chasing away my prospects, then expecting gratitude for it. The bouquets were so *very* Percy. Those stupid flowers were his little revenges. Petty, ineffectual." Her voice climbed even as her cheeks reddened. "But he can be that way, can't he? He's able to stay wrapped in cotton wool, never had to confront reality like I have. No one even noticed when he stopped making any sense."

"And Audrey Keller?" Saffron asked. Amelia was talking now, letting it all out like she was purging a poison. It was taking up time, precious minutes that might mean someone was on the way to help or that she could come up with an escape. "You've treated hundreds of patients—why kill her?"

Amelia's voice turned brittle. "Because she was cruel. I might have stopped after Birdie, but Mrs. Keller abandoned her sixteen-year-old to a horrible, undeserved fate. She could have helped the girl get rid of the results of her maltreatment instead of letting the infection the damned backstreet sawbones gave her fester. She punished her daughter for trying to fix the mess others had made of her life." She spat each word out.

Just like someone had made a mess of her own life. Amelia was desperate to save herself and her family from their undeserved fate. Another revelation, another piece fitting into the puzzle and explaining the things Lee had found in her flat. The jewels, which were found next to a maid's uniform, were likely Mrs. Sullivan's real jewels, stolen in an attempt to provide funds for her family.

Self-preservation might have motivated her first murders, but killing Mrs. Keller had pushed Amelia past that. "You killed three people, Amelia. And you framed Edwards, who is devoted to you. That was not cruel?"

Amelia shrugged, expressionless. "The police needed a villain. If Percy took the blame, no one would stand in my way of securing my future any longer. And without Birdie to occupy him, Lord Vale would be available.. He's always been fond of me." A smile stretched over her lips. "I was almost caught by the man himself when I took the bouquet to Birdie's house. Luckily, I'd disguised myself." The smile turned nasty. "It is shocking, isn't it, how easily overlooked a messenger is. A maid. A nurse."

Had Saffron's eyes not been trained on the needle, she might not have noticed Amelia's fingers tensing, might not have realized she was about to be rushed until Amelia was already in motion. But she was ready, so when Amelia came for her, she ran. She darted to the right, away from Amelia, and leaped onto the sofa. The sofa's back was high, and Saffron's skirt was long, but she managed to climb almost over before Amelia's hand snatched the back of her coat.

There was a distant *crack* somewhere in the house. Another gunshot, but nothing else registered her mind before she was jerked backward and lost her footing on the spongy cushion.

Saffron let out a yelp of alarm as she fell. She landed atop the other woman, who let out a pained groan. She scrambled away, terrified at being in range of the hypodermic. She stumbled toward the door.

"Go on," Amelia hissed.

Saffron jerked around to see Amelia struggle to her feet, chest heaving and pale hair askew. Her eyes burned with malice. "*Run*. Percy will chase after you. He might be an impotent idiot, but he can be frightfully good at following my orders. He's killed that police officer by now. I've already told him how you are to die. This time, I won't have to do it myself." She jerked her sleeve up and pressed the needle to the crook of her arm, barely wincing as she slid it into her flesh. "It's only a matter of time until they come here. They'll find your body, Percy out of his mind, and me drugged. They'll think I was Percy's next victim." She tossed the half-depressed syringe aside and lowered herself to the ground. "So go, Miss Everleigh. Make it a good chase."

A shout and a crash from elsewhere in the house shook Saffron from her horrified stare. Edwards, destroying things as he looked for her? Or the police? It didn't matter. She had to get as far away from this madness as possible.

With one last glance at Amelia lying on the floor, Saffron fled the room.

CHAPTER 38

Alexander was going to get helplessly lost if he continued to run toward the sound of the gunshot, through indistinguishable rooms filled with covered furniture and beams of moonlight. He shoved a shoulder against the nearest set of French doors. Two tries, and the door burst open into fresh, biting air.

He jogged along the back of the house, gravel crunching, until he saw light.

The room next to the glass building was lit with dim golden glow, and as Alexander approached it, he saw motion inside.

A flickering wash of light illuminated the scene: Lee struggling with another man. Fire flickered on the floor atop a small pool of oil from a broken lamp. A gun was discarded on the floor behind them.

Without thought, Alexander kicked apart the doors with a crash and rushed forward through the falling glass.

The man, who must be Edwards, used the surprise of Alexander's appearance to take Lee to the ground with a sloppy blow to the head, then dove on top of him.

Alexander picked up the gun, a heavy, old-fashioned revolver, and cocked the safety. He shoved the muzzle against the back of Edwards's neck. Edwards froze, hands around Lee's neck. Lee's bulging eyes beseeched him, hands clawing at Edwards's stranglehold.

"Let him go." Alexander pushed the muzzle deeper into Edwards's neck. "Now."

Panting, Edwards let go and raised his hands. Lee, rubbing his neck, gasped, "Thanks."

Alexander shoved Edwards away, and he stumbled and fell next to Lee. He made to get up, and Alexander aimed the revolver at him.

His arms were heavy, the cold wood and metal pressing into his hands weighing them down. Darkness formed at the edges of his vision. Everything faded but Edwards. There was nothing but the too-fast pounding of his heart in his ears, and the white-knuckled grip on the gun, and the enemy at his mercy.

Lee said something, distant, unrecognizable words. Edwards was shaking, trembling just like Alexander's unsteady hands. The seconds lengthened strangely, leaving him struggling for breath.

The spell was broken by Lee batting the gun down and away from Edwards, and saying sharply, "Damn it, Ashton, wake up!"

Alexander blinked several times, horror surging as he realized what had happened. He flipped the safety and put the revolver on the nearest surface as carefully as his shaking hands could manage.

Lee was on his knees next to Edwards. Something was wrong with the other man.

"There's nothing I can do," Lee was saying, shoving Edwards onto his side. "Not a damn thing I can do."

"What—" Alexander's voice was too rough, and he cleared his throat. "What's happening?"

"He's having a seizure," he replied, not taking his eyes away from Edwards.

There were footsteps in the gravel outside, growing closer.

"Here, Simpson!" Lee called.

It was, indeed, Simpson, running full keel into the room. He stumbled to a halt, taking in the scene before dashing over to the still-burning oil of the overturned lamp. He threw one of the discarded white sheets onto it, stamping on it to smother the flames, leaving everyone in the gray haze of moonlight.

"Find another lamp," Lee barked. "Edwards is having an episode."

"But you're hurt," Simpson said, staring at Lee.

Alexander saw Simpson was right, blood had soaked through Lee's trousers.

Lee glanced down and made an impatient noise. "Mortal peril after all. It's not serious; I can deal with it later. Find me light."

The blood, the gun—dizziness overcame Alexander, and he staggered from the room. He slumped against the nearest wall. Labored breathing brought him back to the present, only for a hot jolt of alarm to race through him at the recollection that Saffron was still somewhere in the house, alone with Amelia. Any unsteadiness dissolved with renewed purpose. Simpson could find Lee a light; Alexander was going to find Saffron.

He stalked through a room that might have been a study, then rounded a corner and collided with something, something that let out a squeak as it hit the ground.

"Saffron." He was on his knees, pulling her into his arms in a heartbeat.

She struggled and he pulled back. Her eyes were huge and haunted, and she blinked at him a few times.

Relief made him light-headed. His hands couldn't leave her, unsure if he was truly touching her face, her hair, or if he wasn't yet right in his head.

"Alexander?" she breathed, focusing on him at last. "But how—?"

"Are you all right?" Her sleeves were stained, and he turned her hands over to see her wrists were crusted with blood. His throat tightened. "Lee needs to tend to these."

"Lee is here?"

"Simpson too." He carefully lifted them both to their feet. "Come on."

Saffron followed him, clinging to his arm, perhaps in a daze at this sudden turn of events. She paused on the threshold at the sight of Lee and Simpson kneeling over Edwards, who had gone still. Simpson must have found lamps, for there were several clustered nearby.

Lee looked up at them as they entered. He smiled tiredly. "Quite a night, Everleigh."

"I don't . . . understand," Saffron whispered.

At the faintness in her voice, Alexander put an arm around her waist and led her to an armchair. She sank into it, a hand to her head.

He surveyed the scene, thinking to get her a blanket or just one of the dust sheets, but he caught sight of the back of her head. His hands gripped the back of the armchair, his body going momentarily weak. Her scalp was matted with blood.

"Lee," Alexander snapped, "Saffron is hurt."

With a grimace, Lee got to his feet. Blood stained his pant leg nearly to his knee. Alexander's vision swam.

Saffron gasped. "*You're* hurt, Lee. Why are you standing up? Sit *down*."

"Thanks very much for that exceptional medical advice," he said acidly. "Simpson, stay next to Edwards—"

"No," Saffron said. She sat up straighter. To Simpson, she said, "Amelia Gresham has injected herself with the same drugs she's been giving Edwards. She's in a parlor just down the hall. She's . . . she's the murderer, not Edwards."

"Good bloody Lord," Lee muttered, taking a few halting steps toward her chair. "I don't suppose she left a convenient list of the ingredients lying about." He braced himself on the chair's arm and sighed. "Simpson, go see if you can find her and bring her here. I'll need to see to her to make sure she doesn't kill herself by accident. Ashton, we need boiled water, towels, and a damned telephone."

The buzzing in his head at a fever pitch, Alexander was glad for an excuse to escape back into the quiet house.

⁓⧉⁓

Saffron awoke sometime later. Night still darkened the sky, and the sunroom was quiet.

Edwards and Amelia were gone. It had taken a long time for Simpson to find and then convince the local constable that the earl's strange son and his companion—both unconscious—had been drugged and were involved in a crime. The policeman had finally agreed to take Simpson, Edwards, and Amelia to the nearest hospital. From the silence pressing in around her, Saffron gathered Simpson had not returned.

Lee lay asleep on a settee across the room, his injured leg propped up with cushions. The makeshift bandage around his thigh was tinged with red. While he'd tended to it himself, complaining about the indignity of slicing his trousers open to get to the wound, he'd said it was little more than a scratch. But still, he'd been shot because of her.

All the pain she'd put off feeling during the drama of the evening was making itself known. Her head felt like a white-hot lead weight, her body was sore, and she was desperately thirsty.

She managed to stand, then reach the door. After steadying herself, she shuffled through the now lamplit passages until she found the stairs leading down to the kitchen.

The room was like a cavern, with only one lone lamp to light it. It was dusty and empty but for one person.

Alexander sat at the scrubbed table, head in his hands. He'd disappeared after bringing enough hot water and ripped sheet bandages for her and Lee.

Concerned, she asked, "Are you all right? Did you manage to get hurt as well?"

Alexander looked up. His eyes were unreadable, depthless black. They skated over her, as if checking to see if she was all right. When he'd taken all of her in, he dropped his gaze back to his hands. "I'm fine."

He didn't seem fine, but there was a glass on the table next to his hands, one that promised something to drink. "Is there water?"

In answer, Alexander stood and filled the glass from the sink along the back wall.

She drank it down, and the next when Alexander refilled it for her. "Thank you," she said and, in absence of a better alternative, used her coat's dirty sleeve to pat her mouth dry.

"Are you supposed to be walking around?" he asked. "Lee said you had a concussion."

Saffron shrugged. "He's asleep and I was thirsty."

Alexander's frown deepened, the shadows catching on each wrinkle of his brow. "Simpson isn't back yet?"

Saffron shook her head. Lee had mentioned while cleaning her wounds that Simpson was here without Inspector Green's knowledge. She hoped that catching Edwards and Amelia would be enough to save him from trouble.

"I suppose we'll have to keep waiting, then," Alexander continued.

They had one other vehicle, Lee's, since Amelia had evidently ridden in Edwards's while Saffron was unconscious, but Lee couldn't drive it with his injury, and neither Saffron nor Alexander knew how to drive. Unsure what to say, Saffron remained quiet.

"You should have gone with them to the hospital." He'd said as much earlier, argued against her staying when Lee had already diagnosed her with a concussion. He hadn't insisted on Lee's need for treatment, though he had a bullet wound.

"I'm fine," Saffron said automatically. She wasn't, but she would have fought tooth and nail to avoid being stuck in a motorcar with Edwards and Amelia, even if they were unconscious.

Silence fell, heavy with unsaid things. The more Saffron thought about all the things she wanted to tell Alexander, "thank you" being primary among them, the harder it was to get anything out. Perhaps it was the shock of everything that had occurred, but she felt that it was essential she say it now, when they were together in this quiet kitchen, away from the madness of the evening.

Saffron glanced at Alexander, wondering if he felt the weight of words unspoken too. His jaw was tight, face cast away from her.

"Are you sure you're not hurt?" she asked softly.

He gave her a look of incredulity.

It occurred to her then that this was the thing he'd been convinced would happen—that she'd placed herself in danger because of the investigation.

Where concern had been a moment later, a hot surge of frustrated indignation erupted.

Yes, she had been in danger, but through no fault of her own. She hadn't gone searching for it; she'd been walking Amelia to the bus stop, and that was no more than what Alexander had done for her fifty times before. She might have gotten hurt, but she'd also found out the truth. Far more of it than she'd anticipated.

She set the glass down forcefully on the worn wooden counter. She wasn't going to stand here with her heart aching almost as badly as her head from Alexander's judgment. She'd face quite enough judgment for this disastrous conclusion without his adding to the pile.

She started for the stairs, almost able to feel his eyes on her back as she went. On the first step, she paused, hand straying to press against the ache in her chest. How she wished things had gone differently. "Thank you for finding me, Alexander."

She didn't wait for his reply.

CHAPTER 39

Not for the first time that morning, Alexander sighed and pushed back in his chair.

Elizabeth's bloodshot eyes glared at him, matching his subtle retreat with an advance of her own. She leaned forward, poking his arm. "How many more times do I have to tell you, Alexander? You are not leaving until you finish telling me what happened. Lee and Saffron are bound to be occupied for a while, so I have no way of getting information apart from you!"

The moment Elizabeth had walked into the hospital early that morning, she'd forbade him from slipping off to go home or even finding a cup of something hot to drink. They sat in singularly uncomfortable chairs in a hall redolent with disinfectant with the beginnings of dawn showing through a window. He was starting to regret telephoning her.

"What else do you want to know?" he asked heavily.

"How badly hurt is Saffron?"

Alexander's mouth tightened. "She'll be fine. A few nasty cuts and bruises, and Lee said she had a concussion. He wasn't concerned." He'd fallen asleep, after all, he thought sourly.

"But how did Lee get shot? All you've said is that he was! Obviously, it wasn't serious; otherwise, he'd have been attended to before you all came back."

"I wasn't there when it happened."

Elizabeth pushed to her feet, hands propping on her hips. "I am tired of this, Alexander. I know you're exhausted. I know you don't like Lee. I understand all that. But I *know* you care about Saffron. From what I can tell, without Lee she'd still be in that house with Edwards and Amelia Gresham, probably with a bouquet of bloody poison flowers and God knows what else"—her voice shook but only grew louder—"and you should be grateful to Lee that he got shot instead of Saffron!"

He was too tired to try to dampen Elizabeth's indignation. And she was right. Lee had taken a shot that could have easily ended Saffron's life, or someone else's. "You're right," Alexander admitted.

Elizabeth hiccupped. "I know I'm right!" She dropped back into the chair, arms crossed. "Now, tell me the rest of the story."

Though his eyes were gritty with exhaustion, Alexander obliged and took up where he'd left off. "Then Simpson found the local constable, and they carted Edwards and Amelia off to the nearest hospital, in handcuffs, and Simpson drove us back here. Saffron and Lee were admitted, and I telephoned you. Simpson said he'd send the inspector here later to interview them."

Elizabeth nodded, satisfied, and allowed him to sit in blissful silence for five minutes before a nurse came to collect her, to see Saffron. She disappeared down the corridor without a second glance. Unable to keep his eyes open any longer, he leaned his head on the wall behind him.

Someone prodded his shoulder gently. "Mr. Ashton."

Alexander started. Inspector Green's steady, brown-eyed gaze was fixed on him from where he stood a foot away.

He blinked at the sunlight now filling the hall. "Inspector Green."

The inspector looked just the same as he had before, somberly dressed to match his serious expression. "Waiting to see how the others are, are you?"

"Not exactly," Alexander said, stretching his neck against the knot that had formed. "Miss Hale insisted I stay to tell her what happened. She's gone to see Miss Everleigh."

The inspector nodded. "I'm headed that way myself. Since you're here, why don't you give me your statement so you can go home."

Alexander told him all he could remember. At the end, Inspector Green gave him a hard look. "Simpson said it was you that subdued Mr. Edwards before he had the seizure. Something about a revolver."

Alexander didn't reply to the inspector's careful statement. His hands clasped in front of him turned white at the knuckles, the pressure bleaching the discoloration on his right hand. He wasn't sure what he was meant to say, didn't know what Simpson or Lee had said about how he'd nearly lost himself, gun in hand.

"It's none of my business." Inspector Green paused, letting out a tired breath. "It never is. But many who fought go through the same thing at one point or another."

Alexander looked up at him, surprised. Inspector Green had none of the haunted quality he associated with men who'd come back with the same heaviness he had. "Did you, Inspector?"

The inspector's steady gaze didn't waver. "Every time I reach for my firearm, it takes me back to the front. Fortunately, that's not often."

No curiosity nudged him to ask for the inspector's service details. No gratitude compelled him to speak. Sitting in this bright hall, he was suddenly swamped by the disjointed feeling that came with recollections of war when surrounded by peace and order.

He'd avoided reminders of his service for a long time, burying himself in the details of the smallest forms of life instead. Experiencing humanity's violence and pain only reminded him of the fractures that remained deep within him. Maybe he would never fully heal if he kept being reminded of them. He wasn't sure what that meant for him and Saffron.

Alexander stood and offered his scarred hand to Inspector Green, then left.

Cold rain plastering the brilliant fall leaves to the pavement would have usually sunk Saffron's spirits low. Being jolted back and forth on an overcrowded, dank bus would have irritated her to no end, as would the wet tile of the North Wing, squeaking beneath her feet. But each step she took Monday morning was a reminder that she had survived to despise these discomforts. Had things gone just slightly differently, she might have never again lamented her stockings being stained with murky rainwater.

The office was unlocked, and she pushed the door open to find that it was in utter disarray. There were two things keeping her from shouting at Lee, who was sorting papers from his desk drawers into vague piles on the floor around him: he'd been shot on her behalf just days before, and he'd cranked the radiator up to the highest setting so the room was blissfully warm.

He grinned at her as she removed her damp coat and hat. "In one piece, I see."

"Somehow," she said blandly. Her head still ached, but work could only be relaxing after days of Elizabeth's terse ministrations. She'd been tearful and forceful in equal measure after Saffron's stay in hospital.

Lee watched her settle into her chair. "I've decided I feel very foolish we didn't make the connection between the murders and the maid's uniform in Amelia's wardrobe. I thought she was setting herself up for a future position."

"I would have been amazed if you'd guessed she wore the uniform to sneak into her victims' homes. It was terribly clever." Saffron sighed, wishing they were talking about something else. "Or perhaps just terrible."

"The entire progression of her tale was terrible," Lee said. "I think she intended to convince Edwards that he'd killed those women. Planting his card at Birdie's house to implicate him was a master stroke. Pity that the maids recognized her, eh?"

Lee must have received the same rushed telephone call from Sergeant Simpson the day before. Inspector Green had taken photographs of Edwards and Amelia for the victims' former staff to examine. The other maids and housekeepers had recognized only Amelia. From what Inspector Green had shared about the search of Edwards's townhome and questioning his servants, it seemed Amelia had convinced Edwards to go visit his antique collection a day before Mrs. Keller's murder to pick the flowers for her bouquet. After killing Birdie, Amelia had gathered flowers and taken them to the scene, apparently an afterthought meant to implicate Edwards. She'd borrowed his motorcar and driven out to the country herself to get the flowers for her own bouquet. It explained the poor state of the blooms she'd claimed had been left for her; she'd been in a rush to cut them and hadn't had any of the black velvet ribbon the other bouquets had been tied with.

With the new information regarding Amelia's involvement and her access and knowledge of the hospital's stores, new postmortems had been ordered. Simpson mentioned Inspector Green's suspicion that Amelia had been the source of the barbiturate found in the victims' blood, and the original examinations had missed easily hidden needle marks. It had been the perfect way to ensure that a slight young woman could strangle, smother, and stab her victims to death without the rest of the household hearing any disturbances.

Amelia Gresham had confessed to nothing. According to Simpson, she'd played victim the moment she'd awakened in the hospital, no doubt planning to continue hiding in plain sight. But the damage to her carefully crafted web of clues had been done.

Had things not turned out how they did, Saffron would have believed it had been Edwards. She hoped his new physicians would be able to help him recover from the damage Amelia and her solution had caused him.

Silence rested between them for a beat, and Saffron found herself growing warm under Lee's scrutiny.

Eager to shift his attention, she nodded to the piles around his desk. "I see you've decided not to take advantage of your injury to get out of work."

"'Get out of work,'" Lee repeated, scoffing. "I don't need to get out of it. I've been offered more work, in fact. You have as well." He rose to his feet, wincing as he crossed to her and offered her an envelope. "Take a look."

It was addressed to Dr. Aster. She raised a questioning brow.

"He told me to show you." He walked stiffly over to the couch and nudged a sheaf of papers over to sit. "Now that we're finished with all but the finishing touches on our paper, I'm clearing out of the North Wing. But perhaps you are as well."

Saffron unfolded the envelope. Her breath caught in her throat at the heading at the top and the signature at the bottom. "This is . . ." She wet her lips. "This is from the Committee for Imperial Defense."

"That it is."

She skimmed over the brief pleasantries and raced down the page until she saw the words relevant to her. Their study was described—*praised*—and then there was a discussion of terms of cooperation.

Her feet were rooted to the ground despite her head spinning.

"So, what do you think?"

Lee's gleeful question brought her back to herself. "Well, I . . . I don't know what to say."

"Don't know what to say! Egads, Everleigh. It's a stunning proposition, isn't it? Working for the Committee."

"The Committee for Defense. The war committee," Saffron said, irritated at his delight. "The people who sent half the country off to be killed in horribly brutal ways."

Lee blinked. "Well, I suppose if you put it like that, it does lose a bit of its shine. But think, Everleigh—this is government work. Assured positions, salaries. No worry about tenure and gathering more degrees. We could be sent off to run studies out of one of their little research stations."

Saffron looked over at his half-packed desk. "You would want to do that?"

He laughed. "Well, I don't fancy living out in the middle of the country with nobody but a bunch of scientists for company, but it would be a thrill, wouldn't it?"

"No." She frowned down at the letter, then shoved it back into its envelope. "No. It would not be a thrill." She put the letter back in his hands and went to her desk.

"Right," she heard Lee mutter.

She ignored him, looking for something to distract her, but she saw only her mother's face. The bloodless mask of horror when they'd learned her father and his unit had been doused with gas, the confirmation of his death only a day later. Her mother too heartbroken to do more than stare out the window and weep for weeks. She'd lost her husband, and Saffron had lost her father, all because of the sort of people who populated those research stations and government committees. She rounded on Lee. "You would work for them? You'd turn over our research to them? Don't you know what they'd use it for?"

Lee frowned. "It's already theirs, Everleigh. The study was theirs to begin with."

The air left her lungs. "What?" she choked out.

"Aster told me when he gave me the letter. The Botany Department received a commission, and we carried it out." He studied her. "I thought you knew. How else would it have been done? Newspapers across multiple counties, cooperation with hospitals, immediate communication with the university—who else could have coordinated that?"

She pressed a hand to her mouth, suppressing a scream of frustration. When she'd mastered herself, she said with as much equanimity as she could muster, "Do you mean that our study—which documented poisonous plants, their locations and potency—was given to the committee that creates plans for war? What do you think they'll do with that information, Lee?"

Lee just looked at her, eyebrows winging up.

"What do you think they're doing to do?" Nausea had her gulping for breath. "I can't—I can't believe you willingly agreed to do this. I thought you wanted to help people, Lee. People like your brother. Not help the government kill indiscriminately."

Color rose in Lee's cheeks, and he got to his feet with a harsh hiss of pain. "That isn't fair. There is no proof that they want to use our findings for anything like that."

"I don't want anything to do with it." A solution hit her. "I'm telling Aster to take my name off the paper."

"You can't do that. It's months of work. It's an opportunity to be published before you've even begun your master's degree!"

"I don't care," she replied. "I don't want anything to do with it. And . . ." She couldn't bear to say it, not with Lee's green eyes watching her, the slow realization clouding them with an unfamiliar emotion.

"You don't want anything to do with me either," he said, voice flat.

She didn't reply, unwilling to say it out loud. She didn't want to cut herself off from Lee, not when they'd come through so much together, but she couldn't accept this commission—couldn't do that to herself or to her father's memory. She'd have no part of the kind of horrific inventions that had killed him, and she saw no future, not for friendship nor something more, with someone who was willing to work to create more of them.

She had to speak to Aster before she lost her nerve. She strode out of the room, and when she closed the door behind her, she wondered if Lee would be gone when she returned. The thought caved her chest in with dread even as she hoped for it.

She spun on her heel and opened the door again, marching over to the desk where Lee sat, frowning at the stacks of paper. He inhaled in surprise when she bent over him.

With more force than tenderness, she smacked a kiss on his lips.

Voice wavering, she said, "That was for saving my life." She pressed a gentler, lingering kiss to his lips. "And that's because you were shot because of me. Thank you."

He held her gaze for a moment, something like sadness glimmering in the green depths. "Anything for you, partner."

With a brittle smile, Saffron left to go see Aster.

Lush greenery and humid air was a balm to her battered heart. With her hands buried in soil and the sweet scents of blooming *Cochliasanthus caracalla* perfuming the air, Saffron could momentarily forget breaking off whatever she had with Lee, as well as the strange invitation Aster had surprised her with when she'd gone to demand the removal of her name from the study.

She was an hour into mindless work in the greenhouse when the sounds of someone entering interrupted the steady work of repotting small *Ziziphus mistol* trees that Mr. Winters, the greenhouse caretaker, had happily left her to do.

She looked up at the disturbance in the crowd of leafy plants to her left. She almost groaned when she was it was Alexander. And he was angry.

With the intent of a predator locked onto its prey, he stalked over to her. His ears and the tip of his nose were pink, and little wonder that he was chilled, for he wore no jacket, just his shirt and waistcoat, his sleeves still rolled.

When he reached her workbench, he spoke without preamble. "Are you going to Paris with Lee?"

She was surprised he'd already heard about the conference Dr. Aster proposed she attend. He thought the trip would give her the chance to think things over about the Committee invitation. She thought it would give her an excellent opportunity to come up with what she was going to do about her future in the department. "No."

Alexander stared at her for a long moment before his shoulders dropped a fraction. "Good."

Saffron waited a beat to see if he would say anything more, then returned to the prickly little sprouts. "I suppose you didn't hear from Inspector Green what they discovered about Amelia Gresham."

"I don't care," he said, causing her to look up again at the gruffness in his voice.

He was across the table from her now, the intensity in his dark eyes making her mouth go dry. "I don't care," he repeated, quieter. "I'm glad you're done with it. And done with Lee." When her lips parted in surprise, he added, "Your study is done. He took his things from your office. Or so the gossip mill is saying."

Had her heart not been aching, she might have laughed at the sheepish way he said it. "You're not one to listen to rumors, Ashton."

His little smile appeared on his lips. "Let me take you to dinner. I have tales about retrieving your samples that I think you'd like to hear."

"A tempting offer. I'm not sure it's a good idea, though," she said regretfully. "I've made a decision, Alexander. I recently . . . have made certain choices, about my life, my future. I can't"—she exhaled, searching for the right words—"I have to stand by what I believe to be right. And you . . ." Words trembled on her lips, and she hesitated severing another bud before it could bloom. "It seems you can't abide by my helping the police. And that is something I've found is quite important to me."

Alexander's throat worked as he swallowed, eyes not leaving hers. She was relieved that they hadn't shuttered as they had before. "I see."

"I hope we will remain friends," she said softly. "And I would still like to hear about the expedition."

He gave her a searching look, pressing his palms on the tabletop. She bit her lip on a smile when he immediately pulled his hands away to brush away the dirt. "I would like that."

"Good," she said. "But not for a while. I'll be leaving for Paris in just a few days."

He reared back slightly. "You said you weren't going to Paris."

"I'm not going with Lee," she said, laughter bubbling up at his scowl.

"You're going alone?"

"No." She gave up and grinned. "I'll see you when return."

He watched her for another few seconds before saying, "Safe travels, then."

Alexander disappeared through the leaves, and Saffron waited only a moment before she shucked her apron and gloves and donned her coat. She had planned to wait until that evening, but she couldn't.

Anticipation thrummed through her, and she gladly paid the full fare of a cab to get to St. James's, where a certain government minister's office was located. She couldn't wait to see Elizabeth's face when she told her she was taking her to Paris.

EPILOGUE

Chest and feet bare, Alexander sat on the floor in his bedroom. He closed his eyes. He could feel the chill through the thin rug, hear the tinkering of the pipes. He drew in deep breaths, alternating covering each nostril with his thumb or forefinger, and exhaled slowly. The rest of the world faded away. His heartbeat slowed.

The date he'd been contemplating all day, November twelfth, was the one thing that clung to his mind. It seemed like a lot of important things would be happening in one week's time, when a certain conference across the channel was finished. He needed a distraction until then, something to absorb him until he could settle some matters . . .

With effort, his mind cleared. Eventually, he reached that state of mind similar to floating on one's back in a calm sea.

The bell rang, shattering his meditative state.

Alexander rose to his feet, replacing his undershirt and lifting his braces over his shoulders. If his flatmate had forgotten his key again, they were going to have words.

He swung open the front door to his modest flat. Frigid air hit him square in the chest, and a body slammed into him a moment later.

"Alex!" cried a familiar voice.

Alexander staggered back, shoving the door closed. He held the newcomer back from him to get a better look. "Adrian?"

His older brother smiled broadly at him. Tall as Alexander and weighing two stone less, he was a little worse for wear. His black hair curled haphazardly over his forehead, and his narrow jaw was shad-owed with scruff. His tie was loosened, and there was the scent of weary man about him.

"Alex," he repeated, bracing Alexander's arms with his own.

Alexander attempted to return his brother's grin but worry stiff-ened his expression. "What are you doing here?"

It was nearly midnight, and midnight on a Wednesday, at that. Adrian lived and worked in Kingston on Thames, and though it was just outside London, he rarely visited. Their father was to thank for that, something their mother never failed to remind him of. Alexander was actually due to visit Adrian in just a few weeks.

"I came into town Monday," he replied, slipping into their mother tongue easily. Adrian had spent considerably more time with their mother's brothers and their cousins growing up, so his Greek had always been better, just as Alexander's English had always surpassed Adrian's. Alexander had worked to rid himself of the accent he'd spo-ken with as a small child, but Adrian had retained the cadence that sped his words and made everything sound twice as exciting.

Unsure if he wanted to know the answer, Alexander asked in the same language, "What have you been doing since then?" His brother didn't look—or smell—like he'd recently been blind drunk, face-down in an alley. Unfortunately, that was not unheard of.

Adrian's perpetual grin tightened, his eyes darting around the entry to Alexander's flat. There was nothing but coat hooks for his eyes to land on. "Let's have a drink first, eh?"

"No." Alexander crossed his arms, studying his brother. He must be in a poor state if he was asking Alexander to drink with him. Out of everyone, Adrian had been the most respectful of his sobriety, even if he preferred to dull his own troubles with alcohol. "What's going on?"

His smile fell, aging his face beyond his thirty-four years. In the solitary light of the entry, the hollows under his cheekbones and eyes seemed sunken. He ran a hand through his hair, leaving the curls standing on end. "Ah, Alex. It is a misunderstanding. Something hap-pened on the train."

Visions of the scrapes his brother had gotten into over the years flashed through Alexander's mind. He'd never called on him to clean up even the worst of his messes. Alexander took him by the shoulders. "What happened?"

Adrian slumped, releasing a breath. "The man in my compartment on the train—he died."

"Was he ill?" When Adrian didn't answer, he added, "Or it was unnatural? The police interviewed you?"

With a sheepish glance, Adrian nodded.

"And?"

"I was not arrested," he said slowly, wincing slightly. "But . . ."

A sense of foreboding crept over Alexander. "But what?"

"They do not necessarily believe I do not deserve to be arrested." Adrian looked up at him, eyes shadowed with worry. "Alex, I think I might be a suspect in a murder."

AUTHOR'S NOTE

Floriography, the crafting of messages using flowers, existed well before the Victorian era, with every culture and religion assigning significance and symbolism to flowers and plants far back into antiquity. I doubt that any culture did it quite as enthusiastically as the Victorians, however.

Flowers, Their Language, Poetry, and Sentiment, published in 1870, was one of hundreds of books ascribing meaning to flowers, and it happened to be the one that I found, in its entirety, online first. There are many interpretations of the flowers included in the poison bouquets; for example, hydrangea might represent heartlessness, carelessness, devotion, gratitude, or pride, according to three different dictionaries. After seeing the dizzying number of interpretations, I decided for simplicity's sake (and Saffron's) to assign the meanings based on just one source.

Cocaine was available as an over-the-counter drug, an ingredient in all sorts of tonics and concoctions, from cough syrup to tablets made to improve one's singing voice. Packets were sold at train stations and even in Harrod's, with syringes and needles packaged alongside cocaine, morphine, and heroin for soldiers in the Great War shipping out to the Continent. But medical and public opinion had already begun to turn against the free use of cocaine in the decade preceding the Great War.

In May 1916, the British Army Council issued a ban on selling narcotics to members of the armed forces, save for those with medical need, and the Dangerous Drugs Act of 1920 furthered the prohibition. It did not end the sale or consumption of cocaine or other drugs, but it did attempt to stem the tide. With the miasma of war still hanging over much of the world, it is little wonder that the drug was still used as the world tried to move on.

As mentioned in previous author's notes, the realities of shell-shock, or what we now call post-traumatic stress disorder, were barely beginning to be understood in 1923, some nine years after the first recorded cases of nervous ailments in soldiers. At the beginning, those suffering were referred to as hysterical, a diagnosis hitherto identified with women with weak constitutions.

To read some of the accounts of these soldiers—men who might have been no more than eighteen years old and who'd led normal lives up until then, who suddenly found themselves in trenches without adequate supplies, surrounded by the injured or dead, unable to escape the pounding of shelling or the crack of gunfire, and fighting in a war the brutality and longevity of which no one could have predicted—is shocking. But it is no surprise that some conservative estimates suggest that thirty percent of soldiers faced shell-shock to some degree as a result. Research at the time primarily focused on the more dramatic, visible symptoms: muteness, deafness, and the dysfunction of motor skills. Little was known about the inner workings of shell-shock, and those affected suffered for both the lack of medical understanding and the social connotations of the condition.

Alexander's struggles and recovery from his experiences during the Great War, like any other soldier's, are unique and ongoing.

ACKNOWLEDGMENTS

My husband is always first and foremost on my list, no matter how uncomfortable that makes him. When people ask me how I write books as a stay-at-home mother, he is the answer. Erf, you have given me such a gift in making it possible to explore this as a career. Thank you, and I'm sorry about Lee!

My parents, to whom this book is dedicated, are the reason I write Saffron's stories to begin with. I'm the luckiest mystery writer in the world to have my mom and dad as my beta readers, my editors, and my problem solvers. *Flowers and Fatality* would have been an unfinished mess several times over without them. Thank you for giving me this love of storytelling, the encouragement I have always needed to pursue it, your unending expertise and ideas, and the permission to be my quietly (okay, sometimes loudly) weird self.

Thank you to my best friends, Erin and Audrey, for unwittingly lending their names to this story. I promise it has nothing to do with my love for either of you, but a writer's way of memorializing friendships that make me feel both really old and very young. We are written in every line between Elizabeth and Saffron.

Laila and Farokh, my in-laws, are owed endless appreciation for the love and support they have shown me, not just in writing this book but for the past year in particular. In truth, all of my family are almost suspiciously supportive of this unexpected turn in my career path, and for that I am full of gratitude and relief. Lee continues to be the only one making botany jokes at my expense.

Arezou, thank you for being the first person to read this book back when Saffron was still making the stupidest choices imaginable, and thank you for not saying anything about how bad it was. Your support means everything to me!

I've been lucky enough to receive a great deal of love from a number of fellow authors, everything from encouragement to critique, to advice. Thank you all for sharing your wisdom, and thanks, in particular, to C. A. Farran for your unshakeable positivity and generosity of spirit, and Christi Barth for your time and sharp eye.

My wonderful editor, Melissa Rechter, and the brilliant team at Crooked Lane Books: thank you for all you do. I'm constantly amazed at your patience and professionalism and so grateful that I am the recipient of both.

To my readers: thank you for welcoming me onto your shelves or your reading devices, and into your local book stores and libraries. Reading and books have always given me so much, and so giving back by sharing stories of my own fulfills one of my life's greatest goals, so thank you for being a part of that.

Finally, I feel I cannot not acknowledge the creators who have inspired, entertained, buoyed, and at times saved me. This last year was the best and worst of my life, and without the comfort, escape, and reflections of myself that I saw in the media I experienced, I would truly be lost. Thank you for giving me safe spaces in moments of darkness.

Read an excerpt from

A BOTANIST'S GUIDE TO SOCIETY AND SECRETS

the next

SAFFRON EVERLEIGH MYSTERY

by KATE KHAVARI

available soon in hardcover from
Crooked Lane Books

CROOKED
LANE

NEW YORK

CHAPTER 1

Cold rain soaking her boots, splashing her stockings, and leaking from the brim of her ruined hat and onto her face was the least of Saffron Everleigh's worries.

No, it was the lingering nausea of the crossing, clinging to her like a zealous strand of *Galium aparine*, combined with the exhaustion of traveling for over twenty hours, that made her miserable and desperate for the quiet comfort of her flat.

Thanks to the freezing downpour making the November night dreary, there were no cabs available as Saffron emerged on wobbly legs from the train station. She'd resorted to the bus, which had been a poor choice, given her uncertain stomach and London bus drivers' general propensity for driving like hellhounds were at their heels. Rather than risking vomiting all over the passengers of the cramped bus, she'd alighted three blocks before her stop and had to complete the walk with neither an umbrella nor an adequate raincoat.

Given the late hour, her quiet Chelsea street was dark, save for one flat. The warm lights emanating from the top floor of her building drew her like a bee to bee balm, promising a hot cuppa, a bath, and home.

She trudged up the stairs, her numb fingers fumbling with the pins of her hat. At the top, she eagerly pounded on the door. It swung open, and the anticipatory smile on Saffron's lips died.

Standing at the door to her flat was a stranger. He was youngish, tall, gangly, and wore wire-rimmed glasses and a look of haughty indifference. "Yes?"

Saffron blinked, checked the number on the plate next to the door, then looked back at the stranger. He had glossy blond hair in a washed-out shade of flax and very pale skin, which made the redness around his mouth and neck more apparent. His tie was loosened, she saw as she followed the color to his neck and then to his haphazardly buttoned waistcoat. At a loss, she asked, "Er—who are you?"

He lifted a brow. "Pardon me. Who are you?"

"Who's at the door, darling?" asked a voice from within the flat.

Saffron made to look around the man, but he moved with her to block her view. She glared at him and called down the hall, "Elizabeth?"

The man bristled, propping his hands on his hips and doing his best to loom over her. "Now, see here—"

Behind him, Elizabeth Hale popped around the corner at the end of the hall. "Why, hullo! You're back! Don't just stand there. Colin darling, move aside so she can come in!" She disappeared around the corner.

The haughty man—Colin, apparently—grudgingly retreated to the parlor without a word. Saffron stepped inside and negotiated removing her woefully soaked coat just inside the door. She could hear Colin saying something and Elizabeth's husky alto replying.

Just as Saffron discarded the floppy wet felt that used to be her hat, Elizabeth came down the hall in her stocking feet, arms open in welcome. Saffron took her in, sighing in exasperation to see that Elizabeth's clothing was as hastily donned as her date's.

"You look a right mess, Saff," Elizabeth said, embracing her in a warm cloud of Tabac Blond. "Did you swim the Channel?"

"Ha ha," Saffron replied flatly, allowing herself to sink into her friend's embrace. Elizabeth had returned from their trip to France two weeks ago, but it felt like a lifetime.

"You are freezing!" Elizabeth squealed. "Which would you like first, tea or a bath? Or tea in the bath?"

That brought a little laugh to Saffron's lips. "Tea first. You're entertaining, anyway."

Elizabeth winked at her. "Colin was just leaving."

As if summoned by his name, the man in question appeared from the parlor, his suit jacket on and his tie tightened to his throat. "Was I?"

"Yes, darling," Elizabeth said, not looking at him. "My flatmate has just returned from what must have been the world's worst crossing, and she needs tending." She shot him a coy look. "You've been tended to plenty. Scurry along, I'll see you tomorrow."

Colin's fair face heated, and he gave Elizabeth a hard look that only set her giggling. He squeezed by her and Saffron to reach for his hat and coat from the pegs on the wall. He gave Saffron an uncertain look. "My apologies for the confusion earlier. You are doubtless Miss Everleigh."

"I am. And you must be Colin Smith, from Elizabeth's office."

"I am one of Lord Tremaine's private secretaries, yes," he said, placing his hat atop his head.

"Of course," Saffron murmured as Elizabeth stepped forward and placed a gentle kiss on his lips.

"Ta, now," Elizabeth told him and shuffled him out the door. "Good night, Colin."

When the sounds of his footsteps had faded from the stairwell, Elizabeth flipped the lock on the door and wafted down the hall with an air of secretive satisfaction. Saffron made to follow her, but Elizabeth demanded she change from her wet clothing.

Five minutes later, Saffron was wrapped in her warmest and ugliest dressing gown of faded blue flannel, and the kettle was singing. Elizabeth busied herself with the ritual of tea.

"Well, Saff," Elizabeth said, settling the tray bearing teapot, sugar and cream, and cups and saucers on the little kitchen table, "I have all sorts of very interesting things to tell you, but you go first. How was the botanical conference? Did you go on to Belgium after all? Tell me everything."

The warmth of the kitchen, the familiar scent of steeping Earl Grey, and the kindness in her friend's eyes pried away the little that remained of Saffron's stiff upper lip. Her shoulders slumped.

"It was awful, Eliza," she rasped out. "All of it. I don't know what I'm going to do."

❦

Alexander Ashton paced his office. Or attempted to.

Though the space was clear of the accumulation of flotsam that academia encouraged, his legs were long, and there were only so many strides his office could allow before he was forced to turn sharply on the heel of his polished oxfords. His office had become a kind of sanctuary this last week after his brother Adrian had stopped trying to be a pleasant houseguest and retreated back into old habits that left the sitting room and kitchen a mess and him sleeping past noon most days. But even the quiet order of his office couldn't lower Alexander's blood pressure when so much weighed on his mind.

On his fifth circuit of the room, he checked his wristwatch. It was ten past nine in the morning, well past the time he could expect to receive an answer to his question.

He left his office and strode down the hall of the North Wing. Thick clouds beyond the windows left the white-walled corridor gray. Below, the Quad was full of students and staff hustling to reach their lecture halls and offices. Few people lingered in the frosty morning air. The voices of those who'd already sought the warmth of the North Wing echoed through the tiled halls and scuffed wood-paneled staircase.

Alexander climbed the circular stair and saw his quarry at the door at the end of the hall.

"Mr. Ferrand," he called, lengthening his stride to catch him.

Considering the number of times the secretary had seen Alexander this week, the older man should not have looked so surprised as he paused in unlocking the door and turned to face him. But Mr. Ferrand was polite to a fault, even friendly, and so he greeted Alexander with silver eyebrows lifted and a bright smile. "Good morning, Mr. Ashton. How do you do this very English morning?"

His French accent was thick and his tone warm. Alexander managed a smile back, and Ferrand's grew into a knowing grin that might have chafed had it been on the face of a less affable man. "Ah, but I know what you are after. I believe if I just open these messages here"—he waved a hand bearing a handful of papers and envelopes— "I will have your answer."

Alexander followed Ferrand inside. The neat office matched the Frenchman's own appearance: tidy and polished. In all the years

Ferrand had bounced from department to department at the University College London, Alexander had only ever known him to have his shining silver hair cut to suit a younger man and his stylish clothing tailored to perfection.

Ferrand did not move to sit behind his desk, which sat in the same place before the window that the last person to have occupied the position of secretary to the head of Botany had arranged it. He flipped through the messages and his face lit up. "Ah, but this must be it."

Alexander didn't reply. He knew he already seemed like an over-eager boy, asking daily for an updated itinerary, but he was getting desperate. Nothing he'd done to mitigate his brother's situation had borne fruit, and every day that passed wore on both their nerves.

Ferrand sliced the message open with a letter opener and scanned it, his brows dipping momentarily into a frown. "Wednesday," he said at last.

"As in the day before yesterday?"

"*Je le crois.*" Ferrand let the message fall onto the table and shrugged. "Miss Everleigh left France Wednesday. I suppose her plans changed. But that is good news, no?"

It was good news. Alexander had panicked when he'd learned Saffron had changed her plans to stay in France for an additional week following the conference she'd been attending. Learning that she was already back in London should have been a good thing. But it seemed nothing would alleviate the dread that had coalesced in his belly when Adrian showed up at his door.

"Indeed," Alexander said. "Thank you, Mr. Ferrand."

"This means our little daily chats are at an end, I think," Ferrand said, rounding his desk and sitting down with a sigh. "I did enjoy them. Anyone who manages to blink during a conversation is a wel-come change from"—he tilted his head toward the double doors to his left—"the old *lézard.*"

That was an apt description of Dr. Aster, the head of Botany, for whom Ferrand had worked for several weeks. "I will make a point to say hello more often. Thank you again, Mr. Ferrand. And if you wouldn't mind—"

"I will say nothing to Miss Everleigh," Ferrand assured him with a wink.

Alexander nodded gratefully and took his leave. As glad as he was that Saffron had returned ahead of schedule, it meant that the time had come for him to ask her to do exactly what he'd warned her away from doing a dozen times.

He returned to his office for his coat before catching a bus to Chelsea. It was time to ask Saffron Everleigh to meddle in a police investigation.